novum pro

AF003979

Alford Khan

UP THE DEMERARA RIVER

novum pro

www.novum-publishing.co.uk

All rights of distribution, including film, radio, television, photomechanical reproduction, sound carrier, electronic media and reprint in extracts, are reserved.

Printed in the European Union, using environmentally-friendly, chlorine-free and acid-free paper.

© 2016 novum publishing

ISBN 978-3-99048-300-8
Editor: Chennai Publishing
Cover photo:
Rozum | Dreamstime.com
Cover design, layout & typesetting:
novum publishing

www.novum-publishing.co.uk

This story is dedicated to my sister
Mrs Gem Farida Mulroy
(1956–1995)

Acknowledgements

I would like to thank Mr Dave Wakeford. Staff Sergeant (RTD.) Derek Hayes and Mr Harley Nott for their invaluable contributions in providing me with the military protocol required for certain sections of this story. I would also like to thank Dr Keith Mount for his advice on Jewish laws Mr Reg Sandhu for disciplining my computer and to Mr Ian Yardley for his relentless editing efforts.

CHAPTER 1

The Long Journey

My sleep was interrupted at 5.30 in the morning by great shouting and crying. I listened intently for a while when I realised that someone had suddenly died during the night and the relatives were just informed. To add to the disorder, the stall vendors, two streets away, were adding to the confusion with their noisy packing and braying donkeys. When the hubbub was over I was unable to get back to sleep. My thoughts turned immediately to my own uncharted future. I had finished high school and was successful with my exams. My friends and I were so pleased that on the last day of school we thought of being a bit naughty by smoking a cigarette as a way of celebration. No sooner had I placed the cigarette between my lips when a black man approached me; he was well-dressed with a waistcoat and a gentleman's shirt. I noticed the shirt because only my dad and a few other men in town wore them. He pulled the cigarette from my lips and gave me a resounding slap across the cheek and calmly told me to go and tell my dad that Doctor Bristol smacked me. He then crushed the cigarette with his foot and walked away. He knew I would not dare tell my dad what happened. If I did I would only get a telling-off and be deprived of seeing my friends for a week. It was the second time that day I had been punished. The first was because of something I did not care to think about and because I had no control over what caused it. The second was due to teenage naughtiness.

We lived on the outskirts of town in a small community of predominantly Portuguese business men and British administrators. We were classified as Portuguese and not Europeans for the simple fact that our grandfathers came from Madeira. This was of course a political classification and did not have any adverse reaction on the Portuguese community.

In spite of this classification, we lived and socialised quite amicably with the European communities.

For the same political reason, we tended to be aloof from the villagers living less than a mile away; these were the East Indian farmers and labourers and they seemed to understand the reasons for the social divide.

In order to maintain that equilibrium, my mother kept a tight rein on my social activities and all that over protectiveness was not making my life easier. Most of my friends were from the community in which we lived, except an East Indian lad named Persotum Persaud. He was a very bright student and whenever he visited my home he was allowed to meet me in the room on the ground floor. I resented this partly because when my other friends came to visit, I was allowed the freedom of the house.

My father, on the other hand, did exactly what my mother said. I was sixteen and I visited his surgery nearly every day. My ulterior motive was to get a chance to do dental repairs for four dollars which I could keep. I would like to point out that four dollars was more than the weekly wage a labourer would earn. That was the only pocket money I ever got. It suited me fine as I was able to treat my friends each Friday at Mr Choo's luncheon room with his Chinese delicacies.

My train of thoughts orbited in a new direction. Do I find a job until such time that I can really decide where my future lies? The possibility of working temporarily in my father's laboratory did not fill my heart with any enthusiasm. My father was a strict disciplinarian and seemed unable to understand my urgent needs or aspirations. He was the only dentist in town and he had two technicians working in the laboratory, not very bright young men, their social life was drinking with their friends and terrifying the young ladies on their shopping trips.

My journey through my thoughts was interrupted when my dad knocked on my door and invited me to come and have breakfast, "I have a proposal for you." He shouted before marching off to the dining room. I did not like the sound of his voice; it was the tone he used when he was giving rigid instructions to his laboratory workers. Those two would like nothing better that having the boss's son working with them.

At breakfast, I eyed my father suspiciously. He caught me glancing at him. It was at this point he pointed his fork at me and said sternly "I want you to accompany me to McKenzie in the morning. You have all day to get your clothes and personal things together as we will be away for six months."

"Six months?" I asked.

"Is there a problem with that?"

"Yes," I replied. "I have no friends there, my social life will be long and boring, I heard the men there only drink and chase women in their free time; and why are we going there when you have lots of patients here, no competition, and what about mother how will she cope for six months while we are in that lawless place."

"Of course it's a wild place and possibly not the best of places to have a young man of your tender age to mature. You have heard me mentioned my friend Matthew Longhorn. He is the Commissioner of the hinterland and has invited me to do some work there. He kindly offered a place for my surgery at the hospital and also a small house in the Wismar area. I gave my word I'll be there. One important thing to bear in mind I will be earning four times as much as I earn here and you will be paid a handsome salary."

"What happen if the people do not want dental treatment or cannot afford it?" I inquired.

"They will accept treatment all right because they can afford it and the Commissioner has promised to make it mandatory for every employee under his jurisdiction to have missing teeth replaced and regularly examined. Those that fail to obey will be asked to find work elsewhere."

"Is that not a bit dictatorial?" I asked.

"Not at all," my father replied. "It will be money that is well spent and as you know, it will improve their health and also make them look better in the eyes of the ladies."

I was not at all happy. There was not enough time to see and say farewell to my friends. I had recently managed to get a date with one of the best looking girls, who was the envy of all the boys. Marina kept everyone at arm's length. She was fully aware of her potential; this gave her the advantage of spinning us around like toys. My ploy was not subtle. I promised to let my father make a special set of dentures free of charge for her grandmother if she agrees to come to the cinema with me. It may sound like a bribe, but I would do anything to get my arms around her even for an evening. She knew my intentions and warned me that I would not succeed in getting more than a goodnight kiss. Little did she realise that a kiss was beyond my expectations. The thought of having to forego such an offer was more than a young virulent young man can tolerate.

My father was a strict disciplinarian and a strong Catholic as was my mother. I was brought up in the same upstanding order but failed to recognise the importance of rigid religious teachings. I do believe in God and that is where my observance of religion ends. My parents realised this and tried to tolerate it. I thought of going to the reverend father for guidance but I knew he would only want to give me a sermon on life. I soon perished that thought and resigned myself to the destiny that awaited.

The next day we set off at 6 o'clock in the morning to board the steamer taking us across the Berbice River to Rosignol. Here, the men went like cattle for the Tavern to get their glass of rum before boarding the train for Georgetown. I wondered how one could drink a glass of rum so early in the morning. My father must have read my thoughts and explained that since it is a long and tiring journey the drink will relax them in a semi-sleep for most of the time and they will arrive refreshed and relaxed.

The smell of burning coal and steam from the engine was beginning to get me excited in an adventurous way. The thoughts I had before leaving home became something of the past.

I had seen the train from across the river in New Amsterdam, but never this close. To actually smell the burning of coal and puffing steam sent me into a mesmerising world of fantasy. Suddenly, there was a sharp whistle from the engine and everyone went hurrying to find a seat. I took mine in the only first class carriage. Each carriage had a veranda, where passengers can stand to escape the heat. I went and stood on mine and as the train shunted its way, I entertained myself by watching the farmers tending their crops on either side of the track.

Our first stop was Fort Wellington then Belladrum, Abary and Mahaica. The names of these stations I had heard mentioned in conversations only; it sent a feeling of adventurous romanticism through me.

Gripped by this euphoria, my thoughts went swirling back in time to the early days when Essequibo, Demerara and Berbice were three separate colonies. The Governor of Essequibo was in fact the Governor of the other two colonies. It was the time when the Dutch West India Company owned the whole of Guiana. The Van Peres applied to the government in Holland and got permission to prevent anyone other than themselves from trading in Berbice. They built a fort and named it Nassau, fifty miles up the Berbice River. The head of the family Abraham Van Peres sent men and boys to cultivate annatto, cotton, sugar cane, and ground provisions. Since no women were sent, the men cohabited with the local tribes' women and a new race of people began to emerge.

When the British arrived, the Dutch was sent scurrying East across the Corentyne river to create a new colony, those who remained wanted to maintain their monopoly to trade. The British were not having this and drove them out to join their fellow countrymen. The three colonies were eventually merged into one country named British Guiana and the first Governor Sir Benjamin Durham of the newly formed country decided to make Georgetown the capital, where the seat of government was installed. This decision had a devastating effect on New Amsterdam. The capital of the ancient country lost its appeal for traders and investors. My town was reduced to a municipality with an elected mayor and town clerk. The rest of the councillors were men drawn from the business and professional sectors. Eventually the town remained stagnant with the speeded rate of progress in the capital. I wondered what Georgetown would be, a vibrant or sleepy city. I could only wait to see for myself.

At Mahaica, it was mandatory for the train to wait for the incoming one from Georgetown, as it was a single track system, and again the men hurried to the bar for a top up. They were swearing and jostling as everyone wanted to be the first to get their drink. I heard someone shouting abuse at the bar man, one even cast doubts on his parentage. The poor chap ignored their insults and carried on at his leisurely pace. The women, on the other hand, streamed around several large black women selling fried fish and bread, a lot of hot pepper was added and they hurried back to their seats to enjoy their meal.

It was sometime before the other train arrived. The two drivers waved at each other and exchanged batons as they passed signifying that the track is clear.

When we arrived at Georgetown, I was hoping that time would permit me to have a quick look around this big city. It was not to be, we had just enough time to get to the wharf to board the river boat for our final destination. Here, again it was total confusion, tempers flared as everyone was trying to be first to board taking more baggage than they could carry. I ignored the confusion and followed my father up the steps to our seats. The boat itself was larger than I expected. The lower deck was packed with passengers and their cargoes. Our deck was a bit more comfortable. It had a bar and proper toilet facilities. There was also a look out cabin above, where the captain and his navigator stood ordering the boat's departure.

My father went in the bar where the other men had gathered for their ritual of rum drinking. I, being only sixteen, stayed outside and watched with amusement at the monkeys on the other side of the river bank performing acrobatic feats in the trees and irritating each other with their shrieks. My father, on the other hand, was engaged in a serious conversation with Doctor Bristol, the man who slapped me. I tried not to let him notice me. He was quick to point out to my father that it was good I was able to accompany him on this trip. The business and professional passengers were joined by gold diggers and pork knockers; they are called pork knockers because all their supply of food in the bush was made up of salted beef and pickled pork. Their presence is not accepted or tolerated by men of higher standing. They knew this and kept their distance and drinking to themselves.

Doctor Bristol tapped his glass on the counter and introduce my father to the men "Listen fellows, we have Doctor Joseph D'Abrue on board. He is a dentist from Berbice." Before he could finish my father was surrounded by a mob who insisted on knowing when and where he will be practicing, and some wanted to make appointments straight away. Suddenly everyone seemed to have a dental problem. The commotion was so intense it brought the captain down from his perch.

"So you're the dentist? The Commissioner Mathew Longhorn told us about you. I am Captain Danjou, everyone calls me Danny." He stretched his hand out and briskly shook my father's. "How soon are you going to start your work?" "Right now," the mob shouted.

"Look here chaps I can't do any serious dentistry here I need to set my surgery up properly. The doctor can verify that."

The men were not having any excuses. It was Doctor Bristol who interrupted by suggesting that some primary examination and assessment can be made to quieten the men. The captain suggested his observation room on the upper deck could be used for that purpose. It was then he proposed to have an assistant for my father, and he shouted at someone at the corner of the bar. "Bertie! I want you to go down in the lower deck and bring Manny here."

"Up here captain?" Bertie asked. Realizing Manny to be a bit of a drinker and may not be in any shape or appearance to be introduced to gentlemen of the professional class.

"Of course up here, you moron," the captain replied

Bertie disappeared and half an hour later returned with Manny, he was a man of about thirty with dirty clothes and a strong smell of alcohol. Yet, there was a pair of eyes that exuded intelligence.

"Manny, go to the wash room and tidy yourself and make sure you wash your mouth with soap and come back here as swiftly as you can," the captain ordered.

I left the area and went to amuse myself with the monkeys who were engaged in their daily rituals of irritating each other and at times engaged in serious fighting. I sat down for some relaxation. There was no one of my age to talk with, and the novelty of the monkeys' antics soon wore off. I must have fallen asleep in the chair for a while, when I did wake up it was getting dark and I imagined it would not be long before we reach our destination. By the time, my father was in a serious mode of work; and he was by now doing extractions and even taking temporary impressions for dentures and Manny busily helping.

The boat came to an acute bend in the river and started slowing down significantly until it came to a near stop. There were four men in a boat with a cow and were coming to the stern as they approached, the legs of the cow were tied with ropes and the ends were thrown to a group of men standing on the river boat's stern, they began pulling the animal on board. When that feat was successful, the boat picked up speed and we were off again. From here on the boat picked up passengers whenever the occasion arose.

I went back to the make shift surgery to see my father still at it. He looked at Manny, exhausted and all red in the face his tired voice barely exclaimed "I've never seen such a devastating lack of dental hygiene in all my life!"

"It's not so much the lack of dental hygiene, it's the dam food these people eat, no vegetables in their diet, not even a lettuce leaf pass their mouths. It's bound to have the devastation you spoke of. I guess that is why we professionals can make a decent living." Doctor Bristol's remark disturbed me a bit and I wondered why people should remain ignorant of the basic facts of healthy living. We were about to settle down for a snack and my father and the doctor were having a glass of rum for relaxation when the captain came in with a burly young man. He had enormous arms and his legs were like mahogany trees and his size did not hide the fact that he was a handsome man with a mischievous look in his eyes. There was vivid evidence that he was of mixed race.

"This is Benjamin Carson." The captain said and looking at my father he explained. "Ben's got a renegade wisdom tooth that has been giving him hell for some time; it is only his cowardly nature that's stopping him from getting it out. I have made it my business to see it is taken out today and save myself a lot of embarrassing moments with his groaning and moaning." He ended off with hysterical laughter, which seems to affect the others, as they started laughing in the same manner.

Manny closed the door behind me. Doctor Bristol and some of the men surrounded my father as he prepared for the extraction in the middle of the bar. I leaned against the railings of the boat feeling a bit bored. As a teenager, I was not allowed to enjoy grownups jokes that made me appear in their eyes as unmannerly.

There was a sudden groan and a mighty thud as if someone had fallen from a great height. I rushed in the room in time to see Benjamin getting up and adjusting his clothing. He looked at the captain and then at me and said. "Ok! I will sit here, and you dentist can take your time to torture me" Then looking at me he winked and said. "You can stand there sonny and watch your uncle Ben being tortured."

It soon became clear that I suddenly inherited an uncle. It was customary all young boys and girls must address older folks either as mister or mistress or on a more personal level as uncle or auntie and since Ben has decided that I call him uncle I felt honoured. True to his word he sat there as still as a monument during the operation. Without warning he let out an almighty roar. The tooth was out. Triumphantly he held it between his thumb and index finger and kissed it and started laughing like a school girl, his whole body gyrating.

"This calls for celebration gentlemen," the captain announced. He produced a rarely seen bottle of malt whisky and a party began. It was getting dark when we finally arrived at Wismar, which is on the west bank and then on to McKenzie on the other side. I felt sad leaving this boat, there was so much excitement and laughter that went on, it was difficult to imagine. I turned and looked at the boat as if to say goodbye. Still standing on the upper deck was Ben flanked by the captain and Manny, and he looked like the Colossus of Rhodes.

The Commissioner of the hinterlands was a man of immense influence and power a secondary Governor in many ways. As a Commissioner, he was in total charge of all Amerindians affairs. He was also a judge and juror of all crimes committed against the Native inhabitants and a friend of my father for many years. I never had the opportunity of meeting him. He was waiting for us with his car and driver. Matthew Longhorn displayed all the characteristics of a military man. Swagger stick stuck under his arm, he swung around with military precision to greet my dad and at the same time giving me a casual glance. Ben and Manny soon joined us and they were instructed to take care of my father's baggage and to get the equipment to the hospital as soon as possible. They were also told to get a boat to take us across the river to our lodgings.

My visit to this place was not exciting. It was an adult world. Children were allowed to get on with their lives as best as they could. This of course had a devastating effect on their moral and cultural behaviour. There were exceptions. Parents who took time to steer their children on the straight and narrow did not tolerate any mixing with the wayward. I did all I could to make life tolerable, which was difficult, nearly all the young men were only interested in playing dominoes and drinking beer, loitering around the market place for odd jobs and to tease the young unaccompanied ladies. There activities were of no interest to me at all. I longed for the six months to come to an end. Every day was the same routine; visiting the surgery and then the laboratory across the river. Manny seem to cope without my help and I was always willing to let him get on with it. He liked being alone. I sensed a bit of nervousness in him when I was around. He was quick to give me the money collected and the appliances for my dad to fit at the surgery and I was equally eager to dash off to look for Ben. Sometimes Ben and I would visit the plant to see the bauxite unloading and the dust would make it difficult to recognise known faces.

When the six months finally came, my dad could not have hurt me more even if he has struck me with a hammer, but when he told me that we were to go further up the river to some remote villages to take care of the dental problems that the villagers were facing. His friend, the Commissioner, had asked him to help these people and the payment would be a small stipend to cover the cost of his drugs. These people were the Amerindian villages set in a remote part of the Upper Demerara.

Since I had never been to the interior I thought it might not be too boring. I was nevertheless a bit disappointed for not returning home to meet my friends and that date with Marina. I had written her of my dilemma and she promised in her last letter to honour that date whenever I returned. That was something to look forward to on my return. I could not help dreaming of it, if only to soothe the anguish away.

My dad was taking the opportunity of going home to see my mother and restock his surgery requirements before our departure. This did have a joyous effect on me as I was to be left in the care of Ben and it seems the shackles that kept me on the straight and narrow were now gone.

That morning after my father left I went across the river to the laboratory to check what was happening. Manny was repairing a couple of dentures and then Ben suggested that since there was not much to be done here I could accompany him to the town.

"How much money you have?" Ben asked. I checked my pocket and told him I have only eight dollars. "Eight dollars?" He exclaimed. "That's more than I can earn in a week. Come on lets go." He ended rubbing his mighty hands together.

Benjamin Carson was a man like so many of his kind that prefers to hang around wealthy families. They did not earn any salary as such. They stuck around feeling important and getting everything and more than what they needed in life. It was a combination of jobs. Confidante, protector, Handy man and advisor all rolled into one. Of course it was fashionable to deck them out with fine clothing. An unofficial rivalry existed between these families. The more debonair their confidante appeared the greater the esteem. Comments of who has the best dressed confidante were always a topic for gossip.

I was fully aware of this and took pride to see Ben is well looked after even in my father's absence. It was with this pride that I decided to follow him in town. It was not that special, it was a small town as one would expect; there was a market, a cinema and a few shops, further down the road was the company's club house, the meeting place for workers to enjoy a game of billiards, dominoes and also to relax with some beer or rum. Since we were not shopping, and the cinema was not showing 'The Eddy Duchin' film until the evening Ben suggested that we try the club house.

"You like girls?" He asked with a wicked smile on his face.

"Show me a lad who doesn't like girls and I will show you an auntie man," I replied. 'Auntie Man' is a term used locally for homosexuals

"That's what I want to hear, now listen to me when we get there don't be in a rush to go and speak to any of the girls who might be there. Allow them to come to you first," Ben cautioned.

"Why is that?" I asked

"Because if you do they will pretend they are not interested and give you a hard time. Women are like that. They pretend they are not interested and then they get you all sexed up and roll you round their scheming fingers. Just stay by me and I will let you buy me a drink," was his second advice.

It was not long before a pretty young lady appeared and asked Ben whom she seems to know who I was. Ben told her and added that my father had gone back to Berbice and I was left in his charge.

She looked at me and smilingly asked my name. I told her my name was Peter D'Abrue. "Well Peter, if you can buy Uncle Ben a drink I guess you can buy me one too, and if you are interested my name is Jean Brutus. She was a pretty young lady with long curly hair and a subtle hint of lip-stick and a very brown sun tan. At first, I thought she might be the daughter of one of the Canadian engineers or superintendent working in the bauxite plant. Turning my attention to her request I jokingly asked.

"Do you want a beer or rum, Jean?"

"No man, I am too young to drink the hard stuff." Then she explained that she has just returned from high school in Georgetown and was waiting for a friend to bring a typewriter for her to make an application for a job with the bauxite company. Then she added that if her friend does not turn up she will have to wait until the week-end when her father will be able to borrow one. I bought her a cool drink and then she invited me to her home to help with the application when the typewriter becomes available.

"I'd love to help you, but I must have your address and the time you want me to turn up." I replied joyfully. She was about to write her address when Ben stopped her and informed her that he knows where she lives and that she only has to tell us the time she needs me to be there.

Some weeks later Ben decided to take me beyond the Wismar housing scheme where immigrants from St. Lucia and St. Vincent had settled in their own communities. It was tiring walking up the hill in the hot sun but it was worth the effort, when we reached the compound he headed straight for a small house where a woman also of mixed race was doing her laundry. Her house looked like a small bar where men can enjoy a drink. There were ash trays filled with half-smoked cigarettes and it smelt awful. The surrounding area was a huge plantation. I could see hundreds of plantain and banana trees cultivated in neat rows and as far as the eyes could see and in between these trees yams and cassava were cultivated. In another corner was what looked like a massive kitchen garden. There were beans of every sort, peppers, corns, lettuce, and various other vegetables. This I imagine was the source of their income. There were no men around and I assumed they were in the fields tending their crops. I was eager to stay outside in the fresh air and away from the foul air in the house.

We went out and she shook my hand very warmly and told me her name was Norma Wardle, but because of her blue eyes people called her 'Blue Bell.' "It's not my real name but I like it." She was a mixture of Chinese and European and a very friendly lady. She immediately offered me a glass of cool ginger beer and quizzed me about my visit to this part of the world. I told her and then she said she remembered someone telling her about it and promised to make a visit for a check-up. Ben interrupted by saying that my father is married and is a respectable man and it would be difficult for her to curl up in bed with him.

She playfully hit him on his mouth and said "Shut your mouth man. You have no respect, making them wild talk in front of the gentleman's son."

A week later my father had returned and our visit further up river will be in two days. I instructed Manny to give my dirty clothes to Blue Bell to launder and have them ready for our departure. I told him I will go with Ben to collect them the following day. When we did return to collect the clothes we were told that someone had stolen my best shirt from the line. I was furious. That shirt came all the way from England as a gift from my father for my sixteenth birthday and it was only the second time I'd worn it. Bell said she had informed the police of the theft and later they told her they had made an arrest, but we must go to the station to identify the shirt. I have never been in a police station before. The sergeant was very polite. After the identification I was told that I would have to be in court to testify to the magistrate of ownership. I told the officer that we were going up river and there was no way I would be able to delay this trip. The officer suggested that I make the thief an offer for him to plead guilty so the matter can be expedited. I told the officer that if he pleads guilty he can have the shirt. This seems to satisfy the sergeant.

Later that day, I received a note from Jean asking me to meet her at the market. I told Ben and he agreed to accompany me. Meeting her again was a pleasure and we talked about our aspirations and other unimportant issues she told me her parents were going to the cinema that evening and since her father has borrowed the type writer I can come at 8 o'clock to help with the application, but to come alone. I told Ben of her proposal and he then warned me by saying "It's alright you can go alone, but I will have to take you to the house and wait for you outside until you are ready to leave. This young lady is clever she has a motive with you in mind and I am afraid she will trick you into her scheme whatever that is. But here is a lesson I will teach you. A young man must pick all the cherries he can get so by the time he's grown up to adulthood he must have at least 10 or 12 cherries in his bag."

When I arrived that evening she took me into the living area and offered me a chair, as I sat down she brought me a cool drink and we began typing out the application, when that was finished she told me that she need not have made this application as her real father is an engineer in the plant with influence and he could have secured her a job in an instant. I asked her why she did not do that. She told me it was her step father's wish that she get the job on her own merit. She sat on my knees and kissed my cheek thanking me for helping out. Before I could say anything she started stroking my cheeks and kissing me. I remembered Ben's words and a battle ensued in my head whether to leave for decency's sake or to relent to temptation. I relented to her acute receptiveness to my embrace, my body became volcanic, a few minutes later when the magma was released, and I realised I had bagged my first cherry.

As promised Ben was waiting for me a few yards from the house. "Well?" He asked looking for an answer from me.

"Well what?" I inquired.

"Did you or did you not?"

"I cannot tell you that Uncle Ben. It won't be fair for the young lady's reputation."

"So its uncle Ben now. I see you're not going to tell me."

It was customary for young men with or without scruples to boast of their sexual conquest. I was not prepared to do that. Ben seemed to understand and shook my hand to apologize.

My father was furious when we returned to our lodgings; He blamed Ben for misguiding his son and keeping him on the streets until midnight. It was only then I realized how late it was.

He checked my fingers to see if I was smoking and sniffed my breath for alcohol. When he was satisfied he calmly asked me to go to bed giving me a kiss on the forehead. He was beginning to behave like my mother. I guess the time he spent explaining to her why I was not returning home just yet prompted her to make sure I am not led astray by that Mulatto giant.

Suddenly there was a knock on the door. My father opened it and there was a strange man standing there. He asked to see me and questioned me about my visit to his house without his permission. Ben soon defended me by telling him that he was with me all the time and no interaction with his daughter took place. He also told him that it was his daughter who invited me to assist with her paper work. He was not satisfied and insisted we accompany him to confront his daughter and get the truth. Ben argued for several minutes until it was finally decided that we see Jean and satisfy her father's concerns.

My father objected on the grounds that it is nearly midnight and the river would be dangerous to cross, especially with the extra traffic of ocean going ships busy on the waterway.

He was adamant and insisted we followed him or he would report the matter to the police. This really got my father angry. The gentleman was told to do his nastiest and when my father told him that he would consult with Matthew Longhorn of his behaviour, and then he suddenly relented and asked us to see him at a convenient time to resolve this tricky situation.

After he left my father turned his anger to Ben accusing him of reneging on his responsibilities and allowing this to happen. I defended Ben by saying he was in effect helping me from getting in any trouble with the locals.

CHAPTER 2

Into the Unknown

The next day we were prepared to travel to our new destination. First, we boarded a locomotive from the bauxite plant bound for Ituni. On our way the men were pestering my father to take a look at their teeth. Seated at the very front of the carriage was Blue Bell. She was alone and her bags were stuck around her in the seat. Ben and I looked at each other and wondered what she was doing here. The men continued pestering my father

"I cannot do this on the train," my father protested. "It's not hygienic and there is no privacy for me to work. Besides can you imagine dentistry being practiced on a locomotive? We are bobbing and weaving as if on the high seas. Where do you think the forceps or the needle would go if I tried the impossible?"

"We don't care about hygiene and privacy there is no women here and we have enough alcohol to sterilize all your equipment, besides, when we reach Ituni we all go our own way and you would have gone in the bush. So please do what you can at least to those of us who will be going to the mines," they implored.

This seemed to have softened my father's attitude. A make shift screen was installed and he went about his task reluctantly.

The men were so happy they continued their drinking and telling lewd jokes, much to my father's disgust. I, on the other hand, enjoyed it as a new experience and a few more adult jokes to tell my friends if and when we meet.

At Ituni, a truck was waiting to take us on another leg of our journey. Blue Bell and my dad joined the driver while the rest of us scrambled aboard in the rear. With a jerk and spurting black smoke it took off doing a steady 20 miles an hour. After a while it reached forty miles then someone shouted for it to slow down.

I was worried as the track was just wide enough for the vehicle and it was very rough

We eventually arrived at the Demerara for our final journey. We were told we would be met by a Duncan Stewart. We waited for some time and when no Duncan showed up someone asked the men who were already there if they have seen a Duncan. No one seemed to know. I was looking for a Scot with a red beard and totally out of his wits by drink. A few minutes later a small Amerindian arrived dressed in a loin cloth with a bow slung over his shoulder and announced "I is Duncan, I come to take the dentist up river." His boat was in fact a hollowed out mahogany tree about thirty feet long and a yard wide in the middle. Everyone agreed that Ben should go first. The boat bore his weight with dignity and the rest of us got in. Blue Bell came and sat next to Ben. He looked inquiringly at her. She smiled and told him it was a last minute decision. She has some handy work to sell and also she heard that the men up here are attracted to Creole women. "I knew you would be here and if I mentioned it you would try to discourage me," she told him, Ben looked a bit annoyed and asked "What about the men in Wismar, you are throwing them aside like dirty underwear to come and look for a husband?"

Blue Bell hastily defended herself, "Those men only come to buy the cheap liquor and to get away from their boring wives. It's nothing more than that. I am not a whore and you can stick that in your clumsy head. I've never had a man in my life and I don't intend to disappoint the man I marry."

The water looked refreshingly cool. I let my hand slipped in it and felt relaxed. Ben seeing this urged me to remove it instantly as there were vicious fish in that. He went on to say how a man was circumcised recently by one. This brought about some laughter even my dad had a smile to exhibit

The sun was beginning to show its face on the horizon when we finally arrived at the village. It has taken the best part of an afternoon and all night to reach here. I was extremely tired and my legs were almost lifeless, Ben helped Blue Bell and me out of the boat while the others scrambled ashore. We were greeted once again by the Commissioner. This time he was dressed in his official uniform khaki shirt and half trousers, and pith helmet decorated with a smaller plume than that of the governor and it stood at a slight angle on his head. He greeted my dad with a salute and told him he would be staying at the Rest House. Ben, Manny and I would be staying in a smaller house nearby. He looked at Blue Bell and inquired where she would be staying. She told him that she hoped to stay with us. "That's quite alright." He replied, adding "There is enough room for all of you."

The house had three bedrooms two of them had double beds while the third had several hammocks there was a smaller room for personal items and an open area which served as a kitchen and diner.

A woman brought us some dried fish and pancakes made from cassava. It tasted revolting, but hunger forced us to eat some of it. Exhausted and still hungry we collapsed in the hammocks.

Later that day, I had my first taste of roast peccary and wild yam that Bell had prepared. In the morning, I was the first to awake so I decided to take a stroll outside. I can see the Rest House about fifty feet away someone made a very poor attempt to create a flower garden by the entrance. The house was a two storied fortified structure with a tower that was used as a look out. It had a clear view of the river and the surrounding area for several miles in any direction. There was another building, I was later informed that it was the school and on Sundays it was used as a church when the vicar was available for his congregation. Further on were many huts built at random intervals and extending into the forest; here was the main area where the Amerindians live. In between the Rest House and the village was a court yard; in the centre of it was a long house open on all sides with a long table and benches; it is here matters concerning the villagers and the Commissioner were discussed.

Having studied the geographical locations of most Amerindians villages and their population, I thought I'd go down the river to try and get a general bearing of where I was. It was absolutely clear in my mind that the majority of natives lived in the Rupununi area, a distance of nearly two hundred miles North West of the country, and the only other area where a similar number of villages can be found is in the West near the Venezuelan border. I was puzzled why the Commissioner established his base here. This was something I had to ask when the time is right. Sappanam is not a very large settlement, not more than three hundred people live here. The settlement is divided into two separate villages, both with a chief and several headmen.

The village was beginning to come to life. A group of young men scantily dressed and armed with spears and their bows and arrows headed off towards the jungle, perhaps to hunt or fish. This was a daily routine as I came to know later. There were also a few women struggling to light a fire under a tree, with a dead animal nearby and they dragged it towards to fire once it got started. In another part, a bit further away, another group of women were escorting their children towards the school building.

I was soon joined by Ben and Manny after a revolting breakfast. I told myself if this is what the menu is going to be every day I will have to make other arrangements. Ben agreed with me and indicated that he is a very good cook. Bell joined by telling him she is here and while we may not notice it, she is a woman and a very good cook. She also told us with no uncertainty that while she is here all the cooking will be done by her. I can now look forward to some decent meals.

Manny as usual shunned our conversation and crept away quietly to where father was setting up his surgery. He appeared to be happy by himself. Ben and I were not too keen on having him around. It sounded a good idea when Bell told us that she is going down the river to wash some dirty laundry and she will feel safer if we accompany her. With my father and Manny busy setting up the equipment, I felt there was no need for me to assist so we joined her. The water was running at great speed towards the sea and this constant flowing never seemed to stop, I wondered if it was because of the Great Falls at Makuba hill. I must point out that although the water is constantly running towards the sea, the river is subjected to the laws of ebb and flow. During the ebb, the water simply rose to a higher and drops at the flow. I also noticed that it was getting narrower further up. It was essential for me to get my geographical position right.

While Bell was doing her laundering two canoes could be seen coming towards us from up river. They tied their boats, looked at us and without saying a word went in the direction from whence we came. Not long afterwards two more boats arrived until there were about a dozen juxtaposed by the embankment. They all did the same as the first lot, looked at us and marched off towards the village. We were completely ignorant of what was going on. As soon as Bell finished her washing we darted off in the direction they went. They were all seated in the long house. The chief came out last. The feathers in his head gear flowing in the wind and sat among them. A few minutes later the Commissioner arrived in his official attire of khaki uniform and a modestly adorned helmet. He went and sat at the head of the table and started a lengthy conversation first with the chief and then with the visitors. We were unable to hear what was said. Not that it matters, we could not understand their language.

Then the Commissioner emerged from long house surveying the congregation. He joined us to explain what was going on. "Sorry this is happening so soon after your arrival .This has been a sore point for some time and I intend to resolve it." He started out by putting us in the picture. "You may or may have heard it bellowing but behind that school house is a young bull that arrived here three months ago. It apparently got lost from its mother and must have walked the hundred miles or more to reach here. The problem is no one knows exactly whose animal it is, it's a brave bull to have come all the way from Wismar. I imagine dodging caimans and avoiding jaguars is no mean feat. The other villagers wanted it slaughtered and distributed equally between them. I am not prepared to slaughter that brave young animal just because they never tasted beef before. The chief quite rightly suggested that since it has strayed in his village he has the right to say what happens to it."

He looked at us inquiringly hoping for a suggestion. I suggested that since there seem to be enough grazing pastures around perhaps a small herd can be raised to benefit everyone. Bell added that it would be good company for the lonely little bull. Ben added his comment saying that they can have milk, and how he loves milk and he will be willing to help.

"I was thinking along those lines," the Commissioner said. "The only problem is getting a hundred dollars to buy another bull and a few heifers. Getting them here will be no problem. I will go and speak with them and let you know what is decided." He made a brisk about turn and marched off to the gathering. But not before I pointed out that if the cows yield enough milk it can be shared by all the children in all the villages which will be a great improvement not only to their health, but also most importantly to their teeth.

The Commissioner was overjoyed by the many suggestions.

"You have a lot of bargaining powers with you Commissioner," I shouted after him.

Bell was hanging her washing on a line that Ben strung for her and was humming a favourite tune and gently swaying her slender hips to the rhythm. In an instant a man came from the undergrowth and started humming the same tune. "Who are you?" Blue Bell asked rudely, "and why are you singing my song?"

"Lady it is not your song, it is everybody's song. If you want to know who I am then I'll tell you. My name is Diego DeSouza I came along with that lot to decide the matter with the bull. But that is not what brought me I heard the dentist is here and I would like very much to speak with him."

Diego was obviously not a full blooded Amerindian, even his tribal outfit could not hide that fact and more revealing were his greyish blue eyes and huge biceps. Before I could ask him about the falls and how far it is he began telling us the origin of his tribe. Looking at me he said, "I see you are wondering of my origin. Most people from outside are always curious. They think I am a pure blooded Spaniard when I am not wearing my tribal outfit. We are proud to be descendants of the conquistadors their bloody reputation will not deter us from relinquishing that tie. I must admit they were a murderous lot looting and pillaging the continent. Yes! They have destroyed a noble race and their civilisation from the face of the earth and took all the land across the continent, stripping it of the vast mineral wealth in the hills and rivers. They used our people as slaves to get what they wanted and treated them like animals. They were not all bad; some rebelled against the barbarous actions of their fellow countrymen and even went so far as to sever allegiance from Spain. Unfortunately for them they were defeated in a battle with the Portuguese for crossing the papal line."

"Papal line? What papal line you are talking about?"

Diego continued to explain "To understand all this we must go back to the sixteenth century, when the Pope drew a line down a map giving all land west of the line to Spain and those on the East to Portugal. The rebellious conquistadors unwittingly crossed the Papal line and were repelled. Some stayed and took our women as wives. The other tribes called us buffiana a derogatory name for people not of pure blood; I don't care what they call me. I am Diego DeSouza and I am a product of my ancestors and proud of it, more so by the fact that they rebelled against cruelty and genocide."

"Mr Diego," I interrupted. "There are no historical records of what you say."

"History my friend can write what it likes. No one wanted to reveal that Spain had an insurgence in its hands because it supported the barbarous acts carried out by its citizens. Besides, who wrote that part of history? Not you nor I but the lackeys of Spain. Our ancestors have verbal history of their past and it is told generation after generation without altering the truth. To do so will be a violation of tribal laws."

Blue Bell eyes lit up when she spoke. "Mr Diego. I like you, I like your spirit. I am sorry for speaking so rough to you." "I like you too lady. Want me to help you do something?" he asked.

"You can come and watch me bathe in the river, and then help me cook lunch for these hungry lads," she teased.

"You mean I can help you bathe and watch you cook lunch." Diego joked and with a serious note added "Don't ever bathe in the river," he warned. "The best place to wash is on the rocks where those piranhas will find it difficult to attack and I can tell you that they always prefer beautiful ladies."

"Mr Diego," I interrupted, "you said your ancestors rebelled against the barbarous acts of their fellow soldiers. Then why did they not try at least to do something about it and put a stop to this genocide?"

"They did my young friend. No point getting heated with history. Gold is like a whore luring you with shallow promises. It all started with the legend of El Dorado some three hundred years ago. When the Spaniards did not find this mythical city their frustration led them to pass it on to the British who were plundering their galleons and stealing their precious cargo. The British just as greedy swallowed the story. Men like Raleigh and Hawkins came in search of this treasure. Raleigh's failure caused James1 to imprison him for thirteen years in the tower of London. He was so confident this golden city exists and he wrote a book of Guiana and begged the king to give him a second chance. The king did, on condition that if he fails he will lose his head. I imagine being locked up for thirteen years made the offer looks good. Of course he lost his head. It is the same with Cortez and the others. They were not interested in converting the natural inhabitants of this strange land to Christianity, but to steal the treasures they believed is hidden in great quantity somewhere."

I told him that it was the story of Juan Martinez who was set adrift blind folded up the Orinoco River as punishment for causing an explosion on his ship. The Indians found him and took him to their golden city. This story set ablaze a fire in the hearts of the British buccaneers. The Spaniards, content with their diversion set about their destruction of the continent. Eventually they settled in various parts and some stability prevailed.

Bell seemed unable to grasp the history being related and not wanting to be left out changed the topic by asking "Mr Diego what do you do for a living? You seem to be a very knowledgeable person. You should be in the city teaching people of the history of their natural inhabitants."

"I was a sailor," he began explaining, "I worked four years on a bauxite boat from McKenzie to Canada. I read lots of books and became assistant engineer on that ship. My first winter in Canada was a real hell. I lost my way to the small hotel I was staying at and collapsed on the street and nearly froze to death. I was lucky to be rescued by a kind family, they took me home and gave me a hot drink and warm blankets and allowed me to stay the night. My last trip was even more disastrous, my boss took me to his home to spend Christmas, his grand children were visiting and we were to have a big family party. On Christmas day he ordered a reindeer to bring the gifts and he bought to surprise them. I have never seen a reindeer before so I went outside and I felt the coldest wind pass straight through me. I was lucky I had a few whiskies it had the effect of heating me centrally. The next day was all drinking and singing, the kids were enjoying themselves with many cakes and lots of sweets. Barrington and I were so drunk we were unable to get to the harbour in time. Our ship had left. Our immediate response was to notify head office. Barrington eventually got his ship at another port while I was arrested as an illegal immigrant. I can never return to Canada. So my days as a sailor are over. I must now find a wife and become a hunter."

At this point the Commissioner came to join us to explain the outcome of the crisis with the bull.

"Well chaps everything is going to be fine. Our young bull will have a family but it will be some time before that can happen. It's impossible to raise a hundred dollars from these people. They have no money and I will not use my money for this scheme. But leave it with me."

"Is there a way out, sir?" I asked.

"There is a long shot. My brother has recently been elected President of his Rotary Club. I know they can help if they have a budget for their international program. When I get back to Georgetown I will telephone him and make that request."

"I will be prepared to look after the herd for you if you need someone," Diego offered.

"Do you live in Sappanam?"

"No, sir I am from Tacuba near Triangle. You know the area?"

Without answering the question, he told him "Well keep in touch." With those last words the commissioner departed.

My father joined him and they headed for the Rest House. Diego and Bell went to prepare dinner and the rest of us went down the river for a wash. When we returned dinner was ready and a surprise was on the table. It was a bottle of pure malt whisky sent to us compliments of the Commissioner. My dad was not mindful of what I did these days so I took advantage of the situation and joined the group with a good sip of this Scottish nectar.

We were soon joined by three of the local tribesmen. One by one they introduced themselves.

"I is Suru," the first one said.

"I is Guru," and pointing at Suru he added, "brother."

"I is Many fingers," third one said.

Looking at them did not explain much of why they were given such foolish names except Many fingers. It is only when I started looking at his hands that he revealed the extra little finger on both of them, smiling and nodding his head.

"Are you going to ask them what they want?" I asked Diego.

Diego was inquiring why they came by making gestures with his hand and talking in half English half tribal lingo. He himself was unable to communicate fully in their dialect. It seems that a word here and there from his dialect and theirs were the same. After some deliberation he turned and looked at me and said "The one called Many fingers wants you to bond with his sister."

"That's ok by me," I replied "So long as it isn't marriage."

"You don't understand. For you to be his brother you have to bond with his sister. She has chosen you." Diego seemed more perplexed than I was at this request.

"Chosen me? Why did she do that?"

"She is the daughter of one of the Elders and you being the son of the dentist is the ideal choice," Diego explained with some uncertainty.

"This is worse than the East Indians in the Corentyne. The parents choose the wives for their sons. It's a good arrangement. It even goes on in Europe with not only royalties, but also influential families. I must add it always turned out to be a perfect arrangement. But this is ridiculous. I am not royalty or an East Indian…I am not having some savage choosing a wife for me. Tell them to go to hell."

"Calm down, young Peter, I will tell them, you must see her first. Bonding may not mean marriage it is perhaps to be your helper and if you are happy then it can be done." He paused for a while and with a serious note said "Please don't call them savages. They understand that word perfectly."

"This is beyond all absurdities I really don't know what to think of this situation. I will leave it to you to sort it out. No wife. If you let me down I will ask Ben to hold you down while I extract all your teeth." My threat seemed to have a chilling effect on Diego. I was beginning to feel sorry for him and the predicament that has unwittingly fell on him.

Diego told them that I needed time to think about it and only then will I make a decision. They appeared pleased and departed.

Ben and Bell teased me by wishing me a happy married life. Manny looked worried until Ben threatened to rearrange the angle of his neck if he was to say anything to my dad.

After that absurd meeting with the strangers we ate our dinner of roast peccary and yam again. It did not taste as nice as it should be so I told Bell to improve on her cooking. She understood I was annoyed with those strangers and gave me a hug instead. I kissed her cheek and apologised for my outburst. She gave me a squeeze as if to say I am forgiven.

In our beds Ben thought he'd cheered me up by telling some of his womanizing escapades. Some of it I'd heard before and I was not amused. However, the next tale he told us caught me by surprise. He started by saying that he was waiting for the right time to tell us this episode. He began, "I was in love with this girl since I was a boy but because of my size she was afraid of responding to my advances. As time went by I grew more fond of her, she was gradually drifting away from me and my feelings. Eventually she got married to a customs officer. On the night of her wedding I got stinking drunk. Occasionally, I would see her going shopping and we sometimes smiled at each other. To shorten this story, I decided to visit her when I knew her husband was away. She was surprised to see me; nevertheless, she invited me in. I asked her how she is coping with married life to an important man.

"Not that great" She replied "My husband is not a romantic. Every evening he goes to the bar with his friends and when he comes home tight he will hit me if he is not happy with his meal or the way I kept the house. I am married to him so I am bound to a life of misery."

"I'll break his neck," Ben shouted. "By God I'll break the bastard's neck if he lays a hand on you."

"Is that what you want to tell us?" Diego asked.

"No man, after that we met quite often and one evening when he was away. I took courage and went up to the house again. She was again surprised to see me but I can see she was happy I came. Well I don't have to tell you the details. So when her husband arrived unexpectedly I grabbed my under wear and ran the hell out of there. It would have been a no contest if he confronted me but I wanted no more trouble. I ran as fast as I could with my ding-a-ling swinging East to West. When I got in the cemetery I decided to put something on only to discover it was her underwear I ran off with."

"Do you think it's funny making love to another man's wife?" Manny asked.

"Maybe not, but look at it from my angle. She was unhappy and I wanted what should have been mine."

"What happen to them?" Bell inquired.

"I couldn't say. I came down to McKenzie looking for work among other things and here I am babysitting this young gentleman and earning very little."

It was an odd story, funny when you think of Ben running with nothing on to hide his essentials. His escapade got me in a devilish mood. So, when Diego asked me if I had any embarrassing moments in my life I felt manly enough to relate the incident in the last day at school. The incident that occurred on the same day I was slapped on the cheek. It was like this I began. "It was coming to the end of term and our French master had left. Our next teacher was a female Canadian, a lecturer in religious knowledge." At this point I felt a bit embarrassed to continue. Their insistence left me no choice but to carry on.

"As soon as she entered the class room she looked at the blackboard and saw it was not cleaned and immediately looked at the roster and saw my name. She sternly requested me to do my duty. I protested, telling her that I was unwell. To be honest my mother employed a very sexy mulatto young lady who had the habit of discussing her sexual exploits rather audibly I could not help over hearing her relating her latest episode in such details that it set my body inflamed with sexual desire. I went to my lessons full of unfulfilled passion. My predicament was how to hide my embarrassment. Reluctantly I stuck my hand in my pocket and marched towards the blackboard. This infuriated her so much she struck my hand hard with the ruler so hard that it hurt."

"Now get your hand out of your pocket, you are not a man yet." She ordered I gradually withdrew my hand and up popped my embarrassment." "Looking red in the face she quickly tapped my hand this time very gently and whispered." "Put it back, put it back and go and sit down." Her stern stare at the class soon brought their hysterical laughter to an end.

Manny interrupted by saying "You people going to give me night mares. The supply boat is coming tomorrow and we all have to be by the waterside very early. The Commissioner will not be pleased if his supply is left lying on the landing." With those final words we settled down for the night.

I was about to doze off when I heard voices approaching and as it became louder I stood up and took a quick glimpse through the windows. I can see the villagers with spears in their hands and the Commissioner among them. I quietly raised Ben to have a look.

Our curiosity was such that we decided to go and investigate. As we opened the door the Commissioner told us to stay inside as there is a jaguar roaming through the village. I felt a chill through me and when Ben opened the window we could see the villagers standing in a semicircle facing outwards and spears at the ready for any eventuality.

One of the villagers started making an animal sound as if to engage the attention of the animal, all to no avail.

Eventually they dispersed arguing between themselves. I could not understand a word being said as they spoke in their own dialect.

In the morning I went out early to check on what was happening in the night. I was surprised to find large dog like paw marks right up the steps of our front door and all the way down to the river.

I was rather scared to go down the river for my morning wash. I called out to Ben and he came half naked to see what I wanted.

At that very moment the Commissioner came out and told us all is clear as the animal has been spotted heading in the jungle. He also assured us that jaguars are nocturnal and only hunt at night and that we must be careful when wandering about at night.

My first night in the deep jungle and it was more than I bargained for. Ben seems unafraid and flexed his huge muscles to put me at ease.

CHAPTER 3

A Reptilian Battle

It was five in the morning. The villagers were already heading to the landing and we were just about ready to join them. "Hurry up!" My dad shouted to us as he and the Commissioner went pass.

The boat came right on time. The four paddlers worked all night to help the engine against the tide to get here, it appears the engine broke down during the night and they were exhausted. They opened a bottle of rum and had a drink before slumping to rest.

The supplies were divided and each took their share Ben and Diego separated our packages to be transported to the house later. There were more important matters to attend to. Five letters were for me and the rest went to the Commissioner who would eventually hand them to their respective owners. I was too excited to care about anything else. These letters were my only communication with what was happening while I was stuck in the middle of nowhere. I hastily ran through the one from my mother. The usual questions of my health and when will she be seeing me.

Two letters were from England. This did stir me up even more. Aubrey Jacobs the son of a Jewish merchant had completed his degree in law and would soon return to Berbice to be called to the Bar. Persotum Persaud my East Indian friend is going for his masters' degree in law. He wants to be a Judge. There is a slight problem with Persotum. He, being an East Indian, felt he had to go one better to be accepted as a friend by us. This was contrary to our thinking. The truth is there is a racial barrier and the races know their places. It was not a legal prerequisite but a hidden agenda inculcated through generations by Britain to preserve their superiority. The more westernised East Indians did not have that problem since most of them were respectable merchants or professional men. Persotum, on the other hand, was bought up in the sugar estate and his father was a junior administrator in the factory. His subservience to his superiors was transmitted to his children. That was the reason my friend was so keen to keep rivalling me for the top spot in school, a feat I will add modestly that he never achieved. The third letter was from Boston USA, it was my dear friend Freddie. Now there is a man with charisma. On the social front he was dominant and excelled in cricket. He was more of a ladies' man, though he never succeeded with the target he had in mind. My robust friend has a lecturing job at the university having gained his Masters. I felt so happy about their progress it made me forgot to feel neglected and my lack of achievement; as far as my career is concerned it was put on ice.

The fifth letter which was accompanied with a parcel was amusing, it read "Dear Mr D'Abrue this is to let you know that the magistrate has informed me to send you your shirt. Apparently he cannot allow the accused to benefit from his crime. I will have to tell you exactly how it went for you to understand.

"The magistrate asked." "You pleaded guilty? Do you have anything to say in your defence?"

"Yes sir." The defendant replied "Within the boundaries of a layman I am asking for mercy." The magistrate a keen cricketer smiled and said "Talking of boundaries, are you? I will hit you for a six. You will go to prison for six months… Take him away!" He then ordered me to return the shirt to you. Do you know something Mr D'Abrue if that man had not mentioned boundaries he would have been sent down for a maximum of a month? I feel sorry for him. If you come this way again please see what you can do for him. Basically he's a nice person. And he is sorry for what he'd done." It was signed Sergeant Gladstone, Wismar Police Station.

My thoughts were now turned to the matter at hand. With some help from the villagers we were able to get our supplies to our house. I asked Diego if he would like the shirt. I wanted never to see it again.

"It will not fit me," he observed. "I know someone it will fit. Thank you"

The villagers were still carrying their supplies to their huts and the children were playing along the water's edge. Ben advised them to keep away. They of course ignored him and kept on running and shouting. Suddenly there was a louder than usual scream, one of terror. Every one turned to see what had happened. There it was an anaconda its jaws were clamped firmly on one of the little girl's legs and it was rapidly putting a coil around her. The women started screaming and the men threw spears at it. It was Ben to the rescue, he slid down the muddy bank and grabbed the reptile by the neck and tried to squeeze the life out of it, but he was not getting any results the snake made a second coil around the girl and was using its massive length and strength to manipulate the victim into the water. The mud was helping it slide down the embankment towards the water and it intended to drown the poor child. Ben realised what was happening. A desperate battle ensued between him and the serpent. He summoned all his energy and with an almighty roar and resolute determination he buried his legs in the mud and with both hands strangled the serpent. He then unhinged its jaw and released the child, more terrified than hurt she clambered up the embankment and ran to her parents with blood dripping from her injuries.

One of the men threw a rope and the snake was hauled up, Ben looked like the god of mud as he stood triumphantly over the dead reptile.

There were jubilation and praises for this giant. Some of the women wrapped their hands around his muddy biceps and showed admiring smiles. The men, on the other hand, were discussing the snake.

It emerged that the skin would fetch about $5 per foot and since this snake was about 23-feet long it was likely it would bring in a lot of money. The question everyone was asking who gets the money. The Commissioner pointed out that since it was Ben who killed the snake the money should go to him. The villagers argued that it is on their land the snake was killed and the money should be split equally. It was Diego's argument that survived. He suggested that since the Commissioner is unable to get the $100 from London straight away, then the money can be used to buy as many heifers as possible including another bull and in that way everyone would benefit. When this was agreed the Commissioner assured us that he will personally go to Wismar with the supply boat and arrange the sale of the skin and the purchase of the cattle He further promised that he would give the $100 expected from London to make the purchase complete.

He told the chief to brief three of his most reliable men to help drive the cattle here. He turned to Ben and comforted him with the promise that the Governor will be informed of his heroics and maybe he will be given a medal.

Ben broke all the rules and plunged himself in the river washing the mud and sweat away. I could almost feel how refreshed and relaxed he was. He was dripping as he came ashore. My dad came up and invited him to get dressed and meet him in the rest house.

Half an hour later, he came back with a very large bottle of malt whisky, with strict directive from my dad to see I do not over indulge. I hastily started writing my letters to be sent with the boat and eventually posted from McKenzie. Only then can I start any celebration.

Diego did not want to join in the celebration. He felt he has lost Bell. She did not reply to his question of marriage and it has been worrying him.

"What's the matter Diego?" Ben asked. "You not joining us for a drink?"

"I will, but first I must ask Bell again in the presence of my friends if she will marry me."

"Diego you know I will marry you. I thought you were the one who lost interest," she apologetically replied.

"Are we going to discuss matrimony? Or are we going to drink this stuff before it evaporates?" Ben asked.

"We'll do both," I suggested.

As the day passed we drank and planned Diego's and Bell's wedding. It will be the first tribal and western wedding in the jungle. That idea raised everyone's hope of a great festival in the making.

The chief was informed of our plan and I am certain he would have instructed his people to make the necessary arrangements before his departure.

Everyone was overjoyed with the news even the Commissioner joined in by appointing himself as the Master of Ceremonies.

The whisky made me exceedingly merry and I started to sing and held on to Bell for a dance. No one had seen me like this before and I am not sure if I had seen myself like this. If my dad saw it he would have been unsure if this was his son. As it turned out it was the joy of him going away for a month that made me happy. I can practice my method of dentistry on the villagers without supervision and feel a sense of accomplishment.

On the morning of his departure, Commissioner Mathew Longhorn sent a message inviting me to the Rest House. I was very surprised; I have never been inside and was curious. I entered and saw him in conversation with my dad. I said hello and as he was busy I asked him if I could look around in the meantime.

The first place I visited was the bathroom. I was surprised to see flushing water toilet and shower in the jungle I can see how the system worked with a paraffin drum as an overhead tank. It was a crude construction but considering the circumstances it was a novelty. I never expected in all my wildest dream to find flush toilet and a shower in the jungle. On the other hand, it would only take a bit of imagination and little expertise to construct it.

On a table in a corner was sweet smelling soap, a razor and talcum powder. Such luxuries I noted. Upstairs was four bedrooms. His was neat, a large double bed with clean cotton sheets and an elaborately patterned counterpane with tassels. The second bedroom, which my dad used, was less stylish but comfortable I did not look in the other two bedrooms. Instead, I wandered to the back where part of the veranda was converted as a store room. It seemed to be filled with junk. There was an army uniform hanging on the wall and covered with dust and pictures of him speaking with the tribesmen of India's North West frontier. They looked tall, handsome and fierce. Tucked away in the far corner was a picture of the Commissioner and a beautiful

Indian lady dressed immaculately in a silk sari and with jewels sparkling with diamonds. Downstairs was his office on the desk was official papers stacked neatly on one corner, two pens lay side by side one for red ink the other for black and there was the two ink wells. Behind that was a stack of fountain pens bound together with a rubber band. What surprised me most was the presence of a paraffin-operated fridge in the kitchen where two young ladies were cooking and washing. This is what I would call total luxury in the jungle. Now I began to understand why he survived twenty-two years in this wilderness.

My excursion completed, I joined the duo. His orderly brought me a cup of tea, which I sipped while listening to what he had to say.

"Young man!" he began, "I have not had the opportunity to get to know you. I can see you are not very happy here and I may have a solution to put that right at least temporarily. I would like you to stay in the house while your dad and I are away. I shall leave full instructions with my staff to see to your needs and that you observe the rules of this house. In future you can address me as Uncle Mathew as is customary in this country. You are helping your father doing a service for these people who needed the help he is giving. I hope when the cows arrive it will produce enough milk for the children and that will be a big improvement on their health not to mention their teeth as you rightly pointed out."

"I will use your house as my own home in Berbice," I assured him.

"I have never been to Berbice. You must tell me about it. Your dad always seems reluctant to speak about your home town. More to the point I am never in town when he is hosting those famous parties I heard about," he told me.

"Well it may sound prejudicial, but in Berbice, live the most hospitable people on earth. It is even more so as you move into the villages in the Canje and Corentyne areas. We live on the outskirts of New Amsterdam, a small municipality with a population of not more than five thousand. My paternal grandmother left us a very large house. It suits my dad as he entertains a lot. Mostly friends from Georgetown, they would come down to spend weekends with us. When they arrive my father would invite the East Indian women from the village to come with their husbands and prepare an Indian meal which goes down well with his visitors who liked it very much. Since they are never served East Indian dishes at home, it was always a festival when visitors come for their week-ends relaxation. The town's people always joined in and the partying would go on and on. On Sundays they would travel down the Canje River to fish and hunt and swim. It's good fun when you are a grown up. My dad always sent me packing to my other grandmother to make room for his visitors which is always a treat for me. I guess that is why I never bothered about his visitors. My grandmother loves me and pampers me. She even let me go to the cinema to watch western movies. Films, my father used to say is corrupting young people into violence. After a while I got bored with it, the ending is the same, the villain is portrayed as more evil than he really is only to make the good guy look more heroic. In the end as always he'd shoot the villain and after blowing the smoke from the barrel he'd twirl his gun with great dexterity and plant it in his holster. After a pause and with great thought I continued "There is something that always bothered me."

"And what can that be?" the Commissioner asked.

"Whenever his visitors are leaving, they always ask if there is anything my dad can give them to take back. As usual, my dad would give them a bag of vegetables or a chicken. I have never seen them giving him anything in return and whenever he goes to Georgetown they would ask what he has brought for them.

"Is this true, Joseph? He asked.

"Not all of it, sometimes when I go to their city they would invite me for a drink at a bar in a hotel. They never seem to do any entertainment at their homes. The city folks are not sociable as we and they never entertain friends in their homes. It is always at a bar or a restaurant. The only time I would meet their families is to give them what I brought."

"So you are saying. When they come to Berbice they always ask what you have to give and when you go to Georgetown they'd ask what you brought? Don't you find it a bit one sided."

"Well I do. But Berbice is a quiet place, not much socializing and they do give the town a kind of carnival spirit and boost the economy a bit. My friends in New Amsterdam look forward for these encounters and it makes me popular. All in all we do have a lot of fun. What my son doesn't know is that I always get to do some dental work for them at premium rates. So it isn't fair to say I don't get anything out of it."

"I nearly went to Berbice when I came to this country twenty two years ago to establish my base. A place called Oreala." Matthew told my father. He then asked. "Ever heard of it Joseph?"

"I know it very well. I've been there quite a few times. It's about sixty miles up the Corentyne River." After a pause he continued. "By the way Matthew, that is the river that separates us from Dutch Guiana. I've been there also many times. As a matter of fact I have quite a few patients there."

When our conversation ended, I took the opportunity to ask about our position. I was right when I thought the Great Falls would not be too far away. I wanted to be absolutely certain how far in the jungle we were. The most important question I wanted answered without sounding impertinent. Why choose here so far away from the rest of the larger settlements to set up your base. He began to explain.

"This post was started by my predecessors. It was to have an air strip here from whence he could visit the other settlements which are about a hundred miles radius from here. That scheme never materialised. So I am stuck here… I like it here."

"How do you communicate with the villagers in the West and South of the country?" I again asked and again he started explaining.

"I have dozens of rangers made up of the local people and they have certain powers of arrests for illegal loggers or men looking for gold or diamonds in areas where they are not supposed to be. Every six months they arrive here to report to me. If there is any serious trouble then I intervene personally. I must tell you that I find travelling on foot and boat to these far off areas does exhaust me considerably."

"How often do you make these journeys?" father asked

"Since I've been here, not more than a dozen times," he replied.

"How do you deal with the law breakers?" Was the other question from my father.

"I usually confiscate their equipment with the threat that if they are caught again they will be sent to prison. It always worked and I never had to punish any of them twice." He ended up saying.

In the meantime the men started getting the baggage on the boat and I hastened to tell the others of my good fortune. Now I don't have to rely on Ben to shave me with his dull razor or cutting my hair with a pair of scissors that had seen better days.

My dad gave me a hug and made me promise not to follow Ben's rum drinking habit. Ben over heard him and promised to look after me like a brother.

The Commissioner drew me aside after my father went ahead and showed me some books and leaflets he brought back from India and told me that I could go through them and that I may find some interesting, And rather profound.

He also mentioned the fact that not all East Indians are coolies as people here in British Guiana see them.

I thought that for an English man he appears very sympathetic towards the East Indians. I wish I could share his sentiments. Nevertheless, since we are all human beings and creation of the only God, I thought some respect be given to them.

I was beginning to have a deep respect for this Commissioner. I wonder what my mother will think of him.

With the pair gone, I was left to my own devices. I desperately wanted to try an experiment I had thought about months ago. My father thought it a waste of time and materials.

I went to the surgery and there was Manny polishing away at some denture he had repaired. He grunted a reply when I greeted him. I told him I will be here all day doing some experiment.

This seemed to have brightened his spirit. He then asked, "Can I help you?" I told him I was happy to do it alone at this stage.

I tried several times to get my experiment going and always it appears that I was not doing something right. It is better if I gave it some more serious thought. The wasted materials would upset my father. They were very expensive and difficult to buy. The prospect of war was becoming more real every day.

On radio ZFY, the possibilities of war were discussed at every level. Visitors from England were invited to give their views. It was always the same the inevitability of hostilities with Germany and Churchill's determination to stop any further advances by the Nazis if ever they invaded Poland.

I was too young to understand all of it. War to me was a romantic adventure. My teenage visualisation of it did not conjure up a picture of bloodshed and hardships. Ben had a totally different view. He indicated to me that he would rather chase women than do any fighting.

CHAPTER 4

Sugar Bush and Nuggets

After the supply boat's departure Many Fingers came to the camp in the company of a beautiful young lady. He spoke to Diego at length and beckoned me to approach nearer. I looked at her and wondered if this was his sister, by God she was beautiful, her hair was plaited and hung on either side. She appears very young but old enough to be a bride. Her breasts was pointed and looked firm and resilient. I must admit if bonding does not mean marriage then my problem will be over. Diego told me it was not marriage and I would have to make up my mind very soon as she is promised to the son of a chief from another village. I asked her name and she said they call her Sugar Bush but her Christian name is Maureen. What an appropriate name she looks like something rather sweet. Smiling, she looked at me and asked "you bond me?"

Diego was getting impatient and ask me sternly what my decision is. I was angry with his attitude and shouting. I held Sugar Bush by the hand and explain that my dad has gone to Berbice and when he comes back in a month's time I will let her know of my firm decision. Because of her limited English I was unable to convey my thoughts adequately and convincingly. Her brother thought I wanted her as a temporary passing pleasure.

Diego sensing my frustration insisted that this matter can only come to an end one way or the other and that can only be when my dad and Uncle Mathew return. Mention of the Commissioner's name did the trick. Her brother began to relax and his countenance became more amicable.

As he led her away she held my hand tightly with expectation in her eyes she asked. "You bond?"

I looked at her unable to say anything and watched them disappear in the forest. I must consider what effect this will have on my dad, being a man of strong Catholic beliefs.

The next few days were spent wandering and chatting with the villagers. They urged me to bond with her and if my father objects then they can arrange that it happens without his knowing. I was unsure of this arrangement. I cannot have a clandestine affair under the very nose of my dad and more importantly, what will uncle Mathew says about it? I told them my feeling and they agreed they will wait.

It was at this stage that I decided to have a full-scale discussion with Diego in connection with this bonding and what it really means. He told me that the young lady has fallen in love with me and would like to be my mistress, no marriage; this would in effect make her look respectable in the eyes of her people. I told Diego that my father would not allow me to enter such an arrangement. I also have to consider what my friends in Berbice might think.

Diego looked sternly at me and asked "Do you want her to end up as a virtual slave to that tyrant from the next village. He tried unsuccessfully several times to seduce her even the young men at village risked their lives to protect her. These people have their pride and tradition. If this is a respectable way for her to have what she wants, and, I know for sure you are keen to have her. Are you going to allow the dictates of your father to affect your life as a man?"

"I am not sure that is the issue here Diego. I have to be careful how I conduct my life even here away from so called civilisation. I can only promise that when my dad and Uncle Matthew return I will discuss this problem with them and I am sure something decent will emerge."

Diego appears reconciled to my argument. He made one final attempt to get a truthful answer from me he again asked, "If your dad and Matthew agreed that she can stay with you. Will you have her?"

"As what Diego, as a servant or a mistress?"

Diego paused in contemplation briefly, and then suggested, "If things do not go the way we want. Then I suggest that you take her as a servant and this will save her. Her people will be pleased and you will have saved her from a life of bondage. You must understand that you are the son of the dentist a man they love and respect. For a maiden of the village to bond with you is a great prestige for them and that will inevitably put a stop to that tyrant trying to get his hands on her."

It was not long after I was invited by the villagers to go fishing for arapaima the largest fresh water fish in the world. The villagers are known to tell exaggerated stories to people from the outside. When they said this fish can grow to about fifteen feet in length and can weigh up to four hundred pounds. I took it as another of their fancy tales. However, I went along. Diego and Ben soon joined us after inquiring where we are going. With a wry smile I told them what the villagers said about the arapaima. Diego confirm that such a fish exists, but not so sure it can grow to fifteen feet. We told Bell not to prepare dinner for us as we would be cooking arapaima in the forest. She smiled and waved us goodbye.

It was a long walk, nearly two hours continually cutting undergrowth and perspiring until we were completely drenched. We had in fact crossed the Demerara border and were in the county of Essequibo. A county larger than Berbice and Demerara put together. Its mighty rivers are responsible for draining the country. Its main river the Essequibo is so large that an island as large as Barbados could exist in its estuary. A fact no Barbadian wants to hear.

It was one of its tributaries we found ourselves fishing for this great fish. The tannin coloured water was still clear enough to see two feet down. The men cut some dead trees into logs and made a raft. While this was being done, some of the men caught some small fish and tied them to a rope made of palm fibers; it was carefully lowered in the water and then they thrashed the water using their make shift paddles after about ten minutes the water began bubbling creating huge ripples. There was great excitement and more of the rope was let out. Without warning the great fish took the bait and took off. The raft picked up speed as the fish carried us away first from the shore and then back again as it tried to devour the bait. This went on for nearly half an hour. I was informed that this strategy was to tire it into submission. A machete and spear brought an end to the exercise, with Ben's help the fish was dragged ashore. It turned out to be a small one about three feet long its silver scales reflecting the sunlight like jewels. A huge portion was cooked and eaten before we started back home.

The rest of the fish was divided among the villagers and they went their way. We hurried to the house for a shower and relaxation. Two men were hastily filling the overhead tank with water for us. Bell was nowhere to be seen. Diego went in the kitchen and saw a pot that was still on the boil and the vegetables were nearly cooked. Ben took charge of the situation while we went searching for her. She was sitting under a tree with a sad look apparently feeling lonely. It was only the presence of Diego that brought a smile.

In the morning, I felt exceedingly tired and my legs ached so much that I thought it would best to do a bit of walking as an exercise. The village looked deserted except some of the children were singing in the background, and as the wind was picking up the macaws were getting agitated and squabbling for the right fruit. The monkeys soon put a stop to it; clambering from limb to limb they soon put the macaws to flight. Their arched formation of flight and their colours made them looked like a rainbow. I strolled away from the huts to find some peace within myself and to bring back some life in my legs. I must have strolled a long way from the village into the forest when I heard two peccaries noisily feeding on the forest floor. I was too engaged in their activities as they scurried along devouring whatever it has. From the corner of my eye I noticed a stealthy movement among the trees. At first, I could not make out what it was and as it moved into the dappled sunlight I saw it, a jaguar stalking the peccaries. I became afraid that I would make a better meal than the peccaries. Fortunately the wind was blowing towards me. I went behind a tree for better protection as the stalker made swift head way towards its quarry. In a flash it pounced on one of the peccaries and a battle for survival ensued. The peccaries gave the jaguar a valiant fight, blood was dripping from its jaws. Sensing victory they made another attack on the poor jaguar. Bloodied and enraged the jaguar clamped its immense jaws on one of them; a shake of the head was enough to kill its prey. The other one ran off looking back occasionally to see if its mate would follow. It took his kill to a little clearing and as it tore away at the flesh I can hear him snarling and bones cracking. Terrified, I hasten back to relate my observations to my friends.

Diego could not believe what I told him. He closed his open mouth and in a quiet voice asked "Did you really see that? Did you really see a jaguar make a kill? Man I was born around here, I have travelled to many uncharted areas and I have never witnessed such an encounter. You were lucky the jaguar did not see you. From what you said it seems the animal had an unsuccessful night's hunt. It must have been very hungry to hunt in bright daylight."

"You shouldn't let me drink so much whisky in future," I joked. Bell snuggled up to Diego and in a whisper asked "What are you going to do after we are married?"

"I have a plan. When the cows arrive I will be looking after them. There are two things I must do before they get here. First, we must build a safe corral around the area where the cows will be kept as you pointed out jaguars are about and I will not tolerate them stealing our cattle. The other thing I must do is an experiment and I will have to show you as I find it difficult to explain."

A few days later Diego with the help of the villagers were cutting saplings and left to dry. These were the materials needed for the corral. In the meantime, Diego was planning an incursion far into the forest past the point of encounter with the jaguar and peccaries. Diego decided to confer with the Chief and elders of the possibilities of building huts for some of the young male villagers, whom he hopes will help with his cattle project.

His discussion was successful. The chief agreed, suggesting that the young bachelors will become better hunters if they were given the opportunity to live away from their parents with more freedom to do what suited them. Diego was to support them in the project not only by encouraging them, but also to lend a hand in the building of their huts. It seemed that he was hoping that we all would help, and which was exactly what we intended to do.

So, with very little time left before the cows arrive, the construction of the mini village began to take shape. Some young ladies came and gave a hand and cooking for the men while they worked. I presume it is the sweethearts of the youngsters.

It was fun working alongside these fine young men, Diego was having more of the fun as he spoke their language and only intermittently he would explain some of the things they said. Singing and joking among themselves helped to hasten the pace of the work. I began thinking of Sugar Bush. Her loveliness appeared more intense in my mind. The question of morality rested heavily on me and the outrage I expected from my father will be even heavier than the natural urges of nature that were battling for victory. I wonder who will be the winner.

One day, we were having a relaxing time not far from the Rest House, when one of the rangers came running and shouting in his tribal language. Diego came out and calmed him down. It turned out that one of the young men had sexually assaulted one of the young ladies who were helping them at the little village and the chief wants him to be caught and punished. They also demanded that unless the Commissioner ordered his rangers to find and bring him to face justice they will kill all the cattle when they arrive and burn the mini village down. It seems they feel those were the elements that brought about this shame on the young lady. Since the Commissioner was away it was obvious that Diego took charge of the situation.

"This is damn serious. Damn serious indeed," shouted Diego. He then ordered the ranger to get hold of two others and find this young man.

"I will let the Chief know that we can only resolve this situation when we found this young man and punishment can only be given by the Commissioner."

Diego and Ben offered to help. Diego insisted that he knows where to find him, as he has seen them running off together in the forest. We were all pleased with Diego's help. To be on the safe side, he went and brought a rifle from the Rest House and told the servants to lock it and stay indoors.

First, he visited the Chief and he explained the situation to him advising him not to do anything before consulting with him and to wait for the Commissioner to return. The chief nodded approvingly and the party went in their quest. I was too tired to go anywhere so Bell took some of my laundry down to the river to be washed with me in tow.

When we got back to camp a young man was seen standing in the clearing with his hands tied. The chief was questioning him and he was shaking his head vigorously, apparently denying the accusation. Diego came up to him and questioned him about the incident. He vehemently denied the charge and accused the girl of making trouble for him because he refused to accept bonding with her. He realised that she only wanted to bond with him so she could live in the new village and be free to do what she likes. He further accused her of having many men friends and he will look a fool if he should take her as his wife. This, he said, infuriated her to such an extent that she fabricated this lie to punish him.

The Chief instantly summoned her and repeated the accusations made against her. She started sobbing. Diego stepped in and repeatedly asked her for the truth. She refused to say anything. The chief brought a poisoned arrow freshly tipped in a lethal poison. He brought the young man very near to her and after repeating her accusations and his denials he gave her the arrow. They looked at each other for a long time. Diego stepped in and remind the Chief that this is a matter to be resolved by the Commissioner. The Chief argued that this is a tribal matter and must be dealt with according to tribal laws. Diego had no mandate to stop him. He stepped aside and again the Chief repeated the accusation. Without warning she was about to stab herself with the arrow. Diego stepped in, anticipating her next move and held on to the arrow. He had in fact prevented a tragedy. She fell to the ground crying vehemently and still trying to pierce herself, but Diego broke the arrow and removed the poisoned end; otherwise, she would have been dead in minutes if she succeeded. Everyone was in shock. Two young men took her away and the chief, visibly shaken, looked at Diego bowed his head in respect and left.

We were all looking at Diego for an explanation about the arrow. He told us that the Chief gave her the arrow for one of two things. She can stab the young man with it if he was guilty, or stab herself to prove his innocence."

"But why did she not admit she made a false statement and let the matter ended?" I asked.

"She would have been unable to live with the shame," explained Diego.

"I am sorry Diego. I am missing something here. What if she stabbed the young man would this have exonerated her?" I asked to make clear of this interpretation of tribal laws

"She would not have been able to justify her actions with any creditability. The villagers suspected her of dishonesty and as I said earlier she would have been unable to live among them with that shame. By doing what we just saw gave her a chance to redeem herself and her pride. She really had no intention of stabbing herself. She saw I was poised to intervene. That is why she made the attempt." Diego's explanation was not convincing as far as I was concerned.

I thought of the visit I had with one of the young villagers and his proposal of bonding to his sister and that made me very worried. I shall be firm the next time I am confronted with this request. I decided that any decision I make will have to be in the presence of witnesses. Moreover, I was not allowing myself to be dragged in any tribal conflict.

It was several days before we decided to visit Diego and his new village to see what progress was made. Bell came running to greet us and putting an arm around me she invited us to see her new strong house.

"Quite a sturdy building you have here Diego," I said.

"Yes, I copied it from the lodges the trappers build for themselves in Canada; not only does it keep the bitter cold out, but also the bears and wolves. This will keep any brave jaguar away from my Bell." Diego commented then inviting us he said "Come here all of you. Look at the protection I and the young men built for the cattle. This lodge was built here far from the corral we made at the other end." Then pointing at a stream some two hundred yards away he told us that he is using it as a natural barrier and building a fence until it reaches the bend where the stream turns to empty its water in the Demerara. The open spaces are where the cattle will graze until a more permanent pasture is located.

"The fence is not very high," I noted "I heard jaguars can leap some twenty feet over an obstacle."

"That's true. They can leap very high, not twenty feet I don't think. When they are in water they can't leap anywhere." Diego pointed out.

"How long is this stream, Diego?" Ben inquired.

"About fifty miles or so, there is another river some forty miles further on; it comes out of the hill side. I've seen it from a distance and never made any attempt to explore it. One day soon I will."

"Why not let's all go together and investigate it?" Suggested Ben. "It's a bit late to get there and back, but if you don't mind roughing it for the night we can make an early start in the morning."

"Can you rough it Peter D'Abrue"? Ben mockingly asked.

I suggested that we wait for the Commissioner and my dad to get back before we make the journey. And they all agreed.

Several days later, the Commissioner agreed to accompany us to see this river. My father declined the offer. Ben asked him if he would be able to rough it out in bush as it will be a couple of hard days walking and sleeping in the open.

"Young man when I was a soldier in India we climbed mountains higher that you can imagine and all we had to keep warm was a blanket and a ground sheet in a tent in freezing temperatures."

We sat outside sipping rum that Diego brought for us, and Bell was asked to prepare a meal.

At dawn, we were already on the raft. Ben paddled while Diego navigated. At sunset we came to a clearing. The raft was tied and we walked for several hours until we came to the river Diego mentioned. It was gushing out noisily at great speed from the hill down a gentle slope until it came to a barrier of rocks which slowed its relentless effort to go nowhere. Effortlessly, it gushed over this barrier and carried on normally. I suspected it was coming from the Mabura range near the Great Falls. Diego placed his hand in the water and quickly withdrew it.

"It's ice cold," he shouted. We all put our hands in and felt the icy coldness. Diego told us that this water comes from the Andes. Nowhere in British Guiana has a mountain so high to produce icy water and he will exploit it to keep his meat and fish fresh and not having to go hunting or fishing every day.

"How will you do that"? I asked.

"By using one of the paraffin drums behind the Rest House as a storage tank. That is if the Commissioner will let me have it."

"Of course you can have it" was the assurance he received. "I must say you are a clever man. The four years as a sailor and your knowledge of Canada did a lot for you, my congratulations."

We tied our hammocks on nearby trees and lit a fire. Ben and Diego prepared a meal while Uncle Matthew and I went collecting wood for the fire. I am happy my father did not make the journey. He would have been unable to cope with the outdoor activities. The next day without any further exploration we decided to return to base as the skies were getting heavy with rain clouds.

The young villagers turned out in full to see us arrive and to thank Diego for resolving a sticky issue with their friend.

Diego took the opportunity to reveal to the Commissioner the details of events when he was away. He was congratulated for his quick thinking and ability to act decisively.

The skies were getting darker and rain threatening. Without warning a deafening roar of thunder sent us running for shelter. The rainy season has begun. The monkeys started scurrying up the trees filling the branches and huddling together in small groups. One of these groups was harassing a boa constrictor in the tree. Their annoyance seemed to agitate the snake into a great fury and it lunged at his tormentors repeatedly. They ignored his attacks and soon the poor reptile abandoned its attack and glided away.

Soon the river will burst its bank and a bloody wet season was in the making. I suddenly realised it's over four years since I left my beloved New Amsterdam, my friends and my social life, and my date with Marina in ruins. My dad was adamant that my tutelage will be less interrupted here than in New Amsterdam. My mother wanted me home. She was too gentle to argue with him.

Several weeks later the rains subsided and the sun was seen for longer hours, which indicated that the time was right for us to visit the cold stream. The drum was carried by two villagers with Ben occasionally giving a hand. Uncle Matthew decided to stay behind and for us to report back to him.

When we arrived at Diego's Lodge, Ben was given the task of scrubbing the drum clean of the paraffin and the smell that goes with it. It was a tiring task and he did it without complaining.

We took the drum to the stream. I suggested that we cleared the bottom of the stream where the drum will rest to make it more stable, we choose the deepest part and scooped out the pebbles. The water was so cold that Diego and Ben can only take turns of five minute intervals to complete the job. When they nearly finished they threw the spade at me as I was playfully kicking up some of the pebbles and noticed something bright and shinning. I picked it up and behold, it was a nugget. We searched feverishly and found many more. Every pebble was turned over to make absolutely certain that none of it was left hidden. When we were certain of this, more energy was involved to get all the stones we could clear out with our hands while Ben used the shovel. He was doing a better job with the help of his tool and we let him carry on.

We manage to locate a few small ones. Hours were spent hoping to find some more gold all to no avail. Diego theorised that since he was not a geologist and his certainty that this stream came from some part of the Andean range, it is possible that the water may have disturbed a gold bearing area and these nuggets may have travelled here. The handful, we gathered, was placed in a small bag that Diego always carried with him. It was hard to assess the amount in weight; but a rough estimate and my knowledge of gold and its weight, I would say about fifty or sixty ounces which is a considerable fortune. We all agreed that it would be safer if Diego kept the gold in his lodge until we can decide on its division.

Bell was crying with joy when we told her of our find. Diego told her he was proud to be trusted with a great fortune. "It is the second time people have placed their trust in me."

"When was the first time?" I asked.

"The day Bell agreed to marry me," he replied laughing.

We all started laughing. Bell stopped crying and joined in the laughter.

At camp, we explained our good fortune to Uncle Mathew and we also informed him that he would get an equal share. He was mystified why there were not any more of it around.

He eventually told us that he would be going to Georgetown when the supply boat came. He promised to have the nuggets weighed and priced. He, furthermore, told us that the Governor had invited his brother and he would be in Georgetown for a fortnight and that he wanted to come to Sappanam to see the herd that his club had helped to acquire. Also, since he is expecting that the herd will be here long before he returns, it will be ideally suited to present the whole project dedicated to the good work of Rotary. He further added that his brother did some studies in geology, but failed to finish his studies due to a lucrative offer to work for an oil company. His limited knowledge will at least tell us something about the area.

In the meantime, there was work to be done. Finishing the corral and be ready to receive the herd. When it did arrive we were a bit disappointed that we got only half of what we expected. The chief told us his men promised to return when the rest of the herd is ready. The farmer hoped to receive some more from his supplier shortly.

CHAPTER 5

The Visitors

Several days passed since Uncle Matthew and father went to the city and we did not expect to see them for another week or so. It was an unusually hot day and the only cool place was by the river Ben and I went down looking for caiman and enjoy the cool wind. Unexpectedly, I heard some rumbling in the air. I have never heard that sound before; and as it grew louder, our senses told us to look skyward. I saw it for the first time, and I have heard of it but never seen one. It was an amphibious aircraft. I watched it roar past us and turned around descending rapidly until it touched the water sending clouds of spray all around. It came to a stop as it neared the landing. This intrusion upset the caimans. They gaped their jaws and hissed at the craft in anger. One brave reptile swam toward it only to be repelled by the propellers. Ben hurriedly took a boat and helped the passengers off. The party of eight comprised of Mathew, his brother, wife and daughter, my dad and most surprisingly the Governor's envoy and his two aides. I recognised the man and his wife from pictures in the newspaper. He is a Member of the Legislative Council they acknowledged me as they went by to the Rest House, Ben hurriedly tied the boat and we followed a good distance behind. We saw them enter the house and we went to our smaller house waiting.

It was sometime before the two gentlemen accompanying the Legislator came out on the veranda glasses in hand filled with whisky. Like peacocks about to display their colourful feathers they puffed their chests out and breathed in the fresh cool air coming from the river.

I heard the plane take off and realised that they would be here for the night at least. At dusk, I was invited to the House. Ben looked perplexed at being excluded. As I entered the House, I heard the Legislator commending my dad for his voluntary service. My dad mentioned the fact that I was the one that did most of the work under supervision. This appeared to impress him. I was invited to a seat and listened to their conversation occasionally putting in a few words to compliment what was said. The two gentlemen, having finished their drinks, came in and sat next to the Legislator's wife. Their conversation varied from politics to the work we are doing here and reminiscing of their lives as young men. It seems that the Legislator is from an aristocratic family and served with the army in India. It became interesting when Mathew started giving accounts of some of their exploits while stationed there. He began by saying referring to the Legislator.

"Young Gordon was a bit of a hot head. I remember we were sent on an expedition to the North West frontier to rescue seventeen of our men held captive by that renegade Ahmed Khan. He wanted two hundred horses for their release. Gordon told the commanding officer that he would take two instead and bring the men back. The CO told him to obey orders and to remember that he is not in England strutting around his twenty five thousand acres estate. I remember Gordon's face reddening with rage and I thought he would strike the jealous CO. It is a known fact that aristocrats are in the army not because they are trained soldiers, but simply to have freedom from the strictures of a boring life. The CO was a seasoned soldier who would not tolerate the likes of Gordon and his relaxed attitude to military disciplines."

"You said boring, why is it boring. Surely if you are an aristocrat you will have lots to do." My father interrupted.

"Joseph! If you understood Gordon you would understand when I said boring. He is a person if not involved with something or someone of interest, life becomes boring. Allow me to get back to my story. The CO told us to remain in barracks until he decides who will lead this rescue mission. At the same time, reminding him to remain there until further notice. Gordon asked him rather cheekily if they were to be under armed guards. Irritated by this question, he told him not to be impertinent. Pointing out that it would be folly putting him under restraint. "What are you talking about? Armed guards? A complete waste of time. You will only charm the guards and continue doing exactly what you wanted. Now get out of my sight. Both of you… Do you think I am unaware of what goes on behind my back?" He shouted at us. Gordon simply told him that he is aware of his faithful spies. The CO slammed his hand on his desk and ordered us out. With a crisp salute and a precision about turn we marched off. We heard the CO inhale heavily and exhale in anger, muttering something under his breath".

"Was two hundred horses too much for British soldiers?" Catherine inquired.

"200 or 1000 horses the army was prepared to bargain for the men. Anyway, we were eventually allowed to go on the rescue mission with me in charge. It took us several days to reach the Afghan border. We had to defend ourselves from Ahmed Khan's marauding fighters. It was a game with them always harassing us and testing our abilities. They had the upper hand most of the time, you see, they knew the terrain intimately. We were always on the alert and played the game admirably. Our superiority was dependent of the fact that we had superior weapons and fine marksmen. We were sure that he knew we were coming as his scouts were seen on a higher ridge watching the skirmish that went on below. Their presence was to see if we were taking the horses for the exchange.

We eventually found a cave and decided to rest for the night before making contact with the kidnapper. In the morning, we found ourselves surrounded by Pathans. They were fierce looking and each one had a homemade rifle. They deprived us of our weapons and forced us to march to their camp.

Ahmed Khan came forward looked at us scornfully and calmly asked of the horses. Before I could say anything Gordon told him there are no horses, except the two carrying our gear. He addressed us as infidels and asked why we dared come here to tell him that. He lost his patience and threatened to shoot the captives and said that the two of us will be hanged by our legs until the vultures finish us off. Gordon calmly told him that his reputation as a wise leader is known throughout India and that we would not be here if we didn't have something to bargain with. He demanded to know what that was."

"For the sake of Catherine and her lovely daughter, allow me to tell the rest as I saw it," Gordon interrupted. "You remembered when he asked of our bargaining power. I told him it is not wise we speak of it in the presence of his men. I think he understood the time for tact was a better way out to dealing with this impasse. He invited us in his tent. Now, there was a sight to behold. The tent was like something I never dreamt it to be. Silken carpets were laid on camel hides on the ground and Persian rugs hung on the sides. A dozen or more cushions were scattered around which made sitting quite comfortable. Then, he ordered two lovely ladies to serve cups of hot black coffee. This was a kind of ritual that lasts for some time. I was getting impatient. Finally, he turned to me and asked "Who heads this expedition?" I told him Matthew. He told us the British are cleverer than he thought. By appointing Matthew as the head of this delegation has thrown this arrangement in a new sphere of negotiation." "When I asked why, it was most surprising when he told us that Matthew is known throughout this region as a sincere and honest soldier."

"I think you ought to tell us how you came to this conclusion." Ahmed Khan began to tell us by asking.

"Is it not true Mr Matthew Longhorn that you are seen visiting the caves of the mystics, and squatting on the cold stone listening to their mumblings of divine powers? Is it not true you have a sympathetic view of the Indians and their cause for resentment? Is it not true if you had not sworn allegiance to the crown you may have joined us? Deny it and prove yourself an infidel?"

Gordon continued. "It was here that Matthew stood up and threatened to shoot him if he did not retract his accusations, I think brave as he may want us to believe, he became scared and went on to reveal more secrets. He told us he knew of Matthew's wanderings and instructed his men only to keep an eye on him hoping that he would join him. That is why he did not kill him when he had the opportunity. I then told the impatient Ahmed Khan. "We imagined you will want to kill the hostages and us as well. The British army will not tolerate this barbaric action as you know darn well. For the sake of morale they will send in heavy artillery and flatten this mountain with you and your people." It was not an empty threat and Ahmed Khan knew it."

"What happened next?" I eagerly inquired.

"He took all our horses, released the hostages and set us free. He ordered his men to give us enough food to last a few days. Then we walked the two hundred miles back to camp where we were expected to be greeted as heroes."

"I am dying to hear this. A hero's welcome for my daring brother-in law," Catherine urged him.

Matthew reluctantly continued. "There was no hero's welcome, Catherine my dear. The commanding officer summoned us to his office and demanded an explanation for our actions. Gordon told him the fault is all his and he did not have any regrets of what he did. This infuriated the CO to such an extent that he called his sergeant and ordered him to prepare proceedings for a court martial and at the same time reminding us of his displeasure for disobeying a military order. Gordon became angry and told him if he were to proceed with the court martial, it would come to the attention of some of his powerful friends at the Vice Regal Lodge. I need not remind you, sir, they will see my point of saving two hundred horses the Army badly needed as a valid point of disobedience. The CO realised that Major Gordon being an aristocrat and well-connected, would win the argument. He also considered the fact that a military order should take precedence over all other consideration. Nevertheless, two hundred horses were saved by his insubordination so he relented and ordered us back to barracks until further notice."

"You forget to mention the fact the CO was so unsettled he stirred his tea with his cigar and realising what he had done, tossed it at you," Gordon ended amid some laughter.

There was more laughter when Catherine again asked "What did he toss at you, the tea or the cigar?"

When the laughing was over, my father asked if being a knight was higher than a Commanding Officer.

"A knight of the realm would have been the commanding officer," Gordon replied.

"We were awarded the Victoria Cross. Matthew refused to accept his, he thought he was doing his duty for which he was paid and having a Victoria Cross although a prestigious medal was not going to make him a better man or a soldier for that matter. I, on the other hand, accepted it and accused Matthew of being a fool."

"What happened to merit you this high award?" I asked.

"I don't think there is time to go into that. Perhaps one day I will tell you," he replied.

"Please tell us, we will not be here when you tell your story." Catherine pleaded.

"Then I will tell you my dear. On our way home," Gordon told Catherine.

To divert attention from the previous conversations my father asked Uncle Matthew. "Have you ever been married?"

"Never," Uncle Mathew replied coldly. And began to explain the reason, "After our escapade with Ahmed Khan I was seconded to the Maharajah of Rajasthan. My job really was to assess the Maharaja's intention towards the British, a bit of spying to be blunt. Mind you the prince was not a fool he knew exactly why I was sent and played the game with admirable tact. This appointment was an act of splitting Gordon and I. It was the Maharajah who told me who Ahmed Khan really was. Apparently, he is the nephew of one of the Nizam advisors and would have inherited a title if he did not choose to fight us. Ahmed Khan was also being financed by the government in Kabul; they were using him as buffer. The Nizam was our ally and distrusted any dealing with the government in Kabul. The continued harassment of the British Army would prevent an invasion of Afghanistan. I also learnt that he was to be married to the princess. She refused on the grounds that he longer had a title."

"The Maharajah was also aware through one of his advisors that the princess was conversing with me with her eyes and her posturing suggested that a clandestine meeting was possible. She was so beautiful and fragile I thought if I held her too tightly in my arms she would turn to honey. I was also afraid her actions were a trap devised by the advisors to get me sent back to Shimla. I needed to know the truth. Before my plan was put in operation, I was perplexed when the Maharajah asked if I find the lady attractive and if I have any honourable intentions toward her. I told him I did, but I was not sure if this feeling was mutual. He allowed us to meet occasionally and always chaperoned. Eventually, we agreed to be married. ...It never happened."

"Did she die?" I hurriedly asked.

"Not at all, it was blocked by the CO."

"How can the CO stop you from marrying?" I asked again.

"It was only a courtesy for an officer to ask his Commanding Officer's permission to marry. I did not get that consent for the simple reason that I was always mixed up with Gordon's insubordinations. It is not that my friend is that type of person, but the CO was envious of his connections and that always seem to have a countermanding effect on his authority so he refused my request to get at Gordon" His answer was blunt and rueful.

"Was this partly because of the disagreement with the horses? My dad asked.

"Not at all Joseph, The other issue here is jealousy. Mixed marriages were frowned on in the British sector especially by the women.

"Jealousy, why would they be jealous?" My dad again inquired.

"There were a lot of women who were widowed from the regular insurrections, and they believed the single men available would make potential partners. If they all dash off marrying the locals it would diminish their chances of a second husband" Gordon decided to answer.

"So it was not a racial issue?" I asked. Since I was ignorant of military protocol I was forced to ask another question. "When he decided to refuse you permission, Could you have married her?"

"It would not have been possible." Matthew said and started to explain "As I said it was a permission sought out of courtesy. When that was denied, it became abundantly clear that although this was a vindictive decision as an officer of the king I had to accept it. There were many other ways he could have prevented it. So, I refrained from pursuing the matter any further. That was the nearest I came to ever being married. I guess that is why I love being here. It reminded me so much of the carefree time in my younger days. My time spent meditating and listening to the philosopher's sermons. I can tell you they have changed my life so much so, looking back I can hardly believe it myself" Uncle Matthew added with a look of pride.

At this point, I asked to be excused to check on Ben. The visiting family reminded the Commissioner that they have not been introduced. I took the initiative and introduced myself. I could not help noticing how beautiful the daughter Christine was. We looked at each other and smiled.

At the house, I was confronted with a sulking Ben. "No one invited me", he began "You know why? It is because I am black. The white people don't mix with blacks. You know that?"

"Ben all I know is that my dad invited me over. You were not overlooked because of your colour. You are more white than black I …" Before I could finish he blurted out.

"Yes, I am more white than black but no one ever calls me white. It doesn't matter how little black you have in you it is always the black bastard you are called."

"This is getting out of control. You know how much I respect you. Yet, I always treat you as equal."

"You know why, don't you? Ben interrupted "Because your family is from Madeira you are not counted as European. Look at the classification of the races East Indians 40% Negroes 25% European 10%, Portuguese 10% Chinese 8% and Amerindians 7%. I don't see Portuguese included as European and also any percentage of the mixed races."

"Portuguese are excluded from the European classification for political purposes. You should know that. Like Diego said "You are what you are and no one can change it." My words did have a calming effect of him. He poured us both a drink and he began singing a vulgar calypso he knows I hated. I simply let him get on with it.

It was early in the morning when the party approached our hut. Ben was introduced to Gordon as the man who saved the life of the little girl.

"That's a brave act you put on; killing a 23-foot boa it is by no means an everyday event. I'll remember that. I'll see what the Assembly has to say about presenting you with a certificate of courage," Gordon told him.

Ben had the biggest smile I ever saw and never stopped bowing until he was politely asked to stop. He immediately turned to me after the party left and said "The Legislator knows about me. The big boss himself will eventually know who I am. You are right it's nothing to do with colour, sorry my young friend." He gave me a hug that nearly deflated me.

He and I were told to prepare to go with the visitors to the cold stream. It was still cool and the time seemed right for travel. When we reached Diego's lodge we were told Bell was out milking the cows, it was Diego who showed the visitors his corral and the cattle. He told Jonathan that half of the herd is still to come due to a shortage at Wismar. The brother was impressed and took a picture with all of us around the cattle to take back to London. Diego brought the nuggets and showed it to the visitors. There were cries of astonishment at the sight of those beautiful lumps of gold.

There were not enough horses to take the whole party, so we took the raft instead and paddled our way to the clearing before continuing on foot to the stream. Diego showed Jonathan where we found the nuggets. He made a cursory survey of the area and appeared impressed with the geological formation of the rocks and especially the strata formation of the hill. He asked Ben to dig up some more pebbles and more nuggets were found. Christine came nearer to me and asked to see one of them. It was the first close encounter I had. Her perfume sent my head in a whirl and it thrilled me. I felt as if I had met an angel and unable to respond adequately. She smiled gently and thanked me as I showed it to her. Then she asked "Are you a dentist also?"

"I am doing what you can call my apprenticeship or to be more precise my tutelage and hoped to go to the USA to complete my training." I told her with trembling lips.

"How old are you?" she asked.

Her mother promptly interrupted. "How dare you Christine?"

"But mamma, I don't mind letting anyone know that I am eighteen," she defended her question.

"I will be twenty two a week after you leave for Georgetown," I replied trying to unknot a tricky situation. I then asked Diego for a nugget and placed it in my pocket.

In the meantime, her father continued to examine the rocks and was shaking his head. This sent a feeling of dismay through me. He looked at Matthew and told him:

"From what I gather, I think, this area could have gold right under your noses or maybe hundreds of miles away; it depends on where that lot came from. You will need a proper geologist and an engineer to probe into it. The cost as you know will be astronomical, unless you give it to a private company. I am advising you as a layman."

"None of that," interrupted his brother. "This place must stay as pristine as it is. The natives will have it no other way. They are wary of foreigners trespassing and destroying the land and I support them in every way."

"You sound as if you are the master here Matthew," his brother said.

"You are absolutely right. I am the master here. The only person to countermand my decision is the Governor."

"He wouldn't countermand any decision you make concerning the hinterlands unless of course it is tantamount to treason," Gordon calmly replied.

On our way back to the raft, Christine walked close by occasionally holding my shoulders for support as we trod on. In the raft, she sat next to me letting her hand down in the water and flicking it first at her mom then at her dad and eventually at me. We all started doing it until it became laughable fun.

Throughout our final walk to the house, Christine was always next to me holding me even when it was not necessary to maintain her balance. I sense there was something more to it. My upbringing taught me to respect the families of friends. Mathew has invited me to call him uncle which was a great honour and he was a friend of my father and I held him in great esteem. Because of that I tried to ignore Christine's subtle advances. I must admit it did send more ripples through me.

We were all tired on our return to the House. Gordon and his entourage went indoors and we proceeded to our humble accommodation. We needed the rest before joining the others for a party in the evening.

Ben and I took two hammocks and tied it under a silk cotton tree. The breeze was soft and cool. The monkeys were up in the upper reaches peering inquisitively at us before hurrying off. The hammocks swayed in the wind and before I knew it I was sound asleep. It was difficult to tell how long I slept. It was Ben shaking me to announce that we have visitors. I opened my eyes to see the aides standing nearby. We exchanged courtesies. Then, one of them asked Ben about his deed with the Boa.

"Not much to it really," Ben started out. "I really didn't want to kill it. If it had opened its jaws and let the little girl free I would have let it go to find another meal elsewhere."

"That's very noble of you," one of them told him, and then asked "Are there alligators in the river?"

"Not alligators, they are caimans." I explained.

"Do you say caiman or caimans?" The first aide asked.

"I think it's caimans," I replied with uncertainty.

"Never mind all that. Let's go down the river and see if we can find them."

I did not want to go down the river. Ben suggested that we can go bathing at the same time and look for caiman. Reluctantly, I strolled down to the river and was lucky to see two large reptiles on our side of the bank. Their gaping jaws looked more threatening than ever. Sensing they were on the wrong side they quickly went in the river and swam to the other bank. The aides were thrilled and joined us to bathe on the rocks. Ben and I were a bit embarrassed when they stripped off all their clothes and splashed playfully on the rocks like two children celebrating a day out.

Another shock came when Christine appeared and sighting the two nudes ran off back to the House. Later, that evening we were greeted with great courtesy by Catherine, Christine's mother .She held my hand and led us to the party where the two aides were in company with Christine. Mathew was talking and laughing with his brother. Gordon was in deep conversation with my dad. That suited me absolutely fine. I wanted to be in the company of Christine and she sensed it. One of the Aides tried to divert her attention to what he was saying; she discreetly moved away and came next to me. I felt a prayer was answered. We greeted each other with smiles then her mother joined us. I told her mother quietly that I would like to give Christine a gift. Diego and Bell arrived at the precise moment her mother tapped her glass with her huge diamond ring and announced my intention. I was slightly nervous for the simple fact that I was not prepared to do it openly. It turned out to be the correct thing to do. I began shaking due to my nervousness.

"Mr Commissioner, guests and friends I am exceedingly happy that your visit has been a happy one and more so that I had the opportunity to meet a member of the Legislative Council. I would like to take this opportunity to thank Jonathan and his Rotary Club in London for their kind donation towards the herd albeit only half of it is here. I seem to have been caught up in more than I planned. However, my main reason for this interruption is on behalf of Diego and Bell. Ben, Mathew and myself to present Christine with a nugget we found at cold stream. A token by which to remember this place and the people she met." I asked Bell to do the presentation which was done with a perfect courtesy and a kiss. Christine returned the kiss and immediately embraced me and gave me a wet kiss on the cheek.

The applause was loud and clear. My dad looked proudly at me and nodded approval. A vibrant hand shake from Mathew spoke volumes. I was so nervous I could hardly speak. A sip of that malt whisky worked wonders not only for my nerves, but also for my voice.

My mission was completed and as the rest of the conversation became political or more on a personal level. I decided it was time to leave. Christine sensed that and suggested we take a walk to the river. Her mother objected until I mentioned the fact that Ben will be there to protect us. This assurance that her daughter will be safe and well chaperoned persuaded her to agree to let her go.

It was a brilliant full moon; it looked larger and brighter than I have ever seen it before. I then remembered that the moon has reached its perigee which takes place every lunar year.

As we strolled down to the Demerara, she placed her arm around my waist and was singing a song with words of romance in the tropics. She told me at school that they read romantic books of the magic of the tropics and the South Americans and the song she sung was a reminder that she was in South America and in the company of a handsome young man. I was undoubtedly slightly embarrassed and I changed the subject by explaining why the moon was larger and brighter than normal.

She stopped and faced me then asked "Did you order it to be so? If you did then I must say you are a romantic and just the person I was hoping to meet on my South American holiday." Ben was aware of what was happening and excused himself pretending the call of nature forced him to look for a tree. As soon he left we were embraced in a in a long and sensual kiss that nearly left us breathless. Our bodies were trying to bury itself in each other and as we lay on the ground, my penetration told me I was executing a sexual coup de grace. Christine opened her eyes and looking at me she said in a very tender and loving voice. Her lips quivering, "I can see the shooting stars. It is a sign that this is a romance blessed by Eros himself. The stars are like tiny fireworks. I am so happy."

I was too happy to enjoy the display of meteorites streaking across the skies and disappearing just as they appeared. My thoughts then started to focus on a more serious note. I began questioning myself for allowing this to happen. I thought of the years I have been isolated in this place, of the romantic excursions with the village girls and allowing myself to be sexually exploited by their naivety. I was bored and it was one of the only activities that helped cured my ennui temporarily.

Christine was not to be counted as one of them. I held her and her family in great esteem. My Christian teaching forced me to question the moral issues involved and the ethical standards that can prevent the fulfillment of nature's demands. Morality seemed to be waging a war against nature for the preservation of the ethical standards we try to fit into. My Catholic teachings were against the world of human weaknesses. It teaches of the damnation that would follow should anyone stray from the straight and narrow path to eternal life. I did not attain manhood under these strictures. Drinking whisky and participating in amorous escapades with the village girls that came snuggling in my bed without invitations was not the path I would have chosen. In New Amsterdam, I would have been under the watchful eyes of not only my parents but anyone in the town that knows my family. Men like Doctor Bristol who slapped my cheek to prevent me from starting a bad habit. That was the tight rein that would have guided my life.

I tried to think of the teachings of other religions Buddhism, Islam, Hinduism and the Torah the mother of all religion; the teachings are nearly the same ... Love ... Peace ... Charity, Tolerance and all the virtues that can make a man the ideal candidate for heaven. I was not ready for heaven and I was not allowing the effect of the full moon to blur my thinking. The real question here is my feeling of guilt for participating in this seduction. My heart was filling up with sorrow for stripping Christine of her most prized possession... Her virginity. My thoughts immediately reflected on the writings of an Indian philosopher from a booklet Uncle Matthew said I could read and somehow I felt comforted by it, not because it was epitomic of the challenges of life but because it gave me great comfort.

Those words, whether rightly or wrongly, fit my present dilemma. For I am indeed the weary traveller and I am stuck in a wilderness, where my ambitions for my future were disappearing. My obedience to my dad and my love for my mother were all part of this tragedy. Six years without contact with the world I grew up in and the friends and people I knew. A feeling of hopelessness was beginning to grow. It was scarring me internally.

I now make this promise to myself. I will confront the situation head on. As the teachings tell you to behave like a man when you are a man, I am a man and I shall act accordingly. I thought of Sugar Bush and it was at this point I decided that under no circumstance will I allow myself to be forced in any relationship. I have sensed something infinitely strong about Christine. I do want it to remain pure for as long as is necessary.

As we strolled back to the House she told me her head was full of her dreams of South America and the romanticisms of the Latin Americans. I explained that I was a British Guianese and more British than Latin American. On our way home I took her to my lodgings and showed her a bottle of potion left here by one of the village girls. I explained that the natives used it to discourage fertilisation and I thought it best she drink some of it as a precaution of any future embarrassment she looked at it with uncertainty written over her face. "How do you know it works?" she asked looking at it with suspicion.

I find myself forced to tell her an untruth and to avoid any embarrassment "Ben told me that he is absolutely certain of its powers."

She held me firmly and said "It is best we say our goodbyes here in private and again we kissed as before and again I felt myself at the mercy of nature's response. She tidied herself and drank the potion and while she did this I prayed earnestly that it works. Here, again I tried to compromise moral values by telling myself that we were only preventing fertilisation and not terminating an unborn life. At the house, her mother came and greeted us and asked if she enjoyed the stroll.

"I would have enjoyed it more if I were allowed to bathe on the rocks" She answered pretending to be angry "Peter said there are piranhas about. I saw Ben and him and Gordon's aides bathing there earlier in the day and it didn't bother them."

"Never mind darling, we have a shower here and it's much safer," Catherine replied.

Mathew reminded me to return to the House for a farewell drink to his guests and to make sure Ben is here sober.

The party was reaching its end when we arrived. Christine hurriedly brought me a drink and stood with an arm around me. Catherine looked quizzically at us. I nodded and smiled. She returned a smile and I felt really at ease.

Gordon was thanking every one for making his short holiday a happy and memorable one. Looking at Mathew he began "My friend Mathew and his guests have made this a memorable short holiday. Roughing it here reminded me of our exploits in our early days. I thank you for the hospitality and friendship shown not only to me, but to Jonathan and his family and also to our boring ramblings. Today is also a very special day. As you all know it is the birthday of His Britannic Majesty King George V1, I propose a toast to his health, long reign and survival of our Glorious Empire. Ladies and Gentlemen THE KING!"

Everyone lifted their glasses and shouted in unison "GOD SAVE THE KING!"

Chapter 6

The Farewell

In the morning, the amphibious aircraft was at the landing when we got there. The Chief led his people right up the water's edge in two distinct lines. Gordon was escorted by Mathew; my dad led the rest of the party through the line. Christine showed a brave face as she smiled, kissed me on the cheek and before boarding the craft she slipped a ring from her finger and gave it to me. Whispering in my ear "I love you." I knew that it will take a miracle for me to ever see her again. She will, without saying, live forever in my heart.

Mathew summoned Ben and me to the House for breakfast. There my dad told me that he had applied for me to be granted a certificate of registration to practice dentistry. The Dental Council rejected this on the grounds that it will upset the truly qualified dentists in Georgetown. He urged Gordon to assist in changing their minds. This I was told will be undertaken vigorously. The fact that my dad gave years of free service to the community here and I was very helpful in fulfilling that obligation will stand in our favour. Moreover, at the end of the dry season, I will be sent back home and to university if the registration fails.

This was more good news than I had hoped. A glimmer of hope to see Christine again flickered across my mind leaving me with a sense of total satisfaction. Ben it appears would have to find a job. I cannot see him working regularly 8 am to 4 pm five days a week. I cannot imagine him doing any sort of prescribed hours. As for Diego and Bell, the sadness of me leaving them would be heart breaking. A firm bond had developed through the years. The three thousand eight hundred dollars we got for the nuggets will have to be divided in equal shares. What I will do with mine is unclear, maybe I can use it to help with my studies.

I thanked my dad for his efforts and Uncle Mathew who will try to use his influence to get Gordon to do what must be done to ensure I have a career when I leave here.

My thoughts returned to the normal routine. I was at least promised a second class career that will secure my position and respect in society. My thoughts of The Reverend Father welcoming me back to his fold and admonishing me for not writing to him and acknowledging the wrongs I have done and beg his forgiveness gave me a sense of normality. I also imagined the tremendous welcome I would receive from my many friends. Exchange of letters only makes the yearning more painful. I thought of Jean. It was sometime since I last heard from her. Maybe she lost interest in me if so, that will be great. Christine is the one I really cared about. Not because our romance was recent, but because I genuinely know that we love each other. It looks a forlorn dream. Yet, there is hope and I could feel it right in the centre of my heart. I know the way she kissed me on both occasions were not a passing flirtation. Yes! She dreamt of romance in South America; the tropical magic and all that goes with it. I could see she was not an unintelligent young lady. Far from it she has her sights focused on the things she wants in life and with determination she can succeed. I will do all I can to make her dreams a reality. Yet, there is an uncertainty whether when she gets back to England and meets her boyfriend. Will she change her mind? Time has the answers to this question.

Ben came in and looked at me suspiciously. He wanted to know if I heard the vicar is returning to Sappanam. Since this is the first I heard about it, I reassured him that no one mentioned it to me and that I was happy he is coming back to his post. The villagers were having a holiday worshipping the spirits of the forest and indulging in their orgies of getting drunk and in their stupor would indulge in their pagan rituals, some of it rather obscene.

I reminded Ben that we will need some help to tidy the vicar's room. At present, it looks like the devil was having an orgy in it. Ben shrugged his shoulders to suggest he could not be bothered about the room. Instead, he suggested that now the vicar is here it is possible that Diego and Bell would get married and it would be advisable to consult with uncle Mathew before making any definite plans.

My mother had sent me some new shirts and I am certain one of them will suit the occasion.

On his arrival, the vicar summoned a meeting with Uncle Mathew, the Chief, Diego, Ben and I. I was intrigued by this request. Normally, the vicar has a tendency to do what he feels he must do without consultation. At the meeting, he started out by saying:

"The first thing I must do is to get Diego and Bell married I will not have them living in sin while I am here. Second, I have great news from Canada. It's an enormous undertaking, one that needs careful planning and cooperation. I will discuss that later. The urgent matter on hand is matrimony. Now Mathew, I understand you will be the best man. That's good, Diego told me that his wedding will involve tribal rituals and you agreed to it. Mathew, do you know anything about this?"

"I think if the chief is involved he will want some kind of ritual to be displayed to entertain his people, and besides if we are seen to be cooperating by blending the two cultures. Would that not make them see us as tolerant as they thought we are?"

"I get your point. So be it, a joint tribal and Christian wedding it will be. I don't want any tribal ritual interfering with the Christian part of it." Then looking a bit puzzled for a few seconds, he turned to Matthew and said: "There is one thing that always puzzled me. You are a Jew, yet you always fit like a hand in a glove in all the Christian and Tribal ceremonies with aplomb."

"I became a liberal a long time ago. I will not depress you by telling you when it started. But, this I can tell you during my time in India. I saw Muslims and Hindus cooperating in their religious rites in harmony. At the time, there were severe discords between the two religious factions. The clever ones initiate this cooperation and peace prevailed for a long time. Myself was a participant at one of these ceremonies. My task was to negotiate the dowry at this wedding. The groom was a Muslim and the bride a Hindu. It was an extraordinary wedding. The heads of the families held each other as brothers and to consolidate that brotherhood the teenagers became the catalyst for that bond. I really do not care much for religion. I give my support when needed and that is all."

"I will never understand you Mathew Longhorn, but I do admire you for the confidence you have in yourself and everything that you do. What I don't understand is how this wedding arrangement has anything to do with your experiences in India."

"It demonstrates the extraordinary tolerance that can exist between various religions and culture that is why I can fit in," Matthew told him.

"Thank you for that lesson Mathew. Now that the arrangement for the wedding is over I need to meet with the Chief and Diego to discuss plans that my superiors in Canada have dreamt up. Will you arrange that meeting for me?" The vicar asked.

"It's good as done," Uncle Matthew replied smiling.

Ben was helping the villagers butcher a deer that was shot earlier. I decided to watch his skills which even the villagers looked on with admiration. It was his great strength that enabled him to separate the joints with ease. When he was finished we decided to go to the river and wash on the rocks. The sun was extremely hot, not a cloud to be seen and not a whisper of wind about. The animals in the canopy were indifferent to the weather and went about their task foraging for fruits.

On our way to the embankment, we saw a villager all alone peering in the canopy. We asked him what he was looking for and he indicated that there is a harpy eagle about and he must warn the villagers to keep their children indoors. It is a known fact that harpy eagles are capable of snatching young children and taking them away to be devoured. There is a story of one baby being snatched from its mother's arms. I have never seen a harpy so Ben and I decided to have a good look in the trees to see if we can spot it. No such luck. Because they blend so well and are so high in the canopy only an expert eye can spot it.

When the story of a harpy eagle spread in the village, the women armed themselves with long sturdy sticks as they walked their children to school. Some will stay in the Long house until it is time to them take home. This went on for several days until it was certain the eagle had left the area.

We continued to scan the canopy for this elusive bird. A crowd had gathered on the banks squinting their eyes to project their sights. All to no avail and then someone mentioned that the monkeys and macaws were nowhere to be seen. Is this a sign that the bird is up there hiding and waiting for the right moment to make a kill? The answer soon became clear. There was a slight ruffle in the branches and a movement of wings, enormous wings as big as the air craft…Well nearly as big, then without warning it swooped down to the other side of the river and snatched a baby caiman and flew away effortlessly, everyone cheered. It has got its meal now perhaps it will leave the area alone.

Diego joined us and asked if we would like to accompany him to Tacuba, his village twenty miles further up to consult with his family about his planned wedding and also to invite them to the ceremonies. We agreed to this and set about preparing for the long journey. Two light boats will be required for this as there are rapids to negotiate. This trip will take us to the source of the Demerara, beyond the Demerara boundary to a place they call Triangle, where the three counties meet. Demerara being the smallest of the three gave way for the two other counties to merge at that point, hence the name Triangle.

The two-day journey was full of surprises. We passed many little villages and the inhabitants were eager to make us feel welcomed. They invited us to their villages and exchanged some of Bell's handicraft work for their works of art and engravings. When they learnt that I was the dentist's son I was inundated with requests for dental treatment. Fortunately, I did have some emergency units which came in hand. In return for the service, I was given a handful of stones. I did not know what they were and declined their offer. Matthew cleared his throat and told me in no uncertain terms to accept their gifts. Reluctantly, I put them away with the rest of Bell's handicraft works. She was sending those for Diego's family.

On our arrival at Triangle, Diego negotiated with the villagers to give us a tent and some hammocks. He appeared to be well-known and liked by the villagers. They welcomed us and gave us some Brazilian brandy with the tent and hammocks. There were lots of activities going on, huge tents were erected and decorated with palm leaves. It became quite a spectacle. There were men riding their horses from Brazil and a huge market was up trading with the natives. I have not seen so many tribal huts in one place. It must be hundreds spread out in every direction you looked.

Trading was fierce with everyone trying to get the best bargain. The Brazilians were doing a spectacular display with their horses trying to impress the ladies present.

Tiredness forced us to our tent for a brief rest. Later, we joined a group of villagers barbecuing a wild hog. They were generous and let us have as much as we can eat. Ben took a large portion and squatted with a couple of the villagers devouring his portion. They were amazed at the amount he ate and especially cracking the bones to get at the marrow.

Some of the Brazilians started playing their guitars and singing songs of love and adventures. Another group joined in singing and dancing with the young girls of the village. This reminded me of the party my father had at home only not so noisy. Uncle Mathew thought he would visit the market to see if anyone was selling drugs or contraband articles. As Commissioner, he was to protect the area from any illicit trading.

He bought a few trinkets and exchanged some of the nuggets for a handful of stones similar to the ones the natives gave me.

I was puzzled at this purchase and wondered why Mathew would buy such useless items. He was looking at them intently turning them in his palm. He gave them to me with a warning not to think they are useless and to put it away with the rest. He then placed a hand on my shoulders and told me in an authoritative way.

"This can turn out to be a great reward for you when you eventually leave here. Just put it away in a safe place until we can ascertain what exactly it is."

In the meantime, Diego went looking for his relatives. He came back with a huge entourage. They all looked like him exposing their Spanish ancestry and speaking reasonable English.

Mathew explained who I was and what my father was doing in Sappanam. They asked me if I would stay here and give them the same service. Mathew told them that I will be going to finish my studies in England and maybe when I return I can make some visits here.

They shook my hand and thanked me for the promise. More wild hogs and deer were on another barbeque and the smell of cooking meat sent an aroma that stirred hunger. Diego gave them a bottle of rum without Matthew seeing. As we sat down to eat, we were amazed when Matthew presented us with a bottle of his own. This was really a treat and unnoticed to him a drink was quietly passed to the host.

Since we were leaving in the morning I thought it best to say goodbye and have some rest. Everyone agreed. The goodbyes turned out to be an elaborate affair as everyone was in a party mood. More gifts were exchanged and more farewells said. Finally, we returned to our tent exhausted.

There was an argument with the Brazilians and some of the villagers. It looked the inevitable scenario. One of the Brazilian was accused of molesting a maiden from the village. The Brazilian drew his gun and tried to shoot the villager. Diego grabbed him from behind and took the gun away. The gunman snarled at Diego and promised to do something dreadful to him if ever they meet again.

In the morning, the place was deserted not a single person in sight, not even a horse. The tents were still there and the owners had vanished. Diego went to investigate and returned to say the Brazilians have left and since it was their tent we were to keep it. After saying goodbye to his relatives for the final time we departed with great ceremony.

On our arrival back to Sappanam, we found the villagers busy cleaning the Long house and erecting arches with palm fronds. Crotons and ferns collected from the forest and to add to their decorations, wild orchids were tied in the center of each arch, which presented a wonderful sight. Even the vicar was busy directing where his ceremony would take place and a special table was erected to accommodate his wish.

On the day of the wedding, Diego's relatives were brought from the lodge and The Chief had a small fire place erected in the center of the Long house. The orchids were replaced with fresh ones and when all the villagers were assembled. The chief dressed in an elaborate robe made of macaws' feathers, lit a fire. Diego was dressed in his tribal attire that too was decorated with feathers and Bell's shawl was a real work of art. She looked radiant and beautiful as I have never seen her before. The Chief circled the fire once with two garlands in his hands they were handed to some of the elders who in turn placed them on the necks of the bride and groom. Two runners brought a bromeliad with water still in it chanting and making religious gestures to the gods of the forest. Standing nearby was Sugar Bush looking intently at me I tried to ignore her staring and concentrated on proceedings. The water from the bromeliad was sprinkled on the marrying couple and they then spat in it. When that ceremony was over, the runners took the bromeliad and hurried back to replace them exactly where they took it. The chanting was not as noisy and spectacular as I thought it would be instead it was quite, dignified and sung with great emotion. A tear dropped from Diego's eye. It may be that it had some emotive meaning to him. In the end, the couple was given some local alcohol in wooden cups they drank from it and threw the cups in the fire. It burned with a multitude of colours and everyone jumped and chanted blessings to the couple.

The vicar role was a more solemn affair before he announced that they were married he asked Mathew for the ring.

"Ring, what ring? No one gave me a ring."

"As best man you should have the ring," a distressed vicar voiced.

"I have a ring," Ben declared. "It's not gold but silver. Would that do?" He asked.

"Any ring would do the only problem. Will it fit?"

"We can only try," Mathew suggested.

By some miracle it did fit and everyone was happy.

The ceremony over, we all wished the couple long life and a happy married life.

The villagers joined the vicar in singing a hymn of blessings. This brought the ceremonies to an end we all join Mathew in his Rest House for drinks and food prepared by his servants.

Here seated and looking relaxed Bell examined the ring and Diego told her he will have a large golden one made the next time Mathew goes to McKenzie.

Mathew appeared move at the couple's happiness and announced "Friends, young Peter thought I was buying some useless stones for some silly reason. I can now declare that those stones are in fact uncut diamonds. My gift to Bell will be a diamond ring. Peter is a lucky man there is a fortune in those uncut diamonds. They can make him very rich. I need no fortune. My army pension is enough to give me a comfortable life. Since I have no family I adopt you all here as my next of kin and that includes you Benjamin Carson." Before he could finish his declaration, Manny crept in and stood motionless by the door. Mathew invited him to a seat and asked why he was not at the wedding. "I don't like weddings and funerals," he replied.

"You are keeping yourself locked up in that surgery all day. There is no work to be done. Why not join us on this occasion for a drink?" I added.

"Look boss, when I was invited to help your father that day on the boat I swore I would never get drunk. If I start with one drink I will end up getting drunk," he shyly replied.

"I really came here to find out when the big boss is coming. He missed one supply boat already and the next one is coming tomorrow."

"You are absolutely right Manny. I have to get my reports ready as I will be going to Georgetown to see the Governor." Mathew reminded himself, then went to his office to write his report.

After our meal of baked fish and pigeon we all had a drink to toast the couple before they departed for their honeymoon.

The villagers had a platform on two castrated bulls with ropes made of palm fibre and a canopy was erected at the top. Palm leaves were rolled into a cushion and Ben Lifted the two on top. The two runners led them away to their lodge to begin their honeymoon.

No sooner had they disappeared out of sight, the vicar came hurriedly to the Rest house and demanded to see Mathew who came out to inquire what the problem was.

"Did you know the supply boat is coming in the morning? He asked anxiously.

"That is why I left the celebration to finish my report. Now really, how can I help?"

"You forgot the invite the Chief and others for the meeting we were to have before the supply boat gets here. I must have something to tell the Head of Mission when I get to the city."

"Its Diego's honeymoon, we don't want to disrupt that for a meeting. I can arrange it with the Chief and the rest of us are here if that will help," Mathew reasoned.

"That is alright by me for now. The head of Mission is putting too much pressure on me." A distressed vicar complained.

"I don't want to sound ungrateful vicar." Uncle Matthew told him "You are hardly here. I have to do your job in your absence. I think the villagers like what I say to them and prefer it stays that way."

"Are you scolding me Mathew? The vicar asked with some consternation.

Would it not be better if the Head came down with you and get all the facts first hand?

"The head have an enormous task. Coordinating the various missions and looking after the finances. You are an administrator. You know what it takes. You only have to deal with a handful of settlements. The head is in charge not only of the missions in British Guiana but the ones in the whole of the British West Indies. Is that not a monumental task?

"I never realised they were so involved." Mathew conceded.

The meeting was arranged for 2 pm. The chief indicated that he will bring two of his elders. I am still worried that Diego is not here. He knows the region more than any one of us. Even Mathew is not so acquainted with the outer reaches of the tribal zone. I relayed my concern to Mathew and he agreed.

Someone have to put him in the picture and see his reaction. The two runners were called again to contact Diego and to bring a message urgently back.

Against regulation, I gave the runners a drink of whisky as a bribe for their efforts. Mathew pretended he did not see me doing it. I guess he quietly approved under the circumstance.

Instead of bringing a message, the runners came with Diego and Bell sitting precariously on top of the platform.

"I knew it! By God I knew it!" Exclaimed Ben.

"What do you know, Ben?" asked the vicar.

"Diego is here and he has brought Bell along."

"I really don't believe this," I told him.

"Nice of you to interrupt your honeymoon Diego and to bring Bell was not necessary. She is welcomed you know that," Mathew said apologetically.

"It really doesn't matter. I knew it had to be something important for you to send the runners, and besides we had to milk to cows before retiring," Was Diego's answer.

"Gentlemen and lady now that we are all here can we start. This meeting is at the invitation of the vicar and I propose he tells us the plan."

The vicar took out a map and unfolded it on the table. There were several round red circles from Sappanam to Tacuba and further west a dozen or more red circles. These include Kaburi and the united villages at Wakari.

"These are the areas we want to concentrate on to get the tribes together and introduce religion, Christian religion. On the map it looks impossible but the Head of mission had a survey done to find out if it were possible to get the materials necessary to build a church with schools at strategic villages. This will serve very useful to the children as they would not have to walk many miles to get to school. The church, on the other hand, can be reached in a radius of no more than five miles.

The crux of the matter is to get the material there. Mission's survey proves that it is possible. There is a loggers' trail from Wismar to Wakari. From there it would not be difficult to get building materials to the various sites... Now Diego knows more about these areas than anyone here, I would like his opinion to this plan." When the vicar finished his proposal he gave the map to Diego to look over.

Diego began by saying "I know of the loggers trail and it is quite firm it would not flood in the rainy season. Who ever made that trail knew exactly what they were doing. There is a bridge across a stream and that is made of greenheart timbers, we all know greenheart lasts forever. The only problem I see is what we use for transporting the necessary materials there"

"Mules" the vicar replied with delight. The Head of administration in Canada has strong contacts with the bauxite company's Headquarters and it is hoped they will send fifty mules from Canada on the company's ship. On most occasions the ships return empty or near empty, Lots of room for fifty mules and their feed."

"Fifty mules. That should be enough. Why bring these animals from Canada when you can get them at the sugar estates?" Diego argued.

"We tried all that. The sugar estates would not sell their mules. As a matter of fact they are looking to buy any such animals available." The vicar replied. Then he pointed out: "The other problem is that the other Churches are thinking of doing the same. If we don't start this project now we will be overtaken not only by them but also by the Lutherans. Even the church in America is trying to shoulder its way in. We all know they have more finances than us that is why we MUST get there before they do."

"Is this a race between the churches?" I asked before adding "If it is important for the natives to be made Christians. Would it matter which denomination converted them?"

"There are political issues here. Our Church is trying to establish itself in every horizon and it would be helpful if our Church could bring that type of Christianity to these people."

"Now let us conclude. The feasibility of transport is good. The mules as Diego said is ideally suited and the numbers adequate to do the job. It seems to me that your church can go ahead with their plans. Am I right to sum up and say the plan is approved." Mathew concluded, hoping to get back to his reports.

Diego disagree that the decision is unanimous and therefore only the head at the mission can decide on its final outcome. He stated that The Chief is not in agreement. For the simple reason that Sappanam is some twenty miles from where the nearest church would be .He preferred that the make shift church he has here continue to function as it is, rather than having his people walk that distance to and fro, It will take them the whole day and that is not acceptable. So unless the church keeps the mission here, there is no way it can count our congregation to join the others.

"Does that mean a vicar will have to be here at least once a month?" I asked.

It was then Diego revealed his thoughts. "I have some second thoughts about this whole scheme. First there is the problem with the mules. I cannot see why on earth the head of your church wants to put those animals through the ordeal of an Atlantic crossing that will take at least two weeks in rough seas. Has anyone thought about the welfare of the mules? Is your Head so insensitive not to care about their welfare? I have seen the hardship those animals suffer at the hands of unscrupulous handlers, loading them with supplies and gears for their gold mining operations. I tell you vicar this operation will fail and your church will lose thousands of dollars if they go ahead with this scheme."

"I would agree with you Diego." Mathew added "I went through the motion of chairing this meeting in the hope of a swift conclusion. You have brought up some serious points. It needed thorough consideration. The ultimate cost of the project and the people that would be involve in its supervision. It needs careful and detailed attention."

Frustrated by the objections, the vicar went on by saying that he can only put the proposition to the Head of Mission and leave it there. But, before he speaks with Mission he would like Diego, Mathew and himself to go to Wakari to see and make an appraisal of the possibility of this plan.

"If Diego is prepared to go then I will consider it on one condition that Ben will be a great asset if he comes along also. Can I now say that this meeting has ended without any firm decision taken? If so can I have that recorded for future reference? And now if you don't mind I have work to do… URGENT WORK"

"I have an idea. If we are to yoke a couple of the bulls and make a platform like we did on our wedding day so three or four people can ride comfortable on top it will take a lot of stress having to walk all that way and back" Diego suggested and carefully pointed out. "We will have to have two pairs of yoked bulls at least. If Ben is coming, we cannot leave Peter alone he'll be bored to death with Manny and his funny ways. I think that covers everything so far." Then turning to Matthew he ended. "You can finish your report now."

The next day, we all went down the river to meet the supply boat. As usual it arrived on time and the supplies were handed out. For me the most important items were any letters from England. It has been two months since Christine left here and only a brief note from her when she was still in Georgetown to say she will be leaving the next day.

I was so eager about the letters I did not notice my dad standing there waiting for me to greet him I did not disappoint him I said a quick "Hello" before collecting my letters. Two from England and three local ones, I opened ones from England. The first was from Catherine she thanked me for looking after Christine on their short but wonderful stay and if ever I should visit England I must visit them.

I opened the second and its contents were exactly as I hoped. Christine said she missed me and that she had the most wonderful time in British Guiana. She is now working with the same oil company as her dad but her office is in Scotland and she will be staying with her aunt in Aberdeen. She has broken off with her boyfriend. He found another girl friend while she was on holiday. She will concentrate on her career. She also said if she saved enough money she will come and visit me. Her letter has eased a lot of torment that has plagued me ever since she went away. I was uncertain whether that was a passing romance or something real for her. Now that I know it is real I can look forward to some peace of mind and be myself again. The other letters are unimportant now. Maybe, I will read them at a more leisurely time.

In the morning, Mathew will be going to Georgetown. He promised to check the stones and make the two rings for Bell, I wonder if mine will be worth anything. I must wait until his return before I can thrust myself into any future plans. Certainty gives confidence. Then the thoughts of the money from the nuggets came to mind. I know it is a lot but not enough to meet my needs. How much? That is a question only time will reveal.

Hurriedly I went to see my dad I found him in a pleasant mood. He told me he went to see Gordon about my registration and he was given an assurance that it will be approved. I can look forward to a visit to Georgetown when the next supply boat comes. That is great news for me. Today is a blessed day, good news all around. I thought of opening the other two letters and maybe some more good news. It's best to wait when I am more relaxed.

Lying in bed and thinking made me restless. I got up and joined Ben who was nursing a drink quietly by himself.

"You know something, Peter; I wish that Manny was a bit more sociable. He is such a selfish man I cannot understand how he can live like that. He doesn't drink. He don't chase the girls, is he some kind of an auntie man? You'll see when he gets here he brushes his teeth changes his clothes and push off straight to bed. He hardly wants to say a word in friendship. And now I have to put up with you and your antisocial behaviour. You hardly take a drink with me these days. What's come over you man? Is that Christine so sweet that she has you in her magic spell? It can't be Jean she hasn't written you in years. So what's the problem? I can help you if only you will speak to me. I am getting lonely in this place. I think I will join the Commissioner on the supply boat in the morning and go back to McKenzie."

"Please don't do that Ben." I pleaded "It will make me even sadder than I am right now. I tell you what, pour me a small drink and I will tell you my problem."

Without hesitation Ben jumped from his seat and ignoring my request for a small drink he poured a very large one. I told him my problem was getting that damn registration or going abroad to pursue my career. This place is no good for me. The other problem I am facing, the situation with Sugar Bush and countless others.

"Can you remember when you had that fling with Jean and I asked you if you did and you told me it is not a gentleman thing to do. I respect you for that. I am not asking you if the same thing happened with you and Christine. Because I know it did. I will ask you a very serious question and no gentleman's answer; just the truth and I will tell you something very important. After you and her did what you did on the river's bank. Did you do it again here in the house?"

I was shocked by this question. Yet I feel obliged to tell him the truth if only to find out what that important thing is he wants to tell me.

"Yes I did," I replied feeling choked.

"And did you give her that potion from the bottle in the house?"

"Are you interrogating me?" I asked angrily.

"Just answer the question, if you want some serious answers."

"Yes I did. Now, what is so important, you have to tell me?"

"That potion is useless. It's a placebo. You know the thing a doctor gives you when you are ill and he has no cure for you. That's a placebo."

"I know what a placebo is and you are getting me worried."

"I will bet you anything you like, that girl is pregnant."

"Ben!" I replied confidently "I received a letter from her this morning and she is fine. She is working in Aberdeen Scotland. She is living with her aunt. She even said that if she saved enough money she will return here to see me."

"Peter, I am ashamed to tell you but I watched the intensity you made love. Not deliberately, I was looking out for caiman that sometimes patrol the banks at night hoping to get a capybara for supper. I said to myself if that girl is a virgin she will be pregnant. I will not ask you if she was a virgin. You can sort it out for yourself."

"You really have me worried Ben. I can safely say she was and I wish to God you are wrong."

I hastily drank my drink and poured myself a second larger than the first. In disgust at my weakness I threw the drink through the window much to Ben's annoyance. I said goodnight and went to bed.

CHAPTER 7

The Miracle

The mid-morning sun shone through a cloudless sky emitting a warm pleasant heat. Diego arrived before Mathew's departure and brought the stones we collected, also the ones Matthew bought for me. These were to be shared between the four of us. Mathew refused his share and asked Diego to give it to me. For the first time I took a serious interest in it and the amount of money it is likely to be worth if they are genuine as Uncle Mathew thinks. I know about gold and its weight and value, but diamonds I have no idea of their valuation. I can only hope that the stones are real diamonds. I also wondered why Matthew gave them to me. I was reluctant to ask in case he changed his mind. Perhaps, he will tell me in his own time. I then changed my mind and told him the diamonds stayed here until we get to the city.

I was beginning to take a keen interest in my finances as this would become very important if I am to take matters in my hands and sort my future for what it's worth. I can no longer depend on hand out from my dad. I am worried what Ben disclosed about the placebo and the dire consequences for Christine. I read her letter over and over trying to find a clue in between the lines. All to no avail.

Mathew made his way to the supply boat in company with my dad. He asked me what to do with the money he has from the sale of the gold I told him to keep the nuggets until we all get to Georgetown.

"What about the stones?" He asked.

"I will like to sort it all out when I get to the city. It will be an exciting exercise for me. I have bought gold for the laboratory and there are no excitement in that as the price is controlled. With stones you can negotiate and perhaps get a bit more than what is offered." I told him with a bit of excitement, "He is learning. Did you hear that Mathew?" My dad said proudly.

"Well I am off I shall be seeing Gordon and discuss your future with him. I am sure he will get the right results. Is there anything you want me to convey to him Peter?"

"I am sure you will do what is necessary." I told him feeling reassured.

Whatever happens there seems to be a window of hope for me. Ben and I decided to go and watch the men making a boat further down the embankment. They had a tree trunk about thirty feet long and were hollowing it and at intervals lighting fires in the hollow they made. As the fire became intense, water was sprinkled on the outer sides of the trunk to prevent the fire burning through. Ben took an axe and helped, cutting the inside making larger holes and setting them alight. This delighted the men and they began working more vigorously than before.

Tired and sweating profusely he went for a swim ignoring the threat of a caiman attack. He killed a boa, but I doubt if he can subdue a caiman in its domain.

The day the men finished their boat, they came and invited Ben and me to see it launched. There was a small ceremony and some local brew was offered. I did not like the drink as it made me feel sick. However, to please them I took a very small portion and downed it in one gulp. This appeared to satisfy them and the task of launching began. I can see they had an ulterior motive for inviting us as Ben's help was evidently an asset in getting the enormous boat in the river.

Task completed; we were invited to come aboard and go for a ride. The two paddlers sent the boat floating down river with great speed. It was a test to see whether it is balanced.

Back on shore we invited them back to our house and gave them some of our drink which is frowned on. Mathew is not here and we were not going to get them drunk to cause trouble. It was the only way we can show our appreciation of friendship.

I discussed the matter about Sugar Bush and her proposal of bonding.

"She good woman," one of them said.

"She make you happy," the other added.

"Look Peter" Ben tried to clarify "It is simple, all you need to do is say yes you will bond and that makes it proper in the eyes of the villagers. Any other way and she will be seen as a loose woman. Ask Diego, he will tell you exactly that."

"I am sorry my friend, but right now I'm getting a bit fed up with this bonding business. I am not in the mood to create more problems for myself than I think I am already in. Especially, when you told me of the placebo."

The men asked for another drink and I told them no more. The Commissioner will be angry. They agreed and left. It is time I read the other letters. The first one was from my mother. The usual motherly concerns and always when will she see me again.

The other was from my friend the barrister. He was hoping I would come and see him. He is getting married to a girl we all knew at school. He did not mention her name so I was put in a guessing game. I must reply and congratulate him.

The final letter was rather lengthy. It was from my East Indian friend who was installed as a puisne judge. I am invited to visit him and his German wife. He said he told her so many stories about our life at school; she can hardly wait for me to visit them. This too I will have to reply.

I am beginning to burst with excitement. I have never visited Georgetown in a true sense and the thought of visiting old friends and haggling with my stones, if they are diamonds, was more excitement than I can handle.

I was now more determined to make that visit. There are so many reasons. It's hard to know which is more important seeing my friends or selling my stones. I hurried to see Ben and to ask him if he would accompany me when I am ready.

"You don't have to ask me that. You go to Georgetown and I am right behind you. That city is not New Amsterdam. There are sharks about and pick pockets. They will steal all your stones and take the clothes from your back and if you are lucky you will walk the streets naked but alive."

"We have none of those nasty things happening in our town. If we did they are the ones that will lose their lives at the hands of the town's folk. Do you know Ben, sometimes we don't even lock our front door or windows and we can leave all our laundry to dry all night and no one will steal them. Not like what happened to my shirt at Wismar."

On his return from the city Matthew sent a message to Diego to prepare the bulls to take us to Awawuna. It was the central village comprising of nine others. Ben and I packed some essentials for the journey and soon joined Matthew and the vicar at Diego's lodge. When we got there the young men were all ready, Bulls yoked and platform strapped tightly with ropes made from palm fibres.

Ben and I were seated on a pair while Matthew and the vicar who was of diminutive build shared the other pair with Diego.

It took us the best part of two days and a night to get there. The villagers who had never seen bulls before came to greet us running and screaming in excitement. Diego greeted the chief and explained the purpose of our visit. They appeared extremely happy about our presence and hurriedly made us comfortable in their long house. Then, the other chiefs were summoned.

In the meantime, we were fed and had a drink of whisky that Ben brought with him, even the vicar had a drop. As the other chiefs approached we stood up and greeted them in the traditional manner. As visitors, we were the first to open the greetings with these words. "A wiki aye bala." If they are happy, they respond by saying "A wiki aye nou."

Then we thanked them by saying "Soooo," they reply with "Ahwaa."

I was getting pretty good with all these polite niceties and loving it. The vicar and Diego were in deep conversation with the Chiefs, with Matthew listening intently to the discussions. Ben and I did not understand much of what was going on but it looks as if all was going well. It went on for hours. When it was finally over, we were invited to the other villages to see the proximity of each village and the possible site for the church and schools. As always a high ground was shown as the possible site. Every one nodded agreement.

We were given a decent hut with several hammocks and told to rest the night before leaving. In the morning, we started our way back. I did not want to feel left out of what was decided, so I quizzed the vicar. He told me that the villagers were exceedingly happy about the project and they will all help. An important issue was revealed when he told me that the Chiefs agreed to let the church go ahead with their plans on condition that the bright students are given the opportunity to further their education in McKenzie or Wismar. The church owns buildings in both areas and the children can stay there during school times and return home in the holiday periods. I am beginning to see that these people are more ambitious than I thought.

This part of the bargaining was also agreed by Our Chief who suggested that they would make the journey to church in exchange for the same offer of further education.

Mathew, on the other hand, was not at all pleased. He wanted the region to stay pristine as nature intended. When all these advancement are implemented there will be significant changes to their life style.

"A whole culture will be bastardised by these changes." He argued and appearing somewhat enraged. "The forest will be destroyed. I am sure when these youngsters get a taste of life on the outside. The next thing they'll want is to rid themselves of their traditional huts and build proper houses." Mathew seemed to expend the rage in him and continued in a more subdued tone. "Houses need money to build and where do you think they will get the money, from the trees in the forest? Mark my word, loggers will be encouraged to strip the forest of their trees some of these giants are hundreds of years old a whole damn new world will emerge. It is in my power to stop it if I want. I am the Commissioner of the interior and I have to think carefully of a solution to this madness."

The vicar, on the other hand, was not impressed. He argued "That at some point in their lives, changes will be made whether it is in our life time or the next generation but changes are inevitable. Is it not better we supervise these changes when it can do very little harm to their way of life and at the same time make sure the forest stays as pristine as possible? We can be the guiding hand for both progress and conservation. At least we are lucky to have men like Matthew as the conservationist and the Church as their Salvationist."

Uncle Matthew was in no mood to be compromised. He countered with conviction "Most seemingly good intention started with boldness and truth and ended up being the opposite of its main direction. Once so-called progress gets a grip on these people, there is no stopping, it's like the tide, uncontrollable. Some of these same people will curse the church for destroying their way of life. I wish vicar you could inform your superiors of the consequences it can have on a true and natural way of life. I am not God to tell everyone what to do. I am the Master of the Hinterlands and it is my job to do as I see fit." Perspiration dripped from his face as he spoke. It was impossible not to be impressed with his convictions.

The vicar's face fell in his hands in despair and shaking his head vehemently uttered in a hoarse voice, "I will convey your arguments to headquarters; my own conclusion is unclear at the moment. Perhaps when my head is clearer I will determine what proposals to put forward.

"What do you think about what we discussed Peter?" Uncle Matthew asked. This surprised me. I did formulate a view while the discussions were going on. I never dreamt anyone would be interested.

"Since you asked, this is what I would suggest. Let the church go ahead with their project and they can go further, instead of sending the children away for their secondary education to Wismar and McKenzie where they will be exposed to a very disorderly way of life. A school for secondary education can be built here with teachers from your church doing the advance teaching as they do in my school in Berbice. That is of course if your church is really keen about making these people educated Christians. It looks impossible, but it can be done with some effort and resources."

"Peter, Peter, you clever young man, Why did we not think of it before?" Uncle Matthew half shouted with joy.

"I thought of something similar," Diego expressed. "But your suggestion is better than the one I had in mind. The question is what we are going to recommend. What do you think vicar?"

"I am still in a daze at the moment. Let me clear my head and tomorrow I will announce what I will propose to Headquarters."

On that note we had some supper and rested for the night. We were up at dawn getting ready to travel back to base. It was quietly decided not to put pressure on the vicar for his verdict. We agreed that he will tell us when he is ready.

We were half way to base when Diego spotted a young deer lying in agony under a tree. Diego immediately brought the bulls to a halt and went to investigate. There were no wounds on the animal and its breathing was few and far between. Matthew came to assist. He turned the animal over on the other side and saw a little blood on its legs. "It was bitten by a snake." Uncle Matthew yelled after noticing the marks left by the fangs. Then he warned. "Be careful, every one keep your eyes open, it can still be around." Then shouting to Ben, he ordered "Keep the bulls away from the trees. Snakes are as adept climbing trees as wriggling through the undergrowth."

As Uncle Matthew stepped back there was a slight rustle in the leaves and the next we heard was Uncle Matthew shouting. "Lads, I've been bitten."

The serpent tried to wriggle away from the commotion and Ben took a stick and whacked it on the head. It turned out to be a monster of a Bush Master, South America's most poisonous snake. As quick as lightning Diego applied a tourniquet just above the bite and ordered me to get the antivenin from the first aid box. I found it but could not locate where the syringe was. I frantically searched the box and there it was wrapped in linen and stuck on the lid. I have never seen my Uncle so sad; there was a resignation of death on his face. He beckoned Diego and told him in a clear voice. "I shall not survive this bite unless I reserve all my energies and concentrate within my inner self to overcome this disaster. That antivenin is not for Bush Master's bite. I am sure it will have no effect." Then he issued some instructions. "If all fails I wanted to be buried under the tree next to the house in my military uniform. Before you put me in the ground I would like you to fire two shots in the air and then the vicar can say his piece before burial." Half an hour later his breath became fainter and fainter. The vicar was offering endless prayers and Ben was sobbing his heart out. Diego and I hugged each other and the taps were opened, the tears flowed as they have never flowed. We were both sobbing silently. Ben took the stick and whacked the dead snake to a pulp. He then lifted Uncle Matthew on his shoulders and walked the rest of the way to the House.

Uncle Matthew was placed on his favourite couch and covered. The vicar led a prayer and we sang hymns. The servants were in turmoil and Bell was asked to come and help as a night vigil was imminent. Diego asked to be excused and went away. We all thought it strange that Diego should leave at this time.

At early dawn he returned with a large piece of tree bark in his hand and some flowers. During the night he also erected a small stand decorated with flowers to place the corpse for prayers before the burial. As the sun cleared the horizon Uncle Matthew was brought out and placed on the stand. Diego as instructed fired two shots in the air. This had a miraculous effect on Uncle Matthew. First his left hand fell off his chest and a second later his right hand; I can see his fingers moving. We were all speechless. Uncle Matthew tried to turn on his side, Diego gave him a helping hand and his eyes started opening. He was still cold. Ben ran in the house and brought him a large brandy. By now he was gaining more of his senses. His eyes fully opened, he smiled and in a whisper thanked everyone for their support. Then he took the brandy and swallowed it in a single gulp. We all started to cheer. Then I wept as never before. It was Uncle Matthew who embraced and kissed me on the forehead. He looked at Diego and asked what he has in his hands.

Diego looking shy replied "Nothing. Nothing at all."

"Come on Diego it can't be nothing when it is still in your hand." The come alive Uncle Matthew teased. For a man who was near death he had a surprising sense of humour.

Ben took the bark and on it was written what looked like an obituary. I was asked to read what was written. It went like this:

Life was exciting in Sappanam.
When all of a sudden it was calm
And I, a stranger knew not why
My friends sat down and start to cry
So humbly I tried to investigate
The reason for their bereaved state

Soon I learnt that Matthew Longhorn
Was far away from this earthly place
Matthew has said that he will die
In the bush, it was not a lie

Now that he is gone, we did our best
By militarily placing him to rest
An honour given to a very few
As brave and competent as Matthew

The cheers were loud and clear and Uncle Matthew was still weak but strong enough to celebrate Diego's effort to write something. It was still early in the morning. Nobody took notice of the time of day and the whisky flowed. Manny came and joined us. When told what happened, he went and took a glass and poured himself a decent shot. There were more cheers Manny has crossed the boundary to civilisation once again. Bell helped the servants with preparing a meal, we sat chatting and reviewing the incredible miracle. It was the vicar who gave an explanation.

"This is the hand of God. He knows we need our Commissioner for the work in hand."

"God may have a hand in it vicar that I'm certain but I am still too weak from the poison to argue. Nevertheless, I am strong enough to put you right. You always remarked critically when I mentioned my days in India. It is as if you are at war with that country. I can tell you while I was in that coma I was aware of what was happening to my body. The antivenin was helpful in a small way. Foolish as this may appear to some of you I was in command of what was happening to me all the time my only set back was not able to physically react to the commands in my head. I am afraid I had to wait for the strength of the antivenin to help bring back the control of my mental forces. This is going to upset you even more but it has to be told. I watched young men in Rajasthan deliberately allowing themselves to be bitten by cobras. We all know the king cobra is a very poisonous snake maybe more poisonous than the Bush Master, and its bite can be lethal. These young men were in the art of mastering mind over matter. Not only were they building up immunity to its poison. They were also strengthening their will power. When the snake bites one of them he recoils in a yoga position and remain so for a long time several hours or so and gradually he will regain his composure and ability to be normal again. I must point out that the young men who undertook these experiments are extremely healthy, strong both physically and mentally. The trick is not to be afraid of the outcome, but to avoid it with sheer mental prowess and determination. If you go into unconsciousness with the thoughts that you are not going to die, then the chances of survival rapidly multiplies. You all heard Gordon and I speaking of our soldering days and our encounter with Ahmed Khan and my excursions in the caves, listening to the mystics and sadhus They spoke metaphorically, portraying life as an adventure, a journey through time, to strengthen the will and resist the temptations of worldly wealth, which they claim is the source of most evils. I absolutely believe that. When you have made contact with the inner self; a union is born and a new journey begins that can take you to the highest level of the true self. I can never achieve that level for the simple fact that I am content with the stage I reached and the life I am living, at peace with myself. I do not want to be a guru and that suits me fine.

Peter now knows why I gave him those stones. Some people will call me a philanthropist. Unlike the mystics who are fed by their followers. I have no such arrangements. I depend totally on my army pension. In England, I will struggle to survive because I have given away what would have seen me live a life of comfort. Here, in British Guiana I can live better than most men in England."

"But why do they need the snake to bite them when they are able to resist the effects of the poison?" Ben questioned.

"My dear man, to develop a strong will power you must be able to scale great heights in human endurance. Meditation is the key, hours on hours until the body is floating on a new plane. No one knows what level is the ultimate ascension. Not even the great Buddha. To have the power to recognise the usefulness of meditation, you must be able to withstand pain that will kill an ordinary human, not only pain, but also the ability of total self-control. Here is where a new plane is reached."

"Are you saying God had no hand in your recovery Matthew?" The vicar asked in dismay.

Uncle Matthew responded by asking "Is it what I believe that is paramount here?" Is it the force of the spirit that is God? Or is it the mental strength given to me by God? Whatever the truth is, can only be determine by your belief. Humanity is quick to turn to God when in serious trouble. God, on the other hand, would not turn away but pondered why he has given us wisdom to help ourselves. Despair, and lack of courage and determination we turn ourselves into weaklings. God will not tolerate weaklings and if He appears to be heartless it is because He wants us to be strong and to resolve our problems with the same grit and determination I'm always speaking of. That grit and determination He has implanted in our genes. My favourite Guru and philosopher wrote and I quote.

"Man is a weary traveller on the earth plane. There is a load on his back and his mind is shrouded in thoughts of fear and frustration. Foot sore and heart sore he drags on and knows not his destiny. Bound in ignorance, he makes self his God and worsens his lot as he treks on his way in the wilderness of dried up hopes and frustrated designs. Selfishness and sin drags him into an endless chain of misery and suffering. Caught in the snare of illusion, he loses sight of the reality and sinks deeper in the pit of moral degradation. It is only when the sting of conscious bites him and remorse takes hold of him that he seeks freedom from his enslavement. Remorse and repentance open to him a new way of life. His ways are changed. There is no more the cloud of darkness on his face. He is awakened to a new force; it is the force of the spirit that the sting of conscious has awakened and liberated, No longer the weary traveller but a bright soldier. Not sin but virtue. Not self but selflessness. Not greed but renunciation. He knows now as constituting his armour in the battle of life. Does that answer your question vicar?"

"Not entirely, profound, yes, but all the same meaningless to me. I can only say you are somewhat unique among the men I know and alarmingly controversial. I have listened to your stories and your many experiences. You have failed to convince me Matthew, so I will stick with my convictions and let you get on with yours."

"What are your true convictions, vicar? I ask this in honesty and promised not to pour contempt on what you say." Matthew told him.

"I believe in the messages and teachings of Christ and his disciples, the holy Trinity, The crucifixion and the Advent. Does that answer your question, Matthew Longhorn?"

"To a point vicar, to a point. You understand the sermons and all the rest that is relevant for you to become a priest. Let us take Peter here as an example. He is a Catholic, can he understand what his priest is saying when conducting his prayers and blessings in Latin?"

I intervened in the argument only to justify what Matthew said is correct. "It is true most people do not understand a single word of Latin. Not even my dear mother. I understand it because I learnt it in school."

"The Muslims are the same; 95% of them do not understand a word of Arabic, yet they memorise the entire Quran in Arabic and only know of its meaning by what is interpreted by those who knows. It's the same with The Buddhist. They chant endlessly without knowing what it is they are saying. Except what the Monks told them. The Sikhs and the Jains only know their religion by the interpretations of their priests. There is only one truth and that lies with identifying with your inner self. Understanding the true meaning of life and managing your own destiny. A lot of people look at these mystics as leeches, not doing an honest day's work for their survival. I can tell you vicar with absolute certainty that most of them are intellectuals with a university education. Their way of life may appear strange to us only because we are gripped with the idea that only wealth can bring us happiness. Wealth can be stolen or lost or never achieved. What happens next, frustration, which can lead to numerous reactions most of which can be violent or self-harming. When you achieve union with yourself you become the master of your destiny. It is something no one can deprive you of. You become to ultimate human being, armed and armoured for the battle of life. Can you honestly deny the truth in that vicar?" Uncle Matthew expounded.

"We are talking of two different worlds here, Matthew. My world is the spiritual one yours is the mystical, since I cannot boast of trying to find my inner self. My destiny lies in my faith in my Savior. I will not allow anyone, not even you Matthew Longhorn, as Christ is my witness, to implicate me in sacrilege. I would listen to your thoughts as passing conversation and that is all it means to me." The vicar said in defence.

"Are you then saying that if a man tries to seek peace by bonding with his inner self he is diverting from the path of religion? Uncle Matthew appeared to finally ask.

"All I can say is you cannot have two masters. These Indians are using their mystics' beliefs to manipulate the reality into something unreal." Pausing for a few seconds he looked at Matthew intently and asked "Do you honestly believe these people are capable of super powers.?" Without waiting for an answer he continued. "Why then did they allow themselves to be dominated throughout their history by foreign invaders, The Persians, the Moguls and the British only to name a few? Don't answer that Matthew Longhorn, allow me to tell you the reason. Their mysticism cannot stand up to the power of military force. You are always saying how potent these powers are, I see no records of it standing up to invaders and conquerors, I see no records of any great Indian be he a prince or a general, a teacher or a scholar, contributing to the development of modern sciences or inventions. They are a nation of beggars and worshippers. Look at the way they greet you with clasped hands signifying obedience. Their women kissing their men's feet in gratitude. There is the proof that the powers of meditation and ascendency have left them bereft of a stern heart to face reality. The so-called higher plane they were to achieve with their tinkering of the mind. They are a docile race hiding behind a curtain of prayers and magic. I'd like to see you break my defences down with rational explanations not some mumbo jumbo of incantations and mesmerisms." The vicar ended up feeling triumphant.`

"I see you will not accept my interpretation of the true self. You have asked all the questions so far and you did not give me the answer to those questions you posed. Is it because you do not know for sure if the answers you give will stand up to a full blooded argument? Or is it you are afraid that ultimately it will emerge that what I told you is the darn truth. You are a vicar, I respect you for what you represent not for your stupidity and ignorance of something higher. Perhaps you are afraid that you will discover the real truth and your faith in your religion will suffer. You cannot bear that. It is that you are afraid of, aren't you? Afraid of abandoning the religion that has comforted and sustained you? Because you have found something more real, afraid to look out of the open window of your enclosure where the truth abounds? I have a lesson for you dear pastor. A man can choose to be anything if he is convinced that what he has chosen is right for him, his happiness and well-being. I discarded my religion when I was fourteen years old. At my Bar Mitzvah I realised I was not going to be the person I wanted to be but to follow a tradition going back thousands of years. I do not disclaim my heritage. Our people are suffering at this moment at the hands of a fanatic. I may be wrong, but humanity is too precious to be the instrument of people more powerful. It is how is has been ever since man walked the earth. The mass may not have weapons but they do have the ultimate defence no one can penetrate, the barrier to their inner self. The retreat for solace and bliss and from whence scorn is poured on those who dared thought, they have made a conquest."

I decided to join in this debate if only to put the vicar in the picture and not to justify Matthew's argument. I then told the vicar. "I am a Catholic and I am not sure if that is what I wanted to be. I believe in what Matthew said and I am prone to believe there is a higher and deeper purpose to life. That is not a commitment just a thought. You said no Indians have made any noticeable contributions to humanity. I can tell you without any disrespect that you are utterly wrong. It is the Indians who gave mathematicians the, zero a singular digit that is all important for calculations, and do you know that it was a self-taught physicist who discovered the boson particle. It is kept a secret. He did, however, send his findings to the greatest scientist in the world the eminent Albert Einstein who was completely amazed and published it in German. The boson particle can reveal secrets of our world and beyond, the beginning of everything. Mankind is in an embryonic stage of finding those secrets. One day who knows it will all be revealed and the myth of God will no longer exist.

There is a rumour that Britain and the Americans are developing an almighty bomb. One so large even God cannot stop it when it explodes. They are calling it the atomic bomb. It is only a theory, no one knows for sure if they will ever succeed. Some say it will be the end of the world if they succeeded."

"Stop this! Stop this blasphemy!" The vicar screamed. He quickly placed his hands on his mouth in disbelief and in a quieter tone he continued. "The jungle has made you lose your minds. It is God that made everything. It is in the Bible, the Pentateuch, the Quran and every religious text known to man. Is God's words not truth enough. Why do we need the boson particle to tell us what we already know?" Only God can end the world he created. The vicar was clearly distressed and a nod from Matthew suggests that we leave it at that. I was not prepared to leave this unfinished. I turned and quietly asked. "Have you ever met a mystic or a holy man?"

"I have," he answered pondering whether he really had.

"Where did you meet these men?" Matthew asked.

"In Calcutta 1923, there was an outbreak of malaria. The men and women from England were dying at an alarming rate and the doctors were incapable of arresting the disease. There we were burying at least two every day, hoping for a miracle. Then one day a man dressed in a white robe came and offered some herbs for the sick. At first no one wanted to do anything with him until a brave young lady tears dripping from her eyes as if it were a brook boldly brushed past us and took it. She thanked the man and asked the method of administering the herbs. Everyone stood there motionless at her brave actions and unable to speak. She administered the herbs as directed to her young husband."

"What happened?" Matthew asked.

The vicar shook his head and looking at Matthew in disbelief said "It worked. By God it worked. Three days later the young man was as good as new. The doctors were amazed." He then said to Matthew. "This has nothing to do with meditation. It was just a herb that they knew about and that is all there is to it."

"And you said they contributed nothing to science or for the benefit of mankind. Yet, this lonely drifter came to the rescue uninvited and with the herbs he knew would have some benefit. Do you call that coincidence or trickery?"

"It may not be coincidence. It is possible that he may have heard of the dilemma at the fort and came prepared." The vicar reasoned.

"Do you admit that you might be wrong in condemning these people as utterly useless in mankind's progress?" Matthew asked, hoping for a response.

"You are a hard man to follow Matthew Longhorn. I think we go down the river to clear our heads of these controversial discussions." The vicar suggested.

"You don't need whisky to get yourself intoxicated with your truth. Your ego is manifested in that direction. What I cannot accept is your decimation of a race equally responsible for the progress of mankind." Matthew responded with great sadness.

"Matthew you are indeed the devil's appointed advocate. Yes, I decry them for their lack of faith in my ministry. I offered them the chance of finding Christ the only true salvation to deliver them from poverty and deprivation. I was completely ignored. Can you imagine an entire subcontinent waiting for conversion and I, Oliver Heal failed to have any success. To my disbelief the young man who recovered from the herbs converted to Islam. He was immediately sent to a hill station in Maharashtra. I never saw again. Failure is my constant companion. That is why I am sent to this last outpost of Christianity to do something worthwhile. I need this project to succeed Matthew. By God I need it to succeed, if only to redeem myself and regain my confidence. It is a psychological dilemma, is it not? When you feel yourself incompetent and useless you try to find something or someone to ridicule to make yourself feel worthwhile. This was very foolish of me to decry a race for my own satisfaction. What can I say to make amends? My heart bleeds for me and that is not self-pity, it is something more far reaching than I can understand. I envy you Matthew. How I envy you?" They both looked at each other in the eye waiting for the other to respond. Eventually, I ended the impasse and intervened. "I will ask Diego and Ben to help with your project. Matthew will help because he knows it will succeed. He will never be able to live with himself if we succeeded without him."

"Are you trying to seduce me to intervene, clever Peter? Of course, I must be a part of the team. The vicar will be in charge of operations." Turning to the vicar and slapping him gentle on the shoulders he ended "You would take charge, won't you Oliver?" The boyish smile on Matthew's face generated a smiling response from the vicar. The two men shook hands and friendship reigned once again.

Ben was listening intently on the conversation and asked the vicar. "What is it you have to do for headquarters to have faith in you?

"Get the missions running smoothly and in a Christian fashion. No more tribal rituals and drunken orgies. No more excuses for not attending church on Sundays. Or no more help from the church. That is what I intend to tell them in no uncertain way."

"You are certainly getting to grips with your task. Oliver. Good luck old man" Matthew said.

The vicar was about to leave, when Matthew asked "Are you comfortable sleeping in a hammock. In that half-finished house of yours Oliver? You are welcome to stay here and enjoy some real home cooking for a change.

"I will certainly take your offer." A smiling vicar replied.

CHAPTER 8

Revelations

It took several days for Uncle Matthew to fully recover. Bell helped to nurse him back with her funny stories that made him laugh endlessly and the fancy dishes she prepared. Especially, the soup made from the bony parts of the peccary.

One day he asked her if she can cook curry. She gave a big smile and asked. "You know about curry?"

"Know about curry? I love the dish. I ate it all the time when I was in India the only problem is to find someone to cook it."

"Wrong Commissioner, You need to find the powder to cook the curry. The person to cook it is right here." Bell replied gleefully.

"I have such powder in my store room. Mind you it's been there for quarter of a century I don't know if it's still good." He informed her.

Bell dashed off to the store room with Ben and I close on her heels. We rummaged through several boxes before finding it. Locked air tight in a half a pound tin. A bit rusty, but undamaged. We took it in the kitchen and Ben undid the lid. Uncle Matthew joined us and gave it a sniff and pronounced it safe and as fresh as the day it was packed. Venison was removed from the fridge and Ben as usual was quick with the knife to cut it in small pieces for Bell to cook.

We left Bell to get on with her cooking with the help of the maids. They were puzzled with the strange smell in the kitchen. I could hear them sneezing as Bell went about her cooking.

We in turn did what idle men do. We poured ourselves the best malt whiskey from the collection and toasted for the hundredth time the survival of Uncle Matthew.

He was getting a bit fed up with our toasting. He suggested. "Gentlemen if you want to drink me dry, can you please do so without the ceremony. And you Peter not so much drinking. Your father will be disappointed with your behaviour. You may enjoy yourself now but be careful in future. You Benjamin Carson you were supposed to see he lives the way his father would approve." He looked at Ben winked and smiled.

Then continuing in a more serious note he said "I was going to wait for Joseph to return before making this announcement. Events in the last two weeks have given the opportunity for reflection. It is time for serious decision making. I am fifty five years of age. I have been through many battles in life. I have no family for the simple fact that I was not married. It has left me with a bit of sadness that when I am gone there will be no one to mourn me or to put flowers at my grave… Not that it matters, the flowers I mean, but the people who really care for me. Now I know I have been wrong; there are people who still love and care for me and they are standing right before me. You are more than family…You are people with kind hearts.

Let start with Diego here. He came under a pretext to look at our bull. He ended up finding a wife, a very beautiful one at that and ended up starting a small dairy. His pay depends on what he gets for a cow when slaughtered. That's sacrifice. I cannot help thinking that Bell's beauty may have blinded him from the reality of a business venture. Then we have Bell. Coming all alone from Wismar to look for a husband and helping him with the cows to provide milk for the children. Then we must think of Ben. He's been here nearly five years not on a regular salary, as a matter of fact on no salary. Admittedly, he gets all the whisky he can drink and his food. What I think pleases him more is the fact that he thinks he can control young Peter. There again more sacrifices. Finally, we have Peter he came here when he was sixteen because his father wanted him here. Details of which I am not prepared to expose. He left all his friends far away in Berbice. Most young men will have rebelled and disobeyed such a request. Peter quietly went about doing what was asked of him. There were times when he was very troubled. I saw it in his face on many occasions. Frustration is not a strong word to use. Nevertheless, he obeyed his dad's instructions without question I find that it takes remarkable courage and self-discipline to achieve that level of maturity. It was because of all his sacrifices. His obedience and respect and love for me that I gave him those stones. He doesn't know it but they are diamonds." "I wanted to announce that on my sixtieth birthday I will retire to write my memoirs."

"You, retire. I think not. You care too much for the status you hold as a Commissioner and the authority you exercised over these people. It will destroy you if you are to leave here." The vicar said trying to weaken Matthew's argument for a higher level of existence.

"Allow me to finish, Please vicar. Gordon will be recalled to London at about the same time as my retirement. No one knows where his next call of duty will take him. I received news from him that war is imminent with Germany. I cannot believe that only twenty one years ago the devastation of the Great War came to an end and now we are about to enter hostilities with the Nazis. If there is war I shall remain in British Guiana to help with the war effort. Grow more food is what we are told to do I might even take up a large section by the corral for agriculture. Recruitment is vital. I shall help with that. There are many young men here who I am certain will be willing to fight for the Empire. So there you have it friends, the story of my future intentions in a nutshell."

"You said you wanted to retire on you sixtieth birthday. What will happen if someone not as caring as you takes over? These men here will not fight for the Empire. They are not fit enough to do that and it will take longer to train them militarily and to teach them to speak English properly than those in the city." Diego told him.

"I said I am thinking of it. It is the very problem of finding a suitable replacement that makes me reluctant to retire. I have no say of who will replace me. That appointment can only come from the Governor himself or from London. Now you see my predicament." If I were younger I could have persuaded the foreign office to let me take over as Governor when our current one is sent elsewhere. You may pour scorn on that. Remember I have strong contacts at the highest level in the House of Lords. It will mean accepting a knighthood, something that can be a stumbling block to my ambition."

Uncle Matthew has created a dream beyond my wildest imagination, to become one of the richest men in the country? Surely he must be mistaken. He told me why I deserved this. I must think clearly. At the moment I am imagining a wild picture. It is best I leave it until such time when I can coordinate all the facts and the possibilities and put them in their right perspectives. Ben and the others have large sums of money from the sale of their nuggets, but is it enough to set them up for an independent life. We are all friends sharing the same adventures and hazards of the bush, some giving more than what is required of them for the benefit of the team. I am thinking of sharing some of the diamonds with them. Whatever the outcome I must be sure my friends are happy. Diego is a proud man, so is Ben. Will Bell tolerate any unnecessary generosity? She may not be wealthy but she is a proud woman of high moral standards.

I had not until now realised Matthew was a man of such great kindness and above all a great thinker and political manipulator now a philanthropist.

My first task is to go to Georgetown and see what progress, if any, has been made to get my registration. This is important to me. If I do not get it, I shall sell the stones and make my own way to America and study there. I find myself following in his footsteps. By that I mean I am in no hurry to sell those stones and to find myself with more money than I ever dreamt of. I must also visit my friends and catch up with the old days. I cannot make excuses that I spent the last five years in the jungle doing charitable work and all I have to show is five years of non-achievement.

That is why this registration is so important to me. It will show what I have achieved through my own endeavour. Something must be done to get my self-respect in society. This is a country where people only look up to you if you are socially accepted and acceptance comes with being a professional person or a respected merchant. I am neither of these. My last hope lies with the diamonds, I will only use those as a last resort. I will consult with Uncle Matthew as my thinking is still a bit blurred and I will resist the whisky for now and seek solitude by the river bank. I am worried about the regular drinking. Its effects can be devastating if not curbed. Ben will have to be told. He is a huge man and can absorb great quantities at a time. My young and slender physique is no match compared with his and my drinking will have to adjust proportionally. Perhaps some peace and tranquility will give me an answer.

I was sitting by the river bank with my thoughts when I was joined by Uncle Matthew. He saw I was in a contemplative mood; so instead of speaking, he sat a few feet away, his chin resting in his hands. I know he wanted to say something and was waiting for me to invite him to do so. We both sat silently for a long time. Ben and the others joined us. We are such a small community in this wilderness; it is not remarkable that when one of us goes somewhere the others are drawn by that magnetic force of togetherness. It is that magnetism that has forged such a strong bond. Therefore, it is inevitable that when one goes somewhere the others, if not engaged in other activities will be drawn.

We were looking at a troop of monkeys that came down to drink on the other side of the river; one had a young one on her back the others had a drink and looked nervously in the water. Mother and baby took their turn. The caiman was who just beneath the water lunged at the mother and grabbed her, the baby was flung off her shoulder and started to make terrifying cries as the rest ran off. The poor creature kept screaming for its mother. Some of them tried half-heartedly to get to it then looking at the carnage as the caiman trashed its prey to devour, it they scampered away. Ben took a boat and raced across and grabbed it. It became even more terrified as Ben tried desperately to calm it down. He brought it ashore and gave it to Bell. It was only then it settled down nestling in Bell's bosom. She decided to take it home and rear it as a pet. Then they departed.

This distraction left us in a state of loss. Eventually Matthew remembered the reason he joined me. He then spoke with a seriousness I seldom saw.

"I know your father may seem uncaring but that is far from the truth. The next time the supply boat comes I will send a message to get that aircraft here to take us to Georgetown. Don't bother about the cost I will look after that. I have looked on you as the son I never had and I will do all I can to see you are happy.

I have another suggestion for you. I realise that you are a bit young and have other views in your mind. What if I suggest to Gordon that you replace me as the next Commissioner? That will send you right up the social ladder. It will be the first time a local person would have been made Commissioner, a job held by an Englishman from the beginning. You told me of your East Indian friend who has been appointed a judge. The role of the British Guyanese is changing and with war on the horizon who knows maybe one of you will be the next Governor."

"Stop dreaming Uncle Matthew. Your liberal mindedness will lose you a lot of friends." I told him before adding. "That's a bit too much even with the threat of war. For a local to be installed as ruler of a part of the Empire seems unthinkable. I know nothing of your work. Apart from the fact that you have several deputies or rangers as you like to call them, roaming the forest and reporting anything unusual. I have never seen anyone brought before you to be punished for violation of the forest's laws"… I paused before asking this question. "Do you think the vicar will feel you have an ulterior motive for trying got get me appointed in your place?"

"The answer to that question is I cannot be bothered what the vicar thinks. I have no ulterior motive. The only motive I have is continuity. Getting back to what I was saying. There are no real troubles here or anywhere else. Things are settled. In the early days I had to deal with a logger or a poacher every day. I even sentenced a man to death for killing one of my rangers."

"Did you hang him?"

"No, I couldn't, that would have been like committing murder myself. I sent him to Georgetown for the proper authorities to judge him." Uncle Matthew said ruefully.

"Whatever happened to him?" I asked with curiosity.

"He was found guilty and hung. Now coming back to where we left off. A few months training and you will soon get the hang of it. You will have Diego and Ben to help you. Does that sound like a good proposal? He asked.

"I guess it is. Can I think carefully about this? And can it wait until we have seen Gordon and decide on the next step after that meeting? There are some more serious questions I need to ask. What do you think of the gold we found and your miraculous recovery? What about the diamonds? Do you think God really had a hand in all that? I can never understand how you appeared dead and then came alive again. We were all amazed even the vicar was totally perplexed. I understand when certain events are unexplained people always say it is a miracle, the hand of God? There must be something more to it than that. Please tell me the truth. A rational explanation is all I need. The gold I can understand coming from some unknown source, it is possible as Jonathan said disturbing a part of a gold bearing area. Then there is the question of the diamonds. How did the natives get hold of them and why did they give it to us for a few trinkets? The Brazilians must have known they were diamonds and yet they exchanged them for a few nuggets. These questions bothered me for a long time. Do you really think the Brazilians stole the diamonds?"

"You are asking so many questions and putting them so randomly. I can only answer them in the order I see fit. The gold I can never adequately explain. But my revival is due to two things you heard me explained to the vicar, he always appeared agitated whenever I mention my life in India. It is relevant because it was what I learnt there, that has helped me to survive in this place. My dear friend Gordon understands it so well. As for the diamonds I think the Brazilians stole them on their way to the Triangle. There are diamond seekers scattered all around the area. They Brazilians exchanged them for gold even though they knew it was worth many times the price they paid, it was safer to buy from the locals with the nuggets than with stolen diamonds. You see Peter, the locals know who are diamond seekers and who are not. It is what all thieves do. They get something for nothing and the next thing is to change it to ready cash. You do understand what I'm saying?" He tried to explain

"If you thought they were stolen. Why did you not arrest them? After all they were in the territory controlled by you." I argued

"Yes, I could have done that but what proof did I have to make an arrest? Besides, those men had guns and there were several of them. The odds were against me,"

Then in a more thoughtful tone he changed the subject and proposed that I can still do my practice and be Commissioner at the same time. He explained that the supply boat comes every month and returns to Georgetown the next day. I can spend a month in Sappanam and when I go to make my report I can be in my surgery for a month until the boat is ready to return."

It was a wild idea. I think it can work; it appears to hold all the answers I have been seeking. With those words of comfort and reasoning I can see a light in the future. I then asked Uncle Matthew a final question concerning the diamonds. Somewhere in my mind I want to be absolutely certain of the legitimacy of those diamonds. Unless it becomes crystal clear, there is always the doubt that I have become rich from something that should not have been rightly mine.

"Did you give me those diamonds because you are not certain of their legitimacy and to keep yourself pure from corruption?"

"My dear Peter, How could you ask such a question? If I had the slightest hint that they were not legitimate I would have never given them to you. That is my word of honour."

He was adamant and honest. As far as I was concerned I stood clear of any illegal activities. My conscious was crystal clear. No one can believe the relief it has brought me.

"There is another question I would like to ask you Peter, This young lady .What's her name, Sugar Bush? What do you intend to do with her?"

"I'll probably have her around to do odd jobs if that will satisfy her. My stay here is limited and I cannot go messing around with a foolish young woman whose only idea is to establish some prestige in her life. I am in love with Christine and I cannot let anything come between us."

"I knew it! By George I knew it"! Uncle Matthew shouted. "Catherine knew something transpired when you went down the river that evening. She looked quizzically at me and I shrugged my shoulders. Gordon knew something happened also. He is very clever at reading reactions. I shall not ask you for details. If there is anything you would like to say to me? I am all ears."

"This business with Sugar Bush is causing me great embarrassment Uncle Matthew, Ben saw what happened between Christine and myself and questioned me, not because he was being inquisitive, but only to help me solve a problem. I told him everything, also what happened in the house and the potion I gave her to drink to prevent fertilisation. He told me the darn thing was a placebo, which has given me a great headache. Her letters suggest nothing has happened and that she is working and living with her aunt in Aberdeen."

"If she is in Aberdeen then I'm afraid something serious has happened." He explained. "If a young girl from a decent family becomes pregnant and is not married she is usually sent away to relatives until such time as a solution can be found for her problem. No decent family wants to face disgrace because of a young lady's folly."

"It wasn't folly. It was love at first sight for both us. I am not ashamed of what happened, only if something has gone disastrously wrong. I will never be able to forgive myself. Am I not the son you never had any more… Uncle Matthew?"

"We all make mistakes my boy, I could see that she was very attracted to you from the moment she set eyes on you and that play in the boat sprinkling water first at her mom then her dad and eventually you. It was a serious game. We all knew it was to draw your attention. I also notice her holding you when it was not necessary. Gordon saw it and he looked and winked at me. I can understand young people forgetting their responsibilities and let nature guide them to their own downfall. I will get to the bottom of this before long. As soon as we get to Georgetown I will telephone my brother and all will be revealed."

"Thank you. I am ever so much in you debt already. I am glad this has come out. I would have hated it if you found out some other way… Do you know something? We have never spoken like this before. This conversation has endeared me strongly to you. If we had this father and son relationship earlier I might have been able to guide my life in a more responsible way. I know Ben means well; his innocuous behaviour is not the guiding light for someone like me who has entered the doorway of manhood without the proper directives. Do you know his first lesson to me was to pick as many cherries as I can before reaching my twenty first birthday."

"Did you pick many cherries before your twenty first?" He jokingly asked.

"Uncle Matthew you are embarrassing me. I will have to keep that a secret."

"Now I have a secret that will shock you." He revealed "that Sugar Bush was after me long before she came to you. I will now invite her to my house and bond with her and when I say bonding I mean making love. Does that shock you?"

"A little, but it serves our purpose. You can have her. That will save me from committing myself to an unsavoury relationship."

"So that's settled. You will not be offended."

"Not at all, I feel happy for you. I thought you were passed it." I said smiling.

He returned the smile with a devilish look on his face. Revealing more of his secrets he told me.

"I have had many young women in this place; they will come at nights and leave in the morning with no commitment whatsoever. This Sugar Bush is something else. At the time she approached me I thought she was too young and I was involved with some other women who were keeping a close watch on me. These women are very clever. Remember I speak their language fluently."

"Do they still keep an eye on you?" I asked.

"They have their own men folks now and are not interested in my activities. That is why I can take that little beauty to my bed without having to look over my shoulder." He replied with pride.

"I am seeing the more human side of you than I ever imagined. And I like it. You are human after all."

We started laughing with such enthusiastically. It caught the attention of Ben who was loitering not far away. He wanted to know what it was all about.

"Am I missing out on some funny stories?" He inquired.

We were to too hysterical to answer his question. This got him a bit angry. So he simply sulked. After regaining our composure I explained to him it was a private conversation we do not wish to share with anyone.

"Alright then you can wash your own dirty clothes and cook your own food and tidy your own room and protect yourself when trouble gets in your way. Benjamin Carson will keep himself private from now on."

"Now listen Ben this was indeed a very private conversation. I would not even share it with his dad who as you know is my dear friend. So please be the man you are and let the matter drop. We promised each other that no one will hear of this conversation." Uncle Matthew told him sternly.

"Then if it is funny why can I not share the joke?" Ben insisted.

"There is no way we can share that joke. It will embarrass us no end." Uncle Matthew tried to reason.

Ben was the sort of fellow that did not tolerate secrets. I remember my meeting with Jean and his insistence of wanting to know what happened. I am not certain if he did not deliberately watched Christine and me making love, even though he said he was looking out for caiman. I am beginning to have a slight distrust of him in such matter. I looked him straight in the eyes and said, "Benjamin Carson, You listen to me carefully. I am not letting you in on this joke. The Commissioner and I were having some fun that was meant to be for our ears only. If you have any decency you will leave the matter alone." My firmness had the desired effect.

"I am sorry Commissioner. I will not speak of it again." He apologised.

We were reminded to start collecting our belongings together and see that all matters relating to our departure are finalised.

"I think the person that needs the help more is Bell. She has accumulated so much junk I don't think the supply boat will be able to take all her things." Ben told us.

"Never mind all that. Diego will soon sort it out." I replied. Then adding "I think it is better we trudge along and see what the situation is. Women have a habit of not wanting to throw anything away."

"So, you know the habits of women. Do you Peter" Uncle Matthew joked.

"I've learnt it at home. When my dad wants to discard anything that he feels is clogging up the house, he quietly asks the maid to remove them when my mother is not about. In that way he avoids an argument." I told him with conviction.

"I am looking forward to meeting your mother and to see if Berbice can live up to its name as being the most hospitable place in the country. It will even be better if Gordon is there at the same .These parties your dad normally hosts. Tell me a little about it."

"I am not there most of the time. I am usually sent to my grandmother to let the guests use my room. The whole thing normally starts on Friday evening when the guests from Georgetown arrive. Selected people from the town are invited and a party will begin with them taking turns to sing. Eventually, they will play a few records and dance until the early hours.

"The next day it is time to go fishing and swimming in the Canje River. There is some game around and a bit of shooting, mostly deer or wild hogs. Some of the meat is used for a barbeque and they have great fun."

"Sunday is when everyone seems to enjoy themselves the most. Several East Indian men and their wives are invited. The men to curry a whole sheep and their wives make roti an Indian bread."

"I sometimes take my friends for a meal, which they all enjoy. Does that sound like fun?" I ended.

"It sounds great. I can't wait to get there. As you know I love curry. Between you and me Bell can't cook a good curry. I know; I have had it made by experts. I think those East Indian women can do it better. Those men and their wives that are invited to do the cooking, Are they paid or do they do it for fun?" Uncle Matthew wanted to know.

"I think they enjoy doing it for the fun and it is also a great escape from the boring lives they live. They would sing their Indian songs and sometimes the men would do a bit of dancing, creating a party atmosphere of their own. They are allowed to take home enough to feed the rest of their families. There is something else. They get some treatment free. Others in the village often squabble between themselves for the privilege of being there. The men also get a fair amount of whisky while they are cooking." I explained.

"These East Indians?" Matthew asked with curiosity. "You say some have arranged marriages. That I can understand. If the young men are prohibited from courting a young lady and I believe it is most unlikely that a young lady will be seen doing that. How is the couple able to get to know each other?"

"It starts out with one of the young lady's parent having an eye on one of the young men in the village. The next step is to send an envoy to propose a meeting with the young man's father and the possibility of a meeting. If it is agreed then the young lady's parents invite the young man and maybe a few of his friends for dinner. This is a great time for the lucky young man as more often than not he is offered the best rum and the most lavish of meals. Whether giving the young man a fair amount to drink is by design is a matter of conjecture. The atmosphere can be euphoric and most often than not he loses complete command of his senses. He is introduced briefly to the young lady. His friends also have a say in his decision. When he's had a few more, the question is asked "Well son what do you think of my daughter?"

The young man turns to get a clue from his friends if the signal is one of approval then the question of marriage is sealed.

The young lady has no say in the matter. Very rarely an objection is raised.

On the other hand, if he gets a signal of disapproval. Then the lad will say that he will think it over and write a letter to that effect. It is all a polite way of saying No thank you. This is accepted with no hard feelings."

"I must say this is a strange state of affairs. It is a bit different in India. I suppose here in British Guiana and far away from their original culture, they develop one of their own." Matthew concluded.

"I think if they develop a new culture it is because there are multitudes of Indian customs and remember these people came from different parts on India. So it is possible the situation we have here is brought about by a combination of various Indian traditions." Peter suggested and then asked. "Why are you interested in these people?"

"I am only trying to see if I can find a clue why it has to be like that. There is something I must tell you. As in Sappanam if an unmarried girl is seen simply talking with a young man without a chaperone she is seen as a person without moral scruples and would find it hard to find a husband. And as you know no young lady wants to end up an old maid. Did Sugar Bush come to see you alone?" He asked me.

"No. She did not. Nice of you to explain." I replied.

"Peter" Matthew said with solemnity in his voice "A lot of people from the outside see these people as savages. Look at them, their clothes as unconventional by our standards their language sounds mumbo jumbo. To understand what they have in their heads, their thoughts and beliefs you must understand their language. It took me years to manage it. In the end it was worth it. Many would think they have no coordination in their lives. I can tell you, without the slightest hint of exaggeration; their moral standards are impeccably high. Have you seen how they dispose of their dead?"

"It's strange you asked that. No one has died since I got here, or at least I am not aware of it." I told him.

"I can tell you many died since you came and it is because they dispose of their dead very early in the morning that you may have missed out. The dead are bound in palm leaves and tied to a tree in a standing position very far from here. The body is eaten by jaguars and vultures until only the bones are left. These are gathered and taken back to the dead man's hut and buried with the rest of his ancestors. When I asked them why allow the jaguars to eat their dead. They told me that they must give back to the forest all that we have taken from it. At first I was puzzled by what they meant. Then they explained it by saying that a man survived by taking all he needs from the forest and it is only fair to return it back when you die by letting the forest in the shape of its animals and birds take it back. They even quote what they heard the vicar said many times and that is ... The Lord giveth and the Lord taketh away. Only in their case it is the forest that is the Lord. Does that make sense to you?"

"To a certain point. I guess there are more facets in my religion than there is in theirs." I then asked. "Is it not dangerous to let the jaguars get used to the flesh of humans? Surely they must be aware of this"

"I think they do. But it is their tradition and it has been going on for thousands of years." He reasoned.

CHAPTER 9

An Earthquake

When the supply boat arrives I am sure my father will be on it. Now, I can really prepare myself for the most important journey in my life. I must first consult with my friends of the plan I have in mind.

Ben and I decided to visit Diego. It was many days since we last saw him. When we arrived he was busy repairing the corral with the help of the young villagers. Two of them were also milking the cows and Bell was nowhere to be seen.

"Where is Bell?" Ben asked.

"She is in the lodge but please wait for me before you go and see her." Diego replied.

"Is she ill? Ben asked again

"No, she is not ill. I would not be long then we can all go inside." Diego replied casually.

I looked at Ben and he shrugged his shoulders. Bell must have heard us talking and came out to greet us. She looked a bit different. She gave us both a hug and invited us in. Diego stopped what he was doing and followed. In the lodge, Diego went up to Bell put his arm around her and smiled as I have never seen him smile before, the he asked Bell to say something.

Looking very pleased with herself she announced "Friends I am pleased to tell you that I am having a baby. I am so happy I want to cry every time I think of it."

"Please don't cry now Bell or we all will start crying with you." Ben pleaded.

As we sat enjoying a drink there was a tremendous noise and the lodge started shaking. Pots were falling off the shelves. Bell ran and held Diego and asked. "Is it the end of the earth Diego? Are we going to die before my baby is born?"

By this time the vibrations had stopped. The few seconds was like an eternity. Then it started again this time a bit stronger and it lasted longer. We were all huddled on the floor waiting for it to stop. We stayed on the floor for a long time until we were certain it was over. Gradually, we stood up and still holding on to each other waited for the next tremor. An hour passed before we realised that it was over. No one needs to ask what it was. This was the first time I had experienced an earthquake.

By this time our drinks were all over the floor glass and all. Diego poured us a fresh one and we went outside to check the cows. It was chaos out there the cows had spilled all the milk and they were wandering outside of the corral. It was some time before order was restored.

After explaining Uncle Matthew's proposals, Diego gave his view. "I was thinking of this baby and I don't want to bring it up in this place. I want to give my child a better prospect in life, to be somebody. It is alright for Matthew to say this place should remain pristine as nature wanted but my child is going to have a life I think would suit it far better than being brought up in this wilderness. I am hoping to sell my share of the diamonds and go and live in either Wismar or McKenzie where there are proper schools and a library. I know those towns are wild with drunkards and villains but on the whole not bad places if a watchful eye is there for protection. I am sorry Peter I will not be around when you need me. I can only wish you well."

"What about you Ben?" I asked feeling very disappointed.

"You know me Peter. I've lived on hand outs all these years, not knowing what the future holds. I was happy hanging around. I enjoy hanging around. The truth is I can never hold on to a proper job. The money I get from the diamonds will be held in a safe bank for my old age. I will stay with you until you chase me away.

"Well Diego. Can I make a last request before we split up?

"Yes, you can."

"I suggest we leave Bell in Uncle Matthew's house and we all go to Georgetown, sell our diamonds and then go to Berbice for a great party. After that we can go our separate ways."

"That sounds a great idea. I have never been to Berbice. I think Matthew would like to come. Have you asked him?" Diego asked.

"I will and I am certain he will agree. My dad will love this idea."

"Diego," Bell interrupted with a frown "I have not been asked if I would like to remain here while you lot go on your sporting tour of Georgetown and Berbice. I am not going to be left out of it. Baby or no baby if I am not allowed to follow you then you will have to stay right here with me."

"I didn't mean it like that darling. It is just that this is the kind of journey for men only. The fact that you are pregnant might make you tired with all the travelling. But if you want to come then that is what you get." Diego relented.

It was several days since the supply boat left for Wismar and we cannot expect to see it for at least another three weeks. We decided to consult Uncle Matthew and get his reaction to this Berbice trip. As it turned out he was jubilant over the entire program.

In the meantime, Diego was organising the young men to distribute the milk to the villagers and to see the cows are well fed and protected. He was also telling them that the cows are no longer his responsibilities as he was leaving Sappanam for good. This had a saddening effect on them. They appeared to understand, he being an outsider will eventually leave.

Bell, on the other hand, was not so pleased to leave. She looked at her lodge with sadness and all the effort that went into it to making it a home. Manny, hearing the news came to inquire of his position. I told him his position is uncertain as definite plans have not been made about the surgery here. He will in effect remain in charge while we sort things out. I even promised that if we do close down Sappanam's operation there will be a position for him in Georgetown. This pleased him. Ben and I will take things in its stride until the time comes for us to leave.

Uncle Matthew joined us under a tree with a bottle under his arm and Sugar Bush followed with three glasses and a jug of water. She looked at me and smiled. I returned her smile and told her that I was happy with her new arrangement. She nodded and left.

The villagers were assembling in the long house and arguing between themselves. Uncle Matthew ignored them completely which appears to make them angrier. They kept looking at us and waving their arms in a very hostile manner. Unable to stand their noise, Uncle Matthew decided to look into whatever was bothering them. He was there for some time before the hubbub subsided and finally they all sat down and listened to whatever he was saying. We, on the other hand, could not understand a word. I have been here five years and never bothered to learn their language, for the simple reason, Diego always translated for me which I find easier than trying my hand at a new language, a subject I was not good at school.

Uncle Matthew soon joined us after a few minutes and explained that they were upset that we are abandoning their village and the dental service that we provided. He explained to them that someone will come at intervals to see to their needs. As for the cows and their welfare, he told them that it is time they take the responsibilities of their own welfare in that department. They were happy with the explanation and left peacefully.

Diego had joined us to ask that we accompany him to cold stream. He wished to show the young men what to do when they have excess fish or meat. I am sure they understood the procedure, but Diego wanted to make sure they did and most importantly is for them to understand that keeping it clean will prevent any contamination. The young men decided not to come along. The corral was in urgent need of repairs. The rain and minor earth quake had caused some damage. Diego agreed and promised to show them at a later date.

I fear walking all that distance for a mere demonstration. Now the men were not going we can call a halt to this needless journey. Matthew and Diego insisted we go. I must show unity as I had expected from them. So I persuaded myself to follow them.

When we got to cold stream the place was devastated. The hill was broken on its side and tons of rocks were lying at its foot. Luckily, it did not destroy the stream with debris. We also noticed that the stream was not the same. Tons of debris did get in and caused a blockage resulting in it diverting its course in another direction. This caused a serious problem and rendered the cold storage system useless.

Diego and Ben as usual were digging away in turns removing the debris with their bare hands. I was expecting to see some more nuggets. I kicked at the rubble brought ashore only to find more stones. As they dug deeper Ben shouted an unmentionable word "Fucking hell." Uncle Matthew woke up and inquired what it was all about.

"Look," said Ben. GOLD! ... MORE GOLD. We never thought there would be any more of the stuff."

Uncle Matthew rushed to his feet and examined the nuggets. "Second time lucky," he murmured. Then looking at the hill he asked us to examine the rocks on the ground. "You know what's happened here lads, the minor earthquake we had a few days ago disturbed this cunning hill and exposed its secret." He became silent and his brow narrowed. I can see he was thinking of some cunning plan. Then in his official capacity he spoke seriously and grimly. "We can take as much as we can find and after that we will have to cover up the area and all the gold hidden there forever."

"Cover them up!" Ben shouted. "There is more than a million dollars lying there and we are to cover it up. Mr Commissioner, are you mad?"

"No Mr Carson, I am not mad just practical. We have enough gold to make us wealthy and then the diamonds. Remember all the gold and the diamonds we got by mere chance and we are lucky that we did not have to go through the rigors of digging pits in rains and floods to get it. Be thankful it will be more that you will need in your life time. What's more important here is the survival of this community. I do not want greedy men coming and transforming this into a sin city. I tell you this, I will not have it. Anyone that exposes this secret will forever be branded a traitor. We have lived together for many years and always share our good fortune. I say enough is enough. When I am retired I will still continue to keep an eye on this community and that darn vicar, I will have a serious word with him when he gets back. His church and their darn madness of building schools, and what next. The people that will be doing the building will take advantage of these poor souls. I am mad with anger and will veto all his plans. Only the governor can save him now."

I have never seen Uncle Matthew so red in the face. The anger caused his arteries to swell. It was a long time before he got normal again. He quietly asked us what we think.

"I said that we should respect his wishes and bury the darn gold where it is." I also told him that I have my reservations of it being kept a secret and that his paranoia of preservation is veiling his senses of reality.

"I completely agree with Peter." Diego added. "Since you are the Commissioner we must do as you asked."

"I am so happy to agree with the Commissioner." Ben added. "I have enough, besides a man like me would not know what to do with too much money. The girls will have most of it and I have to go back looking for work."

"So, gentlemen, do I have your word of honour that my suggestion be kept a secret?"

"No need for any pledge. We respect you and would abide without question your decision."

With heavy hearts we took our shovels and buried what we could. To be realistic I do not see how this gold can remain a secret. The rain will certainly help to expose it sooner or later, or some clever young buck will discover it accidently. What happens next? Has Uncle Matthew thought this through, or is his stubbornness for purity blinding him from reality? Whatever the real reason, I have pledged not to mention it to anyone.

It was Diego who brought up the subject. "Mr Commissioner. We all pledged to remain silent about the gold and that stays firm by me and I am sure with the others. What will happen if one of the young men find it, what will you do?"

"The thought did occur to me shortly after I made you pledge your silence. I will have to think quite clearly on this. I know it was an irrational thing to ask of you, but I am seriously concerned of the welfare of these people. I will discuss this with Gordon when we next meet. I am certain there is something that can be done to balance things out." Nevertheless, we continued to bury all signs of the gold before leaving.

It was several days since we visited cold stream and the promise we made kept surfacing each time we went there. I was not concerned about getting more gold from the hill. What I was concern more about is the impact it would have on Uncle Matthew if things went dramatically wrong. I realise how much he loves these people and their way of life. It was what sustained him through the lonely years he spent doing what he thought was right. It would be catastrophic for any of us to disillusion him.

I called a meeting of Diego, Bell and Ben, which was held at the lodge. I pointed out that nature cannot be asked to keep hiding its riches. At some point in time it will be exposed. What I was hoping to find was a viable conclusion to this dilemma.

Diego was happy with the gold and diamonds he had so was Ben. I asked Bell what she thought.

"I have a solution. You men are going to laugh at it but I think it can work, if we all try to make it work. We can tell the villagers of the gold explain to them the seriousness of letting outsiders know where it is and see what happens."

"What will they do with the gold when they get it?" Ben quite rightly asked.

"They can give the commissioner to sell and buy useful things to improve their lives." Diego replied

"Useful things like what?" I asked.

"Clothes for the children and young ladies, and other female things which you men know nothing about. They can buy certain medicines which the forest cannot produce and this will enhance their lives. Who are we to say what these people must have and may not have. I love the Commissioner, but I think he is trying to be God. I don't agree with all the things he said. The forest will remain pristine if loggers, poachers and gold diggers are kept away." Bell told us getting a bit red in the face.

"Don't exert yourself darling." Diego warned. "We don't want our child to born with a nervous disposition."

We could not help laughing at Diego's remark. It was agreed that we discussed this matter seriously with Uncle Matthew. Then after hearing what he has to say, we can embark on some other scheme.

Uncle Matthew was busy with his report. He was sitting with his body tilted to one side and a pencil sticking out of his mouth and in great thought. He straightened and took the pencil from his mouth and looked inquiringly at us. As usual it was Diego who explained what we suggested. Without saying a word he took the papers he had written on and tore it up before throwing it in the bin. Then he spoke.

"I imagine this is a culmination of all your ideas, is it not?"

"It is." I replied rather sheepishly.

"Well you have solved a great problem for me. In my report I was suggesting that the Governor declare the area a prohibited site, it will in effect prevent anyone going near that area. That was a foolish and irresponsible thought. Now you saw me tearing up that report proves the point. I will be giving much thought to your suggestions. I guess it was Bell who thought up the idea of clothes for the children and for the young ladies and their essentials. I congratulate you all for your superb ideas. I will add something more to all that when I meet with the chief and elders." Uncle Matthew replied. He looked so pleased with himself he could hardly contain it.

"Gentlemen it is customary when one has acquired victory in a sticky situation. The next thing is to celebrate. This will be a special celebration, for you see gentlemen and of course lady I have successfully made some ice in that old fridge. Now for the first time here in this vast wilderness we are drinking with ice!" Uncle Matthew jubilantly announced then after pouring drinks for everyone he turned to Bell and offered her some tea.

"I don't want any silly tea Commissioner. This is a special celebration, you said so yourself and I am going to be a part of it. So if you don't mind sir, I will have that drink with all of you.

The baby can close it eyes while mamma is celebrating. Besides, it was my suggestion that made you think again. I am sure of it." Bell told him.

"Gentlemen and lady to a successful solution." Everyone raised their glass and thanked Uncle Matthew for being so kind.

Diego then asked the question. "Commissioner, are you going to tell us what made you so jubilant of our ideas?"

"The final point in all this is, when I explain to the Chief and his elders the benefit the gold will bring to the children and young ladies; it may not be enough to prevent him exposing the secret. What I do plan to tell him will be more devastating than you can imagine. I intend to tell him first a lie then the truth.

The lie will be that gold diggers slaughtered several hundred of tribes people to get their land because of gold then I will tell him if that is what he wants for his people he can go ahead and let outsiders know. That ought to do the trick. I will go and see him right away. You can continue to drink me dry if you wish. See you later."

My father soon joined us and I had the difficult task of telling him all that was discussed between Uncle Matthew and me. It was also difficult to explain the possibilities of running a surgery in Georgetown and being a Commissioner at the same time. He point out that it will be an impossible task to do both jobs.

"The travel alone will make you want to give up. Do you notice how less and less I come here? I am so tired at the end of one journey I find it almost impossible to make it to Berbice. It will be far better to accept the post of the Commissioner than trying to get registered. Do you know you will make history? You will be the first British Guianese to get a post held by an English man. It will give Berbice a real boost. The ancient county will once again have a feather in its cap." My dad reasoned.

"I care about Berbice, but I must think what is more beneficial and rewarding to me than what is best for Berbice. I dreamt of being a surgeon like you. Circumstance put an end to that and it is all your doing. If I were not dragged to this wilderness, wasting my time and energy, I could have accomplished my dream.

You wanted to be the Good Samaritan promising more than you could deliver and dragging you son into an empty void. I have enough money to make me the richest man in Berbice if not in the country. But you know something I do not care for it if it cannot bring me the happiness I longed for. My mother should have been stronger and opposed you and your damn wild schemes. You are crushing your own son's dream to satisfy your ego. I hate you for that." Was my damning response. At this point he slapped me across the cheek and shouted at me to be quiet. Then responding to my accusations he said. "Your mother is stronger than you think. She is a religious woman as you damn well know and she has taken a vow when we married. "To honour and obey" and that is all she is doing. Honouring my decision and obeying my wishes. When you young people can come to terms with such understanding then perhaps our world will remain the way it should be. And how dare you say I'm egotistic."

"When, or better still if I do get married I will not have my future wife promising to Honour and obey me. That sound like that tyrant in Germany." I shouted back at him

My dad was absolutely gutted. He was lost for words for a good minute. When he finally spoke it was to ask me about this fortune I spoke of. He knew of the gold we found but it was not enough to make me one of the richest men in Berbice. Of course I told him the rest of the story.

"If what you say is true, then why are you unhappy? You can start up a pawn broker's shop and even become a diamond dealer yourself. What's your problem Son?"

"I do not want to be a merchant it's the most boring profession on earth. It also involves a bit of cheating. Telling people one thing when you mean something else."

"That's the way a business is run."

"I don't like it. One good thing came out from being imprisoned here and that is honesty and sincerity. I have learnt that from Diego and Bell and Uncle Matthew."

"So it is Uncle Matthew now. What brought about this familiarity?"

"When I came here I was nearing my nineteenth birthday and just in case you haven't noticed I am a man of twenty three years old and capable of taking charge of my destiny. I do have a love and respect for you but I will not allow you to dictate what I want any longer. It is not the money. I had other plans that I am sure would have seen me make a happier life for myself."

At this point he hugged and apologised for being blind to my development and maturity. I felt remorseful for speaking to him the way I did. I felt it had to come out in the open. Uncle Matthew must have heard our shouting. He came to see if everything was alright. It was then I told him that I would prefer to address him as Matthew.

"Of course you can. But why the change?"

"Matthew sound more friendly and endearing. That's why." My real reason lies with the way my father asked why I refer to him as uncle.

"Well thank you and you have my permission to address me by my first name."

Diego, Bell and Ben arrived as we sat in the veranda sipping a drink my father served as a compensation for his unreasonable stance towards me. What was more surprising was Manny in their midst. He looked cheerless as usual and sat by himself pretending he wants to rest.

One of the rangers came running towards us. He was almost breathless as he spoke. Matthew calmed him down and he began to explain that the men in the other village are unhappy with the amount of milk they received. Unless the Commissioner does something urgently there will be a tribal war and they promised to kill all the cows in the process.

"This is damn serious... Damn serious indeed!" Matthew exclaimed loudly and ordered his ranger to get the chiefs and the Elders together.

"What action will you take?" I asked.

"I don't know. I never had to deal with an insurrection here. I can only determine my next step when I've conferred with them and Diego." Was his grim reply. Then adding he suggested that

Ben and I be present for moral support. This we were delighted to do. I have never seen a war before and it will be quite interesting to see the outcome of this one.

Matthew went to the Rest House and brought his rifle and several rounds. He then ordered his staff to lock all the doors and remain out of sight.

Diego joined us and we went to the long house where the chiefs had gathered. Before he sat down he pointed at us and told them in no uncertain words.

"These are the people responsible for the extra care your children received from the cows. Not to mention the fact that my brother sent you $100 dollars and Ben. What about Mr Carson. He could have benefited from that skin you all agreed to finance this project. If there is a difference with the quantity of milk distributed then it is an easy problem to solve." Then, shouting as loud as he could, Thundered. "I will not have an insurrection on my hand for a few drops of milk" I can see the terror that sentence brought on their faces.

The matter was resolved when Diego said that apart from a small quantity he took for Bell the rest was divided equally between the two villages. It was decided that the village with a greater number of children be given a larger quantity. This seemed to satisfy both parties. They raised their hand to their chins and bowed before leaving.

CHAPTER 10

Goodbye Sappanam

We were all packed ready to board the supply boat. The villagers as usual came out to see us off. For the first time, I went and shook the chief's hand, my first physical contact with him. He took his other hand and clasped mine as if to say he was sorry we were leaving. There was a somewhat sad look on his face. We finally waved our last goodbyes as the boat sped down the Demerara.

This was the first time I retraced my steps homeward bound. Ituni is a night and half a day's travelling and then the truck and the locomotive to McKenzie. My heart was filled with sadness. It seemed an eternity since I last travelled this way. I was not going to allow sentiment get the better of me. I started thinking of Jean and the passing glory of our meeting and just as quickly my thoughts turned to Christine. I tried whistling the song she sung when we were on the river bank together and tears began flowing down my cheeks. I quickly took some water from the river and washed my face. Then, I remember the last time I did that Ben warned me of vicious fish.

At Ituni, I was looking to see if I could catch a glimpse of Duncan the Amerindian who paddled us up to Sappanam. It was not to be. I noticed the old truck was replaced with a new one. It gave a smoother ride.

As we waited for the locomotive to take to take us to McKenzie, I decided to visit the Chinese shop, not for anything specific just to have a look at what was on sale. There I met Mr Spencer, a man I met casually several times at Wismar. He said "Hello", and inquired if I was the same person he knew in Wismar. He also remarked how much I had changed. Then he told me he is the driver of the locomotive. I have always been fascinated with trains and the romantic fever it sent through me. I then asked if I could ride with him and perhaps do a bit of driving. It may seem odd a grown man asking to ride in the driver's cabin.

"That you can certainly do." He replied happily, then added "driving a locomotive is very simple, you don't have to bother about traffic, except the occasional wild hog that runs across the track." He then bought himself a packet of Lighthouse cigarettes and after I explained to the others I joined him in the driver's cabin.

At McKenzie, we got a car and travelled up to Richmond. Here is where the Canadians working in the plant lived, far from the local people. Uncle Matthew had a house allocated to him which we all shared. It was beautiful with a golf course and all the other luxuries needed for relaxation. We intended to stay there for the two days waiting for the boat taking us to Georgetown.

Some of the Canadian women looked at us suspiciously eventually after Uncle Matthew went up and told them the purpose of our visit they appeared more friendly. Diego had organised a local boatman to take Bell and him to the community where we first saw Bell.

Ben and I decided to go to the Club house where I first met Jean. It was just the same, girls were cleaning the tables and wiping the floor. We sat down and ordered a couple of cold beers. This went down a treat. Then Ben began reminding me of the first time I came here. I did not want to be reminded so I changed the subject. A few beers later we went down the market square to pass the time. There someone heavily pregnant came up to me and said, "Hello! Peter."

It took a while for me to recognise her to be Jean.

"Remember me?" She asked.

"Of course" I replied. Then I told her it was hard to recognise her at first sight due to her pregnancy.

"This is my third child." She told me looking very pleased with herself.

I felt slightly embarrassed and told her I must be on my way as we have friends waiting.

"You don't want to know why I stopped writing?" She asked.

Right now I could not be bothered why she stopped writing. Just for the sake of politeness I told her she can tell me why. What she told me was exactly what I thought it would be. She met her husband and fell in love and the regular bit of nonsense that goes with it. She saw I was not really interested and left. I felt a bit sad as she supported her back with one hand while struggling to carry the basket in the other. I ran up and took the basket from her and Ben in turn took it from me. It was more respectful that Ben was with us as husbands can be extremely jealous if their wives are seen in the company of other men, especially if that man is unknown to him.

She was living in the same house. She invited us in and poured us a glass of fruit juice. I smiled as she gave it to me and she returned the smile.

"You do remember the last time you were here. That is why you smiled. Am I not right?"

I nodded and told her that the past is best forgotten if one is to succeed with the future. She agreed and soon we were on our way to meet Bell and Diego.

I dread going up that hill in the sun but this journey is essential for sentimental reason. The familiar faces keep popping up and all that was required was a brief nod of acknowledgement.

Bell and Diego was seated in the shade outside the house eating boiled ground provisions and salted fish. The folks from her community were returning from their farms and they were all looking at us a few came and exchanged salutation with Bell. They were eager to be introduced to Diego and then they expressed admiration for her courage to leave to find a husband and what a find they said. Some were cheeky to give Diego a kiss and a hug. Bell was delighted with their appreciation. It was getting late and time to head back for Richmond.

The next two days were spent resting. Matthew went visiting some of the Canadians and coming back a bit tipsy. He appears to have lost some of the vigour that kept him going. I am beginning to wonder if he is thinking of his self-imposed imminent retirement and the problems at Sappanam.

On the morning of our departure he was back his normal self. Whistling as he shaved and enjoying a hearty breakfast. The journey to Georgetown was uneventful when we arrive it was late. So we all headed for The Tower Hotel to stay for the duration of the time we would be in Georgetown.

The following day Matthew went to see the Governor while we went in search of a diamond dealer. Bell was asked to stay at the hotel until we returned. She was not very happy about it but Diego insisted.

The Chinese woman examining our diamonds was surprised that we brought in so many and asked how we come to get so many. Diego firmly told her to mind her own business and get on with the assessment. She was unhappy with him and I told her that part of it belongs to the Commissioner of the Hinterland.

"Ah!" She said "If he is involved then I better get on with my job." Then she added. "At first glance I can tell you we do not have so much money to pay you for all of them. I will have to buy a little at a time."

"That's no good for us. The stones will have to be sold so that the money can be shared between the partners. Diego informed her.

"Let me make an assessment and give you a quote. Then you can see why it may not be possible to pay all at once." She took the diamonds counted them and asked us to come back the next day. We were not happy leaving the diamonds with her, so Diego told her we will come back with the stones tomorrow when there is someone who genuinely knows about these stones. She was furious and accused Diego of calling her a cheat.

"I am not calling you a cheat madam. It is just we don't want to leave the stones with someone we hardly know. So if you please we will come back in the morning with the Commissioner and try to do a deal."

With those parting words we headed back for the hotel. There Matthew was having tea with Bell on the veranda. We told him what happened and he agreed with us. At the same time he told us that she is a reputable woman working for a very reputable company. Nevertheless, we did what we thought was the best in everyone's interest.

As soon as we finished breakfast the next day we confronted her, this time Matthew was in charge. Everything went fine another gentleman appeared and gave the stones a good look.

He turned to Matthew and told him "The true price of a diamond can only be made after it is cut and polished and the flaws or flawlessness will determine the price. At the moment if you are in a hurry to sell I can give you a price that will benefit everyone in the end. It's a gamble and I must play safe."

"It seems fair what you said. In that case we will sell only four and the rest you can do as you say cut and polish them before giving a price." Uncle Matthew informed him

"Which four do you want to sell?" He asked.

"The smallest four." Diego told him. "We have hotel bills to pay and we have only recently come from the bush."

"What part of the bush?" He inquired. Fearing if we told him Sappanam he might want to send men there looking for diamonds and find the gold instead. Diego told him we are from Kamarang a place near the Venezuelan border.

"I've heard of that place, but I never knew diamonds are found in that region," he remarked.

"We didn't get the diamonds there. I only said we are from there." Was Diego's firm reply.

"Right let's see, uncut, these diamond weigh in at fifteen carats at eighty dollars a carat. You have…"

"Twelve hundred dollars." I told him

"Smart young man, and very clever with the figures, I will give you your money and a receipt for the remaining stones. In whose name shall I make the receipt? He finally asked.

"My name, Matthew Longhorn Commissioner for the Hinterland."

"I know who you are Mr Longhorn. I have seen your pictures regularly in the newspaper sometimes with the Governor."

"And what's your name if I can ask?"

"Sylvanus Humphries, I own this business. I thank you for coming here first." He paused for a moment and rubbing his chin, he told Matthew that if there is an urgency for the sale of the diamonds. He can send it for Mr Alberga in Paramaribo to cut and polish them in his workshop. "Mr Alberga is the manager of a very large firm based in Holland, a respectable establishment. They are working undercover to protect their stocks from the Germans. He controls most of the stones discovered in South America on that firm's behalf. They have an office in Water Melon Straat and a large work shop in Kankatre Straat. I can send these stones and have them back in less than a week."

"We really don't want these stone sent anywhere. If you can arrange for him to come here then that will suit us just fine." I told him.

"I will telephone him and arrange it." Mr Humphries promised. He also told us that "if the gentleman does come he will not bring cash but a banker's note to honour any amount the diamonds are worth."

"I would of course get my commission from both of you."

This Matthew agreed. To be on the safe side he asked that a receipt and an estimate be given. Mr Humphries took the remaining eighteen stones and weighed them. Then he started writing down some numbers on a piece of paper. He was writing so many noughts I thought he had gone mad. He showed the figures to Matthew who gave a loud whistle. Then Matthew showed me the amount and I felt faint.

"Now Peter you are good with numbers tell the men the estimated worth of these stones you thought worthless."

"One million, eight hundred and seventy nine thousand dollars."

"You are joking of course." A shocked Diego said.

"See for yourself." I showed him the numbers and he nearly fainted.

"Matthew did you realise it would have amounted to so much money when you gave me your stones?"

"I was not far wrong. I must add it exceeds by a fair amount the figure I had in mind." He replied and then looking at the displayed tray in the show case. He asked Mr Humphries, "Can I look at that solitaire ring in the middle of your tray?" He then called Bell and asked her to try it on. It was a perfect fit.

"What this for?" A puzzled Bell asked.

"Remember at Sappanam I promised to make a diamond ring for you. Now that promise is fulfilled."

"But you said two rings one gold and one diamond." Bell reminded him.

"Indeed I said two rings. It is only right your husband buys you the wedding ring. If I were to buy it for you then I think I will have some rights on you." Matthew replied jokingly.

"Okay then since we are shopping I might as well get the lady her wedding ring." Diego added.

We let Diego accept the money for the four diamonds and before leaving, Mr Humphries said. "That sum I showed you is only half of what you would have received if they were sent to Holland or the Middle East. This war is a scourge on business."

"Why can you not send it To Holland or the Middle East?" Diego asked.

"The Germans would confiscate it and you'd never see it again. No one trades in diamonds there at the moment. The Middle East is just as bad." Mr Humphries explained.

On our way to the hotel, Matthew told me he is going to see Gordon and arranged a meeting for me to see the President of the Dental Association in the morning. He also suggested that he accompany me if I so desire. Then he took a taxi and left.

Our next stop was to sell our nuggets. We could have done this at Mr Humphries but the Chinese fellow I normally buy from in Berbice has an extended business in the city. I wanted to see what it looked like. This was a much easier affair, because of impending war with Germany. The price was going up on a daily basis. The Guianese dollar still stood at four dollars and eighty cents to a pound. It has been the same for as long as I can remember and is unlikely to change.

The nuggets were tested and a huge pile of money was given to us. This time we allowed Ben to take charge of it after it was counted. He looked at the bundle of cash and asked. "Why me? Why give me all this money to stroll about town?"

"Ben" Diego asked "Do you honestly think some choke and robber will want to attack you for the money?"

"Not unless he is tired of living." He replied laughing.

The teller at the bank kept looking at us each time she counted a bundle. Ben made a remark of how lovely she looks with the beads of perspiration on her soft red lips. She started counting much faster before finally giving us a receipt.

After a hard day's bargaining, shopping and banking we decided to rest on the veranda of the hotel, sipping tea when someone came and asked for Peter D'Abrue. I was taken aback and followed him as he suggested.

It was a phone call from Matthew. He told me the venue for the meeting has been moved. I am to be present at Government House at 9 o'clock in the morning. He also said the President of the Dental Association would be interviewing me there. I was overwhelmed with joy. At last things are beginning to move in the right direction. My only problem is whether their decision will be favourable. I shall not worry. I decided to leave that problem for tomorrow.

Right now I will ask Ben to take us on a tour of the city. Diego and Bell were happy at the suggestion. A taxi was summoned and we were off. First to Saint George's Cathedral, the tallest wooden building in the world then to the other famous landmark which included the Stabroek Market built by the Dutch, including the buildings at Brickdam, and then the botanical garden. The best laid out public gardens in the West Indies and moderately competing with Kew. Our final destination was the sea wall where hundreds of people went for relaxation and to enjoy the cool Atlantic breeze. We were enjoying ice cream when the taxi driver came up and told us that we are being charged while his taxi is idling. Ben told him to go away and wait for us. This seemed to please him and he went away smiling.

I was up before the others and went down for breakfast. It was not long before the others came down. Diego asked if I needed his company for my interview. I told him I would be fine as Matthew will also be there. "Where is he?" Ben asked.

"With the Governor, I think. He always stays there when he comes to town." I replied casually.

CHAPTER 11

Brazilian Diamonds

I took a taxi and went to the venue of my appointment. A lot of people were in the waiting room. I was relieved when Matthew came and took me to another room where I was introduced to the President of the Dental Association. Two other men were by his side. I was offered a seat and Matthew sat next to me.

The President, addressing me, started by saying, "Now Young man, I was told you and your father were doing a lot of charitable work in the bush and the Commissioner is very pleased with your effort. Our question is. Why do you want to be registered?"

"It has always been my ambition to follow in my father's footstep. My career suffered because of my involvement with the Amerindians and their dental problems, and I was not given the opportunity to go the United States for my training. My father was kind to give the Commissioner an undertaking of helping out and I was caught in midstream."

"What experience do you have in dentistry? If so, how many years did you put in?" The second gentleman asked.

"I began my tutelage when I was fourteen, first helping with the instruments my father needed for his work and eventually taking primary impressions until I graduated to administering anaesthetic for extractions eventually doing the extractions under supervision. At Sappanam, I invented a new way for making temporary bridges. This proved to be a success and I am happy to say I will continue to improve on the method."

"How old are you now?" The other gentleman asked.

"I will be twenty two in a week's time."

"That's not what was asked," the President reminded me.

"I am sorry. I am twenty one."

"Do you think you are mature enough to take on the responsibilities of a dental surgeon?" The other gentleman asked.

"I know I am. I proved it at Sappanam."

Matthew got up and spoke with a serious look on his face. "Gentlemen, this young man came to my attention five years ago. He has been in attendance with his dad constantly. Even in the early hours of the morning when someone came with tooth ache, he helped in the treatment without grumbling. I know that because I observed him time and time again, always calm and polite even though he cannot speak their language. To deny him his request will be a great disservice to a young man who gave the best part of his youth and early manhood to do a service to a people that needed it." He then sat down and held my hand briefly to relax the tension in me.

"Mr Commissioner you have given a very admirable account of this young man's behaviour. However, we will convene with the rest of the committee and give our decision within a week." Then turning to me he said. "The Governor also spoke very kindly of the work you are doing and we will take that in consideration when making our decision. This interview is now over, May I take the opportunity to thank you for your patience… Good day!"

On our way out Matthew came across a friend of his a Mr Simpson. He was the government's surveyor. I heard of him some time back, but never met him. He talked of his retirement. Matthew asked what he would do after all these years in the colony.

"I intend to retire in Barbados. The climate is friendlier there. I am told." Was his reply.

"What about the house by the seawall? Are you going to rent it?"

"Oh no, I am selling it, too many problems in renting."

"I'll be interested in its sale." I joined in.

"Where will you get three thousand and five hundred dollars to buy my house?"

"Oh he has the money. The question is will you sell it to him?" Mathew said in my defence.

"I'll sell it to the devil if he pays my price." He quickly replied.

"When can we see this house?" I inquired.

"I am going there right now. Have you got transport?"

"Not at the moment. But we can arrange something." I suggested.

"You can come in my car and later we can telephone a taxi to take you where you want to go."

The house was in very good order from the outside. There was a small hut at the entrance with a glass window and a sturdy door. His maid opened the front door and let us in while Mr Simpson put his car in the garage. His wife came to greet us and made us comfortable. Matthew seems to know everyone. Their conversation revealed that.

As soon as her husband appeared he went about telling us about the property.

"It has four large bedrooms as you will soon see. There is the dining room and a larger than usual kitchen. This is of course the living room which is divided in two separate rooms. The hut downstairs is for the night guard cum gardener. There is a toilet downstairs and shower room. The main bedroom up here is en-suite and a bathroom with separate toilet is at the far end of the corridor. Now, I am sure you will like to see it for yourself. I would like you to wander through at your own pace and no offer, please. As you can see this house was built as a luxury home. You will not easily find another like it. So please take your time." I told him I did not see any electric fans in the house. I was very pleased with everything else. Then he pointed out that there is no need for electric fans as the wind from the Atlantic is an adequate cooler and it also keeps those darn mosquitoes away.

"Now young man, what do you think?"

"I have no offer to make. I will pay you what you asked, three thousand and five hundred dollars. You can have the papers drawn up by your lawyers and I will sign and have your money ready whenever you are ready." I told him.

"No Offer. By Jove! This is very decent of you. Do you always do business like this?"

"My very first business deal." I told him proudly.

I left the house feeling ecstatic and wanting to share that feeling with my friends. I kept putting off my trip home for the simple reason that when I do get there I will have everything in place for my peace of mind and most importantly to make my mother proud.

Our next stop was to visit Mr Humphries and see what progress had been made on our diamonds. I was hoping the others would be here so we could all go together. Their presence would have some strength in our meeting with this shrewd businessman.

He told us he had received a phone call at great expense from Mr Alberga and that the stones and the money would be here shortly. He took the telephone number of our hotel before we left. I asked to make a phone call to Bookers garage for a proper taxi. When it arrived, I told the driver that I will pay him five dollars a day for him to take us from place to place. He agreed and suggested that he must finish at 6 o'clock or further charges will be made. That suited us and we agreed.

My next visit was to my East Indian friend, the newly appointed judge. I wanted Matthew to go along also, as I intended to introduce him as the man partly responsible for the disruption in my life, a very profitable disruption. The others would not mind being left out and Matthew was keen on going. It was about five in the afternoon when we arrived.

A slim black girl opened the door and asked our names. This we revealed and before she departed to announce our presence. Persotum appeared and came half running to greet me. We were almost choked with joy at this meeting after so many years. I introduced Matthew and we went in the living room. There were more surprises another school friend Aubrey Pistano was there with his wife. We shook hands and slapped each other on the back. I looked at his wife and said "Don't tell me. You are Marina Gonsalves."

"I deliberately did not mention her name when I wrote to tell you I was getting married. Everyone was surprised." Aubrey proudly told me. I also know of the planned date you had with her. We laughed. I told Marina if I had the opportunity to take her to the cinema she would have ended up as Mrs D'Abrue. This brought further laughter.

"Well you did well marrying the right girl. I must say, and Marina, every one of us tried to date you without success...You were a bit difficult with the boys in your young days. We all tried to get you to the cinema if only to put our arms around you. Even Aubrey tried unsuccessfully on many occasions. I wish you both happiness and a successful marriage." I told them and turning to Persotum I asked. "Now Your Honour, Where is your lovely lady?"

"Stop the Your Honour talk. I am the same Persotum. Inge, my wife will join us soon. In the meantime let's have a drink in memory of the good old days." He suggested.

Matthew cleared his throat. I apologised and in the same breath I introduce him to my friends. It was at this point Inge came in. Formalities completed. Persotum asked his maid to get the drinks for us. We of course reminisced constantly until I realised that Matthew was not able to participate in our conversation. It was then I decided to let the others know of the years I spent away from civilisation. I began by saying how much I was enjoying this reunion with some of the greatest friends any man can hope to have. My only pity is that Fred was not here. His last letter to me was that he will be lecturing at the university in Washington and hoped that during the holiday period he will return for a visit. I would have liked to say something very important. I realise now it might embarrass Matthew.

Before I could have finished, Matthew put his hand up and started speaking.

"I know exactly what Peter wanted to say and I know it would not embarrass me. However, I am going to say it. I realise you are very good friends and shared an important part of your lives together. During the years Peter spent in the wilderness with his new friends, who are not here but probably relaxing at the hotel, would agree with me when I tell you of the anguish in his face as he suffered the disappointment of his dream. His obedience to his father, his loyalty to his friends and most importantly his total respect for me. I could be the father of any of you lads here. Unfortunately, I was never married and therefore have no children. That is to say none that I know of." This brought some laughter. Then he continued. "I realise I might be getting boring but the truth must be known and who better to know that truth but his friends."

Matthew continued to tell the story of the gold and the diamonds and he told them what perhaps he felt he had to say.

"The gold was only a small part of our find, yet it would have been enough to make anyone comfortable in life. It was the diamonds that were the crown of our find I must confess as Commissioner I suspected those diamonds were not the legitimate possession of those Brazilians. The truth is I have no evidence and therefore there was nothing I could have done. Had I tried to make something of it we could have ended up dead. Coming to the main point, on our way to Triangle the natives along the banks were keen to exchange whatever we had for the few stones they had acquired from these same Brazilians. Peter was generous in giving them some pain killers and other medicines from his father's surgery and they in turn gave him some of the diamonds. I could see how joyful he felt meeting these people and how happy they lived. I knew then, he is experiencing the same feeling for them as I did over twenty years ago, and it became more evident to me that this young man will make a success of his life. That was the first time it entered in my mind that this is indeed the son I never had. So when I did exchanged the nuggets for a handful of diamonds I did it with a specific view in mind. Realizing his ignorance of uncut stones I decided to give him most of it." Pausing and looking at me he continued "I explained to him my reason for doing this, and if you don't mind I will not be sharing it with you. Later when the division of the nuggets and the diamonds came about I told him in the presence of the others that I want him to have my share I decided to let the others know so there will be no misunderstanding when we took our share. Now young men, Peter sacrificed his career through loyalty, endured tremendous hardships and nearly could have been killed by a jaguar. Do you think those efforts, hardships and hazards deserve some rewards? I am sure you do. There you have it the story of rewards through sacrifices."

"Can I say something? What Matthew told you is true except the tale of the jaguar. I was three hundred yards away and the wind was blowing in my direction, which I knew even by my limited knowledge of the wild that I was safe."

"Not so Peter, the wind cannot be relied on to blow constantly in one direction. If there was a change of direction, you would not have been here today. That jaguar would have picked up your scent and decided that you were a better option than the peccaries."

"Well I must concede it was possible. I am thankful there is a God that looks after the innocents."

"Did you really suffer that much, Peter?" Marina asked with some concern. I told her it was not physical suffering but one of frustration and disappointment. I also told her that my dreams were shattered when I left Berbice. And only getting a legitimise registration to do the job I love best will heal the wounds in me.

"Your friend Matthew told us you have found vast wealth in the wilderness. So why should you be unhappy." Marina asked.

"That is true. What is not true is the reality that all my friends have attained what they set out to achieve, all except me. I, Peter D'Abrue, always top of the class. Leader of the gang ended up being a Good Samaritan and nothing else. If fortunes can buy happiness I am sure thousands of people all over the world will be in a state of bliss." I had to stop as I could see the pain it brought in Marina's face and it was my host who saved the situation when he asked if he can visit me in Berbice. He also said that he will bring Inge on this occasion, as the house maid is expecting a baby and needs time for herself. They were all expecting Matthew to tell them the value of our treasure. I was happy that was not mentioned.

We left and decided to go straight to the hotel. Matthew suggested that we see Mr Humphries at his home and find out what progress has been made with the stones. We were disappointed when he told us that Mr Alberga could not be contacted and that the stones are still in his safe at the shop. It would be better that I stay in the city until I get a verdict from the Dental Council. Then I will have to sign some papers for the house before returning to Berbice.

At the hotel, we found the others having their dinner. We were also hungry so we joined them. Matthew told them of the reunion I had with my friends and the look of surprise in their faces when told of our good fortune. I also told them of the house and my plans for an elaborate party when we eventually get to Berbice. I suggested that we take the stones and go and see Mr Alberga himself. In that way we will have firsthand knowledge of its value and no need to pay our broker a commission.

"I think we should let him try again." Matthew suggested. "The fact is, to go to Surinam will cost a lot and we cannot speak their language. The broker is the best person to deal with this."

"Matthew is right." Diego agreed.

"What you think Ben? You haven't said anything." I demanded from him.

"I am listening and I agree with the Commissioner and Diego. I would also suggest we go back and see this broker and to get some definitive answer from him. We cannot stay here indefinitely while he is negotiating. I am dying to see Berbice and besides hotels and I are not good companions. I hate their food and another thing; they are always cleaning my room. Putting my things where it is difficult to find." Ben complained.

"I am looking forward to going to Berbice also." Bell added.

"So am I." Said Diego. Then he continued "I will want to make that trip to Oreala to see how the Amerindians live there. I imagine it will be no better or worse than those at Sappanam. But it will be interesting just the same."

"My dad has visited that place a few times. Maybe he can tell you what it's like, saving you the trouble of going all that way." I reminded him.

"I still would like to go." He insisted.

"Maybe I will come with you. I would like to see that place, I've heard so much about it." Matthew added.

"I think we should all go and satisfy our curiosity. What do you think Peter?" Ben added.

"I am not planning that far ahead, right now I must concentrate at what lay before me." I told them.

I must be honest that I was getting a bit overcrowded with all this togetherness. I love them all but I needed space for myself to think independently and to make independent decisions. Matthew is doing the right thing by leaving us to spend time with other friends. It was convenient in Sappanam as we were confined in a restricted social circle. Here, in the city and the wide world at your disposal is itself demanding that freedom. My thoughts were not fully completed when Matthew announced that he was going to spend some time with the Governor and will join us in the morning. Bell wanted to go and see The Eddy Duchin Story as she missed it when it showed in McKenzie. Diego chose to go with her. So Ben and I were left with nothing to do. I could see Ben was feeling a bit restless. The same restlessness I was experiencing. His free spirit was screaming for wide open spaces and the freedom to do what he wants.

I suggested we visit a bar out in the city and explore a new world. I have never drunk in a public bar before and to experience what the locals are like. Ben greeted my suggestion with great joy. He told me of a nice place in the city centre where he sometimes visits when in town.

We arrived at his favourite drinking bar, not many people there. I imagine it was still early and most of the men frequenting these premises are still at work. We sat at a table near a window and ordered a couple of beers. There was an East Indian man sitting a few tables away looking very sorrowful. His eyes caught mine and he got up and half staggered towards us. Ben offered him a beer which he accepted.

Then he looked at me and to my horror he said. "You are a good looking so and so." Ben started laughing and I reminded him that this was not funny and that I am not accustomed to people like him talking to me like that. He then continued by telling us that he came in here for a quick drink then he met some men who encouraged him to buy them drinks. And he has spent all his money as they threatened to beat him up if he did not do as they asked. He then said that he has no money to go home as the bus fare is all spent. I asked how much the fare was and gave him with a bit extra. Then he turned to me and said haltingly. "I know you were angry when I said you are a good looking so and so. I was going to ask if you are married. I have a sister just turned sixteen and I think she's got an itch in her groin that needs scratching. Would you like to scratch it for her?"

At this point Ben grabbed him to his feet and asked him to leave. He made a statement that really shocked me when he said. "My brother is a judge and I will let him get the police to lock you all up for assault."

"Is your brother Persotum Persaud?" I asked in astonishment

"Do you know him"? He asked surprisingly.

"He is one of my best friends and I am surprised at your behaviour. I will have to tell him of this incident and the way you spoke of his sister to strangers," was my reproachful reply.

"Please don't tell him." He pleaded. Then he told us he is the chief book keeper at Albion sugar estate and he came to visit his brother. He also said something that nearly sent me senseless. When his brother saw him and asked why he did not wear a suit. He was surprised; he knows I have never had a suit. So he asked me to make an appointment to see him in his office if I continue to dress like that. That is the reason I came to this bar to have a drink and those men bullied me. He said he wants to get back home rather quickly and again he pleaded that I do not mention this incident to his brother. I promised I would not. Then he began explaining why "You see he is our youngest brother and he was very bright. My father could not afford to pay the school fees, so my brothers and I decide to pay for his secondary education. He has always looked up to us for this kindness and he will be disappointed that I have disgraced him to his best friend."

I knew there was truth in what he said, I remember one day Persotum came to school dripping wet from the rain. He complained of having to walk three miles back and forth and when it rains it became an arduous journey. I remember asking my dad to give me fifteen dollars and bought him a second hand bicycle to ease his problem. I was devastated by this revelation. I felt nothing but pity. I told Ben to get a taxi and we took him to get his bus, by the time we got to the bus station the last one to Berbice had left. There were no other alternative than to send him home with a taxi. This was going to cost a bundle. Ben offered to share the cost. I informed the driver that he is a bit drunk and that he is to be taken to his door steps at Albion. I also agreed with the driver that he will be paid only half of the fare now and the other half with a bit extra when we receive a written confirmation that all is well. The little extra I promised did the trick. This incident kept recurring in my mind for days. It vanished when Matthew came with the good news that Gordon had accepted an invitation from my dad to visit Berbice over the weekend and that he would be accompanying him and wait for us at government house.

First, we must resolve this business with Mr Humphries which was beginning to become a headache for all of us. My visit to the President of the Dental Association for a decision was not exactly what I wanted to hear but it was encouraging I was told that Gordon was given their written decision and he will contact me. I asked why they have decided to keep me in the dark. I was told that Gordon insisted that he inform me personally and that he wanted to announce it in Berbice. It all sound like a bit of a mystery to me. I imagine it will all unfold itself.

We decided to make one final journey to see Mr Humphries and to remove this headache that was bothering us for so long.

Mr Humphries was at last able to give us some good news. He told us that he had spoken to Mr Alberga by phone and directed him to come to Nickerie then take the boat to Springlands and finally go to New Amsterdam and await his arrival. This he agreed to do.

"When will all this take place?" Matthew asked.

"In two days," came a prompt reply. Then he asked. "When will you be in Berbice?"

"I'll be there before Mr Alberga." Matthew replied with confidence. He then asked for the diamonds.

"I think that has solved all our problems." I replied. Only one last bit of business of signing the deeds and it will be time to say goodbye to Georgetown. What a relief.

"Now chaps," Matthew announced "I know we have been celebrating quite a lot. This merry go round we've been through has come to an end and I personally think it deserves a celebration. If you agree we will do it in style. I am a member of a very exclusive club here in the city and I will arrange some music and a lavish meal and champagne. Peter, why don't you invite your friends to join us?"

"Excellent idea, it will give Bell and the others a chance to meet the friends I was always talking about. I will arrange it post haste."

So on the penultimate evening of our departure. We gathered at Matthew's exclusive club. It was an enormous building three stories high and the rooms were magnificently decorated, enormous mahogany tables were set neatly in the dining area surrounded by cushioned high back chairs. There were large leather arm chairs in the reception area and also where the members entertain their guests. The chandeliers were sparkling and the light coming from it looked like a thousand stars shining in the sky. The fans which were discreetly set away from the chandeliers made the lights appear to twinkle. The waiters were immaculately dressed with black trousers and white tunics adorned with a bow tie. Ben sat there open mouthed and looking bewildered. He was even more bewildered when the gentle man serving the champagne called him 'sir.' My other friends were relaxed and took the occasion as a normal every day celebration.

The music played softly in the background and the whole atmosphere turned into a dream world I must admit we were dressed in the least formal attire. If it were not for Matthew and his enormous influence I do not think we would be allowed in, more or less sitting down and drinking champagne. This by the way was not a popular drink for either Diego or Bell. They nevertheless sipped it as if they were accustomed to it. Matthew, on the other hand, was drinking glasses of it before we had finished our first. The meal of ribbed steak was perfect. My friend Persotum being a Hindu asked for chicken. I was beginning to look at him in a new light. The power of his position seems to have changed him into a snob. If it turned out that his brother's story is true it will have an enormous impact on our friendship. It's best I forget about it and enjoy a great celebration.

By late evening we were all in a happy mood and Matthew asked permission to dance. This was allowed and all except Diego danced to the most popular tunes of the time. Inge was showing me a dance they did in Stuttgart on special occasions and I took to it rather well much to the enjoyment of everyone even the members who appeared more interested in her décolletage and swirling shorter than normal skirt. I also noticed for the first time that her husband was tapping his glass with his fingers in tune to the music. I have never enjoyed myself as I did on that evening and my thanks goes to Matthew for organizing it.

While he was sorting out the account at the bar, I began feeling a bit uneasy as Inge kept looking at me and whenever our eyes met she showed a broad smile. I tried not to look at her. But I could see that she was continuing to look intently at me. Her piercing blue eyes were like two sapphires, set in a perfect mould to enhance their sparkle, and her movement was full of sensuality. It appears that I was the only one to notice that her skirt was too high up revealing her thighs beyond the limits of decency. Looking at her décolletage was another source of temptation. I wondered how a Hindu with a strong religious background would allow his wife to dress like that. It was impossible for any virile man not to notice the femininity she exuded with that exposure. I was beginning to feel uncomfortable and was beside myself with joy when Matthew joined us and thankfully we parted company.

At the hotel we saw Manny in the lobby looking at a loss. I went up and inquired what he was doing here. "I am here with a friend. He has offered me a decent job at his laboratory and I am leaving Sappanam. No one has paid me any money for all the work I did and I am sick of that lonely place. The chief was in trouble with some men from Triangle...I think they were Brazilians desperados. They said they heard there is gold here and beat up the chief and some other men to tell them where the gold is. I know nothing of gold so when they threatened me I asked them. If I found gold would I be here eating salt fish and cassava? They believe that and left me in peace I am leaving not because of that but I have no money to buy anything from the supply boat. The men treat me like a wild hog."

Matthew became quite agitated with the news. He questioned him about the safety of his staff. Manny was quite adamant that they were not interested in the women only the gold.

"How long did they stay there?" Diego asked "Did they go to where the cows are kept?"

"They spent two days forcing the villagers to dig in the river's bed. It was only when a caiman attacked one of the men they decided to stop. They searched the chief's hut. They dug up everywhere. When they did not find anything they beat up the chief and took all the Commissioner's whisky and got drunk," a distressed Manny reported.

"This bit of news is worrying me." Matthew said with great concern. "It has cast a dark shadow on all my plans. This business with the diamonds is becoming a complication. As it stands I must go to Berbice to support my friend on his first visit there."

I promised Matthew if he were not available then I will meet this Alberga. "What do you think is going to happen in Sappanam Diego?" I asked with uncertainty.

"It's hard to determine. Manny said they left when they discovered there were no gold. That looks as if they are satisfied they had come on a useless journey. The question is. How did they know there is gold there? Who could have told them, and for what reason? The answers to those questions will solve the mystery." Diego reasoned.

"Do you think someone noticed Peter selling gold to the Chinese? Or is it the Chinese who may have informed them?" Ben asked.

He made a suggestion that took us all by surprise. "It's possible they saw the Commissioner paying for those diamonds with golden nuggets when we were at Triangle and they knew where we lived."

"What is the connection between this china man and those desperados?" I asked. Adding "I know the man at the Berbice office has very little dealings with men from that part of the interior. He buys all his gold from miners in the Essequibo region and there is no evidence of a connection between the two groups. I can only assume that it was simple a case of random guess work."

After pausing for a while to think I asked. "You don't think they still believe in the story of Eldorado? What do you think Diego?" I was getting a bit irritable and hastened him for an answer. "Come on. You lived where these men habitually visit. You must know something about them."

"I know very little of them and their business. They buy animal skins from my people in exchange for tobacco. That is all my knowledge of them. They can be very charming and friendly. But as Peter said they may have revived the old story of abundant gold and went wild with the idea. Or even as Ben suggested, which is more realistic. They may have seen Matthew paying for the diamonds with our nuggets. I am sure they visited all the villages along the river in search of their dream. It's beginning to look like there might be more truth in what Ben said. They are too ignorant to know anything of three hundred years ago." Diego replied.

Then Manny said something that really put Matthew in action. "I forgot to tell you. They took Sugar Bush with them when they left."

"Never mind all your theories. Immediate action is needed. Kidnapping my Sugar Bush is a personal attack on me." Turning to Manny he instructed. "This is what I want you to do. Never mind the job that man promised you. I want you to take this money and return to Sappanam and tell the chief that I shall be returning with a constabulary force to track down these kidnappers. In the meantime, he is to contact all my rangers and ask them to be on the alert for these desperados and to report to me at the rest house in ten days' time. You have enough time to catch the supply boat if you hurry."

Manny looked at the handful of dollars and agreed to do as instructed. I don't think he has seen so much money in all his miserable life.

Anyone can see the torment on Matthew's face which forced him to reveal some hidden thoughts "These are the sort of incidence that has made me think of buying a light aircraft. With it I can go anywhere at a moment's notice. The only problem is to get the darn air strips operational again. Since the blasted war and the departure of the Americans, the strips have been overgrown and the natives are using them to plant their vegetables and tobacco. It's a darn disgrace. The Guiana Airways could have maintained them with little cost. They are as useless as an empty tobacco pipe. Now that there is war those strips could have been used for border surveillance. It is something our cartographer was suggesting for a long time. Venezuela has its eyes on a large part of Essequibo for ages. The war could encourage them to make that claim, and as usual London will yield to their demands in a negotiated settlement for concession to use their navy to patrol the Guiana Atlantic coast. I warn you my friends' things are not going to be the same. If Hitler wins we are all doomed to slavery. If Britain wins which we all hoped for then the cost of it will be just as damning. There will be no money for development on the colonies."

Turning to Diego, he expressed further frustrations. "We have got to unite and save what we have. Your village at Tacuba is under threat. If those Brazilians can come as far as Sappanam to terrorise those innocent people, it could be the beginning of a greater agenda for territorial claims. I have always suspected this kind of incursion to occur sometime."

"I think you are over worried. Sugar Bush is not in any danger. Perhaps they simply took her to annoy you. Someone must have told them she is bonded with you. Surely you must see that, Commissioner." Diego tried to calm his frustrations. "It is a good idea of the light aircraft. Perhaps you can get your rangers to co-operate with the Amerindians in the area where the strips are and make it operational again."

"You are thinking sensibly and I am ashamed of myself for losing my nerve. Thank you for the advice." Matthew replied with controlled calmness.

Further instructions were given to Manny. He was to assess the situation in Sappanam and instruct the supply boat captain to report to Matthew as soon as he returns to the city. I was asked for my telephone number in Berbice. This was written down and given to Manny to be handed to the captain.

With Matthew in a more amenable mood we were eventually ready for that visit to Berbice. We informed Mr Humphries of our departure I gave him my telephone number and asked him to relay it to Mr Alberga and for him to ring me as soon as he arrives in New Amsterdam. Then I went to the Law Courts and signed the deeds for the house.

CHAPTER 12

The Pieces Coming Together

We decided to take the train, as the road to Rosignol was in worse shape than the track at Ituni. I was still mesmerised by the steam engines and the intoxicating influence it had on me all the way to Rosignol.

Matthew in the meantime would join the Governor's envoy and his party at government house in Berbice. Their arrival was a grand procession. A representative of the Governor was visiting the ancient county and the people of Berbice were given a magnificent show of pomp and regality. The riders on the horses escorting Gordon and his 'Lady' Caroline were in immaculate military uniform. Gordon himself was wearing his plumed helmet and war medals. This pomp was a gesture to show Britain is the master of the empire. It was a clear message and Berbicians cheered their Governor's envoy as if he was the king himself. This was his first visit to the Ancient County and he was determined to put on a show. 'Lady' Caroline, on the other hand, waved at the crowd, smiling, her broad rimmed laced hat added grace and charm to a beautiful lady. The crowd blew kisses and offered to crown her Princess of Berbice. Matthew sat in a second car with other officials looking at the crowd with total amusement.

When the parade was over, my father drove us home for this long awaited reunion with mother. Diego, Bell, and Ben reluctantly decided to stay at my home. Initially they would have preferred to stay at the only decent hotel in town. Due to Gordon's visit all the rooms were taken. Here again, as fate would have it I am not allowed to meet my mother alone. Nonetheless, I was happy in more ways than one to have them as guests. First my mother was eager to meet the people I kept telling her about and the protection I received from Ben. Not to mention the brotherly affection Diego shared with all of us and Bell, her loveliness and affection did a lot to soften the hardships I endured.

As was expected it was a very warm and tearful home coming, tears were flowing like the tide from the Demerara from both my mother and Bell, I nearly had the wind squeezed out of my lungs from the hugs I received. After that, it was time for relaxation on the breezy veranda for a sip from my father's fine collection of malt whisky.

"I hope you haven't taken up drinking as a hobby son?" My mother asked with concern.

I did not reply, for the simple reason I was not sure if I would give her a sincere answer.

The maid ran in and gave me a squeeze and unashamedly asked. "How many girls you bed down with while you were away?"

My mother gave her a slap on the cheeks and told her to hold her tongue. She was always forthright with whatever she wanted to say even discussing her romantic weekend affairs in vivid clarity. She held her cheek and made an apology of a curtsy to my mother and left. Bell was amused and tried to hide it. Diego and Ben just stood there expressionless. Tired with the travelling we decided to just relax and enjoy the view the village life has to offer.

At breakfast, I sat in the very chair I heard my father telling me of our visit to McKenzie. Nearly five years had passed since then, yet it seemed like fifty. There were endless questions I had to answer to my mother. It was only proper she be given a good account of the life I lived and the hardships I endured and adventures I survived. I deliberately neglected telling her about Matthew.

She looked at me and asked. "Why have you left the Commissioner? Is there bad blood between you all?"

"Not at all mother, I want to do so when he is here." I told her.

"If he is with the Governor's envoy, do you think he will have time to come here?" So many questions yet I have to answer them. My mother will not tolerate insolence in any shape or form.

I finally told my mother "It is getting a bit boring repeating the same things over and over again. The next time someone asked I would simply tell them that I am writing about it and they can read it in the papers."

"Are you going to write of your life in the wilderness, Peter?" She asked knowing full well that I have no intention of doing so.

The Governor's envoy will only be here for two days. Today he is entertaining civic dignitaries and a few business men, my father included. Sunday is the big day for my father. Gordon and 'Lady' Caroline will be entertained in great style in the Canje river area …Berbice style.

My immediate task was to contact Matthew who was staying at Government House and also get in touch with Mr Humphries and set up the meeting with this Dutchman.

Government House was guarded like a fort; there were guards all over the place with rifles. The one at the entrance recognised me and when I told him I am here to see Matthew the Commissioner he let me through. Matthew was standing on the veranda and called me up stairs. Gordon was relaxing in an easy chair known as the Berbice chair a very relaxing bit of furniture with arms that can extend for relaxing the legs.

"Are you happy to be back in your home town Peter? Gordon asked.

"I am sir." I replied. Then I told him how happy I was that he has accepted my father's invitation.

"The pleasure is all mine, by the way I have an announcement to make when we meet again."

"I hope it is good news, sir." was my reply.

"Let's keep it a secret for the moment." He suggested.

Matthew told me that, after Gordon's departure, he would ask Mr Humphries to come here to settle our last piece of business. The Dutchman was on his way here and would arrive at the hotel on Monday. I told him it will be good if you can ask Mr Humphries to be here at the same time.

My mother is a traditionalist and an ardent royalist. She insisted my father do things her way. "It is not every day one has the privilege to entertain the Governor's envoy and it must be done my way or not at all."

My father is also a stubborn man but he dare not disobey my mother in these matters. First, he will have to get one twelve feet square linoleum and to have all the folding chairs and tables varnished. She even wanted candles on the table. She only relented when my father pointed out that the wind will keep putting them out.

The maid was sent to get some of the villagers to help and also for me to select the ones that will be helping with the barbeque. They will have to be briefed as to their conduct at all times. This was a great honour for me. First, they will have to get a suckling pig and a lamb in case they failed to kill a deer or wild hog. It would have been great fun to organise a hunting party. Time was against us.

Fishing was possible. It would be great fun if Canje trout can be caught. These are large sporting fish can reach a meter in length with vicious teeth. Yet, they are simple to catch. Three hooks are tied together and a piece of aluminium foil is attached. The hook is skimmed just below the surface and the fish seized it and started a great fight for its life. The angler will have to tire it before it can be subdued. Actually it is not a trout only that it looks like one. Locally it is called a himara

That would be great fun for the Governor's envoy, who I was told is a great angler himself. We will have to wait and see.

The paraffin-operated fridge in the boat must be cleaned and a case of vintage champagne must be bought. Ice to chill the champagne will be ordered in advance as it will be Sunday and it must be collected very early in the morning. There were so many things to think about it sent my head in a dizzy state. I can rely on mother to sort the other details.

The maid returned with the workers and they were instructed of what to do. I asked my friends to help me with that task. Ben suggested that he be allowed to direct the men with their work and the barbeque.

My next obligation was to take my friends on a tour of the countryside and to show them the true Berbice. I was unable to get a driver's licence so I asked my next door neighbour if he could help. He was keen to oblige and being the nosey sort he wanted to know what is happening. I fed him bits of our program and when I mentioned that the Governor's envoy would be our honoured guest his eyes began to look larger than usual.

My friends were impressed with what they saw in the villages and to prove a point of generosity we visited a family who were about to have lunch on their veranda. I pretended that I was hungry and immediately they brought extra chairs and invited us for lunch. I, of course declined telling them of how I boasted that Berbicians were the most friendly and generous people on earth. They laughed and wished us well.

On our return home, the men had packed all the necessaries in a cart for the big day and were off to the jetty where it would be loaded in a special boat and taken to the site which is about an hour up river. They would spend the rest of the day laying the linoleum and erecting the tent. The whole area would have to be immaculately clean and spotless. Those were the instructions from mother. Ben said it sounds like fun and volunteered to accompany the men. They were overjoyed when he asked that I give him a couple bottles of rum to keep the cold wind at bay, I warned him not to get the men intoxicated and to make sure they obey all the instructions.

At 7 am sharp my mother was up she and the maid were washing all her best dinner plates and silver cutlery. She even packed a twelve piece coffee set with napkins. My father was furious. He explained that this was not a dinner party but a barbeque and people would like to enjoy the outdoors in the usual way. Using their fingers occasionally and even getting themselves soiled with food. "Its supposed to be fun woman." He screamed at her. She poked him in the chest and said that she is sending her things just in case it is needed.

The champagne was placed in the boot of the car for safe transit and the rest of the things were carted off to be loaded. We collected the block of ice and placed the champagne in wooden pails to chill the rest of the ice was set in the fridge.

Our next stop was to collect Matthew. The Governor's envoy and some of his entourage would follow in their own vehicles. Eventually, we were all aboard and off. 'Lady' Caroline went on a secluded part of the upper deck tanning herself in the mild sunshine. I went and joined the main party. Their conversation was centred on the war and the effect it would have on the families whose husbands or sons are sent to the front. It would also have an impact on the citizens of the Empire.

"What if we were to be attacked here in the colony?" I asked.

Gordon then explained that it is unlikely Hitler would attack an insignificant colony as this. He also suggested that should there be an attack on South America it would be Venezuela or Brazil that will be the target. Nevertheless, posters were printed and posted all around the country for people to grow more food and the Commander of the Militia was on alert and giving the volunteers rigid drilling daily.

There was also the prospect the Surinamers might assist in an invasion of the colony. The reason being, that they never forgave Britain for stealing their country. This was dismissed by Matthew who pointed out that Holland is an occupied country and to allow an invasion of our country would leave them with fewer allies. He also told us that young men from the Empire were recruited to join the Royal Air Force and a recruiting office would be set up in New Amsterdam and the Corentyne. This I found to be interesting and though I found the conversation enlightening I would have preferred one with a less serious note; one that would cause laughter. I suggested to my father to tell them the story of the chicken. My father smiled and invited me to tell it instead.

I began by explaining the circumstances of this episode "It was customary that a select group of my father's friends would meet monthly on a rotating basis at their respective homes for an outdoor party. Normally, my father would have the villagers prepare the food which was always an Indian one and drinks were lavishly served and they would have a sing song until it is time to go home. It was David Munroe's turn to reciprocate. The seven friends turned up and saw his cook preparing a single chicken. One of them told him that a single chicken would not be enough. He told him that was his orders. The friend insisted that he prepare another two chickens. Hesitantly he obeyed. At dinner, David was served three chicken legs. He looked at it and questioned his lad. The lad explained why he did it and immediately he phoned the warrant officer at the station to come and arrested the lad.

Fortunately, the officer was also one of the friends that made up their rotating team. He was not able to be present at this fun day due to work. He heard what David and the lad said then he asked David if he ate any of the chicken. With David's confirmation, the officer announced that since this is technically larceny all the participants would be arrested. They all laughed and told the officer to behave himself and to sit down and join the party." I ended by saying "This is how we did things in Berbice. It's our way of life and we enjoy it.

On shore the men were busy preparing the two wild boars they shot. Ben was busy preparing one for the fire which was ready to do its job. Chops were put aside and steaks from the legs were being marinated with ingredients specially prepared my mother. The two men that accompanied Gordon to Sappanam came and joined Ben and Diego. I stood by and let them pass to have a look at what was happening. They watched with admiration as the second hog was prepared and put to boil for half an hour before placing it to roast on a spit.

One of the two men gently tapped me and asked if I remembered him and also why the hog was boiled before roasting. I explained that on a normal day it would have been on the spit hours ago. Due to the time factor it was easier to boil it a bit before to make certain it is properly cooked. Then I answered his first question. I told him I did, and even reminded him when he and his friend went swimming naked in the river.

"You remembered that"? He said smiling.

"Of course I do and I have good reasons remembering it." I told him.

"And what is that reason?" He asked.

"It's personal and besides you would not be interested." I replied.

"It's because a young lady was watching you all with your ding-a-lings swaying in the moonlight." Ben told them.

They all started laughing then one of them asked. "Is it the daughter of Gordon's friend?"

"It is." Ben promptly replied. "I watched you trying to chat her up but she went to Peter instead."

"I wish you'd stop talking and get the food ready." I interrupted.

They then asked if piranha is in this river. I told them they are rarely seen. Immediately they started undressing. For a minute I thought they were going to repeat their antics they did in the Demerara.

I was relieved when they displayed their swimming trunks and jumped in the river. 'Lady' Caroline heard the splash and turned around to watch them swimming and splashing each other. She took a dive from where she was and joined them. I could see they were having fun. It was not long after I saw Matthew and then Gordon joined them, followed by my father. Diego took a buoy and went swimming among them. I realise he was doing that for safety reasons. After their dip they came back on board and I asked Diego to help me serve the champagne. Then he served himself whisky. Bell took just a tiny drop which she drowned with lots of soda. She was so quiet I forgot she was here.

'Lady' Caroline pointed out a boat coming towards us. There was a middle-aged East Indian couple with a dog. In the boat they had produce from their farm on the other side of the river.

Gordon hailed them and asked what they are carrying. The approached our boat and revealed a variety of vegetables and a bucket with fish swimming around.

"What's that you have in the bucket?" 'Lady; Caroline asked.

"It is hassah, lady; we get it in de river. You want some? It nice with a lot of masala." The man said.

"What is hassah? 'Lady' Caroline asked my father.

"It is cassadura. A fish enclosed in bony armour. It looks more like something prehistoric. You want to see what it looks like?" My father asked.

"Let's have a look." She replied.

The man took the fish from his bucket and held it up. Then he began telling her about their behaviour. He spoke in Babu English, a language of English and Bengali.

"You see dem bones all over de body, it is to protect dem from dem other man fish. Dem two things you see here are spurs."

He was referring to the lateral fins which did have two vicious looking sharp barbs. He continued to tell her their uses. "The mother fish lay dem eggs in a nest. The bunch of eggs she lay is big like me palm. Then she left the man fish to look after it. De man fish don't let anybody come near de eggs. If we try to get the eggs, whoosh... he attack with de spurs. If he catch you he make big gash in you hand."

"Did you ever get the eggs?" One of the Aides asked.

"Lot a time. But we no eat all of it. We put some in the pond I gat in me yard and let them hatch. When der is plenty of dem I catch and sell in the market when times are hard." He explained.

"Did you understand what he is saying Matthew?" Gordon asked.

"I got a gist of it. You should get to know the people you govern and their dialects. It will serve you well." Matthew told him.

"Then explain to me what on earth they were saying." Gordon demanded.

"The gist of it that when they got the eggs it is inevitable that the male is caught and they use some of the eggs for food. The rest of the nests are placed in their pond along with the male and allow to mature. When there are hardships they catch the fish and sell them to feed the family." Matthew explained.

Diego gave them two dollars and they left.

"I think you have a point there Matthew. I should get to know them and encourage them to at least speak proper English." Gordon agreed.

After that encounter and a few glasses later they all began to relax, Gordon came ashore and chatted with the workers asking them about their work and families. They felt the wall of social divide was lifted and gladly told him everything. They even spoke of their grandchildren. They were ready to serve the food.

Bell brought my mother's dinner set out and took it where the food was. Then she shouted.

"Lunch is served. Come and get it now or go hungry."

It was fun to see is her in such a happy state. After lunch and when the last champagne was drunk, Gordon announced that he was meeting the town councillors that evening and would like me to be present.

"I would like to expose you as a fine example to the councillors of your dedication to service and loyalty. They are complaining of the state of the roads, which I fully agreed is in a desperate state, my hands are tied, and I can only spend what my budget allows. I must get that through to them and there is the question of a clinic for the villagers in the ten mile strip from Sheet Anchor to Boland. They point out that New Amsterdam has a hospital and many chemist shops. Also Rose Hall sugar plantation has its own hospital and clinic as has the other sugar estates namely Albion and Port Mourant. The roads are so bad that patients travelling to these clinics or hospitals will die before they get there."

"Five thousand dollars would be more than adequate to build a one room ward and dispensary and to stock it with emergency remedies." Gordon told him, adding that the war is putting his entire program on hold.

"What happens if the money is donated, Will the clinic be built?" I asked.

"Certainly, not only will it be built but I can persuade the Legislative Council to guarantee the upkeep and to pay a qualified person to run it."

"Then you can tell them it will be built from private donation. Matthew, Diego, Ben and I will give it to you. It will be a boost to your visit. We cannot have our Governor's envoy making his first historical visit go unnoticed, can we"? I told him.

"I am happy how you are spending our money... Peter... Money we're still to receive." they joked.

"Are you serious about this, fellows?" Gordon asked.

"You heard what Peter said." Matthew confidently replied. Adding "Anything to help an old pal and please let this donation remain anonymous. We would like it that way."

Gordon shook our hands warmly and said. "You are indeed all fine gentleman and truly the sons of a great county." Turning to 'Lady' Caroline he told her "Matthew is rescuing me again. He and those bush men."

With those words the party ended and we were homeward bound. On our way I spoke to 'Lady' Caroline of an idea that we thought might be appropriate and without telling her when it will be announced. She was pleased with my suggestion.

Matthew was given the task as Master of Ceremonies. He sat next to 'Lady' Caroline and Gordon next to her. The meeting with the town councillors went down very well. He told them of the planned building of the clinic and his intentions to have it run by a qualified nurse and dispenser. They gave him a resounding standing ovation that lasted a good two minutes. I was eventually invited to the rostrum and introducing me told them what he knew of my life and work at Sappanam.

He concluded by saying "It is with great pleasure that I take this opportunity to present to this young man, a son of your glorious county, something of great importance. It is the certificate of registration that entitles him to practice dentistry anywhere in the country. I also would like to thank his family, our own Commissioner and the friends from Sappanam for making my visit a memorable one. I have heard it said many times that Berbicians are the most generous and friendly people and anyone who dared question that will have a thick ear."

That was a happy conclusion as far as I was concerned. I was glowing with happiness. I then thanked him and the Dental association for their generosity.

After a pause I made my own announcement. "Dear friends most of you know me through my father and that is why I address you as friends. I have consulted with the persons involved with what I will say and to tell you first hand that the clinic will be given a name to commemorate Gordon and 'Lady' Caroline's historic visit. It was unanimously agreed that it be called the "Lady Caroline Clinic."

The audience was clearly moved with this suggestion. There were cheering and some shouting Princess Caroline. We want to hear our Princess say something. The clamour stopped when 'Lady' Caroline at the Governor's request gracefully stood up and thanked them for their kindness and hospitality. Then she reminded them that she is only Caroline and not a princess. "The king" she added "Would not approve."

Then they all got up and sang the National Anthem.

CHAPTER 13

Goodbye to Old Friends

After Gordon's departure, Matthew decided to stay with us. It was like being in Sappanam again. Bell was not always feeling well due to the pregnancy that is why my mother decided that she stayed here rather than the hotel. Ben's only excuse was that he would help clean the barbeque things and the boats. His main reason was that he can be with the workers and enjoy some of their wild behaviour, not to mention the fact that the maid was giving him the eye. I warned him of her freeness of speech and if anything was to happen the whole village would know about it and my mother would be offended. He assured me that nothing would happen and he only wanted to enjoy Berbice hospitality. The men invited him to meet their families and to have a party for him.

That breakfast table was always the battle station where matters of importance were discussed. It was no different this morning. Matthew informed Diego and me that he will soon be returning to Sappanam. But first we must meet with Mr Alberga who is in New Amsterdam with Mr Humphries. Our journey to the hotel was filled with great expectations.

Mr Alberga was introduced to us by Mr Humphries; he was not the kind of person I imagined him to be. He was tall with rimless glasses and immaculately dressed in a light summer suit. We shook hands and Matthew produced the bag of diamonds. He looked at them with his special lense and declared "These are much larger than I was led to believe and worth a considerable more that Mr Humphries suggested."

Mr Humphries defended himself by stating that his calculations were based on his assessment of the stones. This was accepted without question. I took the smallest one and told my friends that I would like to keep it as a good luck charm they all nodded approval. We were told of the price of the stones and if agreed we will have to go to the bank for payment to be made in an account in one of our names. It was explained that no bank will have such a large sum of cash. A cheque will be issued and deposited in the nominee's name. He then will have to issue cheques to all the recipients and that is how it works. Vast sums of money are not always available unless specially authorised.

At the bank, we decided that Matthew would receive the cheque on our behalf and we would sort it out later. The Bank manager felt that it should be done now, since all those whose signatures are required are here. We saw his point and Diego and Ben not having a bank account would have to open one right now, this was done speedily and the respective cheques were issued. Ben and Diego received a quarter each and I with Matthew's share received the other half as was agreed at Sappanam. I reminded Matthew that he can have his share if he changed his mind. He would not tolerate my suggestion. In order not to upset mother, I asked the others to accompany me to the hotel for a drink. It turned out to be a great suggestion.

At the bar, Matthew revealed a secret thought that was on his mind ever since we left Sappanam. His revelation was that the villagers would not be able to manage the gold at Cold Stream and it will get out of hand and chaos will ensue.

"You heard what Manny said of those Brazilian hooligans. What I have in mind my friends, is this. I will register the mine in the names of Diego, Ben and myself. We will give the villagers all that they need for a better life and pay a doctor to come every two months. The vicar is moving out to the new site where the church is building their new school. Diego can stay on if he wishes but Ben will have to stay with me for protection. I never needed it before. With the gold being exploited one may never know what will happen. The Brazilians may return."

"Am I to be a protector all my life? I have so much money yet I am not allowed to be independent." Ben protested.

"If you had allowed me to finish, you would have heard me saying that I would have appointed you Assistant Commissioner. You wouldn't be paid of course. The title will give your ego a boost."

"Assistant Commissioner? Me? A half black man, and now half a Commissioner. Wait until I tell my friends in Georgetown and McKenzie." Ben half screamed with delight.

"Now Peter, this trip to Oreala are we going to make it?" Matthew asked.

"I am very much for it. Perhaps I can ask my father and he will be able to tell us the best way to get there.

Diego then said that he thinks it is better if Bell is left with my mother due to her pregnant state. "First, let me talk to her and see what she thinks"

My father told us the best way to get there was to obtain a pass from the police station and organise a boat trip with one of the loggers who were idling at the moment. He also said that he would have liked to accompany us but he has a lot of patients to treat. Matthew reminded him that we would not need a pass, as Commissioner he is entitled to visit any part of the hinterland.

Our first step was to make up a party of men that will make the trip a happy one. At Ben's suggestion we were to take some of the men from the village who has befriended him. The cost of the boat would be determined by the length of the journey and not by numbers. We made the forty two miles journey to Springlands to meet the loggers. They were keen to take us, a price was agreed and a date set.

Here, I took the opportunity to show my friends around our last sugar estate on the Corentyne and also to point out to them that the other side of the Corentyne River is Surinam or Dutch Guiana. The manager at the Plantation was an English man and seeing Matthew he sent someone to take us to his office. He was polite and asked if we were interested in seeing how sugar is made. His offer was accepted with great interest. We were taken to every stage of the process which was explained in details. In the end we were given a sample of freshly made sugar in neat packets and invited back to his office for coffee. He asked Matthew what brought him to this part of the country. Matthew told him that he is the Commissioner and stationed at Sappanam eighty miles up the Demerara River. He is here because of the Governor's envoy's visit. He also made a point to tell him that he is also a very good friend of the Governor and the whole visit was coordinated around the wish he had of seeing Berbice first hand and to visit Oreala.

"Are you going to Oreala?" The manager asked.

"We are leaving in two days. The loggers are preparing their boat and when they are ready they will contact us." Matthew replied.

"Never mind the loggers. Give them a couple of dollars for their trouble. I will take you in the plantation super motorised boat with comfortable seating and a fridge, an important item in this weather and on a long trip. That is if I am invited. I had always wanted to pay a visit and as always something or the other comes along and the plans are ditched."

"It will be great fun if you come along. By all means be our guest." Matthew told him enthusiastically.

"Yes," I added more enthusiastically than Matthew. "We would love to have you on board."

He looked at Diego and asked if he is from Spain. "I am from Takuba a further twenty miles from where Matthew lives." He went on to explain his ancestry and how he came to meet us and the many adventures we had.

The Manager told us his name Andrew McIntosh and he was from Scotland, not England as most people believed. He served as manager on the plantation for several years and is due to be retired but with war in Europe that looked unlikely. He seemed a very sociable person and everyone was happy he was coming along. It was time to head back home.

We visited the loggers and cancelled the trip. Matthew gave them two dollars each Ben and Diego also gave them a few coins. We wished them well and left.

Saturday morning saw us in the plantation's super motorised boat. Andrew McIntosh brought his wife which was good company for Bell. The two were chatting away while we relaxed with our glasses of whisky enjoying the fine weather. A strong wind was following us all the way to Oreala. At the landing, a group of Amerindians came to greet us; they assisted in securing the boat and ordered someone to guard it while we went ashore.

Dozens of macaws and parrots graced the skies with a kaleidoscopic array of colours. We were still looking at the marvel in the sky when the head man came and asked for our pass. Matthew introduced himself and we were taken to what appeared to be an office cum grocery and rum shop. We were taken to the office and made comfortable. Matthew told him that it was his desire to visit this place as he never visited Berbice in all the twenty four years he has been the Commissioner.

"This place is not what it used to be. We used to have jewellers, dentist and people selling all sort of things and they in turn bought our handicraft work, pottery and skins from the animals we killed for meat. Now it is all gone... Dead. Occasionally, we get some wild bush Negroes from Surinam. They never have money only things to exchange. They too stopped coming when they realised it was not worth it." He spoke with great sadness.

"My father used to come here. He is a dentist." I told him.

"You mean old Joey D'Abrue is your father?" He then showed us a small denture with a gold tooth my father made for him. Then he continued "He used to come with two young men... they like their drink. But your father kept them in check. He wouldn't let them touch a drop until they finish their work. What made him stop coming? He finally asked.

"Getting tired of the long journeys." I replied.

"Why are those people looking so intently up that tree in the distance?" Ben asked.

"We are trying to kill a bush master up in that tree." he told us pointing to the tree some twenty yards away. It nearly bit of one the children but the boy was quick to run away." He told us.

I was bitten by a bush master a year ago." Matthew told him.

"You were bitten by a bush master and lived?" He asked in disbelief.

"Not only bitten. We nearly buried him alive. We thought he was dead. It was only when I fired two shots as he instructed me to do that awakened him." Diego told the head man.

"Is this true Matthew? Andrew asked.

"Perfectly true," Matthew replied with confidence.

"Now my friends, we have been sitting here chatting and I did not offer you anything to drink. What would you like to have?"

"Anything you have," I told him.

"Not that foul tasting drink the Amerindians make at Sappanam." Ben protested.

"I know what you are talking about. We don't make it here. As a matter of fact I don't think my people know to brew it." He told us.

"You speak very good English." Andrew complimented.

"I went to very good school in Skeldon even two years at high school. I left as I was getting home sickness."

"Now about this bush master, we cannot leave it so perilously close to where children are at risk. I have my revolver let's go and find him." Matthew suggested.

Andrew declined to go saying "I'm afraid I will stay with the ladies. I am too scared of snakes and so is my wife."

Matthew was led to near the tree with us following at his heels. The head man went as near as he dared and looking up he saw some monkeys trying desperately to chase it away. The snake was hissing in anger and lunging at them. They kept a safe distance. I am sure they realised that a bite would kill them, very clever these animals.

At last Matthew was able to spot it. He crept up carefully until he was satisfied the serpent was within range and fired. The snake wriggled and dropped to the ground dead. One of the men cut its head off and buried it in a deep hole and the rest of it was left for the vultures. It was getting late and we wanted to get back before dark. Matthew thanked the headman for his hospitality before leaving.

The next day, my father was preparing to take them to get the boat for Rosignol and their final journey to the city. They told my father that they wished to enjoy some more of Berbice and claiming that they would not have the opportunity for another visit. Ben's excuse was now he is Assistant Commissioner of the hinterlands and Amerindian Affairs.

Matthew looked at him in amazement and agreed. "I think I will stay a bit longer also and get to know this remarkable place better. We must find this hotel and get ourselves some lodgings."

"You are not booking in any hotel." Father said. My house is far better and you will have decent home cooking. Is that not true Peter?"

It was the first time my father had made me happy with a suggestion. I remembered Ben saying that he and hotels are not the best of friends. I told him that I would need his help at home and if he were to stay at the hotel it would make things awkward for me.

He winked at me and smiled. "Thanks for the invitation."

Back at home mother was asking lots of questions about Matthew.

"He is a very pleasant man." She started out. "I can see he has a great affection for you. And why did he give you his share of the diamonds?" She asked suddenly.

"Because as he is not married and don't have any sons. He claims I am the son he never had. Do you know he has given his only brother his share of the family's estate? And he and Gordon were friends since their days at Eton and in India; they were in the same regiment and fought the Indians with great success, Conquering and securing great territories for the Empire."

"It seems sad to me that a man like that did not bother to get married." Mother commented.

"It does not mean he did not try. He wanted to marry an Indian Princess but was prevented from doing so." I told her.

"Who could have prevented a man like him with such a strong personality from marrying?" Mother asked.

"His Commanding Officer," I told her.

"His Commanding Officer," Mother shouted. "Who is this Commanding Officer to tell Matthew Longhorn what to do?"

"Mother when you are in the army you must obey orders and it is a courtesy for an Officer to receive permission from his immediate Commander. Please don't ask any more questions. You should question Matthew when he gets here."

"I thought he went back to his post." A surprised mother said.

"He was all set to go, but decided to stay a few more days to enjoy Berbice." I replied.

She then turned and looked at Ben. "So you are the one who protected my son in that wild world and from all the dangers in the jungle. And taught him to drink whisky?"

"He was young then when we first met and I instantly liked him especially the time when he watched me sitting motionless while his father took my wisdom tooth out." Ben replied gleefully.

"I heard there were a lot of intermingling with the young ladies and the men from the outside. Is this true?" This question from mother to Ben was a bit embarrassing to answer. Ben shrugged his broad shoulders with a bowed head.

"It is true, mother, you don't expect Matthew to live so long in that place without any female companion. And if you must know so did I. I knew this is what you were aiming at. Now you have all your questions answered. Can we have some lunch?" I told her, a bit annoyed. I noticed the maid listening intently and covering her mouth to hide her smile. I turned to her and in no uncertain terms told her if this gets out on the streets that is where she will be.

Ben defended me by telling her the true facts of Sugar Bush's love for me and the sacrifices I made to preserve myself for the girl I really love.

"What girl? The only girl I knew he was interested in is happily married and has two children." Mother told him.

Ben was faced with the dilemma of revealing my encounter with Christine. The fact that she is Matthew's niece seemed to please her. Then she asked an important question.

"What are you going to do about it? All your friends are married. And you are entering you twenty fifth birthday. Is it not time to settle down my son?"

Without thinking I told her I would enlist with the Royal Air Force and be sent to England for training and to fight for Britain if I have to. She was not pleased with that. As a consolation she replied by saying that it is the right for every young man to try and save the Empire from dictatorship and genocide.

I have in fact made a firm decision. Something that crossed my mind only as a passing thought. Now that I have announced it is beginning to make headway in my mind and I am not at all displeased.

The thoughts of possibly meeting Christine increased that determination to enrol. I find myself again surrounded by the same people from Sappanam. I do not think there is any room left for an unexpected visitor.

We were having lunch when the maid announces that my friend Persotum and his wife is here. They were invited to join us for a meal which they declined as they have already eaten. They sat in the drawing room and waited until we finished. Mother had long waited for this meeting. It was a prolonged kiss on both cheeks and praises of congratulation on his successful appointment. Inge was amazed at all the camaraderie showered on her husband.

The story his brother told was beginning to linger in my mind. I was tempted to confront him but the best part of my judgment prevailed. Ben asked the maid to bring us some coffee.

Persotum told my mother that he would like Inge to spend some time here while he is at court. She hardly knows anyone in the town and she might feel a bit lonely at their lodgings at the law courts.

Mother without hesitation agreed and Inge looked pleased. Also mother told her that Easter was coming and she promised the priest that she would assist with the preparations for the Easter festivities.

"How long will you be away? Inge asked

"Not more than two hours the most, I am usually home for lunch."

"Then I will come when you are here." Inge responded.

"Do come when it suits you. I'm sure Peter and his friends from the bush will be able to entertain you until I arrive." Mother said in her most friendly and inviting voice.

Persotum made his excuse and departed leaving Inge in our company. I left her with mother and went to the surgery to meet Matthew. Ben was keen to ask her about Germany and Mr Hitler. At the surgery I met the two wastrels were still working and they tried to greet me with an air of familiarity. I abruptly told them to get on with their work as I am here only to continue an experiment I started at Sappanam. They reluctantly went back to their work.

After a while, I felt a bit sad treating them the way I did. I began encouraging them in a conversation which brightened up their faces. They asked me about my experiment and I told them that the vulcanite we are using will be replaced with a new material which is called acrylic and it is much friendlier that the previous material. The new material will also have an accompanying material that will allow us to make our own artificial teeth.

The war is causing a great shortage of dental and medical supplies and we were forced to use the same teeth over and over again. Patients were amused to find the same size and shape of teeth on other patients' dentures. Even bicycle inner tubes were hard to find and desperate cyclists were forced to replace their inner tubes with pieces of blanket and other rags. It was an ingenious substitute and it worked.

I was happy when I returned home and found Inge had left but with the promise of returning the next day. I remembered her constant gaze at the club and hoped it carried no meaning. It was her sensual posturing that bothered me. Perhaps she is not aware of it. Even so most women know that men can be easily propositioned and I became fearful of my moral safety.

Ben became bored just sitting and talking nonsense to satisfy the maid who kept bothering him with life at Sappanam. We left her with her mouth wide open when Ben related how he strangled a twenty-three feet anaconda.

I decided to take our guests up the Corentyne Coast. Matthew said he would drive father's car instead of taking a taxi. The twelve miles of road up the Corentyne where Persotum's brother lived was dotted with pot holes. Some were so large there were pot holes in them. Matthew negotiated them like an expert. When we arrive, his wife told us that he was at work and would be home soon so we waited. He was surprised and happy to see us and invited us in the living room and promptly poured us a drink of rum. I started the conversation by asking him of the story he told us in Georgetown.

He began by thanking us for seeing him home safely then he told us the truth. "I was a bit drunk when I arrived at my brother's home and he was embarrassed and told me in effect when I am in that state to visit him only in his office. He did not want his wife to see me in that dreadful state."

"You disappoint me with your lies. The only consolation it brought is that they are deliberate lies. Your brother would never do that to you." I shouted. "Now tell me the truth about paying for his school fees." Not that I wanted to know. "It is only to find out, what the truth is and what are lies. You understand what I am getting at." I told him seriously.

"That part of the school fees is true. I swear it on my mother's life. We were not that poor, but twelve dollars a term was a lot of money for an education that probably may not take you anywhere. My father could not afford it. So my brothers and I invested in him and it paid off." He assured me.

I felt happy now the truth is revealed and the ill feelings I had towards him soon vanished, Ben was happy too at the truth. He offered us dinner which we declined as mother was preparing one of her specials for dinner.

To keep Matthew and the others from boredom, I promised to take them to meet some of the villagers and their families.

I did not realise how ignorant I was of village life right under my nose. It was a very warm welcome and I am happy to get to know them on a more intimate level. It also became obvious that though Guianese are tolerant and friendly. There is a lack of social interaction between the very poor and the middle class. The peripheral knowledge I had of their customs and cultural habits was tantamount to snobbery. To be quite honest very few middle class families have any close connections with either the East Indians or the Blacks. The mulattoes were the buffer that separates the cultures. They enjoyed a privilege position which they in turn protected by not socializing with the villagers. It was in fact a racial issue.

Matthew asked them of the arranged marriages and the consequences of a separation. "Separation?" an elderly gentleman asked.

"Yes, if the couple do not get on together do they just split up?" Was my question

"We don't get split up in the villages. When a Hindu arranged for his son to get married to the girl of his parents' choice it is a bond for life. To split up is a bad habit. The British split up when wife or husband find a new lover. The Muslims also have the same custom as we."

"What about legal matters like the division of property when one of them dies? How is that sorted?" I asked because I am becoming interested in their lives.

"Let me explain our customs. We come from India and we brought our traditions with us. It is our way of life. If a man commits a minor crime we don't go to the police. We have the elders who form the panchayat or village court. All disagreements in domestic or other disruption are settled by our courts. Only murder or violent crimes are reported to the police. If those crimes are not reported, we find ourselves breaking the law. It is a recognised system agreed unofficially by those in authority. The Muslims, on the other hand, do get the so-called divorce. It is called a "tallak". The government has nothing to do with it. I'm going to ask you a few questions sonny. Have you heard of any serious crime in this village? Have you heard of anyone committing adultery, or anyone running away with another man's wife?"

"Not that I can remember. I do know of a case when a girl eloped with her lover and caused shame on the family." I told him.

"How often does that happen?" He asked again.

"I only know of that one case. I know her. She was my mother's maid." I replied.

"There you are, when they go out and work for the White man they pick up their bad habits, if she had stayed in the village that would never have happened. By the way she was Hindu and it was a Muslim boy she ran away with. That made it double disgrace." He replied in support for their way of life.

"Thank you Mr Samaroo. I have learnt a lot today." I said to him. I gave his granddaughter a shilling. That was one custom I knew about. A shilling is a lot of money for them. They can buy a meal for the entire family.

"The same situation as in India," Matthew told him

"You been to India, Sahib?" He asked. Then turning to me he again asked "Who is this gentleman?"

"He is the Commissioner of the interior. And yes he lived in India for many years."

Looking at Matthew and wanting to find our more of this mystery man in their midst, He began to question him.

"You were the governor of India?"

Matthew went on to tell him tales of his life there and his meeting with the mystics. By this time a large number of them gathered around us listening intently to Matthew's stories. They told him of their hope of returning to India as the British promised. Matthew told them they are better off here. They nodded in agreement.

As we were leaving we saw some boys playing a game of cricket. Diego never saw the game played. He became fascinated and went to inquire how it is played. The boys had made a bat from the branch of a coconut tree and their ball was made from a gnarled part of a tree. It was a crude assortment of cricket gears. I explained to Diego what a clever compromise it is and at the same time explaining what real cricket gears are. Matthew became involved in the conversation and showed Diego how different strokes are made.

"Why don't we play a game with them?" Matthew suggested.

"Not with those crude things," I said.

Matthew began with a look of inspiration all over him. "I did this in India to help some young villagers like these and by Jove

I feel like doing it again." He called the boys together and suggested a game of cricket. "If you boys lose you give us two shillings and if you win you get a complete set of cricket gears. How does that sound?" The boys looked at him in shock then one of them said, "Where we get two shillings to give you if we lose?"

Matthew discreetly threw a two shilling coin near one of boys' foot and said "Look there is a two shilling coin near your foot."

The lads were more perplexed than ever. The coin was accepted and a deal struck.

We drove down to Rose Hall, a village connected with the sugar plantation and asked the headmaster of St. Patrick's Anglican school for permission to use the school's ground for this event. When the headmaster heard all the facts he readily agreed.

Matthew and Diego sent the boys to the local tailor to be fitted with cotton shirts and white drill trousers. I thought if we can donate five thousand dollars for a clinic a few extra dollars here would be a real investment. My dad and I purchased a set of cricket gears for the occasion.

The big day arrived. The ground was filled with people from all the surrounding villages dressed in their very best clothes. The head master and one of the teachers were the umpires. Our side was made up of Matthew, Diego, Ben, Doc Bristol, Mr Ferreira the merchant and his two sons, my dad and I and three villagers.

The boys arrived showing confidence and waving to the crowd. They won the toss they decided to bat first, a magnificent display of cricket sent the spectators screaming with joy and a decent score was achieved. This was to be a one innings affair.

The score to beat was eighty nine. I went in and made fourteen the others did not fare well And we were thirty eight runs behind when the last man joined Matthew, whose score went up to fifty it was getting tense as the last two took the total to eighty eight with only two runs for victory. Of course Matthew had no intention of winning the match. He had to make it look thrilling, with two runs left for victory and the last two batsmen in. Anyone can see despair from the tense look in the spectators eyes. It was as if the boys had lost the match. The fourth ball in the final over and Matthew deliberately stroked the ball straight into the hands of a fielder. The roar of jubilation was so intense I could hardly hear what Diego was saying.

Match over. It was time for the presentation, a task undertaken by Matthew himself. He congratulated the winning side and asked the headmaster to assist in the presentation. Since this was all pre-planned, Matthew began with these words "I was an extremely good cricketer. I thought I would easily beat these boys single handed but as you saw they are better that I thought. As losers we would like to honour our obligation by presenting them with their prize."

The head master handed it to the captain. His hair shining from the coconut oil on it and he looked very pleased with himself. He thanked us and joined his friends. We joined the dispersing crowd.

Matthew feeling victorious with his ploy told us of another plan he had in mind. "I have this feeling of great generosity in me today and by the power of all the Gods on earth I am going to do it. Diego come here my friend and listen to this idea and let me know what you think." He spoke to Diego for a long while.

Then he said. "I have a feeling the others would love to participate. I'll have a word with them." Diego then explained Matthew's plan for the boys, and we all agreed enthusiastically. First, we have to go back to the village and put forward our suggestion. I know the villagers will be more than happy to discuss it.

There was a little celebration for the boy's victory when we got there. Matthew went up to one of the elder men and asked who was in charge. The man pointed out two older men playing a game of draughts. He went up and announced himself. "I am Matthew Longhorn, do you remember me?"

"Yes sahib, we remember you proper well. We thank you for the nice game. This here is Imam Sattar, Me is Pandit Narine. We two in charge of de village, what we can do for you?"

Matthew went into a long conversation with the two and they in turn called some of the villagers and relayed what Matthew told them. They were clapping Matthew and told him to tell the whole village. The women were gathering around and two wooden boxes were offered as seats, Ben and Diego sat while Matthew and I were left standing. I told him to relate his idea.

He began. "Today was a great day for me. I have not enjoyed such a happy treat for many years. I can see you people need some help. Yes, you did not ask for it. This is all my own idea and now my friends are in total agreement. This makes it easier for me to tell you what I've already told your elders. Talking to your boys today showed that they are very intelligent youngsters. Can I ask a question? How many of you will go for higher education when you finished primary school?"

"Our fathers cannot afford to send us to high school," one boy replied.

"So what will you do when your school days are over?" Diego asked.

"Work sir, we go to work in the factory when there is jobs. If no jobs then we go to the back dam and cut sugar cane or dig canals," a second boy said.

Matthew turned to the two elders and told them "The four of us will set up a scholarship for four boys to go to the Berbice High School for four years. If they study hard they can take all the examinations necessary to get a job with the government. I do not think your family will be able to support you at university. If you work for three years and save enough, who knows one of you can be a lawyer or a doctor."

One of the elders asked a very pertinent question. "How you pick the boys?"

"I will not choose them. I will leave that to the head master. He will chose the four brightest and forward their names to the principal." Matthew told him.

"You see sahibs we have Muslim and Hindu boys here. If head master pick four Hindu boys the Muslims not like it. If he pick four Muslim boys the Hindu not like it, so we make problem in the village." The imam pointed out.

"That's very easy to put right. We will tell the head master to select the two brightest Hindu boys and two of the brightest Muslim boys. No one will then be angry." Matthew explained.

"God sahib, you like Solomon, the king in the Christian bible." It was the Pandit who replied.

"I will go with my friend Diego to see the head master tomorrow and arrange it." Matthew told him.

"Then we will go and see the principal and arrange the scholarship." I told them.

"Why you do this for us Sahibs?" The two elders asked in unison.

"I really don't know." A flustered Mathew said defensively. He went on to sweeten them of his life in India and his relationship with the Sadhus and other mystics. They were in wonderland as he spoke asking many questions and getting the right answers. We were getting bored with this repetitiveness but listened through it to please the villagers.

One cheeky boy asked Matthew "Did you make us win the match?"

"Why would I want to do that? I wanted that two shillings just as much as you." Matthew replied as he ruffled the youngster's hair.

I arrived home to find a letter from the recruiting office informing me that I had passed the medical. This was the beginning of a long journey into the unknown. I had no idea of military life except what I heard from Matthew. That was not real war as such. They were mere minor battles with the Pathans. This is the real thing there are tanks in the fields and bombers overhead. I would not have a chance in hell. I am committed and I have done it by own free will. I wanted to prove I am a man so here was my chance. The idea did brighten my spirits and also that I had a good chance of meeting Christine again.

In the meantime mother was getting worried. We had been away for hours after the match was finished and she had prepared a special dinner especially for Matthew. As we sat down to dine, she started asking questions about why we were so long getting back. Matthew told her why and she continued to plague him with more questions.

"Why you spend your money on those people?"

"It's only a small sum." Matthew told her. Then he explained. "I am attracted to that little village it reminded me of one just like that, somewhere. What that village needs is a little push in the right direction. I can see those lads have potentials and I thought why not give them the nudge they deserve."

"And you Peter. How much did you spend on those wastrels?" she asked

"Just as much as the others, Diego and Ben, It is not a lot when you think of it and it has not been taken from our capital. It's bruised the interest a bit, we can afford that." I told her reluctantly.

"And you Matthew Longhorn. What happens when you are forced to retire? Who will look after you in your old age?" Mother probed.

"I have enough to see me very well taken care of. Mind you I must admit it will not be enough for me to live comfortably in England and I will not be a burden to my family. Yes! Mrs D'Abrue I intend to live out my life in British Guiana. My army pension is enough to make me live like the king himself. I have no family so I don't have to make any plans for that."

"You are still a young man there is still a chance for you to start a family." She pointed out.

"No chance of that Mrs D'Abrue. Please let's stop here. I find it a difficult point of conversation."

My mother was not the kind of lady to leave a stone unturned. With one of her persuasive smiles she asked. "Assuming you retire. Have you secured a home to live in? I am sure your friend the Governor will not be here when that time comes. Have you thought of that Mr Longhorn?"

I told her. "Matthew can live in the house I bought in the city, as a matter of fact the house is partly his and you don't need to know how. So save yourself an embarrassment by not asking."

"Mr Longhorn. Can you see how impertinent this boy has become? Telling his mother what she can't do. I have one more thing to say before I finished. "Why did you not consult me before you bought that house? I have not seen it and I don't know if it is suitable for a D'Abrue."

"It is suitable, mother I promise you. I have asked Persotum and Inge to live there when I've gone to England. They promised to look after it." I assured her.

"That man may be a judge and married a European but he is still an Indian with his Indian culture. That house will never be the same when you get back. It's the same you are doing for them in the village they will kick you in the rear when they achieve what they set out to get. You mark my words. Mr Longhorn I understand your family is well connected in England and so is that nice Governor. Will you be able to see my only son is saved from disasters and come back to me?" She pleaded.

"It is true my family is a bit connected. The Governor is of the nobility and that reminds me of something very important. The Prime Minister has made his brother The Honourable Cavendish overlord for the Medical and Dental corps. So maybe I can ask Gordon to help."

I became a bit angry. Here again I have my life being planned for me. While I appreciated their concerns I am forced to decline. "Mother!" I snapped. "Did anyone ask me what I wanted? I am again having my life surrounded by protectors. What I have been reading very recently about the solar system appears that the same is happening here in front of me."

"I don't see how the heaven has anything to do with me." She said.

"It's too long and complicated to explain. What I am trying to say all along is for my parents and friends allow me to try at least. You can step in only when it becomes necessary. Surely you will not deny me that. You must let me go and find myself. If I am to die in war then so be it, At least I would have tried to brave the tempests of life. You can make yourself happy and useful when I'm gone by giving those boys the room downstairs to study. There is no electricity where they live and you will find them entertaining, courteous and amusing. Go to the village and introduce yourself tell them you are my mother and you want to help. Take them some meat or fish as a token of your good intent. They will love you or make you a God, as Matthew said in

India they do that sort of thing. Once a year they make clay statues of their Gods and celebrate with offerings. It is like what we did with that clinic that will be built at East Lothian. "The Lady Caroline Clinic", it is similar as making her a God."

"I do not want to be a God. What will the Father in heaven think? Is he going to be made redundant? No thank you. I will go and see them and give them offerings of goodwill and I will let the boys have the room and a biscuit and a cup of cocoa before they go home. Now how is that for a mother who cares for his son's wishes."

There were tears in her eyes as she spoke and gave me the biggest hug I'd had for a long time. She gave the others a hug before asking the maid to clear the table. Then she took us to the drawing room and to my surprise she brought out my father's favourite malt whisky and gave it to Matthew to pour.

The maid came in to take her leave at the end of her day's work. She saw us with the bottle and half shouted. "That is Massah favourite drink. I will tell him I did not drink it. He is always accusing me of something somebody else done."

"Never you mind." My mother told her. Then she said. "You will find your wages in the old teapot take it and be early in the morning. These gentlemen have a boat to catch."

My dad arrived just as we were about to pour a second drink. He looked at the bottle and said in jest. "I bet it is that woman that opened that bottle. It must be something important. Are you going to tell me? Or do I take away my bottle?"

He joined us as mother told him of her new role when I am gone. He was very pleased and congratulated me for giving her something to do and remarked. "It will drain her energies and there will be little time left to antagonise me."

After Matthew and Diego and Bell left, the house looked deserted and little conversation at the dining table. The maid kept Ben amused with her funny stories. I have heard them many times so it was of little interest to me. Boredom can have a devastating effect as I am experiencing. So I invited a few friends on a fishing trip up the river. We took a lot of essentials to last us a few days which turned out to be wonderful short holiday.

The next day I received another letter asking me to get my passport ready and to report to the recruiting office when that was done. Things appear to be moving faster than I expected and I was not all too happy. I have learnt to take things at a steady slow pace. If I am to come to terms with being a military person I imagine I will have to be a bit more alert.

Matthew had indicated to me that he would be able to help me settle down in England as I will find life there completely different and the winter weather will be the biggest problem to cope with. I will have to get acclimatised he also asked me to come and see him before I leave.

My mother was not too excited either when I told her that I have been a successful candidate. She gave me a note for things the maid has to buy in the market and I passed it on to Ben to deliver it.

"I think I will go with her to the market and buy myself some fruits." He told me. At the same time giving me one of his wicked boyish smiles "It's a long time since I ate fruits. What about you Peter do you want me to buy you some."

"You are not talking of cherries. Are you? I joked. Then I told him to buy me some mangoes. "But only if they are fully ripened."

The next morning I was having breakfast alone. Ben went with my father to do some shopping in the town. Mother had gone to the church and the maid was busy in the kitchen. I heard the car honk its horn and looked I to see Inge coming towards the house. I hurriedly went and put some clothes on before opening the door. I told her I was having breakfast and offered her some coffee which she declined saying that she had just finished her breakfast. She sat in a rocking chair and when I finished my meal l went and joined her. We sat for sometime not saying a word which was becoming tiresome. I began by telling her that Ben and I went to see her brother-in-law.

"Oh, how is he? She asked "I've met him briefly once, when we first arrived."

"He is alright. We did not stay long; we only took the drive because we were getting bored." I replied.

She laughed and repeated the word 'Bored'. Then she told me that boredom is a constant companion ever since she came to British Guiana.

I was surprised to hear that and began to inquire the reason why.

"We were very happy in England. Our marriage was blissful and we went out a lot. He had a lot of friends then, so were always on the move visiting constantly. Ever since his appointment he has gone through a metamorphosis, a complete new person. He blames his work for his neglect of me. His appointment was a great milestone for him and I understand that but to let it take over your life is unforgivable. That is why I was happy when he said that I can come and spend the days here when he is in court. I have seen how much he is loved by his friends. The first time you visited us I could see the great friendship that existed with all of you. I feel relaxed now that I have opened the truth to you. Please forgive me for burdening you with my problems." She ended saying.

The tension soon disappeared and we talked of more pleasant things. I told her of some of the troubles we got into when in town and even mentioned the incidence where I was slapped and a cigarette taken from between my lips and then the gentleman told me to go and tell my father.

She laughed hysterically and asked. "Do people do that sort of thing here in Berbice?"

"They do." I replied and then told her. "It keeps the youngster out of trouble. If you don't tip your hat to someone older than you it will be reported to your parents and you can expect some punishment. That is why we have very few criminals here."

As we talked she was moving herself in such a way that her dress was wrinkling its way up her thighs and exposing a major part of it which was less tanned. She saw I was getting red in the face and tried unsuccessfully to cover herself up.

Then she said "We don't have that system in Germany nor in England as far as I know."

"Is Inge your whole name"? I asked. "It sounds as if it is shortened."

"It is shortened." She told me "My maiden name is Ingeborg Freidrich and we used to live in Stuttgart. The Nazis as you know drove us out of our country because we are Jews."

"You met Matthew the English man; he was with me when I visited you the first time. He is a Jew, but not a good one. He cannot be bothered about religion." I was happy to say. "So you are Ingeborg Friedrish."

"Not Friedrish but Friedrich." She corrected. "The C is sounded like a soft S." She came up to me and held my face and said. Put my lips together and pronounced Freid. Then let the tip of your tongue touch your palate and say Rich."

I did as she said and hooray it came out as she said it would. I repeated it several time until I got the hang of it.

"There you see, anything is possible if you put your heart in it."

With her hands on me I felt exactly the same when Christine made those furtive moves holding my shoulders when it was not really necessary. I became sexually aroused when she held my lips and asked in the softest of whisper "Are these the same lips that held that cigarette when that awful man slapped you?"

I was unable to answer that question my mind went blank for a second. Then l held her tightly in my arms and my kiss was returned voluntarily and with an intensity I have only experienced once. She looked me in the eyes and poured her heart out. She told me of the long and lonely sexless nights when she cried herself to sleep for want of an arm to caress her and the fulfilment of a woman's needs. Her words inflamed me further I lifted her in my arms and took her to the bedroom. We spent an hour there until I was getting afraid Ben or the maid would come and discover her infidelity. I am part of that infidelity and no blame should be attached to anyone for obeying Nature's most important ritual.

"Would you see me tomorrow?" She asked a bit uncertain.

"Of course. How can I not see you again? My heart right now is filled with the affection for someone who belongs to another. Yet, I do not find it easy to make love to you. If I am making someone very happy, that makes me happy," was my loving response.

She held me and slightly bit my lobe and whispered. "Why did I not meet you instead? I seem not to have any real opportunities in life. First, our disaster in Germany and now this very unhappy and possibly irretrievable marriage. I am happy at least we have no children."

It was not long after when Ben arrived. He brought me some beautiful ripened mangoes. I shared some with Inge; Mother also was coming through the door. The maid hurriedly went in the kitchen to see it was clean enough for mother to start dinner.

Ben joined us and offered us some of my father's whisky. Inge was taking her second drink when her husband arrived to take her home. He was invited to join us. Reluctantly, he sat down and took the drink Ben offered.

After they left I went and hurriedly made up my bed to make it look as if nothing happened there. If the maid had seen it she would have let the whole town know of her suspicions. Ben came in to see me putting the final touches and tickled my rib.

"You've been at it again. I see" He teased.

"You are imagining again. I see," I also teased. Then I explained. "I was lying in bed before she came and you know mother, she examines all the bedrooms to see that they are tidy. He accepted this.

CHAPTER 14

A Murder

The next few days we spent idling and drinking not excessively just to keep boredom at bay. I was contemplating going to Sappanam to confer with Matthew about my impending journey to England. I thought of the long and tiresome journeys I would have to make and my heart was set against it. Ben totally agreed with me. He told me when he returns he will hire the amphibious aircraft that Gordon used for his visit. It was then the idea came to me, perhaps when I have definite orders from the recruiting office I can go and see Matthew as Ben suggested. I can now go there and back in a single day, with that lovely aeroplane.

Killing time can be a lethal pastime. Ben and I went to the luncheon rooms for a snack. There were a lot of people there. Sitting next to us was an East Indian lady whose husband I knew. She nodded acknowledgement as our eyes met. She was having 'Chicken in the rough' with fried chips. I was surprised that she was eating. Muslims do not eat meat at restaurants. It was not long before she stood up as if choking. Ben rushed up and held her neck to make her breathe. She collapsed in his arms a few minutes later she was found to be dead. What an extraordinary disaster. The owner called the police and everyone was pointing at Ben and claiming he choked her.

The police arrested and took him to the station; I was completely devastated by this event. I went to the station to make enquiries of what was happening. The sergeant told me that he cannot see anyone as he is being questioned about the incident.

When I returned in the morning I was told to my great horror that he had been charged with murder. To say I was devastated was an understatement. My parents were in shock. So was the entire town. Everyone knew him as a jolly easy going man always polite and friendly.

I engaged Aubrey Pistano to take charge of the situation. I told him not to leave any stone unturned to get the truth, the sooner the better. I was asked to make a statement of what I saw. I told them exactly how the situation was. The woman was choking and Ben tried to help her.

It was several weeks before the preliminary hearing was held and again he was remanded in custody. His trial would be in the next session of the Supreme Court. I told the officer in charge that I was due to travel to England as I had enlisted in the Air Force. I was told they would have to inform the recruiting officer that I cannot leave the country as I am a vital witness in a murder trial. This news only added a bit more to the torment I was going through.

What on earth is happening to me? I asked myself. Am I doomed to failure in all my undertakings?

My father and a friend of the Commissioner of the police came with even more distressing news. The prosecutor would be a Mr Adrian Myers a man with a renowned reputation for convictions. This was indeed chilling news. Nevertheless, Aubrey will have his hands full when the time comes.

In the meantime messages were sent to Matthew and Diego of the sad situation. A week later they were both at the hotel waiting for me to give them the details of events. Matthew informed us that even the Governor is unable to prevent the chain of events. This we understood. We were allowed special dispensation to visit him at the prison.

He looked paler and drawn. He told Matthew the facts that he only tried to help the lady to get her breath as he could see she was choking and by holding her neck he was trying to ease the passage for air to get through.

We all assured him that we believed his story and we would try our best to see justice is done.

I did not have to wait long before my passport was sent and I forwarded it to the Recruiting office. I knew when they had all the other recruits papers together they would send us off to war. The thought was not comforting. I asked the recruiting officer whether he received any instructions from the department of justice and if they were informed of my delayed posting. This he said is in place. I will be informed of my departure after the case is finished. I just have to wait. He also told me I must do my initial military training with the local Volunteers in New Amsterdam.

"They are not as good as we would like. It will keep you in shape until we get hold of you at Grand Parade." There was a wicked smile on his face.

I told mother that I would have to start my training with the Volunteers. She started crying and told me she hoped I do not get killed as I am her only child and I have not left her a grandchild through whom she could remember me by. I told her to pray that it did not happen as I too wish to live a long life if it is my destiny. She asked an age old question why countries have to go to war to solve their problems. My response is that this was a war Churchill had to wage to teach that parvenu a lesson of civilised nations. There are thousands of men from all over the Empire who were giving their lives to the cause. British Guiana with a population of less than half a million is doing its part.

She nodded in agreement and made me promise to see the reverend father before I go. It then occurred to me that I did not visit him since my return from Sappanam. He sent many messages to me which I ignored. It would seem that my only reason to see him was to get his blessings. Perhaps I am getting like Matthew. Believing only in yourself and steering your life with the power that God gave you. Mother will never understand that. It would be pointless telling her. So I promised to see The Reverend Father.

The Reverend Father looked at me with dismay. Nevertheless, he greeted me with courtesy and asked how my life was in the wild.

"It is not really wild Father. There are people living there. Headed by a very respectable English man who happens to be a friend of our Governor," I said. I felt happier that the conversation was not about my religious side of life. I then told him of Ben and my involvement as a witness.

"Yes I heard of that unfortunate incident. It's a pity he is your friend. This puts you in an unfortunate position." The inevitable questions came soon after. "Did you attend mass while you were there? Was there any one to take your confessions?"

I was determined not to let him draw me into making apologies for my lack of spiritual guide. I told him there were no Catholic priests in the area and the only priest that visited the area on rare occasion was a Methodist. This infuriated him.

"Methodist, Has our church let you down my son?" he asked with concern.

"You will not like what I am going to tell you Father. The truth is I've drifted away from the conventional way of worship. I find it easier to speak to my God when it is necessary and not to molest Him with tiny details of inconvenience. He is already protecting millions caught up in this war. Who knows how many people are calling on Him day after day minute after minute for help. I think we should leave Him to help those that do need it. You may think I am not qualified to think what God wants or what he should do. It is because of that uncertainty I acted the way I did. Just thinking of Him is worth more than wasting hours congregating to pray, which to me is nothing short of a publicity stunt. Have you seen the ladies on Sunday trying to make each other jealous with their new expensive dresses and hats? It is blatant hypocrisy. What worries me more is that you know they are only there to show off. You can curse me and send me to hell if you wish. It will make no difference. Where I am going is hell indeed." I told him and I felt good with what I said. He is such a gentle soul. I felt a tinge of sorrow. This induced a surge of remorse to fill my breast of the brutal fashion I expressed myself.

He looked at me uncertain of what I had become and almost in a whisper he asked.

"You said you were in the company of an English man? A friend of our Governor, Did he not have any religious connection?

"He is not a Christian. He is a Jew, a sincere man with greatness about him. God will be pleased with him and what he does." This I told The Reverend Father with conviction.

"At least allow me to bless you before you go and I do hope your mother is not aware of your thoughts and your friend if he is innocent or guilty I will pray for him. But now I want you to let me bless you before you leave."

He placed both hands on my shoulders and with a gentle pressure I was forced in a genuflect position and I let him get on with the blessing. I felt a bit different after that. My arrogance was overshadowed by a feeling of humility and sadness. I eventually shook his hand and told him that mother is spared my views. He smiled and nodded. He stood and watched me leave. I turned around and saw him still standing, hands clasped as if in prayer.

I came home and did not quite finished closing the doors when mother asked if I had seen the Reverend Father. I told her I did. She wanted to know what was said and I told her everything was in order. I had made my peace with him and we understood each other. This she found pleasing and gave me a kiss. Then she told me the trial would resume on Monday. This gave me the whole week-end to prepare myself for it.

The court room was packed. No one was allowed to stand when the seats were filled so it was no wonder when we arrived there were dozens of people waiting outside. We shuffled our way to the room set aside for witnesses and waited. We could still hear what was going on despite the fact that we were not supposed to know anything.

Many witnesses gave their testaments. It was fair to say that they only relayed what they thought. They all saw Ben supposedly strangling the woman.

It was the testament of the owner Mr Choo that cast a semblance of doubt. The prosecutor tried to discredit his testimony.

"Are you saying that Mrs Ali cried for help before the accused held her throat"?

"Yes I did."

"Is it possible that you heard her cried out after the accused held her? You were busy serving your customers were you not?"

"Yes sir."

"If you were busy serving. Is it not possible that you may have heard her cry out only after the accused went and deliberately strangled her?"

"No, sir, I saw what I saw and that's the God's truth."

"I put it to you Mr Choo that you are lying to this court because the accused was in the company of one of you regular customers. The son of the dentist who is currently treating you,"

"I would never defend a murderer. Would you?"

"I am asking the questions. So please answer them truthfully."

"I told you I will never defend a murderer. You know me since you were a young man going to our high school and I think you know me to be truthful and honest just as I know all you boys though a bit mischievous are good at heart and just as honest."

"That will be all Mr Choo. Thank you." The prosecutor felt a bit uneasy by Mr Choo's last words.

Aubrey was saying something to the Prosecutor which I failed to hear. The judge asked him if he is satisfied with the x-ray pictures showing a lump in the deceased throat.

"I am not your honour. These pictures only show a swelling in the trachea. What it does not show is what that swelling is. Is it as the defendant said that she choked and he tried to help? Or is it a swelling the prosecutor is conveniently claiming made by strangulation? The only positive answer lies with a post mortem. I move that the court order the Exhumation and a post mortem of the deceased."

The Judge then asked both the Prosecutors and the defence councillors why there was not a post mortem, a mandatory procedure in a serious crime.

It was the prosecutor who told the Judge. "As you know this is a small town and we only have the services of a single surgeon, he is attending a seminar in the city and because the deceased is a Muslim is was mandatory for her to be buried before sunset the next day. No one could contact him. So the radiographer with the consent of the physician decided to do the next best thing. The x-ray showed no broken bones only the swelling."

"This is totally unacceptable by any court of law. I therefore rule that an exhumation and a post mortem be carried out posthaste and I am to be informed with that same urgency when that is done." The Judge then adjourned the court until further notice.

Mr Ali, the deceased woman's husband objected that his wife's body be subjected to this unholy ritual. His protest was over ruled when the Judge told him that the order of the court precedes all religious laws. A tormented Mr Ali left the court with his children crying.

While my father went and tried to comfort Mr Ali, Aubrey asked us to go with him to his home to review the situation.

Marina was ever so pleased to see us she offered us coffee and cakes and we sat down to listen what Aubrey had to say. As was customary when men are in discussions the ladies find something else to do elsewhere.

Aubrey started out by saying "If it is a piece of chicken bone that was the cause of death, then the case against your friend is a fore gone conclusion, an acquittal. I want to tell you a true story that happened twenty five years ago. Perhaps Mr Longhorn can remember that murder trial, and I would like you to tell me truthfully what you think. In Port Mourant sugar estates a young Scottish overseer was accused of shooting the field manager. No one saw the shooting. It seems that another overseer had a grudge against the accused and testified that he saw the shooting. Let's bear in mind the gun belonged to the accused and also the fact that he had a verbal battle with the deceased. It was enough to send him to the gallows. As we all know Britain will not allow that to happen in one of their colonies."

"Why is that? Is it not the law of the land that all capital punishment is meted out with the death sentence?" I asked not sure of the laws.

"Gentlemen I am sure we all understand that Britain is the ruler of her Empire and she would not tolerate one of her English subjects be seen as a murderer." Aubrey tried to explain.

"Why is that?" I again asked.

"There are two distinct reasons. First, it would undermine the authority of Britain. Secondly, for an English man to be hanged as a common murderer would further undermine their authority in the colony. We must come to terms with reality." Aubrey tried to explain.

"The English gentlemen we have running our country, are a show case of that supremacy. The poorer Blacks and East Indians look on them as Gods; they have that status to preserve the integrity of the Britain.

So the trial judge who was an Englishman deliberately misdirected the jury for a guilty verdict. After the sentence was passed, the defence lawyer naturally appealed of the grounds of misdirection. It became a lengthy affair. Eventually, it reached the House of Lords and the conviction was quashed. The accused was eventually sent home. What became of him no one knows."

"I remember the case very well. The judge retired and went to live somewhere in the West Indies.

Mr Pistano, what are you trying to tell us? I can hardly see any relevance," Matthew told him.

"What I am saying is that there are ways we could save your friend if it is matter of life or death. My question is. Would any of you tolerate such extreme measures to free your friend?" Aubrey asked. There was a devilish look in his eyes.

"Mr Pistano." Matthew said, "I would never go along with that. For the simple reason that I strongly believe in justice although I have no strong religious beliefs. I think there is a power stronger than any of us to see that justice is done. Also let me tell you this, I am an English man born and bred. I spent most of my young days in India and I had the opportunity of meeting men in the administration of that country. I am talking of men that actually ruled in the king's absence and that load of rubbish you just put forward is absolute nonsense."

"I have the same feelings as Matthew" I responded without the slightest tint of hesitation, "So do I." Diego added.

"The reason I told you that story is to see what your reaction would be if such a situation was to surface. Let's be honest my friends. These things actually happen. Anyway we are not home and dry not by a long shot. The post mortem will have to prove conclusively what that lump is." Aubrey ended with a note of seriousness.

"What will happen if the post mortem proves she did not have a chicken bone in her throat?" I was getting desperate to know all the alternatives.

"I will encourage all of you to remain calm and let truth do the talking. It is pointless to rouse any other ideas. I say this because we all know Ben would not attack or kill anyone on an impulse. A lady he's never met in his life before?" Aubrey concluded.

The long wait for the post mortem results finally arrived. The surgeon could only give that to the court. It was all tension when the usher called everyone to their feet and announced the judge as he entered the court room.

The surgeon appeared with something that looked like decaying meat in a jar of alcohol.

The judge asked if he had carried out the autopsy. He replied he had and found that it was indeed a piece of chicken with a small portion of bone attached. He further stated that if the bone was not present the piece of meat would have gone down unhindered. It was the piece of bone that was stuck in the airways.

Aubrey immediately demanded that the prosecutor withdraw the charge. Aubrey made the legal submissions and Ben was released amid great jubilation from his friends. I have never seen Matthew so joyful.

He went up to Ben and shook his hand and said. "If you thought you were escaping from your new job as Assistant Commissioner, you are mistaken. Let's go and celebrate."

It was indeed joyful. We celebrated until the early hours of the morning until we were asked to leave by some of the hotel staff.

I was in a celebratory mood when I arrived home. Mother waited up as I had to travel to George Town to start my drilling exercises.

"Do you want me to help you pack?" Mother asked, referring to the fact that I would be travelling in less than two hours. I declined her offer knowing full well she would pack enough to last me a year.

I went to rest for the short while. The villagers were packing up their carts as usual and the continuous racket made me restless. It was still very warm so I opened a window to let in some air, I saw Ben coming towards the house leaving the maid to go her way. I was puzzled by this behaviour. Ben had told me he had no interest in her and I believed him. He is a man of immense sexual appetite and was not the least embarrassed to reveal that fact. I was not going to upset him with what I saw. The only problem was. Did he renege on his promise and if so will the maid keep it a secret? We'll have to wait and see.

CHAPTER 15

Military Training

Grand Parade turned out to be exactly what it said, an enormous open space filled with men in military uniforms and marching like robots at commands given by their instructors.

The new recruits were allowed to watch and observe their every movement. I stood mesmerised with their precision marching, and was only brought to my senses when the sturdy uniformed soldier called us to attention. We were given verbal instructions of military drill and the reasons why it must be obeyed at all times. "Discipline," He shouted. "Without discipline a soldier will be lost in battle and jeopardises the lives of an entire infantry. So what is important?" He shouted louder than before.

We all replied… "Discipline"

"I cannot hear you," He shouted again.

"Discipline." We shouted as loud as we could.

So for the next three weeks we were roused at six in the morning and after breakfast congregated for another two hours of drilling. After lunch, we were to get familiar with our rifles. We were taught to strip and reassemble it until we could do it with our eyes closed. Then it was more drilling.

I became so fed up with it I was tempted to break a leg and be excused altogether. My thoughts of Christine soon made that idea vanish.

We were then told that we would be sailing for England in ten days' time. We were to return home and sort out our businesses and say our goodbyes and report here on the eve of our departure.

Ben occasionally came and watched us parading and I can see the smile on his face when the Drill Sergeant shouted at us. I was glad this masquerade is over. I hope it will not be like that in England.

Ben and I took time to go and book the air craft for a flight to Sappanam for the next day. We were told the plane needed some repairs and that can take several days. We were offered the chance of the first flight when that repair is done. My telephone number was taken. Then I visited Inge when I knew her husband would be at home. She had told me that they were thinking of renting a larger house. My instant response was to offer them my house, since it will be left unoccupied for the duration I will be away. They were happy with my suggestion. He offered to let me stay there the night. I declined with the excuse that I was with Ben and we were off to Berbice very early in the morning.

He asked to see the house which I readily agreed and we set off to the sea wall. The watch-man cum gardener was sitting outside. I introduced him to my friends and told him they would be living here while I am away. And he will be paid two dollars a week. He protested and I told him he can supplement his earnings by planting vegetables and other cash crops.

"You saw the posters the government has posted on all government buildings urging people to GROW MORE FOOD. Well my lazy gardener you can start moving yourself in that direction or find a job."

He did not like the alternative and protested that only a little space is left for vegetables.

"Dig up the flower beds and plant… Plant until you drop. You have all the tools and water handy on a hose, more than most people have."

Inge was smiling at his sluggish behaviour. I showed them around and they were quite happy with our verbal arrangements. Instead of returning to Berbice we lingered around Georgetown until after the weekend. Occasionally visiting the office where we booked our flight. Repairs were still under way. It would be a further few days before it was completed.

Ben was eager to return to Sappanam. So we returned to Berbice to wait for that phone call. I was a bit worried that my passage to England would prevent me from making that trip. I wanted desperately to meet Matthew.

The few days in Berbice were uneventful. To break the ennui I visited the laboratory to continue with the experiment I started at Sappanam, until even this failed to inspire any enthusiasm.

I made several attempts to visit Inge who was in Berbice but failed to do so.

Eventually, out of desperation I surprised them with a visit. They thought I was still in the city. I did not stay very long. Before leaving, Inge asked if she can come and visit as she still has not made any friends in the town. I told her she need not asked. Just drop in as every one used to do in the old days.

On our way home Ben asked if it was the right thing to do. "Remember I am an old cock at this game. You tried to dissuade me from prying into your private life once before. I appreciate that because you only wanted to protect the lady in question. This is a respectable couple. Surely you would not want them to split up?"

"No Ben. I do not want them to split up. I will be careful." I said quietly, then screaming at him with these words, "I need a woman right now to cheer me up or I'll go mad." I remembered how I felt towards Ben when he told us of making love to a married woman and the reproach he received after that.

"But I am here. I can cheer you up. I've done that for many years. Am I becoming boring? You find no more solace in my company?" He asked in an appealing voice.

"You know I do, but there is something deeper that is worrying me. It could be the thought of leaving all the best friends behind and going into the unknown. That is why I wanted to see Matthew to give me confidence and reassurance. The past is repeating itself, like when I was asked to go to McKenzie for six months and it turned out to be nearly six years. This war is going to last forever and I will not survive to return to see my mother or my friends. Not Diego or Bell, Not you or Matthew, the people I loved and cherished will be a distant memory after I leave here."

Those words nearly brought a tear to my eyes. Ben was there to comfort me. He told me that the recruiting officer will give me a couple of days' notice for my departure. Recruits are scattered all over the country. Since they do not know what form of transportation is available and from where they would be travelling. We can go and visit Matthew and Diego all in one day. His words made sense and I was beginning to feel relaxed and my confidence returning.

The next two days that Inge visited we just chatted and she helped mother with her cooking. My patience from making any physical contact with her was wearing thin; I kept reminding myself of Ben's words of caution. I was torn between my desire and decency. I remembered her words of loneliness and sex deprivation and it became the propelling force in me. It also occurred to me that unconsciously I was remembering those words only to give me an excuse to have her. At this point I decide to let events take its course. Inge had a charismatic and sensual way about her. The way she spoke and her words which had a strong German accent sounded sexy and appealing.

I knew mother would be going to the church in the morning and my heart was set with desire for her. So when she arrived the next day I was happy that Ben went with the maid to the market. He wanted to see the catch the fishermen brought in from all night sea fishing. They would sell their catch to the retailers and on occasion one can have a very good bargain dealing directly with them.

My conversation with Inge was only small talk. She sensed it and told me what I wanted to hear. She has still not had any physical contact with her husband. She was beginning to think he might have become impotent. I told her that is unlikely. Hindus have their religious beliefs that prevented them from any intimate contact during that period and maybe he was going through that period. Of course, I had no idea of what I was talking about. I simply said it to make conversation. She joined me on the settee and asked in a whisper if we are going in the bedroom. I did not need to be asked a second time. I was quick on my feet and lifted her to the bedroom I gently threw her on the bed and as she lay there in the corpse position limp and helpless slowly lifting her clothing and removing her underwear.

Again her untanned thighs above the knees looked more inviting than before. I looked at her trophy. It was an invitation no man need to be offered twice. We stayed longer than usual, not caring if mother returned and found us in bed. It was not my mother but the maid who burst in without knocking and was aghast when she saw us entwined. She apologised profusely and ran out to the kitchen. I hastily put some clothes on and followed.

There I confronted her "What did you see?" I asked.

"Nothing sah." she replied lips trembling.

"Now look here, I am going to tell you something only to protect you from going to prison. That lady's husband, do you know who he is?"

"Yes sah. He is the judge."

"Now, if you go telling people what you saw it will cause a scandal and you will not be able to prove it. I will be in England and the lady will deny it. You will be sued for slander and then you will find yourself in court. Her husband's friend will sit in judgment. Who do you think that judge will believe the white woman or a servant girl?

"The white woman sah," she replied still terrified.

"The punishment for slander is five to ten years in prison. Do you want to go to prison?

"No sah. I swear on my life I would not say anything not even to your nice friend."

I calmed her down and she became a bit more relaxed. I was happy Ben stayed back at the market waiting for a bargain, and happier still that he would be unaware of this incident.

I returned to the bedroom and found Inge had dressed and was waiting in the drawing room. She asked me if the maid was going to speak about it.

"No" I told her. "I threatened her with imprisonment for slander and I can assure you no more will be heard of it."

"I think I will not come here when we would be alone. It is best I go home now."

With those words she kissed me and said goodbye. I asked her if I would see her before going away. She told me they were returning to the city and I should visit them before my departure. This I agreed to do.

No sooner had Inge left when the manager from the sugar plantation at Skeldon dropped in without warning. I was pleased to meet him again. His presence became a shield for the unpleasant event with the maid. He inquired of Matthew and I told him he had returned to his post in the interior.

"As a matter of fact, it is your father I wanted to see. I went to his surgery and I was told he has gone home, that is why I dropped in."

"Please have a seat and let me offer you a drink. He will be here soon." I sent the maid to fetch Ben who had returned and was relaxing in a hammock in the garden. I then told Andrew of my impending departure to fight for the Mother country. We discussed the impact the war was having on supplies, building materials and spares for the crusher at the mill. Luckily, they have an engineer who is good at improvising to keep the mill running.

We were joined by both Ben and my father and drinks were served around for the second time. Ben told him that we have booked a flight to visit Matthew and it will be a day trip by plane.

"Fascinating, those aircrafts, I never flown in one it would be a great experience." He said.

"You can join us if you so desire. We are not sure when they will finish with the repairs but I hope soon as time is running out on me." I suggested

"I will think about it. If it's a weekend it will be great. Leaving the factory on a week day can be tricky. Let me think about it. I will leave a phone number that will enable you to get in touch with me at any time." He handed me the piece of paper with the number and began explaining to my father the dental problem he was having.

Ben and I left the two talking while we went to see the fish that Ben bought. It was a huge snapper and mother had already prepared it for baking.

A few days later, we were having lunch when the telephone rang. It was a message from the air craft pilot telling us that they are ready to take us up the Demerara when we are ready.

I telephoned Andrew in Skeldon and relayed the news. He was excited and promised to be here early in the morning to get the train to the city. We will not arrive until late afternoon so Ben began repacking his things with the help of the maid.

"You have to leave her a present for Christmas." I suggested to Ben.

He quickly agreed and I promised her a nice new dress from England if she takes care of mother when I am gone. She was overjoyed and would not stop kissing Ben until he gently pushed her away.

I telephoned Persotum to ask if he has moved into my home. I told him I will be staying there for a night with a friend or two. I was not sure if Andrew would bring his wife. Persotum said that he will move in only when I am gone and the house is free. At the same time he asked me to visit him when I arrived and Inge would prepare dinner for us.

Andrew was as punctual as he said he would. I was happy he brought Ismay with him. She is easy to speak with and her conversation is always topical.

When the train arrived in the city we headed straight for my friend's home, as promised there was the table nicely laid out and the smell of something delicious came from the kitchen.

"I am sorry the food is not quite ready. We were not sure of the exact time you'd arrive." She apologised.

Ismay went and sat next to her while my friend brought us his best malt whisky. I knew Andrew would appreciate it more than Ben. We discussed our plan for the next day.

Inge then asked. "Do they charge for the flight or for how many passengers on the flight?"

"We pay for the flight and we can take as many passengers as the plane can hold." Ben told them with certainty.

"Is that true Peter?" Inge asked.

"I am sure it is true. They did not ask how many people were going to be on the flight." I reassured her.

"Thank God for that." Andrew exclaimed. "I forgot to ask if there were to be any payment. I did not bring much with me. But I am sure I would have been able to meet my obligations one way or the other." Andrew added feeling a bit more relaxed at the explanation.

I told him "We were very pleased when you offered to take us to Oreala with the company's super boat. You can consider this as a thank you."

"I don't want to take advantage of your generosity, Peter. But can we join you if there is room for us as well." Inge politely asked.

"I don't see why not. The aircraft I'm sure is capable of carrying a dozen people or more." I replied.

"If it cannot take all of us, we can always leave Ben behind. Look at him he is the size of three grown men." I added with some humour.

"Why don't we go with them, darling," she suggested to her husband. "I have never been to the interior and you always promised to take me to Bartica."

"I don't see why you cannot go, if you feel you can cope with the hazards of the wild." He told her and expressing regrets that he has a lot of preparatory work for tomorrow.

Normally Hindus do not allow their wives to go out anywhere without their husbands. I guess the presence of Ismay was a deciding factor. I was very surprised. It confirmed what I thought was happening all along. He was drifting away from her for many reasons. He has strong family ties and I am certain he was not connecting with the rest of his family because her and their different cultures. This alienation was having an impact on him. Since they are not sure if she will appreciate their way of life, they kept aloof. Also maybe her husband is reluctant to expose her to it for the same reason. I am absolutely certain this is the reason for their estrange relationship.

I then told him the jungle is not that wild and besides you have Matthew there. I am sure he will protect her and not to mention Ben. "Look at him. Do you think a jaguar or caiman dare come near her when Ben is there?" I wanted to reassure him that his wife would be safe.

It seems most of my life I was doing something for the first time. Flying was no different. As it turned out it was rather exhilarating. The only problem I had was when the pressure changed and I had to activate my jaws to release the pressure. Inge did not appear to have that problem.

The plane landed just as it did when I first saw it and the villagers came rushing out to admire the sight. When they saw me they ran jubilantly and tried to lift me up. Ben told them that I have two ladies with me and they might become jealous.

"You bond with this lady?" One of them asked pointing to Inge

I told him she was a friend's wife and she is here only for the day. Matthew by now had come down to the river. He greeted us with great friendliness and we went to his rest house for some refreshments. He expressed surprise when he saw Andrew and Ismay. My first question was to find out if he had news of Sugar Bush.

"Sugar Bush!" Inge asked "What sort of name is that?"

"It's not her real name" Matthew told her. "No one knows her real name except her parents."

Matthew told us that she was located by his rangers and is left in the care of Diego's family until it can be arranged for her to join him here. In the meantime, Matthew sent a villager to tell Diego we are here and would be leaving late afternoon.

"This Sugar Bush, Is she your wife?" Ismay asked Matthew.

Ben as usual took up the conversation. He explained that she is bonded to him and because of that she is under his protection.

"So what does bonding entail?" She again asked and again Ben went into details of explaining. His explanation left Matthew a bit embarrassed. To avoid any further misunderstanding, Matthew told her the truth, "she was initially invited to be bonded with Peter, but Peter thought she was too young and decided against it. The truth is she is twenty two years younger than me." Matthew told her unashamedly.

Ismay turned to me and asked "Have you bonded with any of the girls here."

Ben again took the lead and said "He came here when he was sixteen and would not leave until he was twenty three. Of course he bonded, not with one but many. He was a young man full of energy. Bonding was the tribal system, their tradition, to prevent inter breeding."

I could see Inge was bemused by all this revelation. Was jealousy the reason?

Matthew agreed with Ben.

Diego and Bell's arrival put an end to an embarrassing subject. She was heavily pregnant. I was greeted with such warmth and kisses from Bell it made me happy I came. Again I could see Inge looking unhappy with what was happening.

Matthew continued by telling them of the gold and the co-operation he is having with the villagers.

"Look!" Diego interrupted. We even made a cart to be drawn by bulls. No need to walk all that way to the lodge. The cart is much faster. We even brought the gold we found at cold stream in the cart. Show him the gold we found Matthew."

Our guests were intrigued by this revelation. So Matthew took them to his study and making sure none of his helpers were around he opened the lid and there to my surprise the drum was nearly half full of nuggets. Inge could not believe her eyes.

"How much is there? She asked.

"I think they have about two and a half ponds of gold there." I told her.

"Here have a nugget." Everyone that visits us always gets a nugget as a souvenir. Matthew handed her and Ismay a nugget each. They looked at it for a while and promised to keep it safe.

Then turning to Bell, Ismay asked. "When are you expecting the baby?"

"Very soon," Bell replied. Then Diego started speaking. "I think it was God that sent you here with that plane. Bell did not want to have the baby here, just in case there are problems. Would it too much to ask if we can come as extra passengers? I will pay if there is anything to pay."

"The plane is chartered and paid for by me. You and Bell are welcome to be my guests" Ben told them. "I am not going back so you will have as much room as you like."

While we were having lunch the two of them set off to get their things together. Matthew also suggested that Diego can take the nuggets and sell them at the assayer's office. It was abundantly clear how fortuitous it is that we came when we did.

Matthew asked to be excused and he went to his study and started writing. After a while he came out with three letters one was for Jonathan and the other for Granville Cavendish, Gordon's brother. I was to post the letters when I reached England. The other I was to hand to the Colonel when it was convenient. I wished there was time to show Inge the cold stream and the place where we are getting the nuggets.

Before boarding the plane I spoke to Matthew at great lengths about the army in England and what is expected of me. I did not want to look cowardly. I have been put through many uncertainties in my life and I was not prepared to face more of it in a strange land.

His explanations put my heart at ease and the letter to Colonel Bray contained all that is needed to make my stay as comfortable as is possible. I did not want VIP treatment nor did I wish in any way to be treated different than the recruits.

The words of the Guru came tumbling in my head, "Foot sore and heart sore he drags on and knows not his destiny."

Soon we were on the plane for the two hours flight to Georgetown.

As soon as we arrived, Bell was taken to a private hospital. The flight had caused her water to break and Diego was not taking any chances, once she was admitted and made comfortable we left the two and waited for Diego to join us. This he did sooner than we expected. There was fury in his eyes. He wanted to be present at the birth but the Matron refused to let him.

He left a number for the matron to call when the baby arrived and then we took Inge to her husband. I took the keys to my house and the rest of us went to spend the night there.

Andrew was not having a quiet night on his rare visit to the city. Message was left with Inge to inform us of any news of Bell. She rang the hospital to give her telephone number and to be informed when there is a development. This put Diego's mind at ease.

Andrew took us to the same club we went with Matthew. The man at reception recognised me and remarked that I was not wearing proper clothing again and so are my friends but as you are here with an esteemed member you are again excused. I told him it was not deliberate as I am leaving for England and had to make a hurried trip up the Demerara to see Matthew who he knows very well. He nodded in recognition of my apology.

We were enjoying Champagne and brandy. A concoction introduced by Andrew.

"This is the 'Admiral'," He announced "It's a name I gave it when I was in the Navy. What you think of it Peter?" He asked. "It is the only alcoholic drink Ismay likes," he informed me.

"It is really excellent. It is not the drink I will have every day, I can assure you. It is excellent."

Ismay sat quietly sipping her drink occasionally skirting the rim of her brandy glass with her index finger and listening to the sound it made. Diego sat silent and only listening to our conversation. I am sure his thoughts were back at the hospital and a worried frown soon appeared. I told him she is in capable hands. He shrugged off his worried look and sipped his drink. A few minutes later Inge rang to say Bell had a successful delivery and we can go to see her as soon as she is prepared for visitors. Ismay calmed Diego by telling him to relax and the hospital would have relayed a message if there were complications.

At the hospital, Bell was smiling and cuddling her baby with great tenderness. Diego had a quick glance and expressed delight at his handsome son. It was then we all knew what sex it was.

Diego was so happy. He told Andrew that to celebrate the birth of his son he would charter the plane to take him home. Andrew tried to dissuade him but he was adamant. A couple of phone calls to alert his captain to watch out for the plane and be ready to collect him on the Corentyne River.

True to his word the plane was chartered and we flew home in great style. It was great fun sitting with the pilot in the cockpit to direct him to the Skeldon wharf on the Corentyne River. He never flew to this part of Guiana before. From Skeldon he located the Berbice River and again I had to show him where to land. Two boats came and collected me. A huge crowd was at the stelling, cheering the flier as he took off.

I arrived home to find my papers from the recruiting office ordering me to be in Georgetown in forty eight hours. The time has eventually arrived and I was not at all unhappy as I thought I might be. Instead there was a feeling of adventure and the unknown and using my initiative to face it with human dignity and resolve. I did what was expected of me, packing my personal belongings, telephoning my friends and saying goodbye and most importantly writing Matthew, Diego and Ben to give them the news.

So on the morning of the 8th May 1942 I left my beloved Berbice. Whether it will be for the last time only time will tell.

Mother insisted in accompanying me and my father to Georgetown. I did not want that as I knew it will be a tearful farewell and perhaps embarrassing for me in front of the others.

Most of the recruits were young blacks and East Indian men. The only other white face apart from mine was that of an English Officer. He was coming all the way with us. Probably to make sure we did not change our minds.

CHAPTER 16

Finding Christine

The British Overseas Airways Cooperation was the airline that transported recruits to Gatwick, then known as "the Beehive."

After leaving Atkinson airfield we headed for Port-of-Spain in Trinidad, then to Jamaica collecting recruits. When the plane finally landed at Gatwick it was almost midday. From there, most were taken by military vehicles to Catterick. I waited with the recruiting officer in the lounge as more recruits were expected. When they did arrive we were driven to Aldershot.

After six weeks of rigid military training. I was sent off as second lieutenant along with another South African to the Cambridge Military Hospital where soldiers from the Royal Army Dental and Medical corps were treating the wounded.

On the morning of the following day I was summoned to the Lt. Colonel's office. He had my documentation before him. He explained to me that since I am registered as a dentist in British Guiana, I am allowed to practice there but not in England. However, since there is a war on and we are in need of as much help as is available. He was instructed to allow me to work under a dental surgeon and I must attend lectures when not pressed with causalities. This sounded like exactly what I wanted and I knuckled down to it with great determination and enthusiasm.

I hardly noticed the time slipping by. I was working such long hours I nearly had a nervous breakdown. I was sent to rest at the hospital. Two days later when the doctor came to see me he was in the company of the officer in charge of Southern Command and also an official from the War Department, referred to only as the Honourable Cavendish. Their visit was to assess the casualties in the hospital first hand.

The Honourable Cavendish looked at my chart and mentioned the fact that his brother is Gordon Cavendish, a member of my country's legislative council. I told him I had the opportunity of meeting him on two occasions once when he visited Sappanam where Matthew Longhorn is the Commissioner and another when the two of them were guests at my father's barbeque.

"So you know Gordon? How is he? I haven't had a chat with him for some months. Not for the want to trying. It is almost impossible to get a good connection these days. Anyway get well soon."

After he had gone, the doctor told me that Jonathan had been assigned to the Royal Engineers and has brought the family to live in Alton which is only a few miles from here. I found this to be very interesting news. The letter I posted to him was an address in Somerset. This war for me sad to say is something of a blessing. It may sound heartless especially for the families of the men who lost their lives and those with serious injuries. But I was thinking selfishly and felt no remorse.

I needed to get out of the hospital as soon as I could. There was an urgency that had taken hold of me. Try as I might it would not go away. The doctor refused to let me out and I was forced to remain until such time he deemed me fit for duty.

Eventually, when I did get back to my duties I was faced with another obstacle. I could not leave my post until I was given leave to do so. This really infuriated me. There was nothing I could do. I must remember this is not British Guiana and the opportunities I am having is not worth the effort to disregard orders.

That night I wrote my mother a letter explaining my situation and for the first time telling her of my feelings for Christine and how I would find no peace until I meet her and get the truth of her feelings for me if any still exist. I even asked that she go to the Reverend Father and ask him to pray that I find peace in my suffering. This request was contrary to all the beliefs that sustained me in times of distress. The situation was beyond me. I am controlled by powers I did not know existed and they are not divine powers but the military might of an empire.

A few days later I went to see the doctor as ordered. It was a follow-up to see how I was progressing. My heart was checked and my pulse showed a reading of higher than normal. The doctor questioned me about it. I did not give him a reasonable reply and then he asked me if I missed home and my surroundings. I told him I feel fine and my only problem was...

"You must tell me what your problem is if I am to help you." Dr Adams insisted.

"You could be developing a high blood pressure syndrome which can lead to heart attacks or stroke. What do you think can happen to you? I will tell you one of two things. The first and most serious is permanent paralysis and the other is death. The choice is yours."

"Why is paralysis more serious than death? I asked.

To which he replied "I leave that for you to think about."

I summoned up some courage and told him some of the truth. I did not want to compromise the family. He shook his head and told me some very pleasant news. First that he knew where I could find Christine. He told me that she had joined a group of women volunteers helping families whose sons or husbands died or were seriously injured, and are finding it difficult to come to terms with their grief. Furthermore, he can tell me that the office is in the town's centre. The only problem being is that those involved are not there all the time. Most of their time is spent visiting the unfortunate families to give comfort, and assess their immediate needs. The only time they can be located is when they decided to make their reports, and that is mainly early morning or late in the evening.

I was determined to meet her even if I have to sleep at the doors of that office. The doctor promised to arrange for me to get some time off soon. I decided the only way to ignore my feelings was to immerse myself in my work until the time came.

I reported fit for duty and set about doing what is expected of me. I asked the Lt. Colonel who had recently taken charge if it was possible for me to continue an experiment I started. He was intrigued by this request and decided to have a look at what I was doing.

He showed some interest in the experiment and asked me to write about it with a promise that it will be handed over to the right authority for scrutiny. This I did and gave it to him.

Walter Douglas, the South African asked me about it. I told him what transpired and he shrugged his shoulders and told me that I would never hear anything about it. That was a bit worrying.

Days went by without a word. Eventually, I asked the Lt. Colonel about the experiment. I was told that permission was given for it to be sent to the dental hospital in London. They will determine whether there is merit in proceeding with it. I told him I unaware of that decision and perhaps he will see that I am informed. He agreed.

I decided to leave the whole matter aside as it was giving me some headache and to concentrate on my work and attend lectures as often as I could. This decision calmed me a little.

Dr Adams saw me in the mess and told me that he had contacted Christine and she would come to see me at the hospital as soon as she could. I was overjoyed at this unexpected news and thanked him for his efforts. Suddenly, a dark cloud descended over me. I thought if Christine knew I was at the Cambridge Military Hospital and if she really loves me, she would be here in a flash. Perhaps I am too optimistic of our relationship. After all it was the briefest forty eight hours romance. I was also aware that intimacy can have a long and durable impression on the minds of young foolish lovers. She was young but not foolish. I rebuked myself for thinking that an intelligent young lady would hang around waiting for some romantic colonial to whisk her off her feet for a second time. Being foolish once is enough. Yet, deep within me I felt something positive. Is it my mind teasing me? Or is it that same mind is telling me the truth? There were a hundred questions I wanted to ask. I realised it would be futile and decided against it.

By telling me of Christine, Doctor Adams was doing what any doctor would do, looking after his patient's welfare and no one can ask for more.

Several weeks went by and no sign of Christine. I felt I could no longer depend on others to solve my problems. Instead of going to the mess for lunch I went to the office where Christine worked. I was told she had been transferred to London where there was more urgent need of volunteers, I asked where about she was posted and the young lady told me that she was living in the Victoria area but that she did not exactly where. She gave me some encouraging news when she told me that Christine had left a letter to be posted to me. Unfortunately it was left lying on her desk.

I realised there is a war and the urgency of volunteers caring for those devastated by bombs was a far more important issue than my romantic inclinations. I tried to tell myself that the only way to secure a normal frame of mind is to divert my attention completely away and to continue to concentrate on my work. After all I was helping with the war effort at the hospital and to a certain degree enjoying what I was doing. I looked at the letter and thought I'd better read it later just in case it was not all good news.

Walter was becoming friendlier and sometimes we went for drives in his car to Farnham. One day, I saw the road sign indicating Alton straight on. I told Walter part of my story and he agreed to take me there the next time we come this way. I drew on my reserves of patience and diverted my thoughts of having a pint at the Kings Head a public bar not far away.

The torment of being so near to finding Christine and the frustration of not being able to locate her was more than I could bear. I went in my locker and took out a bottle of whisky and started drinking from it. I wanted to get senseless and maybe some sleep. Walter came and found me imbibing and forcefully took the bottle away.

He began telling me of his problem in South Africa. He started by saying. "Women are not as sturdy as men when it comes to relationships. I was happy with my Virginia. We hoped to get married when the war is over. She knew I would be in England indefinitely, so we arranged that when the time is right she can come over and we will be able to continue our relationship if only to keep it alive. On the morning I kissed her goodbye she promised to see me in England at the right time. I've been here nearly a year and only two letters I received from her. I sent nearly a dozen. It was my mother who wrote to tell me that she has married. That did not hurt me so much. It was when my mother said she was seeing someone else weeks before I left that really broke my heart. I eventually wrote her a letter wishing her a happy married life. That letter I wrote her was the healing oil for my heart. I felt supreme and never grieved after that. What I am saying my friend, if you find it difficult in locating the people you are after then I suggest you put it down to a lost cause."

After a long silence, he told me that on Sunday we would go to Alton.

"I do not have their address." I confess to him.

"That's not a problem. The office where she last work will have her address." He assured me.

The following day we went and got her address from the same young lady I spoke to previously. She was very polite and seems to understand my concerns.

It was a very large house with an enormous garden attended by what looked like a very able gardener. When he saw us he told us to wait as Mrs Longhorn was at the back. She came and stood rigid for a minute then came running towards me. I was not sure what to do so I just embraced her and kissed her cheek. She looked at me hardly wanting to believe her eyes then gave me another hug before inviting us inside.

"Quite a pleasant home you have." I remarked.

"Lots of hard work keeping it up, this was Matthew's house. As you know it was part of his share in the family's estate he gave to Jonathan. I must say he is a wonderfully generous man and Jonathan is equally grateful."

"So where is the family estate?" I asked.

"It's in Somerset. The Americans have rented it and promised to return it as it was. I could never be happy there. It is much too big for me to handle."

She began reminiscing of the week-end at Sappanam and inquired of Gordon. I told her of his visit to our barbeque and the wonderful time they had. They thoroughly enjoyed the unique Berbician hospitality. I sensed that she avoided speaking of Christine and I was not sure if it was proper to talk about her in the presence of Walter. She asked of Caroline and she gasped in surprise when I told her that Matthew and I gave the money for a clinic to be built and that it be named The 'Lady' Caroline Clinic. During the polite conversation many questions crossed my mind. Did the placebo worked? Did she become pregnant? Is Catherine aware that I made love to Christine? Is she avoiding the issue because of Walter's presence? As I sipped the coffee I felt unnerved by all the questions turning over in my mind. I felt less nervous when she said "I wish we had been at your unique barbeque and with Gordon and Caroline there it would have turned a perfect holiday into a heavenly one."

"When the war is over you must visit us again. Matthew will be so pleased." I said

"In his last letter, he did mention the fact that you enrolled to join the RAF. He also said that since you left Sappanam he was in a sad state for months but he has found love again and hoped to make her a decent woman." Catherine said half laughing and looking pleased.

"I know the young lady he is talking about. She is twenty two years younger. Did you know that?" I asked and immediately wishing I had not said it.

"Oh yes, he did not try to hide that fact. I wish him well. He deserves it" she confirmed.

"Those women aged very quickly; very soon she will look as old as him. I've seen it happen." I told her.

Walter listening to our conversation broke his silence.

"Where did all this happen?" He asked.

"It's all happening in the jungle in South America." Catherine told him.

"I must visit this place. Maybe I can find a beautiful maiden twenty years younger," and adding "This bloody war is preventing everyone from doing what they wanted to do."

"If it was not for the bloody war as you put it .You would not have not met Peter to know of that place." Catherine reminded him.

After finishing our coffee I got up to leave. She then asked me where I am staying and promised to visit me within the next couple of days. Disappointed as I was, I put on a brave face and left.

"I thought you came to find your girlfriend." Walter almost shouted.

"It was just as important talking of the past. It brought back a lot of fond memories. There are a lot of important issues you do not know about. That is why perhaps you are a bit angry." I told him.

"You did not make love to her daughter when they visited? Did you, Peter?"

"You heard what she said. She will visit me in the next couple of days. That's good for me for now. In any case Walter, you reminded me of Ben, a mulatto and my body guard for five years. He is capable of defeating the Germans single handed." I joked.

"Do you think I can defeat the Germans single handed? He asked.

"No not at all. It is too complicated to explain. Maybe someday I will tell you everything."

"I can hardly wait for that day," he commented.

There was hope that the war was coming to an end soon, when we read in the newspapers that the Big Four were meeting at a summit to put end to the war. This was greeted with joy and expectations. To add credibility to this news was the fact that there was an increased movement of troops in Aldershot. Hundreds of Australians and Canadians were housed in nearby barracks and the Americans had taken over an air base in Brandon. We heard Vera Lynn singing "The white Cliffs of Dover" over and over again and soon everyone was humming it as a national song.

My heart pounded when the orderly came and told me that a lady was waiting for me in the CO's Office. Catherine was sitting legs crossed and immaculately dressed in a light blue silk dress. She immediately stood up and gave me an embrace. At this point the CO left the office to give us some privacy. She then offered me a seat and spoke softly. "I am sure that you are unaware that Christine has had a child. She refused to let you know as she felt it would put you at a disadvantage. What I mean to say, is that she felt she might be a hindrance to your plans of going to America to pursue your studies. I wanted to let you know through Matthew. Jonathan and Christine forbade me from doing that. The whole issue now lies with Christine. She and Elizabeth will be at home for the week-end and they are dying to meet you. I could not speak about it while your friend was there. Will you come and have lunch with us on Saturday?"

"I can hardly wait. I will have to order a taxi. I would not want Walter to know where I'm going. Please tell me. How is she? I heard that she was in Victoria with the women Volunteers."

"She was in Victoria but is sharing a flat with a friend in Sloan square." She paused, then said "Never mind the taxi I will ask Jonathan to come for you. I'll see you on Saturday." Again she paused then continued. "I felt I had to come in person as this is a very sensitive situation. We are all hoping for the best for our grandchild. Her aunt who is very fond of her is most distressed and cannot come to terms with the idea that her beloved Christine has made a mess of her life. Jonathan, on the other hand, is taking it rather philosophically."

After she left I felt like someone who had committed a gross immoral act and it was like a noise in my head. I wore the most forlorn expression anyone can imagine. It was so obvious Walter tried to cheer me up by making up funny stories. He was distinctly a very funny character who is capable of making anyone laugh. It was remarked on many occasions that he could make a cadaver smile. I was not immune to his jokes and soon my composure returned.

We became very busy with an influx of causalities. There were so many of them with facial injuries I was given the rare opportunity to tending to their problems without supervision, and I took it to prove to my superiors that I was capable of handling emergencies. The men told horrifying stories of front line fighting and the causalities were of such proportion they thought they'd lost the war.

The newspapers, on the other hand, were saying the contrary. The Russians were recovering from their humiliation in St. Petersburg and were heading towards Czechoslovakia with their new tank division and gaining the upper hand on the Nazis. When I showed one of the injured men the news, he told me it is all propaganda to boost morale. I imagine the newspapers would not go to such length to misinform the public. I was beginning to have a feeling of what it was like to be in the front line. The despair and misery those brave men had to face. Walter as usual was there to cheer them up. He made two puppets, one British the other German and imitated the German accent perfectly. The men forgot their pain and laughed hysterically even though in great pain. It made my work a lot easier.

The Officer in charge of Southern Command again visited the hospital having heard of the high number of injured men. He spent a few minutes watching me cope with my work and tapped me on the shoulder with words of encouragement. I was too busy to respond to his compliment. And I knew he understood.

I began to worry that this influx would prevent me from visiting Christine. By Friday midday several technicians from the university college came and gave support making splints at record breaking speed and these were fitted as soon as they were made. By evening, we fitted the last patient with his splint and headed towards the mess for a meal but not before having a double whisky from my locker. At last, it was all over. It looked like God was on my side after all and who could have asked for more.

I was all dressed and ready long before midday on Sunday. Walter wanted to know my agenda for the day. I told him I was invited for lunch and Jonathan would be taking me and I would see him in the evening for our regular trip to the Pub.

On our way to see Christine, Jonathan told me that he may be leaving for the front very soon and he is not at all sure how Catherine would survive without Christine being around for company. I offered to look her up occasionally when time permits. In the meantime I must try and get a driver's licence.

He volunteered to give me a few lessons as a beginner and to ask one of his friends to help if he has to leave before my test. Our conversation came to an end when we arrived at his home.

Christine opened the door and started crying as soon as our eyes met. I comforted her with a jesting threat that if my presence was upsetting her maybe I should leave. After the social preliminaries the parents left us alone in the drawing room and we went over events that took place up the Demerara.

"I have no regrets of what happened there." She told me. "My only regret is that you were not here to prevent my embarrassment and the wrath of my dear aunt. The seriousness of the situation must be taken head on, a respectable solution can only be found by what we do if only for the sake of Elizabeth. I do not want her to be branded a bastard."

"Christine, My darling Christine, if only you had told me I would have been by your side in a matter of days. I had my suspicions. Ben told me. You remember Ben? He was the huge man that escorted us on that moonlight night. Well, he told me that he will wager any amount of money that you would be pregnant. I did not know what to believe. But he was right all along."

"Why did he say he was sure I will be pregnant? She asked puzzled.

"The potion you drank in my room is a placebo. He only told me that after you had left."

"How did he know I drank that stuff? Did you discuss our love making with him? I am surprised at this disclosure." She asked a bit irritated.

I told her the truth. "He saw us on the embankment and when he asked me if you did take that potion. I refused to say anything until he swore that I would be in serious trouble if I did not tell him the truth. It was only then he told me about that stuff was useless. Please let's look forward and put the wrong right. My darling Christine, I love you so much." I could not finish what I wanted to say when we were both gripped in an embrace only seen by people really in love. Then I showed her the ring she gave me in Sappanam. She pulled a chain that was hanging from her neck to reveal the nugget I gave her. She had it made it as a pendant and it was beautifully polished. We touched the two items as a symbol of reunited love and sealed it with a kiss.

We must have spent an hour talking and reviewing the situation with only one solution in sight and that is marriage. Catherine must have psychic powers. She knocked on the door at a convenient time and we let her in.

"After lunch we will have a serious discussion. First, you must meet Elizabeth." She said firmly.

Jonathan sat next to me and Christine next to her mother. A woman brought Elizabeth in the room and she sat next to her grandmother. It was a painful meeting. The four-year-old was taking it like a matured person and when she was told I was her father. She came and kissed me, it was like heaven. It became more heavenly when she addressed me as Papa and told me that she was named after the king's daughter.

We decided that we would marry at a civic ceremony in the town hall as soon as the documentations were completed. Catherine insisted I stayed over and have a proper Sunday lunch before returning to base. Since I was not prepared for an overnight stay Jonathan said he would lend me some of his sleeping attire. A magnum of champagne was uncorked and we talked until midnight of that wonderful week-end at Sappanam.

After Jonathan and Catherine took Elizabeth away, Christine asked me without warning.

"Did you have a girlfriend when I was away"

"A girlfriend? Now let's be honest about this. I did not have a girlfriend when you went away and that I can swear to." I told her, because it was the truth. I may have had a short relationship with Inge, but to admit that she was my girlfriend was strictly not true.

"Well. Are going to ask me if I had or have someone? She asked.

"My darling Christine, if you had a male friend it is understandable. If you have a current one then I expect you to tell me.

I could not expect you to be lonely especially due to the uncertainty of both our lives and relationships."

"I have no current boyfriend and I never had a serious one. The stark reality is with so few men to choose from because of this bloody war, no man wants an unmarried woman with a child. Elizabeth kept me from going mad and lonely. My aunt although she was angry with me gave me all the support when it was most needed.

Later in the week I was told that Walter and I would be sent to Mill Hill in London to assist the dental surgeons who were unable to cope with the large number of recruits who, having finished their training would be sent to France preparing for the big push which will involve hundreds of boats of every size and shape. It looks like the newspapers were right after all. The tide is turning in our favour.

First, I would be interviewed by our Commanding Officer in the presence of The Honourable Cavendish. Will the presence of Gordon's brother be of any significance? I wonder. His role in the Medical and Dental corps was made abundantly clear by Matthew. I dare not question it.

The Honourable Cavendish sat next to the General on the right and our CO was on his left. I was quizzed about my work with my father and the time I spent with him in the interior. I explained everything in details. And of Gordon's involvement in helping me get the registration I so badly needed. The General addressed me by my new rank.

"Captain D'Abrue you appeared to have spent more years than is required to become a fully trained dentist. You will be sent to Mill Hill to assist the over worked dentist there. We have every confidence in you. Captain Douglas will work with you. May I remind you gentlemen that we are nearing a crucial part of this war and all hands are to remember Lord Nelson's words. I don't need to remind you of it." He then turned to our CO and asked if there were anything he would like to add.

"Only to say, that both Captain D'Abrue and Captain Douglas have served this hospital with all the energies at their disposal."

He then asked The Honourable Cavendish for any remark.

"Only to ask Captain D'Abrue, Why did Gordon got involved with getting you the registration? Gordon can be a bit reckless, as you can see in his military records, when he and that dare devil Longhorn were in India," his Lordship wanted to know.

"I first met Gordon at Sappanam where Uncle Matthew is stationed as the Commissioner for the hinterland. And again at my father's barbeque," I replied.

"There are two things I want to clarify here. The first, did your father's invitation to his barbeque have any influence in that decision? And finally why do you address Matthew Longhorn as your uncle?" His lordship again wanted to know.

"The Commissioner told Gordon of my obedience to my father; the relentlessness with which I helped with his work. That must have convinced the Governor. The answer to your second question, he is not only an adopted uncle he is also my friend and benefactor. Without his help I would not have been able to achieve the things I longed for. It was his recommendation and advice that made the Governor persuade the Dental Council to ratify the recommendation." I told him with great confidence.

"You must tell us more. We are unable to understand how he became your benefactor. You don't have to tell us. We are only asking because as you know Gordon is my brother and Matthew is his best friend. My implication is that we are all like one big family and these colonial postings can have a remarkable ability to change a person's orientation." He asked with great curiosity. Then looking at the others he asked. "Would you like to hear what he has to say?"

I was beginning to think that, because I came from the colonies I was being made a target for ridicule. Also it seems from my point of view that Gordon and Matthew are not held in great esteem in the eyes of these gentlemen. I was not for one moment saying anything to discredit them. It was only a thought that kept recurring during this interview.

"Intriguing information won't you say General?" my CO commented.

"I'm all ears." replied the General.

"With due respect to you noble gentlemen, I would like to refrain from speaking about it. It is rather personal. Matthew Longhorn is a gentleman of repute, very much loved and respected. He is held in high esteem not only by Gordon but also by the Governor himself." I told them firmly.

The Honourable Cavendish then told me that like his brother he too would bestow on me an award that I will find pleasing if I am to fulfil my obligations to the Armed Forces.

I remember Matthew telling me that he needed his CO's permission to marry. Courtesy demands that an officer ask for permission to marry. So I took the opportunity and asked the CO for his, at the same time telling him it was the niece of Matthew Longhorn. Without saying anything one way or the other, he merely remarked that he hoped I would be happy and not to let it interfere with my work.

CHAPTER 17

The 'Royal' Visitor

That evening in the mess was an important visitor from India. From information gathered he was the Rajkumar, who is here to bolster his men's morale as they were to be sent to Ypres to reinforce the battalion that were hard pressed to save the port being overrun by the enemy. We were told that the fighting was escalating and our boys were putting up a strong resistance.

I was determined to meet this visitor as I knew exactly who he was by reputation. After dinner, I met him smoking and introduced myself as a friend of Matthew Longhorn.

He looked at me half smiling out of courtesy and asked "So you are a friend of Major Longhorn?"

I was unsure of how to address him. It took a lot of nerve to ask but I did. I was surprised when he thanked me for asking and told me that he is a Rajkumar which is his title it would be appropriate to address him as His Excellency. He was a very friendly man and made me feel easy conversing with him. We were soon joined by two of his body guards. Tall, turbaned and moustached, they stood rigid by his side with their hands resting on the hilts of their sheathed swords. I felt threatened for a while until the prince waved them further back and offered me a seat.

He asked politely. "How long have you known Major Longhorn?"

I told him the history of our meeting and the strong love and admiration I have for him. I also told him of the stories Matthew told us as a soldier and his involvement with a beautiful princess from Rajasthan.

He showed a very warm smile when I mentioned the princess and asked. "Do you know who I am?"

I replied.

"So you wanted to confirm Major Longhorn's story. Is that what this meeting about?"

"Not all your Excellency, I would never cast doubt on what he said. As I told you I came from the colony in South America and I just wanted to meet someone who is a real Indian. Not only did I get that opportunity but the honour to meet a Prince." I said.

At the same time wishing I had not initiated this meeting. He saw I was getting nervous and asked me if I wanted a drink. He signalled one of his body guards and spoke to him in Bengali. The orderly asked what malt whisky we would like. I was surprised when the malt he asked for was my favourite. Douglas came in and sat a few tables away looking incredulously at me. I acknowledged his presence. The prince then asked if he is a friend and suggested I invite him over. I found this very friendly indeed. My nervousness disappeared completely when Douglas joined us. During our exchanges I was able to see further into the Indian way of life.

It was then he asked. "Do you have Indians in the colony?"

I told him we have but they were second and third generation and wholly unfamiliar with present day India. The conversation was not what Douglas liked and made an excuse for leaving. After he had departed the prince began telling me the story of the Princess. The part Matthew did not know.

He started by saying. "I knew of Major Longhorn's involvement with the Rajkumari. His would have been a marriage of love. Mine is a political one. If this war is over soon as we all wish, I will come to your country and see for myself the things you told me. I find it fascinating. Perhaps meeting Major Longhorn will be more fascinating."

He then looked at his watch and announced that duty calls and he must attend a meeting with the Generals. As we stood up and nodded at each other, his parting remark was surprising. "When my men are safely away I hope to meet with you and your South African friend for some more interesting conversation."

The last snow had melted and spring was in the air. It felt good to be able to shed all the heavy clothing to which I was unaccustomed and found to be burdensome.

There were an enormous amount of military activities around London. The Americans and Australians were filling the pubs to capacity. Douglas warned me not to visit these pubs as the Australians can turn nasty at the slightest annoyance from any one especially a non-combatant. The military police were finding it difficult to maintain order with so many disturbances all over the capital. At least their presence was reassuring to the public.

Douglas and I were returning to our base from the East end when a bomb struck an office block the explosion was so deafening it sent me sprawling to the ground. The fire engines were there in minutes trying to save what they could. We helped some of the casualties with minor injuries to safety, while the more seriously wounded waited for help. The land lord from a nearby pub brought a mug of tea and his wife served it with comforting words.

We thought it best to remain and help in any way we could. It was a very long time before the ambulances arrived and took the injured away. The military police arrived on the scene and dispersed the crowd. That was my first and only experience of what war was like. I began to imagine what it must be like in the war zone, of the men digging deep trenches in snow and rain and bullets flying everywhere. The devastation surely must send some of them out of their minds. My heart was filled with sorrow and again I questioned rather loudly the existence of the Divine power that would save us from these terrors. Douglas was in disbelief when he heard me. His remark was that it is not God that caused this war and since we, humanity, is engaged in it by our own will. He is leaving us to resolve it ourselves.

My plan for the wedding was put on hold. There was a notice on the bulletin board that had the names of officers to be sent to Gibraltar. Both our names were on the list. Douglas was philosophical about it, stating that he would go to hell if that is where his destiny lies. I, on the other hand, looked at this posting as another adventure partly due to the fact that I was getting bored with London. Just when we expected to be flown out orders came cancelling all movements. There was a strong suspicion that something was afoot and it was kept a secret. The Americans and all soldiers not including the non-combatants had disappeared from the Capital only a handful of the military police were seen patrolling the streets.

Christine wrote to say that her father had been sent to France and her mother was worried. She advised me to be careful as London is expected to receive a lot of bombs and it can strike anywhere. I wrote her of the cancellation of the Gibraltar posting and to tell her that I am expecting to see her at the week-end if she can make it.

There was comforting news that the Americans were making head way towards Germany and General Paton's army was in Italy. The news was filled with morale boosting stories of the Nazis capitulation in Eastern Europe and the Russians were making great head way towards Poland. One can sense a feeling of happiness in the Capital. There were, however, exaggerated talks of Hitler running off to a haven in South America. The premature celebrations in some of the pubs we visited were alarming. What if the Americans failed to capture Germany? What if Hitler had some master plan with his much improved bombs and is only waiting for the right moment to use it? These were the questions the sober minded individuals were asking openly, only to be ridiculed by the dreamers.

When we got back to base, I could sense the same feelings in the most senior officers as the dreamers in the pub. "Victory is in sight." The CO told us in a hushed voice. "It won't be long before our boys will be returning home." Coming from the senior officers were more encouraging. I felt there is some truth in the rumour.

I began to wonder if this war would end as quickly as everyone thinks. I would be able to finish my training and return to British Guiana. I heard from Christine that Gordon's tour of duty had come to an end and it was possible that he would return to England unless he is posted to another colony.

Some weeks later The Honourable Cavendish was at Mill Hill as part of his routine visit. I sought an appropriate moment to ask of Gordon. He was surprised I had this information. He did confirm what I was told and added that if victory is achieved sooner rather than later he may be asked to remain a bit longer until normality takes its rightful place in society.

Douglas and I decided to present the final stages of our experiment to the board as a joint effort, hoping that this would expedite a result that would enhance our chances with the written final test. Everything seems to hang on the outcome of hostilities. We, like everyone else were held in limbo.

Now that our posting had been cancelled, I could concentrate on the wedding. Douglas has agreed to be a witness and Catherine said she would find another.

In the meantime Douglas and I decided to put some finishing touches to our experiment before trying it out on some unfortunate candidate.

Catherine came to London unannounced to see me. At first I thought something had happened to Jonathan. It turned out that the wedding would have to be delayed once again as Jonathan insisted that he must be present at his daughter's wedding. This was totally accepted by me. Catherine was also pleased with my acceptance. She told me she did not know how I would react to that decision and only came to reassure me that it was the right thing to do.

Jonathan's presence in France was giving her cause for concern. There were rumours that the boys were holding off a German advance at Ypres, whose intentions were to take the port and cut of the food and ammunition supply for our troops. It appears that the German army is losing the war on all fronts. No one can believe all the stories being told. It was comforting just the same. So when it was rumoured that General Eisenhower was poised to take Berlin it became a real morale booster not only for the citizens in the capital but nationwide. There were premature celebrations in the pubs. Here, again we have the realists and the dreamers. It can sometimes get very tense between the two factions that caused the Military Police to intervene. Douglas had a glass thrown at him for suggesting we listen to the official news. He spent nearly a week in hospital for a suspected fractured jaw.

In bed I thought of the circumstances that brought me here. I wondered if my father had not forced me to go with him what road would I have taken. I am beginning to see a new perspective of events that is shaping my life. My mother; was she too protective, did she really love me for what I am, or what she wanted me to be always adhering to my father's demands? Yes I was the top academically and socially. The friends I had, looked to me as a God because I had more pocket money to spend. Let's face it, although all our parents were either professionals or merchants it was not customary for young boys to have too much pocket money. Their appetite for other non-essentials such as dining in the luncheon rooms and going to the cinema was a great asset to attract the girls who were always dependent on the boys to foot the bill. I became an asset through my father's generosity. I was allowed to keep all the money I received from the dentures I repaired. This could sometimes be more than I needed. I wondered whether that was a reason for their friendship. I am always surrounded by a host of people. If not friends it is family. I wondered if I was ever to be left alone to my own devices, to sort things out without the help or advice from those too keen to help. I might have been stronger in will and more decisive. Then, there was Ben who played an influential part in shaping my life on dependency. His protectiveness was stronger than my mother's. Even Diego and Bell treated me as an ornament delicate and fragile, nudging me always towards what they thought was right. If I had the will of someone determined to find his own footing would I have been a different person on another stage looking at life from a different perspective?

What about the encounter with Christine. Was it destiny that brought us together, and what about the romantic affair that ensued? Yes! I was torn between morality and desire. I justified myself by saying the urges of nature can overcome any sense of decency. I have let myself down, my thoughts of purity. I remembered the Indian sage's words of wisdom and yet I failed to take notice.

Matthew was a man of immense strength. To give away his share of the family's estate to his brother is something anyone can understand. To give a fortune to a make believe son was sheer generosity. He sees the world not for the material things we all tried to achieve. In a sense he was a religious person, perhaps not following a specific religious doctrine.

He was just the same religious in the fact that he admits the existence of God and followed an almost puritanical way of life. Though it would not appear on the surface, it can be detected in his words and the way he lived not all of it in the highest moral standard but then we are all mortals. We set our own standards and hoped to live up to them. To this day I am still bewildered by the fact that he gave me all those diamonds. Was it because he believed them to be stolen gems and he is protecting his moral values. Or was it because he wanted to reward me for the sacrifices I made by accepting isolation and hazards? No man no matter how decent will give away millions to justify his puritanical way of thinking. My thoughts ran back to the day he accepted Sugar Bush as a lover. Was that a declining moment for him. All men I think have an Achilles heel. I am not sitting in judgment of him. I am not that clever to ascertain what is right or wrong in the mystical sense. The fact is I have a strong love for him, so has Diego and Bell and I think even Ben.

My father, on the other hand, sees me as the heir to carry the family's name to the next generation. What would happen if I was a girl, would I be forced to marry a man whose surname is D'Abrue? Then there is Elizabeth, she will not carry the name Longhorn or D'Abrue into the next generation. Perhaps it is better I formulate a new code for my life, an independent code, a code that is embodied in morality and justice only. I am getting tired and need to sleep and wash away these thoughts or face insanity. My thoughts of what we did for the lads at the village worked like a charm. I wondered how they are doing; my mother I know will keep her promise. How will the boys react to her if she gets in her domineering mood? Father will be lonely if she gets too involved. Maybe she will try to convert them to Christianity. That would be a tragedy. Those people are firm believers in their faith any such attempt would be seen as a betrayal of our generosity. Their pride would force them to relinquish the scholarship. I must stop this train of thoughts and get some rest.

In the morning, Douglas came to tell me that we were wanted in the CO's office. When we got there he was in a humorous mood. I imagine it is all the talk of victory. Victory...Victory that is all I kept hearing and no real sign of it. I think I might ignore it even when it did eventually come. The CO asked what I was discussing with the Prince. I told him that it was not important. He became suspicious and demanded I tell him the truth. I was also adamant and told him exactly what I said previously.

He began by telling me that the rulers in India are there only as a figure head and that we are in effect the real rulers. I was most surprised when he asked me to make an attempt to see him again and to inquire what plans he and the Maharajah have about merging their states under one ruler.

I told him under no circumstance will I be a spy for him. "May I remind you that the Crown has special men for such tasks and if you insist, I shall confer with the Honourable Cavendish as to the precise nature of my work."

"No need to go to Cavendish. I was hoping you would do this as a favour for me. You may not know this but the Indians are hostile to our occupation. They may appear friendly and cooperative but they are always plotting to kick us out." He told me in the most friendly tone.

"Now I will like to ask you a question. Are we not fighting a war to preserve the rights for people of every denomination to remain free from genocide and enslavement? Would it be impertinent to ask another question? Is not the right for the Indians to seek their independence and shed the yolk they carry?" I asked a bit confused by the double standards in which I am engulfed.

"That statement can be seen as sedition. Do you understand how serious that is? I warn you Captain D'Abrue. You are treading on thin ice. Before you go I would like you to think careful of what I asked, If only as a favour to your Commanding Officer."

I told Douglas what was said and he was extremely angry. He nearly shouted as he made this remark. "I would have told him to go to hell if I were you. You know what he's trying to do. He is planting seeds of suspicion in you. I wonder what the poor bugger will think of it, if you start quizzing him of State Affairs. No, I am sorry; I will not support you if you go ahead with this vile scheme."

I eventually thought of two ways to avert any further altercation with the CO. The first was to avoid meeting the Prince or secondly if a meeting did occur I would avoid all political discussions. The fact that I did want to meet him again was very high on the agenda.

Douglas and I went to see the Honourable Cavendish concerning our experiment. He was amazed that no one told us of the possibilities it has; but only for children under twelve years.

"Is it not worth pursuing even though it benefits only children?" Douglas asked .

"So what are we to do now that this is approved?" I asked.

"I did not say it is approved, not by a long shot. It has to be decided by those far more senior than I am. I mean from the War department. I am sorry to have to tell you this. I cannot see anyone taking time to go through your experiment right now. You all know what this means it will have to wait until this cursed war is over." Cavendish said with some repentance in his voice.

There were other important things I can do to keep myself busy. I thought of getting a driver's licence, this will give me greater freedom to visit the Longhorns and the possibility of planning a way forward. Douglas although keen to get me there is doing it to acquaint himself with my personal life. I would not say he is deliberately nosey. It is difficult to converse openly in his presence. Catherine is always nervous when he is around and falls short of asking me not to come with him.

I knew the Prince was here for a short visit. The only problem is trying to reach him. I thought of asking the honourable Cavendish to initiate a meeting but that would arouse suspicion if it reaches the CO's attention. I am going to wait for the opportunity.

A few days passed and time was running out. Douglas and I decided to visit a special club where very senior officers went for their relaxation. We needed a special pass to get in. So I thought of a plan. I can ask the CO for that pass on the pretext that I wanted to interview the Prince concerning his intentions towards British occupation.

The CO was more than willing to give it to us. He was as happy as a dog who successfully stole a bone from its rival. "Don't screw it up Captain D'Abrue." He warned me and as a word of encouragement he said. "Be tactful. Show you are a colonial sympathiser who shares his views. If Captain Douglas is going with you make sure he keeps his mouth shut."

We did not have to wait long when we went in this very private club. The Prince seeing me standing and talking to the usher signalled him to take us to his table. There were other Indian dignitaries drinking tea and conversing in their language. We were introduced and then offered a drink.

I was somewhat perplexed at this invitation. I came to see him but did not expect it to be so easy. It did not take long for his reason to become abundantly clear.

He reached in the inside of his tunic and produced a letter for Matthew. There was only his name on the envelope I was to fill in the address and post it with the other letters I was sending. Again he asked of the Indians in my country. What I told him were simply the bare facts. They were indentured labourers from Calcutta and as second generation migrants knew very little of their language. The only thing that they appeared to be interested in is their religion. I felt slightly embarrassed telling him that there is a culture, racially motivated that prevented any social interaction, hence my ignorance of their life style. He seemed to understand my position and made references to the caste system that still exists in his country.

I then took the opportunity to tell him of the East Indians living in nearby Suriname, this caught his interest. He then encouraged me to tell him what I knew. I started out by telling him that the information I have is from what I gleaned from my father, he is a regular visitor there and can speak a little of their language. He told me that they wear their traditional clothing. "The ladies wore sari and the men, the older ones, still dress in their dhoti."

"Why only the older men?" He asked.

"As in British Guiana the East Indians are discouraged to speak their own language. I think it is because they must try to be British. So the younger men, they dress western style. It also helped them get good jobs." I explained.

"You say the ladies wear their saris. Is this not discouraged? He asked again.

"It is rather funny this. The European women like it and sometimes wear it at parties."

"I understand." He said and then commented "It is the same in India some of the English women wear it when they are entertaining wives of high ranking Indian officials. If I came to British Guiana would your father take me to see these people?"

"He would be absolutely delighted and you can be assured Major Longhorn would come along. That will be a good meeting for you, will it not?" I asked feeling confident.

"Absolutely, do mention this to him in your letter?" Then abruptly he said. "I am afraid I must say goodbye and hope to see you sometime in the future."

Douglas sat there throughout our conversation without saying a word. When we were alone he said he wished he could be there at that momentous meeting.

A few days later Douglas accompanied me to the garage to collect my new Morris minor a pale blue little beauty, I now have total independence. I drove down to the mess to see the CO and tell him of my encounter with the Prince. He was obviously impressed with what I had to say. I told him the only thing of importance that was discussed was coming to British Guiana and also to visit some of the East Indians in Suriname.

"Suriname!" He shouted "Where the hell is that?"

"It is also known as Dutch Guiana" I explained.

"Still apparently angry with my lack of information from the Prince," he almost shouted. "Why the hell did you not say that in the first place?" Then he asked with a roguish smile, "Did he mention any pact with Rajasthan?"

"Not specifically. He did say that there is an understanding among the 'Royal' families of the two states to respect their borders." I told him to make him happy. Life can be difficult if dealing with an angry CO. As a passing remark I casually mentioned that the 'Prince' is married to the sister of the ruler of an Indian state. To cheer him even further I also said that she and Matthew Longhorn were in love.

This had the desired effect I was hoping for. He was smiling and tapping a tune with his lips. Before dismissing me he said in the most amicable way. "You must allow me to buy you a drink. I am pleased with your information. I understand there will be a meeting with the 'Prince' in the Honourable Cavendish's office and that you will be there also. Do let me know how of the outcome."

I told him I would, only to make him happy. I had no intention of declaring anything confidential to that upstart. I felt I had somehow betrayed the 'Prince' by mentioning his marriage. I have had enough of the CO's under hand inquisitions. Using me as a spy was going over the top. I resented it and his tantrums were becoming unbearable. It seems to me that the CO is a man of intrigue and loves it. Douglas had the same opinion.

The only obstacle of returning to my homeland is this bloody war and everyone is totally fed up hearing of victory and not a sign of it.

The Prime Minister Churchill made rallying addresses to the nation. Giving much needed hope and encouragement. After his broadcast, quite a few of the officers called him unmentionable names blaming him for declaring war on Germany and wishing we had leave them to get on with whatever they intended to do. Most senior officers had a different view and that caused a lot of arguments in the mess. Quite rightly they argued that if Churchill did not do what he did at the time, Hitler would have seen us as an easy target. I must admit I think that was the right course of action. Anyone who could not appreciate that decision was very short sighted. Maybe it is not short sightedness but frustration. The rationing was a big factor that caused dissent and the number of our men slain in battle was another. Each day dozens of women are made widows. For some it can be far more serious, having an amputee to care for. I heard many women saying it was better if their husband had died rather than made a useless cripple. That would have provided a widow's pension to make life more tolerable. I can see the logic in that but just the same it is a heartless thing to say. War can bring out the best in man and also create monsters. That is how I viewed those women. Monsters!

I imagine coming from the colonies had shielded me from the harsh realities of European life. I can see why Britain must deal with the diversities of its empire and keep a tight hand on its purse. We who lived protected all our lives cannot begin to believe the enormity of the burden this country has to bear. The same size as ours and with thousands of times the population.

I am resolved that on my return to my homeland I will gather the others who are fighting in this war to help explain the responsibilities of the mother country. Our relaxed and devil-may-care attitude will have to be readjusted to fit in with the new world order that is emerging.

I am happy that Gordon was asked to remain at his post for the time being. I must write him a letter of my feelings and especially my encounter with the 'Prince' and to thank him for the courtesy his brother extended to me. From Matthew's letter I was told of Gordon's interest in my career prospects.

I have not written to my dear friends Ben and Diego for many months. I am sure they think I have lost interest. I will put that right as soon as I can.

My next course of action was to follow in Matthew's footsteps and meditate. He said it helped him to find peace of mind and the happiness that goes with it. First, I must find isolation to concentrate. Not even a hardened mystic can meditate in these surroundings and I knew just the place. I could find a room in Catherine's huge house for that purpose.

The sun is getting hotter with every day that passed by. I imagine it will be summer soon and another year would have gone by. We wrote our final papers and that went well. We can now look forward for that long-awaited diploma. Going down to the pub for a cool drink looks the ideal thing to do.

The saloon bar was unusually packed, mostly with American servicemen. We sat in a corner far away listening to their loud ramblings. Douglas became annoyed when one of them suggested that we should be grateful that they have come to fight the war for us and that Montgomery only stopped Rommel in his tracks because of American intelligence.

"That is total rubbish you yanks are talking. You are jealous that it was us and not you that stopped Rommel." Douglas replied to their accusations.

"And who the hell are you to say we are jealous .You are nothing but a cowardly colonial bastard." The American shouted back as the rest of them cheered.

"It takes a colonial to recognise another. You are still trying to shed that colonial stigma that is blatantly recognisable in what you say. I am a colonial and proud of it. Your overseas states are colonies with a different name. Like the French calling their colonies Departments of France. It is all the same with different names." Douglas was getting in fighting mood.

I wished Ben had been here, he would have slung the whole lot through the window, I was getting worried this whole thing would escalate into something more serious. This looked obvious as the American sergeant came over to hurl more insults at us. I was extremely agitated by his aggression.

He pointed his finger at Douglas and said. "We at least have a democratically elected President not like you lot. You with your unelected kings and queens."

"You were once ruled by the same queens and kings as we were, mate!" Douglas laughingly told him.

"Never. We were never ruled by pomp and arrogance, we have democracy. You ever heard of the word or know what it means." The sergeant told him and getting nearer to Douglas.

"Apparently, you are simply ignorant of your history. If you read foundation and growth of the British Empire you would have seen how wrapped up you were in it. Now go and finish your drink away from me." Douglas replied.

The sergeant drew a few feet away and pointed his gun at Douglas and shouting. "Apologise for that f****** insult or I'll blow your brains out."

Now this is what I would call a real disaster. Gun play, I have seen it in the movies. This is occurring right in front of me. This is real. I could not explain what came over me. In a split second I stood up and went in front of Douglas and tried to appease the sergeant. I thought if I spoke to him quietly and with reason he might think twice before pulling that trigger. He was not listening to me. Instead he ordered me to move away or he would put a bullet in me. I stood firm and told him Douglas is my friend and I will not allow you to be charged with his murder. That had a sobering effect on him.

He turned to Douglas and asked. "What would you say if I had shot your friend?"

With steely nerves Douglas said "I would have called you a coward for shooting an unarmed man."

Senior American officers were sitting there watching what was going on as if it was some kind of show on a stage. This could have been a tragedy and yet no one tried to defuse the situation. I took Douglas by the arm and led him out. As we went out the military police arrived. I can only guess that the landlord must have phoned them.

The day we received our diplomas turned out to be a low key occasion. The diplomas were handed out with very little ceremony. For me this was an anti-climax to all that I was looking forward to. Nevertheless, I got what I always wanted albeit it is only a licentiate degree. Unlike my father who has a doctorate. I was happy all the same. It would have been nice to have Christine and her mother watching me receiving this long-awaited reward. It was time to leave London and return to Aldershot.

Later that day I met The honourable Cavendish at the Cambridge Military hospital and asked about my experiment and how do I go about having it recognised as a useful means of treating children with acute protrusive mandibles. His response was that I would be given the opportunity to illustrate it to the board of senior surgeons. That time is to be announced at a later date.

I was beginning to give up on it. I can only comfort myself with the fact that when I return home I will be able to put it to practical use. Douglas was even more frustrated as the experiment I was doing was almost a replica of his. It was the reason I decided to do it as a joint effort.

It had been several weeks since I last saw Christine. I did not want to appear impatient in getting married. Her father's absence had put everything on hold. Even Catherine was getting impatient. She wanted this to happen more than I did. Each time I visited her home I was half expecting to find Christine there; my only consolation was Catherine's repetition of her plans for the wedding. It was to be an enormous affair to be held at the family's residence in Somerset. I shudder to think of the people who would be attending. This was strictly a Jewish affair. I am a catholic. I wonder what mother would have to say about this. I have no objections whatsoever. If my mother cannot come to terms with the religions of others I will feel very disappointed, she was the one who always told me to respect other peoples' religion. I cannot remember the last day I went to a church. It means that Elizabeth is a Jew and so will her children. This was beginning to get more complicated which I ever imagined. I thought of Matthew; he is a Jew and yet for all that his generosity had made me an extremely wealthy man. It was beginning to look like a myth that Jews are mean and heartless. I will have to explain this to Douglas. I wonder if he will still want to be a witness at my wedding.

My visit to establish a room for my meditation looks pointless Catherine had no objection to my request. She even suggested that she might try it to help with her recent acquired nervous tensions.

Once again I appeared to be rolling out the carpet heading towards my goal and once again I am faced with unusual obstacles.

My first attempt to meditate was proving much more difficult than I thought. Perhaps I am not the right frame of mind, or maybe the atmosphere was not right. What I needed was a guru to teach me.

On the evening of 28th May, I met the Honourable Cavendish in his office it looked very quiet and everyone was whispering. There were some very senior officers and even a General and Admiral were trying to keep a low profile.

It was several minutes before the Honourable Cavendish strolled into the room accompanied by The Prince.

They sat in deep leather armchairs and the General and Admiral joined them. Standing like two statues behind the Prince were his two Indian body guards, eyes looking straight ahead. It was the Honourable Cavendish who spoke first. He began by saying, "Gentlemen, you are selected to be at this meeting for specific reasons and I do not need to ask your undertaking that whatever will be discussed remain confidential and not a word to be said outside this room. Is that absolutely clear?"

Everyone nodded agreement.

The prince then produced a short letter and before starting to read it made this comment. "Gentlemen it has come to my attention a rumour that I find disquieting and after I read the contents of it I am sure you will agree with me of its gravity. This letter was sent from someone I know and is currently working in the Prime Minister's office. It is a confidential letter typed and unsigned."

He then put on a pair of reading glasses and started reading. "Your Highness, I choose to send you this letter not for any vindictiveness but to confirm your beliefs in the rumour that is quietly circulating among some very prominent people not only in Government, but also in the highest circles of the aristocracy. The Prime Minister is contemplating conversion to Islam. If this rumour is true then I need not guess of the impact it will have not only here in England, but throughout the Empire. I trust you can use your influence to get to the bottom of this affair and save your country from disintegration."

"Then the rumour is true." The General said and looking at everyone for support.

"We don't know if it is true. The fact is all rumours have a base of truthfulness in them." The Prince interrupted.

Then he continued. "Can you imagine the implications this will have on the Empire? The peoples of Canada, Australia and New Zealand, whose land covers two-thirds of the Empire, they will want to seek separation and the other third though small has three quarters of the Empire's population. Then there is the Middle East. They will be celebrating as a great victory for their religion. Most importantly is India. It is, as you all know, an Empire within an Empire. The majority of the population are Hindus and Muslims. This will be the wedge that will split the subcontinent and possibly bring about its disintegration. We have to consider the Sikhs and Buddhist and the Jains will they want their own state?

As you all know currently the world's richest man is the Nizam of Hyderabad. If this were to reach his ears it will have catastrophic consequences globally. The tribal areas in the North and North West have a great population of Muslims. The Nizam can use his wealth to encourage this separation."

He took off his glasses and wiped his forehead before commenting, "I sincerely hope this is exactly what it is, only a rumour or a very bad dream."

It was the Honourable Cavendish who tried to assure everyone that there can be no truth in this rumour. "I have been personally assigned as overlord of the Medical and Dental Corps. Because of that I had many private meetings with the Prime Minister and at no time did I see any hint of his inclination towards Islam. I can only say we dismiss this allegation as a hoax."

The Prince looked at the Honourable Cavendish for a good few seconds then asked. "Cavendish, is it not true that The Prime

Minister in 1940 gave £100,000 for the building of the mosque in Regents Street?"

"That is absolutely true but it was not his personal donation. That money was set aside. As you all know, 1940 was a terrible year of this war and we needed friends. The middle East holds a strategic balance for this cause." The Honourable Cavendish tried to explain.

"Whether it was his or the state's is irrelevant. Is it not odd that the man accused of conversion is the very man to oversee the funding for the construction of that mosque?" The Prince argued.

"I can categorically say, and as Cavendish said the Prime Minister's motive was to gain support from the Middle East to help with the war effort. Remember the Germans could have easily misled the Arabs to side with them instead of Britain." The Admiral said.

Then what he said came as a great relief for all concern. "I know just the Lady who can stop all this nonsense. This I promise with absolute certainty."

CHAPTER 18

Homeward Bound

I was beset with mixed feelings getting on board that plane taking me home. I have accomplished what I set out to achieve academically. My personal feelings were mixed with both sorrow and happiness. Happy that I was eventually married to Christine, sad that I must return alone until such time as Christine and Elizabeth would be able to join me. There were a lot preparatory work to be done, setting up a surgery in the city can be time consuming, getting the house ready for personal occupancy was another, and finally to meet my benefactor and consolidating his plans for Sappanam.

Christine thought Elizabeth coming to a strange country would find it unsettling and it would be best for her stability that I sort these matters out. My thoughts keep turning back to the last few days.

I remembered being half conscious with uncertainty at the wedding. I have never been to a Jewish wedding and I was not sure what mine will be. It was not dissimilar from other weddings. I did not understand what the Rabbi was saying most of the times. My only consolation was an occasional smile from Catherine. Elizabeth stood next to her grandmother, with a posy in her hand and her shinning silk dress reflecting the sun. I had two rings made one from the nuggets we found and a large fifteen carat diamond ring. I could not help noticing the congregation eyeing it with delight or perhaps jealousy.

After the reception I asked for a private meeting with Christine parents. Before I could say anything Catherine said to me. "Peter, Jonathan and I think we know what you wanted to say. We feel you should not express regrets of what happened at Sappanam. We do understand. You are now our son and not Matthew's."

I felt I had to clear the air with Christine. After her parents left I asked "Why did you not write and let me know you were pregnant? Can you understand how I felt? Especially when meeting your parents and trying to hide my guilt."

"My reason is perhaps a selfish one. You must try to understand I fell in love with you the moment I saw you and I think that feeling was mutual. I did not plan to get pregnant. It happened. I thought if I kept it away from you and you really love me then you would try and find me. Uncle Matthew would have helped you."

"You said your reason was personal. You haven't said what it is."

I asked

"I thought if I should have mentioned it you would have come perhaps earlier. I did not want any other reason to motive you to come to me. It must be for the sake of love and love only. Did I do wrong?" She explained almost to tears."

It was a valid explanation. I was happy that I did clear up that mystery before I left.

As the plane took off I settled down trying to read. This was useless; my thoughts kept going back to that wonderful day Victory over Europe was announced. The surge of jubilation was so intense. It seemed to invigorate every muscle in my body. I remembered we were busy in the surgery when the car flying the pennant of the General of Southern Command came to a screeching halt. His aides quickly opened the door and he hurried past them into the building housing the most senior officers. Not long afterwards I heard great shouting of joy and congratulations. Loud salutary remarks of Churchill and Monty followed. It was rumoured that Monty had a special place in the hearts of the inhabitants of Hampshire, for it is claimed he lived not far away round the corner in Alton, the same place where the Longhorns have their secondary home.

We were in no mood to adhere to protocol and rushed in to share the good news. I have never seen the General in such a jubilant mood; he was shaking every one's hand ignoring their rank.

Douglas held his hand with both of his and exclaimed with extreme delight. "We did it sir. By God we did it."

There were plans for those that wish to travel up to London to join in the main celebrations. The Royal family will be on the balcony of Buckingham Palace to acknowledge the crowds cheering them and Churchill and his Generals will probably be among the most senior officers joining the Royal Family to review the situation of the occupation of Germany. This was completely out of our league. Most of us declined the offer of celebrating in the capital. Instead we joined the locals; which was not low keyed by any standards.

The celebrations continued as one would expect for several days until it finally sunk in that the war had ended. The harsh reality of normality appeared. The struggle to get enough to eat was still there. Rationing was the stark reminder of the hell the people of this country suffered.

The pieces will have to be put together and only time will dictate when that will happen.

I have got what I came for and more now is the time to really roll out the carpet and follow where it takes me.

The first thing I did was to persuade The Honourable Cavendish to accept my resignation and allow me to go home. I hoped he will not feel I have used the army for my own benefits. I have after all done a massive amount of work not only in Aldershot but also at Mill Hill. I remembered his words at the wedding. "We are sorry to lose Captain D'Abrue. I know Matthew and Gordon will welcome him with open arms. His contribution to the war effort as a non-combatant will never go unnoticed. I can only wish the couple a blissful married life."

The plane landed with a jolt at Atkinson airfield. My father was there to greet me. Several of my friends were waiting in the arrival lounge among them was Inge and Isme the wife of the sugar estate's manager. It was really pleasing to see them. I wondered why Isme was there. I had only met her on two occasions. I guess those meetings may have left her with a feeling of deep friendship.

A hard day's drive home ward bound was more tiring than the nine hours flight from London. However, I sat through it without complaining. My father thought he was a rally driver. With roads like we have it is no wonder.

Mother was crying as if she had unlimited tears to shed. She only stopped when she saw I was getting a bit irritated. The house was filled with people I hardly knew. The maid came running and hugging me so hard mother had to pull her away.

My mother had employed a handy man and he served the drinks with a hint of professionalism, I guess my father must have taught him. I hardly noticed Matthew and Diego standing in a corner with Bell next to her young son. How handsome he looked possessing all the fine points of both his parents. Bell unsure of what to do soon rushed to greet me and introduced him to me. She told him he was just a baby one day old when I held him in my arms and cuddled him. He was smiling with satisfaction. Ben came forward and lifted me like a toy and gave me one of his almighty hugs and the tears from his eyes spoke volumes. After Diego's greeting, it was finally Matthew's turn. He turned to face mother and said "Miriam, you and Joseph will probably throw me out of your house. If you do you have all the right. Ten years ago in Sappanam. I once told this young man that he was the son I never had. He stood up to the rigours of hardship in a land torn with war. He accomplished all he set out to achieve and I am proud of him. I was never a religious person but today I can see that he has made my life complete, and for that reason I will surrender my soul to my maker and ask forgiveness for my errors. Peter D'Abrue. I salute you and the wonderful parents and friends you have. I pray God that now you are back, a happy life is here waiting for you to enjoy. I know I may have stolen your father's thunder. Because I feel I am a member of this great family. Thank you all for listening to my boring rambling."

The applause that followed was reminiscent of that given to 'Lady' Caroline. My mother went up to him and cuddled him for a long time then she asked "You said my son is like the son you never had. You also said that you feel like a member of this family. So are you the brother I never had?

The laughter that followed said everything. It even brought out a seldom seen big smile from my father as he cheered a bit longer than anyone else. It took hours for me to personally chat and toasted with the friends and neighbours present. I seized the opportunity to set the record right with Matthew, I told him "Mathew, you have said it so many times I am the son he never had. May I remind him that I am no longer that son but a nephew by law?"

Tiredness was beginning to show and soon they all drifted away. I was too tired to undress and simply collapsed on the bed and orbited away in dreamland.

When I awoke the next morning I discovered to my great pleasure that my four friends from Sappanam was still here. There were so many things I wanted to know only they can update me.

Before I can get to that stage, Mother brought a set of keys and told me that my East Indian friend has left the keys to my house in the city. She told me that they bought a small estate on the East Bank of the Demerara River. I nearly forgot about owning a house.

Diego looked a lot older than I expected. Bell was as radiant as ever. She and her son went with mother somewhere in another part of the house, leaving us men to chat.

Diego began to give me a description of what Sappanam is like now "I have nearly two hundred cows which is mostly for the beef market. I continue to let the villagers have their share of milk. The young villagers have left and gone to the township. So I was forced to hire two Brazilians that came to trade. They have established themselves and getting on fine with the locals, we continued to thrive. I heard there are a lot of Brazilians in Great falls. That is what attracted the young men there. Matthew is having is having a tough time maintaining order it is like the wild west. Now the Americans are gone things are beginning to return to normal.

The good thing we are still getting gold in smaller quantities. We managed to keep it a secret from outsiders. You would not recognise Sappanam or the people there. They have become westernise wearing fancy clothing and boots brought in by the Brazilians traders from Great falls. There is now a shop and a jeweller and hucksters peddling a lot of nonsense to the villagers. The Americans have established an airfield in the area and small shops are cropping up like maize in the fields. Actually the place below Great falls is nothing but a township."

"Do the Brazilians, working for you or the traders, know of the gold?" I inquired.

"We never mentioned it to them and they are happy working and tending to the herd." Diego told me.

"These are not the same desperados who kidnapped Sugar Bush and terrorised the villagers?" I asked.

"Not at all, these men actually fought a battle with the desperados and I understand they wipe them of the face of the earth. No, they are gentle folks. They have their families with them and they get along just fine with the villagers." He replied.

Ben told me that being Assistant Commissioner was not doing any good for his life. The ladies are afraid of his title and the men do not drink with him anymore. The only pleasure he has is when he comes to Berbice. He complained that Matthew promised to send him to Oreala years ago and he is still waiting.

Matthew was a bit more realistic. He quickly explained his plans to me "Peter." He said. "I once made a proposal to you fifteen years ago to take over the mantle of Commissioner and you can still have your surgery in the city. The way I see it is this. Manny is running the surgery your father left in Sappanam and he is doing fine. You can let him deputise for you when you are not in Sappanam and you can live in my house for the short periods you need to be there. The rangers will do all the work, it will take about two days to put all their reports together and bring it back to the Governor's office, another day going through them with the clerks and you are free to do what you want."

"What will you do if you retire?" I asked.

"I am sixty six years old. The Governor expects me to announce my retirement. As you know I do not want to leave that place in the hands of someone who will bring more traders and build shops and make the place a small town. That is what is in the air and it frightens me. There is another reason a selfish one I may add. If you accept this post I can live there with Sugar Bush and feel comfortable. It will be like old times again. I will send Ben to Oreala to please him. It will be like the old days." After a short pause he asked. "What do you think of my proposal?"

"Let me think about this." I told him, then asked, "who is the new Governor?

"He is a nice enough fellow not as sociable as Gordon. By the way he wants to meet you. I told him of the proposal I put to you and he appeared to like it. He is not keen to send Ben to Oreala. He feels Ben is not the right candidate as assistant Commissioner. Personally I feel he is a bit prejudiced by the fact that Ben is mixed."

"Did you tell him that I am Portuguese?" I asked.

"He did not seem to mind. He realises your classification was political."

"Well there is something good about the man, a realist. How long are you staying here? And when are we to see the Governor?" I asked.

"He is not like Gordon when I can drop in anytime day or night. He sticks to a rigid protocol. An appointment must be made in writing and a formal reply will be sent with date and time. I can understand that Gordon is my friend this chap isn't. There is something important I must tell you before it slip me. The Americans are selling some aeroplanes they call war surplus and I have made a bid in our name when I heard you were coming home. It's a reasonable bid. There are people who thought they can get it for next to nothing. I have a contact with one of the Americans and I was told that my bid looked like a winner. I think when you're fully rested we go to the city and see how we get on. Also in the meantime you can get one of the clerks in the solicitor's office to type a letter for an appointment. We might as well coordinate all our activities before we get to the city. Well, what do you think?"

"You have been doing a lot of planning for me, Matthew; I do like what you planned. I must tell you that when I was in England. I made a vow not to let anyone take over my life. The things I do must in the future be my decision and my decision alone. I fully understand and appreciate what you have done so far, I am grateful especially the part of the aeroplanes. What kind of planes are they? Did you see any of them?"

"I saw the lot; there are some Jeeps that will be put up at auction. That announcement will be in the papers. The planes are light aircrafts used for short journeys in different parts of the interior. They will be quite useful. Did you know they built several airfields at strategic points from Essequibo to Oreala?"

"Oreala, why there?" I asked.

"To keep an eye on the Dutch There were some rumours that German spies were filtering through Cayenne into Surinam pretending to be refugees and the darn Surinamers were letting them through. It's only a river that separates us from them." After a pause, he said. "I noticed you never said a word of my niece. Is everything working well with you?" He asked with some concern.

"I will discuss all the details with you when I am in a more relaxed mood. OK dad." I said jokingly.

"Then let's have a drink and go for that swim we promised ourselves." A joyful Matthew suggested.

I told him I am not in the mood to swim and that maybe tomorrow I will be fit enough for that. Mother came in and sat next to Matthew. She stretched her hand across the table and held mine. The she spoke. "My son, I told you before you went away that the four boys you and your friends helped with their further education will turn out to be ungrateful. You thought I was being prejudiced. I did all the things you asked me to do for them. I let them use the room below just as you asked and to take meat or fish when I visited their village. All this I did because you asked me.

Those boys after their graduation got jobs in the civil service and developed into politicians. They are asking that Britain give British Guiana its independence. If Britain refuses they will bring the country to a standstill with strikes in all government departments. The Governor promised to sack the lot and throw them in prison for sedition. This got them more inflamed. They are now forming a political party called "The Freedom Movement" and people are saying they are being financed by an outside power. Every one is saying it is the Russians but no one knows for sure. They accused the British of reneging on their promise to send back to India all the Indentured labourers they brought from Calcutta and elsewhere. They are going to ruin this country. In the name of God we just finished a war. Is it not time to settle down and count our blessings that almighty God has made us victorious? You must go and see them and talk to them and you Matthew Longhorn, you and your good deeds helped to put ammunition in their hands, you and my son and his friends."

In the morning my father lent me his car and we all drove down to New Amsterdam to let the clerk type the application to see the Governor. We left home deliberately skipping breakfast as we intended to go to the luncheon rooms for Mr Choo's special Full English breakfast. Without telling the waiter she brought each of us a plate of lovely fried sausages, bacon, eggs sunny side up and black pudding with fried bread. Except Ben he was given two plates. It was a pleasure to see him eat. These were breakfasts I heard about in England but never saw one being served. I imagined the rationing is responsible for that.

I planned to visit Andrew McIntosh in Skeldon; It is a good two-hour drive, Hence the lavish breakfast. I was perplexed at Isme's presence at the airport to greet me and perhaps I will get to know why. It is usually near relatives and close friends that turned up to greet arrivals from abroad.

We stopped at various villages to admire the new aqueducts that were recently built for the farmers to produce more food for the war effort.

At the sugar plantation in Skeldon our meeting with Andrew was short. I told Andrew of our plan to buy some light aircraft and wondered if it was possible to use the plantation's air strip on occasion. He immediately agreed and asked to be excused.

He told us that he had arranged a meeting with his staff and he must return to the office. We were invited to sit in the meeting as it would have given us an insight into the running of a sugar plantation. We declined and he left us in the company of his wife. I told her what my mother said of the boys' threat with strikes and asked if it will affect production at the factory. She was not certain but will ask Andrew and let me know. It is then she told us that they will be visiting the manager at the Rose Hall factory later that day on a dinner date. I told her the importance of this information and that I intend to speak with those boys to get to the bottom of this affair. Without warning she began telling me why she was at the airport. "Inge and I have become great friends recently. We spend a lot of week-end together sometimes here or in the East Bank at their small holding. We were visiting that week-end when you arrived. So Persotum asked if I can accompany her to greet you on his behalf. In any case Andrew and I are very fond of all of you. And it isn't because of the great hospitality we received from you." She ended up smiling.

We drove home amid thunder and lightning, just as I thought it would not rain an almighty downpour came with a vengeance. The pot holes were beginning to fill up and my windscreen wipers could barely cope. Thankfully we do not have the traffic as in London. Here in Berbice, there are no more than fifty cars and only a handful at any one time on the road.

Mother had arranged for the boys to come to the house to meet me. They were very happy with the invitation and were already there when we arrived. Courtesies were exchanged and as usual I offered them some refreshments. It was mother who brought up the subject. I immediately asked her to leave this to Matthew and me. She was a bit annoyed and went away.

"Now, young men I heard you are all in the civil service. What department are you in Satar? I asked trying not to be seen as an inquisitor.

"I am a custom officer." He answered and looking a bit apprehensive.

They all told me of the positions they held and expressed gratitude. I told them we are not here to be thanked. It is only we heard disturbing news of their involvement trying to disrupt the government.

"We feel it is time that we take hold of our destiny. Britain and the investors are milking this country dry. They are reneging on their promise to repatriate the indentured labourers back to India.

There are men who claimed that it was promised and now they are old they will never see the families they left behind" Satar told us

"I seem to have had this question with your parents before I left to finish my studies and they agree that they are better off here." I reminded him.

"The truth is they changed their minds. They heard India will become independent and things will be better there among their friends and families." Satar who appears to be the spoke person answered.

"And you Rohit, What do you think? Matthew asked him.

"I am not sure, Sir." He replied

"What department are you in?" Matthew again asked.

"I'm assistant supervisor at the Transport and Harbours Department, Sir." He sheepishly replied.

"You Ali and Naraine where do you work?" I asked.

"I am deputy head post master. Naraine is assistant superintendent for prison." Ali told us, and then he exploded. "Can you not see what is happening? We are all either assistant or deputy of every department we worked. We do all the hard work and the white man just laze around giving orders. When everything is going fine he takes the credit when it isn't, it is the dam coolies to be blamed. I am fed up with it. I hate being called a coolie. If the white man's want respect from us then let him show us respect. IS THAT TOO MUCH TO ASK? Was this loud reply we got from Ali.

Matthew was astonished at his behaviour and told him so in no uncertain terms. Then looking at Sattar he asked. "Why are you looking so apprehensive?"

"I feel disappointed that we have let you down. Not angry, But disappointed. Our parents do not agree with what we are doing and are pleading with us to stop this fight. To be honest with you, sir, our parents do not want to be repatriated. There are a handful of older people that likes the idea but that is all." Sattar explained.

Matthew then went on to tell them the realities of India. "It is a great country many times bigger in size and population than England. To know how much people live there, you take our country for instance; we have less than half a million. India has a thousand times more. It is so large; it is what you call a subcontinent and it is not just a country it is an empire." He took out a shilling from his pocket and showed them the king's head and around the corner of the coin the title of the king. "It says here. King George VI. Fid def Ind imp you know what that means?"

"No, sir, I was not good at Latin." Satar told him.

"It means. "Defender of the Faith, Emperor of India." There are many men who have similar power as a king; they rule their own state with Britain safe guarding their territory with its own soldiers. Is that not caring for the people under her rule? I have met great Indians philosophers, mystics, sadhus, and poets on one side of the coin, and on the obverse side is that great dividing line the caste system. That is more an infringement on the dignity of humanity than it is to be prejudiced or racist. A cruelty so unkind you will not believe it is real. You are right, India will become independent and there is talk of dividing the country one part for the Muslims and another for the Hindus. You want to go to India? I will buy you the tickets tomorrow if you are brave enough to face the harsh realities that await you. If not; your loyalties is to the crown until such time as you see fit to don the mantle of leadership and create your own destiny. When you are ready Britain will not stand in your way. This I promise."

Matthew reached in his pocket and took out what looks like the cutting from an old newspaper. He unfolded it and showing it to them. He said "what is written here has been my guidance through life. Your father is a religious man, the pandit of your village; I would like you to read it for all to hear."

After reading it he folded the page neatly and returned it to Matthew. The he asked "Have you met the man who wrote this?"

"I have" Matthew proudly told him. "He was one of the many intellectuals I met on the banks of the Ganges. Anyone who looked at them would not believe that he possess such a great intellectual capacity.

I would like you to think what Peter and I did for you, not to be ever grateful but to understand why. When you have found the reason then I think you will have a different view of us. I have had my say. Is there anything you would like to add, Peter?"

"You have said all that is needed and I think they are intelligent enough to understand our position. Having said that I would like to tell you something I learnt during my stay in England. It is a wonderful country. The people are not like some of them who came here only as administrators and feel they are more superior to all of you put together. In actual fact, they are just as ordinary as any of you. Just the same you must show respect, they are the bosses. I had the privilege to meet a Rajkumar. Do any of know why he was there in the heart of England dinning with Generals and Field Marshalls and even had an audience with the King? His men came to support the main army in France and he was there to give them a talk of loyalty to the Crown. His men went with renewed fighting spirit and some made a name for themselves earning medals of gallantry presented to them by the King himself. If those men did not see the good Britain is doing fighting suppression. Do you think they would risk their lives?"

"Did you meet the King?" Ali asked.

"I was not worthy enough to have that honour." I replied.

"Did you not fight in the war, sir?" Narine asked.

"No Narine! I told him not everyone in the army is a combatant. There are lots of people who have to care for the wounded, the Doctors, nurses and dentists. I was one of those persons. In between I was studying for my degree.

Now I am going to tell you something I only just this minute decided to do. Commissioner Longhorn wants to retire and ask me to take the post as Commissioner. Not because I am married to his niece. This offer was made before that. Until just a few minutes ago I was uncertain. Now I have decided if it were offered I will accept. Do you want to know why?" They all nodded. I then said. "This is to prove to you that a local man can have the job that was set aside only for the English but he must prove himself."

"Are you really married to the Commissioner's niece? Sir… Narine again asked, I nodded.

His response was surprizing. "This will make our town very important. We are proud of you and we will take your advice. Be patient with us. We are learning."

We watched them walked away with heads held high. Matthew and I went upstairs to enjoy mother's cooking.

Ben was already eating when we reached upstairs. He told us that Diego and Bell are preparing to return to Sappanam in the morning. Any business left unsettled will have to get sorted out before they go. No sooner we sat down to our dinner they appeared with their young son. He looked at me inquiringly and I asked. "What's your name sonny?"

He replied confidently. "My name is Diego Matthew Peter Ben DeSouza"

"Will I remember all those names? I asked.

"You can call me Young Diego if you want." Again confidence was written all over his face. "It is easy to remember. First my father's name then the Commissioner's and yours and uncle Ben's." It was amusing the way he said it.

As I said before the dining table was always the battle station where all matters of importance are discussed. This was no different. Here we reviewed our agenda and came to the most important decisions, the aeroplanes. Matthew assured me that it is a certainty we will win. He also told me it would be to our advantage to buy some of the jeeps as well when it comes up for auction. It will make travelling in the bush much easier and we can fly to any destination where there is an airfield.

CHAPTER 19

Getting at the Truth

We arrived to see mother and father sitting their hands across the table and clasped. Their faces looked sad and worried. I went to cheer them up. Instead my mother asked quite seriously. "Tell me again son. Are you really married to a Jewish woman?"

"That is an absurd question, mother! Why this sudden change of heart? You told me you were happy that I found happiness in myself finally now this nonsensical question. I am getting absolutely frightened of your attitude."

"Now look at it from my point of view. We are Catholics. Margot Ferreira was very much in love with you. Did you know that?"

"I flirted with Margot for a while I was more interested in Marina. Everyone was. Why this sudden change of heart with Christine. You knew Margot had a nose like a screw. Did you not notice that?" I said in defence of my choice.

"Her nose was not like a screw as you say. I must admit it had a graceful curve." She pointed out then returning to the original topic she began to give her reason. "I was thinking of the future of this family. Your children will be Jewish and so will your grandchildren. Can you not see the future of this family as Catholics will be dead?"

I was getting really angry with my mother for the first time. My father was not helping. He sat there listening. "I will tell you something you may forget. It was with Matthew who is a Jew, made me a millionaire and it is his niece I married not because I wanted to put things in their right perspective but because I really love her. Yes, she is a Jew. She did not choose her religion when she was born. She was born in it like I am. Now I feel disgusted that my own parents are denying me the chance to choose what religion I may follow. That condescending and bigoted priest they sent from Rome should go back and preach his sermons there and leave us to get on with our lives in a more humble way."

I looked at my father and with a stern voice I said. "Look at my father sitting there all quiet. In fact he is a bloody bully and you mother! Don't speak to me about religion I never cared much for it. I want to live like Uncle Matthew. Yes mother, Uncle Matthew. I love him more than I care to mention. I was stranded in the jungle doing my father's bidding. He was getting all the credits while Manny and I did all the hard work year after year. Who do you think nudged me to achieving my goal in England? It was the same Jewish family you so much wanted me to forsake just for your own idealism. What about Lord Cavendish and our very own Governor. Are you going to deny them hospitality because they are Jews? I am ashamed of my parents. You should have had more children. To share your love with them instead you are suffocating me with love, selfishness and religion for your own ends.

If the Governor confirms my appointment I shall take the post of Commissioner and live the way I wanted. I shall always have a love for you both irrespective of our differences. I shall grab that rudder with both hands and steer my own course in life. If I should founder on the rocks it will be my mistake. I may even learn from that and not blaming anyone for my misfortune. If father was so interested in my affair he would have done much more to see me through university and a first class career. Instead, I had to settle for everything second class. Registration, Registration my arse, Degree in dentistry... Second class, Citizenship... second class because I married a Jew." I was getting hysterical and could not care if I died this moment. It seems happiness is only shadowing me, showing its face for one brief moment and disappearing the next."

My dignity was restored when mother hugged and consoled me with the promise that Christine will be very welcome in this house as a daughter and the woman her beloved son loves and married. Remembering that I mentioned the fact that I had become a millionaire through Matthew, she then asked with concern.

"I did not know you had so much money, son. What are you going to do with it?"

"I really don't know. The source of that money has a grey past and it bothers me. I understand Uncle Matthew's explanation but it still has a grey area. Maybe I will do what he would like me to do." I replied.

"And what would that be?" She asked.

"Helping those poor unfortunates down at the village I imagine." I told her.

"I'd rather you give it to the church than those ungrateful miserable people." She suggested.

"I'd rather burn it than give it to the church. They are all exploiters. Pretending to take religion to the unfortunates instead they are nothing short of spies for the country they represent. And I am not going to refer to the conquistadors. I will leave it in the bank for now until I can see a way to use it properly. I will have a decent salary and pension if my appointment is confirmed and besides I will make enough to live quite comfortable on what I earn as a dentist. Perhaps father will want to retire and I can take over his lucrative practice. First and more important of all, I must attend to the security and happiness of Christine and Elizabeth." I felt good telling my mother what I really thought.

Matthew and the others must have heard the loud talking. I hope they did not hear the entire story. Ben came next to me and put a comforting arm over my shoulder. I dried my eyes and asked that we conclude our plans for the aeroplanes.

"Not yet." Mother interrupted. "Now that you are leaving this house and Matthew is here I would like him to explain to me the source of those diamonds you say has a grey past."

It was no point telling her it is not her business. I decided to remain quiet while Matthew gave his explanation.

He began by saying, "It does not have a grey past. Those Brazilians could not buy anything with those diamonds from the traders."

"And why is that?" Mother asked.

"The traders were ordinary people who do not know a thing about diamonds." Matthew began to explain. "They recognised gold and that is the currency they accept. If the Brazilians could not purchase their supplies they would have been stranded and left hungry and perhaps die. I know the pound of nuggets we gave them was only a fraction of the worth of those stones. They had no alternative but to hand over the handful of diamonds for their survival." He then turned to Diego and Ben and asked. "Did you not notice that they were gone before we woke up the next morning?"

"I was wondering that myself." Ben told him and giving his own explanation. He continued "I thought that because they had a fight with Diego they decided to break camp."

I felt relieved now that the truth is out. I told mother. Then I turned to Matthew and asked. "Why did you not say so the first time?"

"I only wanted to add a bit of harmless mystery in it." He replied with a school boy grin. He then continued. "I heard you were talking about religion. We couldn't help over hearing what was said. So I would like to ask your mother a question." Turning to my mother he asked "Can I Miriam?"

"What is the question? She inquired.

"Your mother's maiden name was Rosenberg. Was it not?"

"What's this got to do with what we were discussing? Mr Longhorn?" She asked brusquely.

That question unsettled her and it showed when she referred to Matthew as Mr Longhorn.

"The only Rosenberg I knew, and remember, I have been here for over a quarter of a century. Is a jeweller in Georgetown? I think he usually comes to Berbice every month to sell some of his work."

My mother put a hand up and stopped him from going further. She then announced that she will tell us the real story.

"You were right he is the same gentleman. One day he was coming to catch the last boat from Rosignol but missed it. As you know there are no hotels or guest houses there. So he hired a fisherman to take him across the river to New Amsterdam. Half way across a heavy wind turned the boat over. He was desperately trying to save his sixteen year old daughter, his wife and the box containing his jewellery.

Unfortunately by the time the fisherman righted the boat he found that his wife and the jewel box had disappeared. You could understand how distressed he was. He eventually got a taxi and went to my grandmother's house. He always stayed there when he visited. My grandfather gave him and the girl some dry clothes and asked my father, who was only twenty at the time to make them a hot drink.

In the morning they reported the incident to the police and a search went on to look for the body. Weeks went by and no body was found until this day. Mr Rosenberg was so distressed that he was unable to think properly. Eventually, he and my grandfather decided that since Mr Rosenberg was unable to cope with a teenager she was allowed to remain in my grandparents care. I am not going into all the details. The short of it is that Esther Rosenberg and my father were married in the Catholic Church after some negotiation with the priest. Is that the story you wanted to hear Mr Longhorn." She started to cry and apologised to Matthew for addressing him so formally. She invited Matthew to tell the rest of the story.

"Well the truth is," he stopped and asked my mother. "Do you really want me to tell everything Miriam? My mother nodded. He continued "Simon Rosenberg was a Jew from Germany. He came here after the Great War. I met him and his young wife at a hotel I was staying in. He was much older than me. So we were never close friends but I occasionally visited the family when time permitted."

Matthew reached in his inner pocket of his jacket and produced a diamond crusted star. He showed it to my mother and then turning to me he said. "This diamond encrusted Magen David was given to me by your grandfather on my fortieth birthday. I never displayed it around my neck but I kept it as a memory to his generosity. This is worth quite a few thousand dollars. Why would a man who I only met a few times give me a birthday gift? Was it because he knew he was dying and wanted to leave something to be remembered by? I really don't know the answer. I would like you to have it Miriam, a memento to remember your father."

Mother told him to keep it and give it to Elizabeth when she comes. "It will be the perfect gift from her great grandfather. Don't you think?"

There was a pause and without replying to mother's request he insisted that mother tells us the rest. She was still distressed and would not say anything. Matthew proposed to finish the story as gently as possible.

"The truth is, Miriam you are a Jew according to Jewish laws. Peter is also a Jew by the simple fact that his mother is. There you have it. What the hell does it matter what religion you are. It is these small things that cause nations to split, creating civil wars and upheaval in society." Matthew concluded.

"I really don't feel different, as a matter of fact I think I feel a sense of pride." I turned to my father and asked. "Did you know this?" He nodded without showing any sign of his thoughts.

Matthew decided to make a point that in comparison between the plight of the Jews in Germany and that of the East Indians in this country. "In Germany the Jewish people are accused of hoarding vast wealth and depriving the ordinary Germans of their birth right. What the hell gives them the right to make those accusations and embark on a mission of genocide? That is exactly what will happen to the East Indians here. I heard on many occasions the Blacks accusing the East Indians of hoarding their money. They own all the businesses, buying all the land in the villages. One Black man remarked by saying to me that wherever you look you see an Indian name on all the shops in town: Samaroo, Persaud, Sukhoo, Khan, only to mention a few. No Black man has a shop he told me. When I told him that it is their fault they did not try to establish a business for themselves. He defended himself by saying that if they had the money they would. I then pointed out that the East Indians plant their rice fields and vegetables gardens and worked twelve hours a day to get the money for the things they needed in life. Establishing businesses and sending their children to be qualified as doctors and lawyers. They, on the other hand, wanted to have a nice suit to go to dances and spend their salary before the month's end. It's a nonsensical situation, if you want something go and get it. Don't wait for someone else to get it and then say. That should have been mine. I am happy to adapt to my way of life. Inner peace is real happiness. A treasure no man can take from you. I am happy Peter is beginning to think like that."

My mother was sobbing quietly and my father tried to console her. I knew she was distressed when she started singing a hymn… "Oh come, on come, Emanuel. And ransom captive Israel."

It was the kind of hymn that sent a feeling of sadness. I could not help thinking of the millions that perished in the concentration camps undoubtedly the majority being Jews. I thought of my own new found identity and wondered how on earth I would be able reconcile myself. This new found religion with the path uncle Matthew showed to inner peace and happiness.

Matthew noticed I was in deep contemplation. He knew I was troubled by what was revealed and the only way forward was to suggest we leave with Diego for Georgetown tomorrow as the jeeps will be auctioned at the sea wall that afternoon. Obtaining the aeroplanes is out of our hands at the moment. It would not be long before that is announced. I have confidence in Matthew. He seems to know the right people and although the Governor is not his close friend they do enjoy a healthy working relationship.

With our agenda firmly fixed I went and fetched a bottle of my father's best malt from his cabinet. I saw him looking at me from the corner on his eyes and wondering why I have chosen that special bottle. That was because it was going to be a special occasion. Bell was in shape to take the odd drink, so I asked the maid to bring my mother's crystal whisky glasses from the side board and a bucket of ice. Ben was eager to assist her. We all knew he had an ulterior motive.

"Gentlemen" I began. "Today is a historic day for me. Not only has my identity been revealed. It is also the last day I shall be a resident of this house. I leave tomorrow for the city and a new life. I have friends I can trust and that is worth more than all the diamonds there are in the earth. I shall miss this house I grew up in, its cherished memories and the parties and the love I enjoyed from my parents and especially my grandmother. She perhaps is thinking that I have forgotten her. She lives in my heart at all times. When I visit her the next time she will get the surprise of her life. So join me as I drink a toast to my friends, my memories and to the future."

"I have something to toast about." Matthew started. "It has become an old joke but this has a significant connection. Some years ago I met a young man keen to undertake any problem without complaining or asking for help. I recognised the quality in him and that is why I am now going to repeat that famous statement of "Him being the son I never had." Deep down in my heart it was as realistic as I meant it to be. By a strange coincidence he is now officially my nephew-in-law and I am proud of him."

There was a genuine tear in Uncle Matthew's eyes. My mother saw it and handed him her handkerchief. Even the maid was crying. I hope Ben will not join them, then we will have a wake instead.

My father turned to me and said "Son I did not know you were so hurt with my selfishness. It was unintentional. I am going to make amends. First let's have one of my special parties. The ones I reserved for my friends from the city."

Turning to the maid he ordered "Isabellala go to the village and bring some of the men and their ladies. Tell them I am having a special party for my son and his friends and be quick about it."

My father for the first time in his life put a comforting arm on my shoulder and looking at the special whisky I cheekily took from the cabinet said with a wink. "I have lots more where that comes from."

Ben wanted to go down stairs to see the village folks dancing their Indian dances and singing in their high pitched voices songs of love and tragedy. It was a welcoming sight and to everyone's great surprised Matthew joined in the dancing and even humming the tunes to their songs. It was really hilarious watching him doing all the right moves. The ladies gave him as much room as he wanted. They did not want him stepping on their bare feet with his desert boots. They were so proud that he joined them in their dances they knelt and touched his feet with their forehead. It was a moving scene, their humility made me felt sad only for a short while. I was soon in the party mood again. It was Ben's turn to show what his sixteen stone can do and when the maid joined him it was even more hilarious than Matthew doing his bit.

Stranger still was when mother came down to see the fun and grabbed my dad and tried doing the impossible. The village ladies was so overwhelmed with what they were seeing they threw flowers at her and encouraged her movement with their clapping.

Eventually, everyone was dancing which drew a crowd looking on from the street and clapping to the rhythm of the music. This caused mother to hastily withdraw and went upstairs.

It was a well-established fact that Europeans or Portuguese are not seen in public to socialise with the East Indians or Blacks. If it is done it must be away from prying eyes. What was happening in my garden was a spontaneous reaction to joy. The villagers were well aware of this protocol and even though they enjoyed it did it with reservations. It can easily be seen that they are trying to assert equality in that brief social encounter. Nonetheless, they were extremely happy and will boast of it for generations.

I thought of the complexities of human behaviour that generations of servitude were able to transform an entire civilised culture into one of subservience. Here, now for the first time in the history of British Guiana peasants were dancing with the white elite of the empire and both sides shedding their inhibitions and enjoying a moment as human beings. It would only take a man of Matthew Longhorn's calibre to create such an atmosphere. My dear mother was embarrassed that the folks from the village were watching and enjoying the show, afraid of the gossips that would ensue.

I was disappointed when it came to an abrupt end. Even Matthew looked disappointed and made it known to my father.

The four young men kept a low profile. I could see they were enjoying themselves all the same. Clapping their hands and wriggling to the tune. I went and told them of my plans and we were expecting that they honour their promise to us. I even promised that I would try to get them to Sappanam if and when I settled there. It was time to say our goodbyes and left them enjoying the rest of the evening. Matthew gave the head of the village twenty dollars to split among the rest. He deliberately gave it in full view of some others watching. This was to prevent him pocketing it all for himself.

Before we departed the four young men came and started speaking to Matthew. My attention was drawn to the sound of unfamiliar laughter. Then I saw the four laughing and joking with Matthew. I heard Ali ask Matthew. "Have you brothers and sisters?"

"I have one brother and no sisters" Matthew told him.

"Your parents sent you to the best school they could afford. Is that not true?

"What school is that? Another asked.

"It is called Eton and it is the best school in the world. Only very few privileged boys are sent there." Matthew answered and then asked. "Why all these questions Ali? Is there a purpose to it?"

"There is, Sir. One more question. If you had a sister where would she be educated?"

"I suppose at some girls' finishing school in Paris or Switzerland when she finished her formal education. There they will be taught to be ladies, a trait that must come as natural as drinking a cup of tea and acquainting themselves with the arts and music and in general to be the perfect hostess at parties when they are married. I hope that answered all your questions."

Ali smiled and responded by saying. "It is no different to our world. We do not have the schools you have in England. The pattern of life is just the same." He put up his hand as if to stop Matthew from saying anything. "In our society the boys are given all the chances for as much education as money can buy. The girls are taught to cook and keep house and look after babies they are never given the same opportunity as the boys. You see my point Mr Commissioner."

There was a short silence then they all started laughing at Ali's comparison.

The party came to its end and as we retreated for bed I felt clean and free it was like walking on air. The only thing to make it better was if Christine was my side. The truth of the diamonds has lifted a great weight from me and the fact that my real identity was established only made me happier. It was a pity Diego and Bell did not participate in the dancing. I was just as happy as the time when Matthew invited us to his club for that champagne dinner. Inge came momentarily to mind. I soon dismissed the thoughts and went upstairs.

I started feeling nostalgic leaving this house, not knowing if ever I will return. I went to the dining room and looked at the table where important decisions are made and challenges overcome. Where truth is wriggled out and sanity prevailed. I thought of the maid, she joined us when her father died in an accident at the factory and mother, out of pity gave her a job. I never knew her name until my father ordered her to bring the villagers to prepare for the party. It is a nice name. I shall call her by it before I leave and do something significant to make her life better. I will ask mother to do the same.

Matthew is a marvel in my life and he will live there forever. No kinder man exists in the world as far as I am concerned. Revealing the truth of my heritage took a lot of courage. He is only a friend and to meddle so deep in our private lives was indeed heroic.

I am beginning to feel a sense of camaraderie with the new Governor. He may not be the same friendly type but there is a sense of fairness in him.

Tomorrow the result of the winning bidder will be published in the Gazette. It will be interesting. This has nothing to do with the government of British Guiana it is entirely American.

It should have given me concern to be restless but as it is I am too immersed in the outcome of the auction. Diego promised to remain with us. It will help; his knowledge of engines can be invaluable. I remembered him saying he was assistant engineer on the bauxite ship.

On the morning after my last night at the home I had always known, I heard the maid Isabella instructing two men to remove my bed from my room. I ran and held them back for an explanation. I was told my mother had given the bed to one of the men in the village. I was furious. I knew I would no longer be a permanent resident in this house, but I was not allowing my bed to be given away.

My mother came in and ordered the men to carry on with her instructions and she invited me to the dining room. I knew it had to be something serious for her to give away the bed and ordering me to the dining room confirmed my fear. The only trouble is, not knowing what that problem is.

"Sit down, son" she said with a calmness I seldom heard. "I had hoped the men would come and take that cursed bed away when you were gone. Unfortunately, you witnessed its removal so I am obliged to tell you the reason. I heard that Inge and you were found cuddled up together and I am devastated to learn that my son has brought pollution in this house."

"Just a minute Mother, Who told you that?"

"I am not at liberty to say. You have no right to ask me that question."

"Why do I not have that right?"

"Because you know it is the darn truth." She shouted.

"So Isabella has opened her big mouth yet again, I'll strangle her." I yelled.

"For telling the truth?" she asked and continued. "And what will happen to you after you strangle her. Become a murderer? What will your wife and daughter think of you? Gather your senses and leave this house with peace in your heart. Think of your uncle Matthew and all the friends you have. Isabella has an unrestrained mouth. You know that. It should be no surprise to you that she spoke out.

Before you leave I want to tell some simple facts. Those East Indians that went abroad and married European women did it not so much for love but a trophy to exhibit for social acceptance. That Ingeborg, you said she is a German refugee, did your friend know of her family's back ground before they married. I should not think so. She knew the reason he married her, if she was not the refugee she claimed to be do you think she would have married him? I leave that for you to sort out."

"You are wrong mother. She and her father fled Germany because of persecutions and arrived in London just before the war. A Jewish society for displaced persons provided them with a house in Golders Green and assisted the father to restart his export business. When her father died she went and worked at a club and that is where they met. Maybe he is not aware of the family's entire back ground but that does not make her a loose woman." I thought I had my argument all sewn up when my mother asked me. "What sincere woman would make love to another man when she is married? Would you be able to defend her truthfully?"

"The women from Europe that marry the boys here know of the life style. They can expect a big house with servants a life beyond their wildest dream. What stopped those young men returning home and marrying a decent girl from the village is beyond me. I am so happy you are married to a woman from a great family" Mother then hugged and squeezed me as hard as she could and kissed both my cheeks while the tears flowed.

Christine will not be a trophy to be exhibited. I do not need that. No trophy or labels to say who I am. I am Peter D'Abrue a qualified dentist and the first local resident to be given the second most important job in the land. Commissioner of the hinterlands, those are my labels and I am proud of them. Isabella came to tell me that that my friends were waiting and the taxi was here, Then she hurried away afraid I might do her some harm. Eventually, I confronted her as she placed the last suitcase in the taxi. I held her by the arm and reproached her for exposing my secret.

She swore it was not meant to be; it only came out during a conversation about European women and their status in the country.

CHAPTER 20

The Great Auction

The beach at the sea front was packed with bidders from all over the country. They were milling around and poking at the jeeps that lay on an orderly line. Also there were two wind chargers and half a dozen lighting plants. I looked at what was exhibited with great interest. Some of the men sat in the seats and pretended they were driving. It looked rather foolish. Matthew looked around to see if he could spot anyone in authority but to no avail. He tried clapping his hands to attract the crowd's attention. This did not work. Frustrated by the commotion Ben took a stick and started beating an old oil drum next to one of the jeeps. This had the desired effect, Matthew stood in one of the jeeps and told the crowd not to meddle with the machines and that they could be held responsible for any damages. He did not quite finish when an American came and asked. "Who the hell are you?"

Matthew stretched out his hand in welcome and told him. "I am Matthew Longhorn, Commissioner of the hinterlands."

He was impressed and shook Matthew's hand enthusiastically. I left them chatting and went with Diego to have a closer look at the articles on auction. Diego pointed out the ones he thought would be in better condition motor wise, and also the wind chargers would be ideally suited for Sappanam. They would be quieter than a lighting plant. This is solely for the wild life's benefit.

I agreed with him and made out a list of what to bid for, it was no contest with the opposition. Their offers were ridiculous. Matthew soon made them look like amateurs and we secured all that we wanted.

After the auction, Matthew offered to buy the American a drink and his Club was the right venue to impress the American further. Diego and Bell decided to return to Sappanam. So we left Ben to take charge of our properties and secure them at the warehouse by the wharf and then to join us at my home.

I sent Matthew and the American upstairs while I instructed the gardener of his next duty. I was surprised to find him sleeping in the rest room. Part of his duty was also as a guard, this was certainly neglected. He was more surprised when I roused him and he hurriedly tried to put some clothes on and freshen himself.

I scolded him for his neglect and gave him the instructions for the garden. "Now do you understand what I wanted you to do?"

"Yes, sir, you want me to dig up the all the vegetables patches and to prepare the ground for flowers, is that what you really want sir? What should I do with the vegetables?" He asked unsure of the instructions.

"Yes, Carmichael, I want you to dig up all the vegetables and prepare the ground for a flower garden. I shall employ a professional gardener to show you what to do. I want this to look like the gardens in Buckingham Palace. As for the vegetables you can do whatever you like with it. Eat them or sell them," was my final instructions.

He shrugged in a nonchalant way and went about his task. I went upstairs to find Matthew and his friend in deep conversation. I thought we'd have a drink while waiting for Ben. I was finally introduced to the gentleman and we sat down to enjoy a drink. It was in between drinks that Matthew's idea for the future became evident. It emerged that Sebastian is a Spanish American and he is one of the finest flyer in our country. He was not keen to return to the USA. Instead he preferred to go to Sappanam and prepare the landing strips that were initially laid down by Matthew's predecessor.

"I wanted to be my own man for a long time. This is the first opportunity I have had and by Christ I am not going to let it go." He told us like a man who has found his El Dorado.

Moreover, he was prepared to teach us to fly, which sounded great and exciting. He then told us. "First we must win that bid. If we did not win he could find us some decent ones left in the Essequibo. The American Government could not be bothered to send them back home, so they will lie there and rust. I will never let that happen. Of course, I will have permission to do that. A few dollars under the table will secure my rights to those beauties."

"Why were they left there?" I asked.

"They needed some repairs and no one was troubled to do that. I can make them air worthy." He assured us.

"What will happen to those planes in Essequibo if we win the bid?" I asked.

"We can always dismantle those that are beyond repairs for spare parts. The others we will use for our business. That's what we will do." He was delighted with his own suggestion. So were we.

Ben arrived and told us the jeeps and the others things were safely locked up. We told him that we are going to Matthew's Club for dinner and he must get some proper attire for the occasion. He became grumpy about the idea. He relented when Matthew insisted that an assistant Commissioner was to show his class where it matters.

A quick trip to Bookers stores was easy, finding him a tuxedo was another matter, we did get the in store tailor to do his best and he looked handsome in it.

The usher was surprised to see us dressed like four grooms going to the altar.

"Welcome to the Club gentlemen and I am indeed impressed that you see fit to come here for the third time, and properly dressed."

Matthew gave him a huge tip for which he was thankful. Sebastian wanted to impress also gave him a five US dollar bill. This really sent his eyes popping.

Matthew ordered a magnum and when that was finished Sebastian ordered another. We were half way through when Aubrey and Marina came in accompanied by Persotum and Inge. We invited them to join us which they gracefully accepted. We discussed our success at the auction and also told them of our hope in securing the aeroplanes. They seemed baffled at our success.

As is customary in a close knit community and confirming with social colonial etiquette Marina turned to Matthew and asked.

"Can you afford all that military hardware?"

"I cannot… Peter can." He replied casually.

"Well you see Marina when you have a wife and daughter to look after you will have to look to the future." I said proudly.

"We were not in the knowledge you were married and have a daughter" She said in surprise. Then added, "Was there a reason for this secrecy?"

"There is a reason I did not mention it before as I did not have a bride and daughter to show. But when they come this Christmas This town will see the biggest party in its history. I will set it ablaze with fireworks you have never seen before."

"Are you going to invite us poor people to your extravagant celebration?" She again asked.

"You are my friends poor or not there will be an invitation for all my friends. Besides, I heard Aubrey is doing rather well." She blushed at my remark.

Persotum volunteered to get another magnum. This was declined for the simple fact that we had a meeting with the Gordon in the morning.

As usual we were punctual arriving at the Governor's office. We did not have to wait long. In the office we were received with a smile and hand shake from him then he offered us a seat. He turned to Matthew and asked. "Is this your final request? You wanted to retire and for me to approve the Commissionership to Mr Peter D'Abrue."

"This is a courtesy request." Matthew told him and went on to say. "I was appointed by the foreign office and as such I should have submitted my resignation to them. I did write, and told them of my decision to consult with you on this matter as it relates to the fact that I wish to name my successor and also to retain a non-stipendiary post as a consultant to my successor an assistant Commissioner."

"I was not aware we had an assistant Commissioner," the Governor told him.

"This was mutually agreed with your predecessor and me. I pointed out to him that Berbice is an ocean away and that by having an assistant Commissioner it would give the government a better insight of what is happening in the hinterlands." Matthew told him feeling a bit embarrassed.

"I will not object to what was determined before I came here. It is good thinking Matthew. Good thinking indeed." He then turned to me and asked. "Are you prepared to accept this post and all the other requirements Matthew forwarded?"

I told him I was happy with all the proposals. He then said that an official letter would be sent confirming the date of my appointment and salary. He was about to say something further when his aide brought in the Gazette and showed it to him.

He looked at it and announced to Matthew. "You have won the bid for the aeroplanes. What do you intend to do with them?"

Matthew turned and gave me a victory hug. The Governor expressed his delight at our success. We then shook hands and departed. We must now inform Sebastian and the others of our good luck.

We met Sebastian and asked him to take control of events. We were not trained pilots and did not have a clue of taking the aeroplanes to their destination. He soon put our minds at rest by forwarding his own idea of setting up a business in partnership with us.

It turned out that Sebastian intended to do regular flights to the West Indies and break the monopoly of the other privately run Air Company. His share would be seventy per cent of the gross takings. From which he would take his salary and maintain the aeroplanes. This sounded fair to us and we immediately agreed. In the interim he would have to teach us to fly and leave at least one air craft with us for our personal use. This was agreed instantly.

I was so excited. There are so many things to be done. I must await the official letter before doing anything. Planning will not hurt. I decided to do this with Matthew, the Rest House was still after all his and I would not want him to think I was ejecting him from the home he had known for quarter of a century.

All the proposals I put forward were agreed enthusiastically. I would extend the house for my family and give him his own quarters and bring it up to modern standards the smaller house will be for Ben and Sebastian. The wind chargers will supply electricity for all our needs and a pump to bring the clear clean water from cold stream. It will be luxury.

Matthew was not so keen about all these changes. I pointed out to him that his niece will be happy with the new arrangements. I also pointed out that the severe changes she will experience might not encourage her to stay and then there is Elizabeth, her young mind needs gradual acceptance of her new surrounds. Eventually, he reluctantly relented and expressed delight at the prospect of having a family around.

Ben was not too excited of being sent to Oreala. I was not too keen either as I would miss him enormously. He will be a great asset to Christine in helping to look after Elizabeth. We would have to wait on the confirmations.

The airfield at Sappanam would not accommodate an aircraft without proper preparation and we were not willing to take a chance of landing there so would have to charter the amphibious one to get us there. We were making use of the jeeps to take us around while Sebastian and Ben went about preparing the aircrafts. Matthew and I went around visiting friends as there was nothing else to do.

It did not take that many days for the confirmation to come through. At last I was officially the Commissioner and Mathew is my consultant. The sad news was that Ben would not be given the post as Assistant Commissioner. In no uncertain terms the Governor stated that his advisors were against handing such an important job to a man with no experience. It further stated that Matthew and I would have to make regular trips to Would and Matthew would be paid for every trip he makes. Not what we wanted but it did have a bright side to it. Ben can remain as my unofficial assistant without pay the honour will please him. Matthew and I knew the real truth in the advice given to the Governor. If Ben had not had a trace of black in him the post would have been his. That was why we could not tell him.

When he and Sebastian came home that evening he saw the envelope with the crown stamped on it and knew it was the letter of my confirmation.

He looked at me and asked, "Well did you get the job?"

I told him I did but his was not confirmed.

"I am so happy about that." He said which surprised us both. He then said "I would have been unhappy there without you around me giving me orders and getting me drunk."

"You are not getting off that easily. Peter has made you his assistant child minder when the family gets here." Matthew told him.

I have not seen Ben so happy for a long time. "Me a child minder Are you sure? I can't wait to boss around your little daughter when she gets here." He was so jubilant, it was hard to imagine.

CHAPTER 21

Sappanam Revisited

It was the gentlest of landing this aircraft made as we touched down on the Demerara. As usual the entire village came out to greet us. There were shouts of greetings and the chief came and personally greeted us in the traditional tribal manner. Matthew as usual expressed his thanks in their language and at the same time told them of my new position. I now know that I must learn to speak their language if I am to succeed, not only as a Commissioner, but also as their dentist. It immediately sprung to mind the promise I made to the people at Triangle that I would visit them and check their teeth. Right now my priority was to extend this house and make it habitable for my family and Matthew.

After breakfast the next morning I asked Matthew what is my first task. He told me to recall all the rangers and give them the good news and to report to me directly of any incident. It appears simple enough. We were still having breakfast when Diego and Bell appeared. Young Diego has grown a lot and into a handsome lad. Standing next to sugar Bush made him look rather taller.

Sebastian and Ben went about measuring the house and the extension to be built. He was also busy drawing plans for his own dwelling. He came up and told me that the first thing we must do is to get the wind charger up and running then the pump for the water from Cold Stream. "I tell you what sir, you leave everything to me and I will give you a big surprise." Sebastian assured me. I was beginning to like and appreciate this American.

Diego was not sure what part he would play in all these undertakings. It was Matthew who told him that he was a partner in all our enterprises and we expect him to give his full cooperation. He willingly agreed and hugged his young son to show delight. He quickly assisted Sebastian with the measuring and planning. Which freed me from matters I am totally unacquainted.

The pilot of the amphibious plane came to remind him that the tide would be turning and if the level of water drops and exposed to some of the rocks the plane would not be able to take off. Eventually, he finished his work and Diego offered to accompany him to Georgetown and send the jeeps up with the supply boat. Ben would have to assist with the cows. I left this place for nearly three years and I was eager to visit the lodge and see how things have changed. I was so excited about the proposed changes I could hardly contain myself.

After the plane took off, I asked Matthew to send word to the rangers to attend a meeting as I would like to discuss a few changes I wish to make. Matthew looked at me inquiringly. I assure him that he would be pleased when they are unfolded.

Sebastian had accumulated a band of enthusiastic young men from the other villages to assist with the building. They were progressing faster than I thought. Their expertise in house building was a great asset.

It was several days before the supply boat arrive. Thankfully Diego was there with the Jeeps and the wind chargers and also the pump. He looked in amazement at the rapid rate of expansion of the two buildings. He asked Matthew's permission to use his store room. The pylon for the wind charger had to be left where it was.

The next few days Diego and Ben were busy digging the foundation for the pylon. Some of the villagers offered to help and the work was done on time. I watched in amazement as the wind charger was placed on the pylon and hoisted on its foundation. There were two harpy eagles made of wood with mobile wings that can move in the wind. Matthew asked what purpose they served and Diego explained to him that the imitation harpy would deter the local birds from flying into the propellers. It serves two purposes one is to save the birds and the other to prevent damage to the propellers. All that was needed was to wait for Sebastian to arrive and connect the electrical wires. The pace of progress was satisfactory.

By this time, Diego had fiddled with the engines of the jeeps and was using one for his daily travel to and from the lodge. As always there was a crowd of children following him and he would sound the horn to amuse them further. I thought if he could go to his lodge with the jeep then it would be possible to go to Cold Stream with it also. Matthew liked the idea and it was agreed that the following day we would make that trip. Ben was busy painting the inside of Sebastian's house so I thought it was time for a drink before he gets here.

It was my first ride in the jeep. I sat in the back with Matthew while Ben sat next to Diego in the front. Diego made a detour via his lodge to pick up his son who sat comfortably on Ben's lap and we were on our way. To see Cold Stream again and it would bring back memories of our first find of nuggets and later more of it.

The place had completely changed, the hill was a mere mound and the water was flowing faster than usual. Diego said that it was summer in the Andes and the melted water was rushing down to this outlet. I asked if more nuggets were found since I went away. Diego assured me that they were constantly finding them at this time of the year. I went to look and there to my great delight I picked up a few and held them as I did that first day of their discovery. I was beginning to be filled with nostalgia.

The rangers returned sooner than I thought. I invited Matthew to sit in on the meeting. He introduced me as the new Commissioner. Then I addressed the rangers with these words. "Friends and guardians of the forests, I would like you to serve my office with the same loyalty as you did your old Commissioner and you will receive great rewards for the work you are doing. I want to create a two tier working relationship with you. I will elect the most experienced rangers as executive officers and the less experienced as guardians of the environment. This means that all instructions will be given by my executive to the guardians, he in turn will report to me.

You may ask why change at all when everything is working fine. The answer to that question is to relieve me of the burden of giving you instructions that might not be feasible and to establish a chain of command. It works perfectly in the Army. The executive officers will discuss all arrangements with me before passing it on to you. He can also punish or reward you for your work. Finally, in all these years not one of you had a holiday."

"Holiday, what is that?" One ranger asked.

"They are days when you do not work but have time to spend with your family and do things together and you will be paid. Does that sound like a good deal?" I finally asked.

"We chose to be rangers so we can get away from the women and their nagging. We will take these days of holidays to go fishing and hunting but not to visit our women. If that is acceptable then it is fine." Another added.

"You speak very good English." I said. "Who taught you? May I ask your name?"

"It is old man Matty who teached us and my name is Jango."

I was inclined to correct his grammar but refrained from doing so as it may make him look silly among his friends. "Well Jango I appoint you chief executive ranger. You may bring another four of your friends for a private meeting before you return to your posts."

I could see Matthew was impressed with the changes. He told me in no uncertain manner, remarking how much I have changed since returning from England.

It took days to rearrange everything to my liking and see that Matthew was comfortable in his new surroundings. It went without saying that he was free to visit anytime he feels like it and be a part of his old house. I am sure when my family arrives he would use his discretion.

Sebastian was chatting with a young lady with two male villagers standing nearby. He tried to hold her hand but was immediately prevented from doing so by one of the men. This appeared to irritate him. I could see that this little incident could turn into something nasty. So I intervened and told him it is not customary for young unmarried ladies to be seen holding hands with visitors.

He appeared angry and demanded to know why. "These are not the savages people from the outside think they are. They are just as sophisticated as you and I. Besides the young unmarried ladies have their reputation to protect." He became subdued, apologised, and bowed, which was the most honourable way to say you are sorry. They smiled and shook hands before departing.

"I must expend my energies on the painting of my house and making other comfortable arrangements. I shall use one of the pumps to make a fully operating shower and toilet with a huge overhead tank for water from that clear stream fifty yards from those trees." He told me.

"What stream are you talking about?" I asked.

"Behind those trees about fifty yards away." He was surprised I did not seem to know of its existence. Matthew hearing us talking joined in. He was also amazed at the revelations of a new stream just yards from his house.

We hurried to where Sebastian said the stream was and sure enough there was a stream with water as clear as crystal trickling gently down to the river. Matthew and I stood there amazed. He lived here for quarter of a century and I for six years and neither of us knew of its existence. It is not that it was hidden behind some hill or in an inaccessible part if the forest.

We decided to send for Diego and consult him of this phenomenon. Diego was a man who would stroll through the forest always looking for something or the other and I am sure he would have known about it.

When he arrived he was as baffled as we were. He suggested we trace its origin. It was many hours following it towards Cold Stream. The mystery was solved in an instant. It appears the Cold Stream must have burst its bank at some point in time, maybe during the heavy rainy season creating a new stream.

A serious question came simultaneously to our mind. Is it bringing nuggets with it and if so what are we to do? If it is bringing nuggets along, Sebastian would inevitably find them and probably claim it for himself. We could not discuss this problem while he was here with us. So Matthew, the wily old hand, told him that this stream is a tributary of Cold Stream and this is where we found the nuggets he heard us talking about. Because of this we have the rights to all that it carried. We would of course make an exception. Since he was now part of the team the nuggets we find in Cold Stream would remain ours and all other nuggets found in this tributary would be divided between the five of us. It was only fair as he discovered it.

To everyone's surprise Sebastian was overwhelmed with our generous terms and shook hands all around. Ben who was absent would have to be told of the new developments. He was still painting his part of the house when we called. He looked like the clown you see at the circus, paint everywhere on his face. We started laughing at the spectacle he presented. Not understanding why we are laughing, irritated him.

He finally asked. "What's so funny and why all of you looking so darn pleased with yourself?"

We told him everything and the decision about the gold did not go down well with him at first. It was after we explained why, that finally made him see our point of view and he quickly forced the brush in Sebastian's hand and told him to get on with the painting. Smiling and tapping him on the shoulders. Sebastian took the brush and vanished.

The next day we went back to the stream with spades and asked Sebastian to start digging. No sooner did he get in the water when he made an almighty noise. Something I have not heard since that bomb exploded in London.

"This water is as cold as the Arctic ocean." He pointed out and shivering.

"Never mind all that cold," Ben told him. "Take the oil from this drum I brought and paint your legs with it then go in and work your heart out."

Sebastian did as he was told and sure enough he was able to stay longer digging up great abundance of pebbles. We could see some tiny nuggets shining in the sunlight. We allowed him to collect all he could before departing.

Back at base, Sebastian was counting his nuggets while we sipped a malt under the silk cotton wood. We could see him weighing them in his palm trying to assess the amount in dollars.

"I guess I have about six hundred dollars of nuggets here." He told us.

Matthew poured him a drink which he swallowed in one gulp. Seeing this prompted Matthew to ask the question. "Tell me Sebastian have you got a grievance against whisky?"

"I don't get it. Are you asking if I like the stuff? Of course I like it."

"Then why don't you nurse it, savour the bouquet, and sip it so it can flow smoothly down your throat." Matthew tried to explain.

"I can never understand you Brits. Everything has to be done with ceremony. God man, it is only some whisky that relaxes you. But I'll take your advice and see what charm it does to me."

The trio from the village must have noticed us gathered under the tree and they came and explained to Matthew the young lady's intention. She wanted to bond with Sebastian. When this was revealed to him he became quite excited and again tried to hold her hand. Again he was prevented from doing so with the intervention of Matthew and again he apologised and bowed to show remorse.

It was a simple ceremony not like the lavish one we had for Diego and Bell. The parents were invited along with some of the Elders. Matthew interpreted the proceedings to him its relevance and implications and the duty he is bound to observe during their period of bonding. He instantly agreed they then embraced with hands tied together. She was then told she would have to stay in the village until all the paint work is completed. This was agreed and they disappeared in the forest to collect berries... So they told us.

Matthew sighed and commented. "It appears we would soon have a sizably community here after all. You would be having

Christine and Elizabeth, Diego with his small family and who knows how many brats that young lady with her child bearing hips would produce. I could see changes here gradually creeping in whether I like it or not. It is up to you Peter to see it doesn't get out of hand, you should always remember my wishes if you have any love or respect for the things I treasured and for this place to retain its pristine state."

It was sad to hear him speak like that. I wondered if I would be able to hold back to tide of progress.

CHAPTER 22

News from England

On the other side of the river and a good distance from the caimans usual habitat, Sebastian and Diego were using the small bull dozer "A TD6" or tracked diesel powered machine to clear a hundred hectares of savannah land for cultivation. This land was on the other side of the river and not much use to wild life. It was dry, with not much vegetation. I can only guess that only birds can survive the harshness of the landscape.

The noise the tractor made attracted many villagers who came to see the might of machine against hardy bushes. Some of them were so overwhelmed by the sight that they went across and helped with the clearing. We stood in silence and watched.

Matthew remarked about the welfare of the caimans and what impact it would have of them.

"Surely they are too far away to be bothered by a bit of rumbling." Diego told him.

"They are sensitive reptiles. Huge and vicious as they are, they are suspicious of anything that is not normal. They do a good job keeping the piranha population in control." Matthew pointed out.

When Diego and his party finished their task they came over, followed by the villagers who were perspiring profusely. Matthew invited them and made a drink which contained a small amount of whisky. Diego told us that all the work for the new agriculture farm was done. We only had to wait for the rains to water it before cultivation. I told them that the two pumps we had could do the job in a couple of days. Sebastian pointed out that they thought of it but decided that the cost in gasoline would be astronomical. Diesel, he said, was still cheap, which is why we were using the TD6 and it is a blessing that the jeeps use the same fuel. We would only use the pumps if the rain fails.

The next few days went by before the supply boat arrived. I have been eagerly waiting this moment as I was expecting at least one letter from England. That prayer was answered. I hastily opened it and went into a blissful state.

Christine suggested that we send Elizabeth to a boarding school and Catherine volunteered to visit and look after her. I had to think carefully about this. I did not want my child to grow up without the close contact of her parents.

The next day we were having a drink under the silk cotton wood. I told Matthew of the contents of the letter and he suggested that I ask both of them to come and he knows of a small Jewish community in the city that has a private school which would be ideal for her.

I then proposed that he took Ben with him to make the arrangements on my behalf and for them to go to Berbice and get my mother's maid Isabella to come to Georgetown and stay with my family in my absence. Of course I will be writing my mother asking her permission and also to arrange the training of a new maid. Matthew thought it a great idea.

Sebastian heard what was said and insisted that he would join them, "I have never been to Berbice and the stories I heard from you is damning proof that I visit this place."

He also told us that it would give him an opportunity to check the land planes and see if one of them could be converted to an amphibious one. If it fails then he would have to go to Essequibo and make the one there air worthy and safe.

"How long will that take?" I asked.

"Not more than a month." He replied casually.

"What do you think Matthew?" I asked.

"The truth is we need an amphibious air craft to take us around. There are rivers everywhere in this country; that is what the name Guiana means land of many waters. I say let Sebastian do what he thinks is best." Matthew concluded.

I must hasten and write that letter for mother before the supply boat departs. I gave the finished letter to the man in charge and we all strolled along the river bank to see how the caimans were faring. It appears, as Matthew said, they are sensitive to changes and are moving further up river. We followed them until they came to a point where the bend of the river created a small island. They clambered on to the island hissing at their neighbours, another small group of caimans whose home the interlopers now occupied; realised that it would be futile challenging the new comers who were bigger, stronger and many in numbers. They soon settled down peacefully basking in the early morning sun.

The next day after the supply boat departed, the houses looked empty and deserted. I felt terribly lonely and longed for Diego to come visiting.

Later that day Sebastian's bride ambled in and I told her he was away for a month to get an aeroplane to take her for a honeymoon. I was getting used to speaking a little of their dialect and I seemed to be making good progress. She looked a bit disappointed; eventually she smiled and went into my kitchen to speak with my maids and housekeeper. I did not try to stop her as it is not allowed for other female members to enter the house without special permission. I thought this is Sebastian's bride so she is exempted from such restriction.

My spirits went on a high when I heard a jeep coming. I knew it had to be Diego. He arrived with his family and I greeted him as if I had not seen him for years.

"Where is everybody?" He asked seeing the place deserted. I explained to him events that took us by surprise and of the new arrangements. I hastily poured us a drink with Bell looking inquiringly as to why she was not given one.

"Sorry Bell I thought you were pregnant." I said in jest.

"How did you know I was pregnant?" She asked in amazement.

"I was only joking." I told her, then asked "Will you have a drink?"

"I am not sure of the pregnancy but the indications are there. Since I am not sure I will have that drink." She said smilingly.

Sebastian's bonded bride joined us uninvited and I was not sure how to handle this situation. She was not a member of our community as far as I was concerned. I looked quizzically at Diego and he did not have an answer. Bell asked for her name. We soon learnt it was Daisy, a name given to her by the vicar at her birth.

I said to her. "Daisy, I think you should go back to the village and wait for Sebastian to return and then we can have a good party. You will then be free to visit anytime you feel like it."

"Me no welcome now?" She asked looking disappointed.

"It is customary for your husband to introduce you properly. That is our custom." I told her firmly.

She went into the kitchen and said something to the maids before leaving. The matter rested heavily on me and I felt I had to speak openly about it to release the tension.

It was Diego as always who spoke. "You did the right thing Peter. I know this appear as a bit of a social blunder on both sides. The trouble is Sebastian should have done his duty before leaving in such a hurry and you had no alternative but to tell her the truth."

"You know what your problem is Peter? You still have that Berbice attitude of social class and until you shed it you will find yourself in this situation over and over again." Bell's reproach was painful but truthful.

I had found another hidden side of my personality. I could not believe I acted so cruelly. It was the years of training that was difficult to cast aside. I wished I could be like Matthew. I remembered the day he danced with the East Indians at my home as if he was one of them. Speaking their language unashamedly, laughing at their jokes which I found unamusing. His years in India as a young man and the Indians who made him their friends must have created a deep impression in him. Shedding his inhibitions and absorbing the Indian life style. Their culture and language was something the Army thought was a good thing and encouraged it for their own Imperial purposes. I found it painful to adapt to anything that is not within the confines of my thinking. By God how I wish it were not so and the more I longed to be like Matthew. I confided these inner most thoughts to Diego and Bell. They were sympathetic and could do no more to help me.

I had to start readjusting myself and be strong in my resolve. My family would be coming and I must show tolerance if I expect them to adjust to life in this desolate land. The people in the city are unforgiving as the devil himself and any social blunder would be a disaster. I had managed to join the elite in the social order of things and I must observe all the criteria it embraces.

My thoughts were interrupted when Young Diego asked. "Uncle Peter, Why are you sad?"

"I am not sad sonny, I was only thinking,"

"You promised to tell me of the fighting you saw in England. Are you too busy to tell me now?"

"Yes young Diego. I am a bit busy now, but not too busy to show you where the caimans have made their new home."

"That sound like fun. Can my parents come along too?" He asked looking very pleased with himself. The four of us drifted towards the river heading for the caimans new found home.

Sitting on a rock and throwing pebbles in the river was Daisy. She saw us coming and got up and started walking away. I sent Young Diego to bring her back and she looked perplexed at me. I held her hand and invited her to walk with us. She placed an arm around Bell and they walked ahead of us.

I had broken the unwritten rule. I thought it was a step forward and damn the unwritten rules. Peace with myself was what I strived for many years to achieve and I was beginning to realise how hard that can be.

Back at the house I asked Diego and his family to have dinner with me. The maids have cooked some tapir's stew and I knew how they liked that. Bell started licking her lips and decided to go in the kitchen and help with the cooking. Diego and I poured ourselves a drink and I gave his son toy army tanks to play with.

We had just finished our delicious meal when there was a knock on the door. Young Diego went and opened it and announced that two men wanted to see me. I saw they were my two most senior executives. They had the most worried look on their faces. They told me that one of the rangers had been found dead under a tree where he was sleeping and a great wound was in his left side. They buried him and brought his personal belongings to give to his wife. I took them and promised to deliver them personally and express my sincere regrets. I sent them to the kitchen to have a meal and against regulations I gave them a drink of whisky. It was an emergency and surely that must take priority above all else. At the same time I must remind myself that I cannot be doing this too often.

Diego promised to accompany me the widow's home. We did our best to express our sorrow and promised to see that she would receive all the care we could give, to make her life tolerable.

We were not far from where the vicar was busy with his workers constructing his school and church. Apart from the two buildings we saw a third building going up.

Diego asked what that building was. "Oh, that will be my home. I decided to stay here and concentrate on this community. That way I would achieve my life's ambition."

"May I ask what that is vicar?" Diego asked.

"Making it a successful Christian community; that is my life's ambition." He answered confidently.

"I wish you luck and hope you achieve what your heart is set on." I told him.

"If you need any help please don't hesitate to ask. I can always send some of the young men to help." Diego offered.

"Why don't you come around when you are finished? and have supper and there is always a glass of something for you. You looked famished." I said to him.

"Sounds like a good idea. I will hold you to that."

We headed back to the Rest House and waited for the vicar.

It was not long afterwards when he appeared and asked for a towel and permission to use the shower.

"You used to live here temporarily. Why ask for permission to use the shower?" I reminded him.

"Because you are the new occupant and I'm not so sure if you would take kindly to me just helping myself." He explained.

Looking refreshed he sat down with his drink and asked in a matter of fact way. "I heard your family will be coming soon. By the way what do I address you as Mr Commissioner or doctor or simply Peter?"

"Stop being so formal, you've known me since I was only sixteen. I was catapulted to this height and that should not preclude you from addressing me as you always did. I shall, on the other hand. continue to address you as the vicar and not Oliver."

"I would prefer if you address me as Oliver. It will be prestigious for me when we meet in the higher circles. Ah! They would say The vicar is on first names with the new Commissioner. They will whisper and gossip about it among themselves. That I'm sure of." He chuckled in a roguish way I had never heard before.

It was several days since Matthew and the others left and I was waiting eagerly for his return. The sound of an aircraft set my heart thumping. As usual we raced down the river to investigate. Sure as it is mid-morning it was Matthew and three other men wearing yarmulkes and well-tailored suits.

Diego had to deputise for Ben to get them ashore. He in turn ordered two villagers to bring them ashore.

At the Rest House I was introduced to Rabbi Solomon, Mister Robinski and Mister Weisman. Matthew told them that it was my family coming from England and my desire to get Elizabeth to their private school. I felt honoured meeting these men and more so for them to come and see me here. Oliver seemed intrigued with their visit but remained silent. I persuaded Diego to stay and listen to what was discussed. He was very pleased with my suggestion.

"Well young man." The rabbi started. "Matthew told me of your situation and we are happy to assist. First, we must tell you that if you do decide to send her to our school she must be prepared to follow our instructions on Jewish laws and customs and all books will be provided at a very low cost. The rest of the details will not be of any interest to you at this point. It will, however, be of interest to her mother. We will discuss fees and other matters when the time comes."

"Did you come all this way to tell me that?" I asked without appearing to be rude.

"No, not at all, it was I who suggested that we meet you in person and get to know you a little, and more importantly we wanted to see what the Commissioner of the hinterlands was like. I can say that we like what we are seeing and now if you would be so kind, may I have a glass of water?" The Rabbi replied.

"Would it be impertinent to ask if you would like something stronger?" I inquired.

Much to my surprise they accepted my offer of whisky. I then turned to Matthew and added "I like these gentlemen, Matthew, I was certain that you would not have brought them here just to see me and for the ride. There is something else to all this. Am I right?"

"Maybe... Remember she is my niece and I feel responsible also for her welfare." He replied with a note of seriousness in his voice.

He got up and spoke while walking to his desk. "There is something I wanted to give to Peter a long time ago. It is appropriate that I give it to him now."

He came back and sat next to me, then he unfolded a yarmulke and took out the small diamond encrusted Magen David and presented me with the yarmulke, "An appropriate gift in the presence of three wise men."

I tried it on and they all clapped and told me how magnificent I looked and laughed heartily.

Mr Robinski then joined in by saying. "We like you, and look forward to meeting your family soon."

"Perhaps you would like to come fishing with us and we can barbeque our catch on the grill outside. I will have the men clean it thoroughly."

I assured them of the strict kosher standard I would try to maintain. It was a lesson taught to me by Catherine. I did well to remember. They appeared pleased. We finished our drink and went fishing. It was Diego's expertise that produced a dozen very large himara, a delicate fish akin to trout.

Bell took the maids and went to the new stream to prepare them. She does not like the smell of fish around the house. At Oliver's invitation we strolled down to where his construction was taking place. He was rather happy explaining to the visitors his plans for the settlements. They were very attentive to what he was saying and it was not out of politeness.

We then showed them the area cleared for agriculture and our plans for developing it into a profitable business venture. This surely delighted them. Diego brought his jeep and we clambered aboard and went to the new stream. Bell and the maids finished what they were doing and were returning to base. Diego told them to wait for him to do the cooking. We drove off to the stream and if this was an excursion to impress the visitors it was a success.

They could not believe what we told them. Diego took a shovel and scooped up a few spade full of pebbles and without fail there were a few nuggets among them. Diego presented the Rabbi with the largest of the nuggets. Then told him "We always present a nugget to important visitors as a reminder of this place."

To impress them further, Matthew told Diego to take us to Cold Stream. Here again they were mesmerised with the stories Matthew told them and also of the benefits the villagers got from it. The dairy herd was next and the mention of Rotary donating towards it made them happy.

When they saw Diego's timbered lodge Mister Wiesman asked. "Who constructed that lovely building?"

Diego explained that it was copied from the lodges of the Canadians trappers. The only reason being that there were jaguars roaming around and it was protection for his wife.

Back at the Rest House, after they had their fish and a glass of more whisky. The Rabbi looked at his watch signalling that it was time to return. They thanked us for our hospitality and tried to urge me to be more Jewish than Matthew ever hoped to be, if only for my family. I could not promise anything. I was not sure if I wanted to go down that road. My conception of God was sealed in my heart. No religion could change that and Matthew understood it so well.

Matthew decided to remain here and sent the visitors with instructions for the pilot to see they are safely home; he wanted to brief me on what happened in Berbice and my mother's response to my letter. He first apologised for bringing the visitors before telling me.

Then he began. "I told your mother of your wish and she was happy to comply. Ben insisted on remaining until Isabella is ready to come to the city. He planned to bring her first for me to give her instructions."

I interrupted by asking, "Why here? I would have joined them in the city and finalised the arrangements. I know Ben has a motive for this behaviour."

"I have no control over him. Peter. He is your man and only you can deal effectively with him. He appears to get on the wild side in Berbice. I noticed it the last time we were there. Sebastian, on the other hand, was very pleasant and enjoyed his stay he could not convert the land planes so he went off to the Mazaruni in Essequibo to salvage what he can of the amphibious aircrafts there."

"How did he get there?" I asked.

"He went with one of the land planes to Bartica and then by boat to his destination. He will be useful to you Peter so we must treat him kindly. He told me the police station in Bartica has a telephone and he will ring McKenzie police station to relay any news of progress to you. You are the Commissioner and any news they receive will have to reach you the quickest way possible.

There is also some troubling news, not only for you, but for the four of us who sent those boys to further their education. They have formed a political party and their aim is to get independence for British Guiana. I don't think they are doing what we expected. I spoke to the men in the village and they know nothing of their intentions. Every week-end they stage a rally calling on the villagers to join their movement for independence. Quite honestly I do not think they are getting the support they hoped for. They call their party 'The Freedom Movement' or some ridiculous name like that. That is all I have to report and I must add things are going rather well in all other directions.

Diego and Bell will have to be told. By the way I brought a couple of bags of seeds I must get some of the villagers to bring it here. It seems we will be getting that long-awaited rain soon. We do not want the seeds star germinating before we are ready. I am really looking forward to this venture. It will keep me busy until I can find time to settle down and write my memoirs."

No sooner had the men brought the seeds into the store room than the rains came pouring down bringing thunder and steely flashes of lightning. It looked like all the water in the clouds was coming down with all the fury of nature. We were happy. The wheels of progress are turning faster than anticipated.

The final hurdle is the arrival of my family. I consulted with Matthew and suggested that he deputised for me as I want to go to Berbice and oversee the necessary arrangements. I cannot rely on Ben especially if that Isabella is around.

I shall have to take Diego with me to help with the many arrangements and to send a telephone message to Bartica police station requesting that the message reached Sebastian as soon as possible. I will have to say who I am to make it official and urgent. That should do the trick

Matthew agreed to deputise and brought up the question of the dead ranger. This incident rested heavily on our minds. There was nothing we could do and ordering the others to try and catch whoever did it was a hopeless exercise. The rangers told us there were no illegal loggers or prospectors in the area. It could have been a personal attack by persons unknown. I decided to close the matter and to record the death in my reports.

I took the other jeep and drove with Matthew to meet Diego. I told him of the situation and the report Matthew brought back. He was willing to accompany me on condition that Bell and their son stayed with Matthew while he was away. It was a reasonable request. All we had to do was to wait for the supply boat to take us to McKenzie.

Young Diego came running to greet us. He had the squirrel monkey we saved from the caiman on his shoulder. He brought it near to me and asked that I stroke it. It had such an appealing look in his eyes I could not resist the request. A moment of tenderness greeted me. I held it close to my chest and felt his little heart beating as it snuggled up to me. I felt painful telling Young Diego that his pet would not be allowed to stay at the Rest House.

"Mother told me that. He breaks things and makes lots of mess. She has arranged for the men in the village to look after it. He gets on well with them." It was wonderful to hear him speak with such confidence.

CHAPTER 23

The Final Touches

The supply boat arrived earlier than expected and with some very good news. Sebastian took the initiative to send me a telephone message via McKenzie Police Station. They knew if it were for the Commissioner then it must be urgent. It read "Like to inform you that all is going well and plane will be ready sooner than expected. Sebastian." That was all we needed. All we have to do is send a message urging him to come here as soon as possible and to give us an idea when that will be. I was prepared to wait for him and save myself the long and painful journey to the city.

Two days after the supply boat left Sebastian landed at Sappanam. We were so delighted we hardly noticed that two caimans had returned to their old home and looking around to see what changes were made. We ignored their presence and went and collected our American flyer.

He was beaming with delight seeing us and immediately began to give us a detail account of his absence. "The plane is as good as new," he started out. It was only one of the propellers that was out of line. I soon put that right and here I am." He then showed us a sign he made. It read

"SAPPANAM ENTERPRISE. UPPER DEMERARA RIVER TRESPASSERS NOT TOLERATED"

"Allow me to introduce my friend. This is Hector, he lives in Bartica and what's more he is an unemployed electrician. I brought him here to wire up my house and connect the wind charger.

"Now that is what I call constructive thinking. I have some more constructive thinking for you laddie," Matthew told him, then went on to say, "If you were to erect that sign you will have to register with the land registry office. You will be given a grant to farm the land and also to pay a yearly rent of $1 per hectare.

You have one hundred hectare so you calculate it. It will also give you the right to this land for ninety nine years."

"I'll pay the darn rent. I am not sure I'll live ninety nine years. There is one question resting on my mind. Who are the people involved in this scheme?"

"Well" Matthew told him. "It is Diego, Ben you and myself. The Commissioner cannot be involved. It will compromise his position.

"I don't want to be involved. I wouldn't have the time." I told them. Turning to Diego I told him

"You should think to safe guard any future misunderstanding. The grant should be registered in all the names of the shareholders." I also told them that any of their future children might see things differently and may want to continue with the project and again the legality of this will have to be done with the help of a solicitor. It is not that no one is trusted with a verbal arrangement."

They all agreed.

asked Diego to assist me with planning our visits to the city and eventually to Berbice. He suggested that we go to the city first and then to Berbice.

After saying goodbye to Matthew and the others we were on our way. During the flight Sebastian asked me to show him where exactly my home was at the sea front. I took the map and indicated a rough distance where it might be. "That looks great I will have to make a low altitude flight to see if the sea is calm before attempting any landing," he told us.

When we reached the estuary of the Demerara he made a sharp right hand turn and a few minutes later I could see my house. I pointed it to him and he flew lower and saw that the sea was calm enough for a landing. I again thanked the stars for their blessing.

"I am going as near to the shore as possible. You will have to wade ashore after we secured the plane." He advised.

"I don't mind getting my socks wet," Diego told him.

The plane came to a gentle halt a few yards from the house. I could see my gardener running and waving towards us. When he recognised me he waved more enthusiastically. He helped secured the plane and took our bags away.

I explained the purpose of this visit and the new role he must play in the future. He became agitated. I asked what is troubling him. "All this new duties, Will I get extra pay for it?"

"You did not have to ask that." I told him. He was very pleased and helped Diego prepare a meal of ribbed steak and vegetables. It must have been several years I last ate ribbed steak and Diego was a master chef.

With Sebastian having a short rest we enjoyed a few drinks before starting on the second leg. The trip to Berbice lasted forty minutes and as the plane neared the stelling to land, a flotilla of fishermen's boat came to fetch us.

My mother was ever so pleased to see us she hugged and kissed me as if I have been absent for years. I asked what progress she made in finding a new maid. "I have not found a single lady willing to work. They all have families to look after and their husbands would not tolerate their wives working as kitchen slaves, "Where is Ben?" I inquired.

"He has gone to the market. Your father took him this morning and he will be back with your father." She replied.

"Now then mother since this is my responsibility I will find you a maid. I am going down to the village and see what information I can get." I tried to comfort her.

Diego and Sebastian accompanied me to the village. There I met Ali's father cutting his grandson's hair. He stopped what he was doing and greeted me. "You look fine Mr Commissioner." He said smiling. I did not get used to the idea of being addressed as Mr Commissioner.

"What brought you to our humble village?" He asked.

"You know my mother is looking for a maid. Is there any way you can help?

He scratched his head for a moment and suggested that perhaps his niece who lives in Albion and recently widowed might be interested. This was fantastic news. I immediately suggested that we go and see her. He told me he must speak to his people first. They gathered around him and in babu English he explained my visit. They were nodding agreement as he spoke. This was a good sign it indicates that they are in agreement.

He turned to me and said that it can happen. I must agree that he comes with me to speak to her. This was quickly agreed. There was a problem. My father had gone to the surgery with his car and I needed a vehicle for the many visits I planned. I suddenly saw my neighbour and asked if he was willing to take us. He did better than that he handed me the key and told me to replace the gasoline I used on my return.

We could not wait for Ben. Our journey was a bit painful; I could hear Mr Ali groaning each time the car went in a pothole.

This widow lived only a few houses from my friend's brother so I asked Mr Ali to walk up and inform his niece why we are here. My friend's brother whose name I still cannot remember came out and ask us in. "Welcome Mr Commissioner. Welcome to my humble home. This is indeed an honour for me. I wonder what Persotum will say when he hears that you visited me."

"My visit is to ask of the widow a few doors away."

"Very sad cast that. Her husband contracted malaria while cutting sugar cane at the back dam. He died so suddenly. It was a real shock." He told me.

I explained why we came and again he said it was a blessing for her and her two children. "She is a proud woman. Only take the hand outs to feed her hungry kids." I was a bit worried about the children. Mother will not have them around in the house. It is not that she is prejudiced. She likes her house to be spotless more like a museum. I conveyed my feelings to Mr Ali and he shook his head vehemently and told me. "The children will stay with me. My wife will expect some cash to buy food and care for them. We are poor people as you know and have barely enough for ourselves."

"Your niece will have to see to that. She will be paid handsomely if she pleases my mother. I will be contributing to her wages you make sure you tell her that." I told him.

I then gave him five shillings for the bus fares.

"This sugar plantation? Sebastian asked. "Do they actually make the sugar here?"

"Of course nut head." I replied jokingly.

"I really would like to see how it is done," he indicated.

"You will. But not here I will take you to another sugar estate. The manager is a friend and he is a Scot. I told him.

"How far is this place?" He asked.

"Then I insist on driving this jalopy. You will never be dropped in a pothole." He assured me.

Andrew McIntosh was the most surprised man I have seen in years. He congratulated me on my appointment. Isme came and gave me a hug and a kiss. "This is Sebastian an American. He flies our aeroplanes. Of course you know Diego." Formalities ended. Andrew asked "Why are we standing? Come on gentlemen be seated."

Isme shook her head in amazement and uttered "My how you have changed. I would have hardly recognised you." She asked all the polite questions about my family and when I am expecting them.

I told her very soon and this is one of the reasons I came up here. I could have telephoned but I thought of doing it personally to invite them to the city when they arrive.

"Is Ingeborg going to be there?" She asked suspiciously

"You are the first people I have invited. Invitations will of course be extended to all my friends. The other reason we are here is for Sebastian to see how the sugar is made."

"You are out of luck laddie. The factory is suffering a break down. One of the boilers is not functioning. So production had come to a halt." He told us. Then asked "Why didn't you come with your plane? I did say you were welcome to use the air strip."

"We had some business to sort out at Albion." I said.

When I arrived home mother was furious. "I have been waiting hours for you to tell me if you succeeded getting a maid for me."

"I'M sorry. I went to see Andrew in Skeldon. I did get your maid. You will have to assess her competence and attitude." I told her in a matter of fact way

"Well where is she?"

"At the village, you can either come with me or ask her to come here. You must make up your mind quickly as I have a lot to do."

"Let's go to the village." She said firmly. "She will be more at ease answering my questions."

Father and Ben arrived just as we were leaving. Ben greeted us with his usual gusto and decided to accompany us.

I left my mother to interview the woman and I went to speak to Sattar and the others about their political movement. They knew they were going against the principles of the four of us that helped them and reneging on that promise should make them feel ashamed. Sattar came and shook my hand and then called his other friends. There was no way to sit so we stood while they tried to explain their motives for going into politics. I did not want a confrontation only to make my feelings clear to them.

"Mr Commissioner, we are not apologising for what we are doing. We are not ashamed of not doing what was expected. I strongly believe that our course of action is far more important than educating a handful of youngsters." Sattar began. "We can see the direction this country is heading and now the war is over, Britain has a lot of other responsibilities for her white colonies. If we don't take the initiative and propel ourselves to a new future we will be the dust bin of the empire. Our idea is for us to forge a continental destiny for this country. Our immediate neighbours are Brazil and Venezuela. Trading and forming a close relationship would be the best course for us."

Ali then joined in and said. "There are others mostly the blacks who would prefer a relationship with the West Indies. I agree with some of their arguments that the West Indians are more culturally akin to us. While that may be true I still prefer the former suggestion not for any political advantage but to secure a good trading relationship. There is another dentist who has formed a political party and we are hoping to join him. I want to make this absolutely clear to you Commissioner. I make no excuse for what we are doing. If you feel that because you and your friends helped us to acquire a formal education and that we must be a slave to your wishes then I honestly wished you name your price for your kindness and we will repay you."

"You are indeed an ignorant man. I am more disappointed with your comments of not helping other youngsters than with you futile political ideas. Britain is still the head of the greatest empire mankind has ever known and you in your tiny minds think you can manipulate the leaders of this great power? I am sorry but I wish you have a good look at what you are getting into. I cannot say I wish you luck. I will undoubtedly follow developments with great interest." I was angry with their fool hardy ideas and I was happy when mother came and told me that she is happy to employ the woman.

My father was intrigue with what I told him of those lads. He thought they were on a course to disaster. My mother agreed and hurriedly pointed out that she told me so. Ben told me to forget them and let them get on with whatever they see fit. He then looked at Diego and asked, "Anyone for a drink?" He knew it was what we all we wanted and went about being bar tender.

Sebastian and Diego went to check the aeroplane. While we were enjoying our drink mother brought the woman and introduced her to father. "This is Beda, our new house maid. She clasped her hand on being introduced, Indian style and bowed. Isabella was observing her with the eyes of a hawk. After they departed, Isabella told us that she did not like her and that she will not be able to manage all the work by herself. "Why is that?" I inquired.

"Look at her, she is so skinny and her hands are so small."

"In that case I better take her to Georgetown and you can remain here." I teased.

"Oh please don't do that sah. I want to go and help your wife. She will need me and all me experience." She pleaded.

"To tease her further I said "Let me think about it." She started to cry and ran off to the kitchen.

There were important things to do. I must wait on the return of Sebastian and Diego to plan the next journey. Father was silent for some time and only spoke when spoken to. I knew something was bothering him. I invited him to the other room to seek a reason for his silence. He told me he is worried I am undertaking too much and should delegate the others to help. "What should I delegate and to whom? I asked.

"This Sebastian looks like a dependable person. Let him and Ben look after the house until the wife comes. Get Diego to write all the invitations and see that they are delivered. Isabella can keep an eye on the gardener to see he is doing what you asked. She will enjoy bossing him around and you will have more time to see clearly the overall picture. I know how much you wanted to impress my daughter-in-law and I appreciate that, but you will have a nervous breakdown before they get here. Trust me I know what I am talking about. You shouldn't be running to Albion and Skeldon sorting things out. Delegate! That is the key word. You delegate responsibilities to your Executives to make your life easier. Follow that example in your own personal life." He ended with an arm on my shoulder and the look of a worried father on his face.

Perhaps he is right. I do get tired easily these days.

When I arrived at my home in the city I decide to put my father's advice to the test. I called them together and explained what my father told me and surprisingly they all agreed. So Diego was given his task with the invitations. Sebastian and Ben was to carry out all the necessary painting work on the house, Isabella and the gardener was given cash to find suitable new pots and pans, bed linens and curtains.

I went on the veranda relaxing with a large whisky and enjoying the cool Atlantic breeze which I found relaxing. A smile of contentment occupied my face and as I sipped my whisky and relishing the coolness of the wind I drifted into a deep sleep.

It was Isabella shaking me to get away from the rain which was soaking me. I must have been in a coma with the magic of the cool breeze and the whisky. No sooner did I get changed, the rain ceased. That's typical in these tropics a light shower one moment and bright sunlight the next.

I began to think of Matthew and how he is dealing without us. As soon as we finished here it is Sappanam bound.

That evening Persotum rung and invited me for dinner, I told him Isabella is doing that right now but he can come around if it is something important. When he told me it was important. I agreed.

He brought a young East Indian man along with Aubrey and Marina. The young man told me his name is Singh and he was in the Royal Air Force where he learnt to fly and he heard that I have some planes in store and it would be advantageous for us if he can lease one on them to start a tourist business. First, he would fly tourists to the famous Kaiteur falls for a day's outing and also to Surinam and Trinidad.

Aubrey suggested that an agreement be drawn and a sum is deposited for the lease. "That is why I am here Peter." He explained.

"No need for that you are always welcomed in this house." Marina gave me a big smile of appreciation.

"I have brought a prepared agreement for you to sign if you are willing. Since I am acting on his behalf I suggest you get an accountant to look at the proposals before you sign."

"You are my friend and I trust you implicitly no need to throw money away to an accountant. But allow me to introduce you to my flyer." I sent Isabella to fetch Sebastian and the two discussed their knowledge of flying. It was a subject I am totally without any knowledge.

It emerged that they would form a partnership and go in the tourist business in a very big way. It looks appealing and my only concern was what to do with the planes. Do I sell two of them or do I lease them.

Sebastian told me he did not have the funds to purchase any of the planes and he would prefer to lease them.

Singh said he can raise the money to purchase them if Sebastian will agree to pay his share with interest in stages. It must be the fastest business deal in history. In less than two hours all the documents were signed with Aubrey earning himself a big fee.

Such a deal did warrant a celebration. Here in British Guiana, life can be so dull that anything out of the ordinary calls for a celebration.

Aubrey decided to entertain us at the club Matthew first took us to. I was making my first appearance since becoming a member. I wonder what the usher will think when I marched through the door with an entourage not appropriately dressed.

I was not surprised when he tried his best to halt our progress. I turned to him and said in a very polite manner. "I am the new Commissioner of the hinterlands and as such I was made a member of this club by introduction of Matthew Longhorn."

He politely showed us a table set is a discreet corner. A magnum was ordered and when that was finished a second came up, the usher came to me and whispering asked if the ladies wanted some music for dancing.

"What is all that whispering?" Marina asked.

"The usher wanted to know if we need music for dancing." I revealed.

"Are we allowed to dance?" Ingeborg asked.

"I am sure if it weren't allowed, he would not have asked." I teased.

Ingeborg went up to the gentleman and express her desire to dance. That was what started a new phase of the celebration and again Ingeborg did not fail to impress the membership. When it was over I was formally introduced to the rest of the members.

There was a sudden silence as Ingeborg danced. Again displaying her décolletage and shorter than normal skirt. We were all used to her style of dressing. It never fails to entertain the members who were mostly middle aged men waiting for their retirement. I guess this is one of the reasons we were always allowed special treatment.

The sleep I had earlier energised me and I participated in the dancing. Some brave members joined in the party and the champagne flowed as I have never seen it flowed before.

We were all exhausted and decided to go our separate ways. Aubrey promised to come over and review the agreement all over to make certain I am happy.

CHAPTER 24

Back to Base

In the morning. we were on the beach to board the plane for Sappanam. Isabella seeing that she would be alone with the gardener started crying. She did not want to be left alone with him and pleaded that I take her. I hesitated for a moment and eventually agreed.

It was a nearing Christmas and I thought of getting something for the villagers and their children, some of the apples, Grapes, walnuts and other goodies that we get only at this time of the year. I asked the others to wait as I must go to the market to purchase some fruits. Isabella insisted on accompanying me to the Stabroek market a majestic building constructed by the Dutch.

After purchasing several boxes I needed it to be transported and I hastily went to the dispatch clerk to get the necessary transport. He gave me a ticket and hailed a driver of a dray cart. He was a middle-aged Portuguese man who drew alongside my boxes and started loading them. I was so shocked a Portuguese doing jobbing one of the lowly jobs in the city.

"What the hell you think you are doing?" I asked.

"Loading your boxes." He replied meekly.

"Damn you!" I screamed, then asked "How long you've been doing this?"

"This is my first hire, sir." He again sheepishly replied.

"Stop calling me sir. You are not working as some jobber, and drop those reins down right now." I demanded.

I called the dispatch clerk and told him to get someone the load his cart. The man was unsure of what to do. I told him to get on with it as I am going to see The Town's Clerk. Hearing that soon got him going about what he was asked.

The Town's Clerk was a diminutive English man about fifty and walked with slow deliberate strides towards me. I told him my name. He looked quizzically at me and asked.

"Does that name supposed to mean something to me?"

"I did not want you to think I am being self-important by telling you who exactly I am." I told him politely.

"Then make yourself known. Man" He retorted.

"I am the Commissioner of the hinterland."

He became subdued and said "Well commissioner what can I do for you?"

I turned to the man and asked his name which he said was D'Costa. I then pointed out that it was a shame to issue him with a dray cart's license to patrol the city like a coolie. He in turn told me that he would issue a license to anyone with a good character and sober. I thanked him for his time and left. I asked D'Costa why on earth he did not find a job with one of his own. I then told him what was on my mind ever since our encounter.

"You are a disgrace to your people and a disgrace to me."

He lifted both his arms to silence me. So I gave him the opportunity to explain.

He started out, "I did have a good job. I was an engineer at the distillery. You may not know what it's like working in a place like that. I eventually took to drinking until I was unable to stop. This led to my sacking and the downhill road to poverty. My poor wife died of heart break and that was when I woke up to the realities of life. I have two children; my son got a job with one of the sugar estates in Berbice and has ignored us. My daughter was offered a job as a 'hostess' in one of those funny clubs where she would have been introduced to prostitution. I took this job as a last resort if only to save my daughter. I owe two months' rent and the threat of eviction hangs over me."

I stopped him. I could visualise the picture, I went and told the dispatch clerk to get someone to load his dray and take it to my address. After some protest he agreed and a black man came and took the address and went his way. I took a taxi and the three of us went to my home.

"What am I going to do now you've deprived me of the only means of getting some food for my daughter?"

"How old is your daughter?" I asked.

"She is nineteen and very smart." He replied.

I told him of my situation and the imminent arrival of my family. Perhaps I could employ her as a confidant and helper for my wife. Christine would need someone to talk to and to get acquainted with life in the tropics. I turned to him and still pretending to be angry told him.

"I have to think what to do with you. In the meantime when the dray gets here I want you to tell the man to put all the boxes in the room below. I will pay you whatever you think is a fair price for your horse, you can dispose of the dray as you see fit. Here is a dollar go get yourself a bus after you've bought some food then bring your daughter here as soon as possible."

Diego and Sebastian were having a swim in the sea and they came running when they saw me. "All set for Sappanam, boss? Sebastian asked.

"All set except for one small matter I have to attend to."

I told them of the situation and my proposal for his daughter but I was unsure of what to do with that reformed alcoholic.

"You said he is an engineer? I think with a bit of training I can find him work servicing our planes. He would not receive any serious money until he can prove he can do what is required." Sebastian suggested.

"You are a wizard Sebastian." I told him joyfully. "I only have to wait until he gets back here to let you put the proposal to him." I ended.

"I thought it best we have a drink before he gets back. We don't want to put temptation to him." I told them.

When he arrived I was told the young lady's name was Margaret. I told her exactly what I proposed to her father. She was ever so pleased she came and kissed me on the cheek and thanked me. I then invited Sebastian to put forward his proposals, which he did in a more pronounced American accent. D'Costa agreed to everything and was prepared to take the minimum salary in the interim. My next problem, if D'Costa would be taken to Sappanam with us we can leave Margaret with Isabella. Isabella would have none of it; she protested and threatened to walk all the way to Berbice if I did not take her to Sappanam as promised. She is an obstinate woman and one who does not make empty promises. This left me with no alternative but to take them both. I hope I may not live to regret this decision.

It was mid-afternoon when we got air borne and after an hour's flight we were back at base to be greeted by Matthew and Bell, "Where is young Diego?" His father asked, Bell explained that her son was trying his best to get his pet back with a family of squirrel monkeys and every time the little devil returns with a fruit as peace offering hoping for a chance to remain with him. I guess he has grown so attached to my little boy he does not want any of his own kind."

I left Bell to sort out the ladies accommodation and to direct their daily routine. I told Ben to take the fruits down to the new stream to keep fresh and the rest of the non-perishables could be left in the store room. The rest of us went to the study to finalise our plans.

Although Matthew is not a partner in these ventures we still looked on him as one and cherished any suggestions he made. I got a pleasant shock when he told us that he had received a letter from India. The Prince wants to visit British Guiana and reminded him that I promised that my father would take him to Surinam to meet the East Indians there who still preserve their language and culture. I had forgotten all about it and thought at the time that it was only passing conversation. I never dreamt that he took it seriously. Nonetheless, I am delighted. I can only hope his visit does not coincide with Christine's.

Matthew asked an important question, "Since this is not an official visit. He, being a 'Prince' must be given some accommodation by the Governor in recognition of his status. We cannot have a 'Royal' person roaming the country without some official recognition. Protocol will have to be observed.

"You are a good friend of Gordon and he has the Governor's ear. Why don't you speak to him and see if a low key governmental invitation is possible" I suggested.

"It's a bit much to ask but it's worth a try. That means I will have to go to the city. Well since nothing much is happening I will do as you ask." Matthew agreed.

We discussed all the necessary programs in hand and it was Matthew who suggested that he take D'Costa and Hector with him to complete the two-bedroom flat on the ground floor of my house for Isabella and the gardener. Matthew thought that Isabella may not want to share a flat with an older man. Margaret, on the other hand, will be given her accommodation in the main house.

"Isn't it worth building a further two bedrooms over the flat just in case your mother-in-law decided to come and stay for a while?" He asked, knowing that I would agree with his suggestion. I relented to his arrangements only because I wanted to follow the advice of delegating. Then, I thought maybe he is getting bored and wanted something constructive to do. Bell would be more than happy to advise him and probably arrange things much better than both Matthew and myself. I relayed this idea to Matthew and he cursed us both for being mindless idiots.

Bell was so happy she nearly stumbled as she hurried to tell Diego. I was really beginning to feel on top of the world. I have people who know exactly what I wanted and are prepared to do it for me. What more can a man ask.

My family would be here in less than a month. I promised the villagers a good Christmas party for the children and they kept reminding me. Bell will see to that, with Margaret and Isabella giving a hand. I will have the time to make my reports for Matthew to take to Head office. I do not have a type writer so everything will have to be done by hand.

Margaret came to see what I was doing and asked if she could help. I showed her the brief notes and asked if she could translate it in readable English and to make sense of it then by all means go ahead and she would have earned her first wages. She smiled politely and sat down to do her job. I left and joined the others who were resting under the silk cotton wood.

I reminded Sebastian of the electrical work to be done in The Rest House. All other connections were done. The wind charger was working perfectly and there was no accident with any of the birds or the wild life. The carved harpy eagle is doing a wonderful job.

I suggested to Matthew that he should buy a new electrical fridge and one of those new things they called a deep freezer and also a type writer.

"There are going to be a lot of changes in this place Matthew. It will not affect your precious wild life or your environment. It's all done for my precious wife your niece." This did have a sobering effect on him. He sighed heavily and downed the drink.

Hector had made himself a neat little hut not far from the village. I sent Ben to fetch him to give him instructions for the wiring and some electrical points for the new fridge and freezer. This place would soon become a modern home right here in the middle of the jungle. I entertained a wicked smile when I thought of Matthew's slight displeasure.

Sebastian sat next to D'Costa and casually commented for the sake of conversation. "You have a very pretty daughter. I understand you hurriedly left your house. What will become of the things you left behind?"

"I left a note for the land lord to sell them and that would be for the rent I owed. As for my daughter she inherited all her mother's beauty. She loved her mother intensely and did not speak to me for several months after her death. Now that she has found something useful to do it will make her happy and perhaps she will forgive me for the shame and disaster I brought on the family." He told us looking sad.

I told D'Costa that if our drinking upset him he is welcome to stay indoors.

"Stay indoors! And miss all the nonsense people say when they have a few. No sir I will join you and even have a small one occasionally." He looked at me and placed his hand on his chest and declared.

"As God is my maker and on my life I WILL NOT! AND I SAY IT AGAIN I WILL NOT EVER GET DRUNK EVER AGAIN! This promise is for my daughter." He told me looking like the man who just a minute ago woke up to the realities of his failure.

Hector came and I showed him what I needed.

I asked. "Do you feel isolated living by yourself among the villagers?" He appears to be someone who could not be bothered living all alone with strangers.

"I like this place it reminds me of Bartica and the life I lived there," he told me. He was all ears and seemed to know exactly what was to be done. I left him to get on with his work and went to see how Margaret was progressing. She did a very good job; better than I could hope to do. I congratulated her and told her to go to Bell and get acquainted. She was rather petite and pretty, but I could see some of the torment still visible on her face. I knew exactly how she felt and I was determined all the more to try and see that she is liberated from her woes. I told her of her father's pledge and my commitment to see that they get a new start in life.

She held my hand ever so gently and said "You are a good man and God will bless you for this. I shall be loyal to your wife and child. I know I cannot repay you for your kindness, the least I can do is to serve your family as best as I can."

"It is your God that has caused me to meet your father. I did it initially to protect my race from disgrace. I was wrong to think like that but in this colony one must follow the dictates of society. You would have repaid that kindness when you have fulfilled your end of the arrangements. Now go and meet Bell, she will tell you your duty."

Women are not generally tolerated when men are having a quiet drink and talking men talk, even in our society, except of course when we are out celebrating. I wonder what Christine would think of this arrangement. I would have to leave that to the wisdom of Margaret to explain.

I began rolling the ring she gave me when she left Sappanam on that memorable holiday and the fire of love that ignited in that short space of time. I remembered her quivering pink lips as she told me how the meteors looked like a fireworks display that the angels arranged just for her at that moment.

I also remembered her ploy of first sprinkling water at her mother then her father before turning her attention to me. The struggle I had in England finding her and all the complications of a Jewish wedding. It appeared strange to me to have my daughter at my wedding. I wonder if she was old enough to realise she was born out of wedlock. That thought rested heavily on mind and I wondered if it would have any effect on her later.

My catholic upbringing still has its roots in me and I find it difficult not to take heed. As for my newly discovered identity only heaven knows how I will reconcile myself to that. I kept telling myself that I was not a religious person and the way Matthew has shown me was the right path to happiness. Then there was that other problem; my daughter was brought up in the Jewish tradition and she will look for guidance from her parents as she grows older. I thought of inviting Rabbi Solomon for a fishing trip and seek his advice. I was sure he would come if Matthew were to tell him that I would contribute generously towards the proposed building of his synagogue. All this I put to Matthew to see if he could find an answer. As always he suggested we do exactly as I thought. Another problem solved.

It was time for Matthew to go to the city and see Gordon to negotiate a decent way forward for this 'Princely' visit and to bring the Rabbi here if possible.

CHAPTER 25

All Good News

The Christmas party was something of a novelty for the village children. Bell and the other two ladies did their best preparing the best meals for them. The children behaved just as children anywhere. They made a racket amusing themselves by blowing their balloons and causing it to explode. That stopped when they were served the grapes and apples and all the other sweets children liked. Apples and grapes are fruits that are imported from England and Canada for the Christmas season; as are Walnuts and other exotic fruits from the Middle East. These children never saw these things before. To see the joy in their eyes was overwhelming. Whatever prompted me to buy them is beyond me. The boys took their toy guns and went pretending they were hunting jaguars it was a good exercise for them for later life. On the whole these children were enjoying themselves beyond their wildest expectations and I could not help watching them in their ecstasy.

Their parents came and joined in their activities and were just as thrilled with everything before them. I suggested to Bell and Margaret to ask Ben to help prepare a meal for the village ladies. "All of them?" Ben asked and dashed off with the two ladies.

Events were in full swing when we heard the amphibious air craft landing. We instantly knew it was Matthew. I remember him saying he would not miss this Christmas party for all the gold in Cold Stream. He brought some of his own gifts including party hats and decorated the ladies from the village with them. They looked quite comical and the village men just stood there laughing. That came to an abrupt halt when Matthew placed a party hat on the chief and gave the other elders one to wear. They took it rather well. They were also looking at Sebastian pouring a drink. It was at this point I turned to Matthew and told him that I was now the Commissioner and did not need his advice but I am asking for it out of respect.

"What is it you are asking?" He wanted to know.

"I was a bit reluctant to say. Then I told him confidently. "It is Christmas and it is against regulations to give the villagers any alcoholic drinks. They drink their cassiri which is alcoholic and probably more potent than ours. Would you consider it a dereliction of my duty to offer them some wholesome whisky? Remember this is Christmas a time of goodwill among men."

"Peter my dear troubled friend. You are the Commissioner and you do as you see fit. You can always explain the circumstance under which you gave them if it comes to the attention of the Governor."

"I am quite capable of explaining myself. I will feel more at ease if I know that you give your blessings." I told him.

"Under these circumstances, I would do exactly as you suggested. Thank you for showing me this respect." No sooner did I finished speaking, Matthew marched off to the house and brought a bottle and handed it to me which I gave to the chief and told him to take the others to their homes and celebrate there with a warning that this will not happen again.

In the morning I woke up with a sore head and trying to recollect what happened the evening before. The others also appeared to have a sore head and they went to bathe in the cold river to regain control of their senses.

The ladies had smiles all over looking at us in utter disbelief they told us what a spectacle we were dancing with the ladies of the village and eventually with each other.

"It was Matthew who started it," Bell announced. "I know men can be ridiculous when they had a few but last night surpassed everything imaginable. Sugar Bush was so annoyed she threatened to go back to the village and never to return. It was only when Matthew told her that he will find another she changed her mind."

It took the best part of the day to regain control of my senses. There were lots to do. I must discuss with Matthew what plans the Governor is making if any for the 'Princely' visit. I also have to visit Triangle as promised all before my family gets here. It is not the place I would like to take Christine. The other big question, will Christine's arrival coincide with the 'Prince'. I will not know that until I receive a date of her arrival. This Christmas is holding up the post. I may have to go to the central sorting office to see if there is a letter. Matthew told me not to flap about. He telephoned Jonathan and got all the information. They will arrive on the 8th of January Three days before the 'Prince's' visit.

Manny came and asked if he will be needed to travel to Triangle and what should he take. I told him to use his imagination and do what he sees fit.

Sebastian and Diego were busy checking the aircraft. Ben was over the other side with the young villagers planting young orange and lime trees along the perimeter of the prepared field. It was to serve a double purpose, first as a fence from wild hogs and inquisitive caimans. Secondly and more importantly was it was a source of income. The fields look great and any shower will signal the time has come to put the seeds in.

Matthew now fully rested came over to reveal the plans discussed with the Governor.

"The Governor quite rightly told me that the 'Prince's' visit is not an official one, therefore, his hands are tied to make it look official. He suggested as a favour to his Commissioner and to me he will arrange for him to have two escorts and to use his official car while he is in the city. I reminded him that the Prince will have his own body guards as well. His other suggestion was that he will attend any function the 'Prince' may be planning and in return he will have a private dinner party on the eve of his departure. Gordon was very helpful by suggesting that when the 'Royal' visitor is in Berbice he will have use of the Governor's Berbice residence and be allowed to inspect a police guard of honour. He stressed he was going against the protocol normally reserved for official foreign dignitaries. I thanked Gordon for his efforts. It occurred to me that when the 'Prince' arrives I will be in an embarrassing position. I cannot tell him how I met his wife and our feelings for each other. Not unless he brings the matter up. I will have to be very tactful.

I visited Rabbi Solomon and he was overwhelmed by your suggestion of a generous contribution for the synagogue. He took me to the site where it will be constructed. It is in a good location, quiet and just behind the botanical gardens. He will be coming up with a delegation when I can arrange transportation and discuss any problems you have. I think he understood what the problem is without me telling him. Finally I went to the land registry and paid the $100 dollars for a year's rent and the documents will be ready in a fortnight." Matthew told me and looking pleased with what he had accomplished.

"That is more than I expected. You have been busy. You realise the 'Prince' is our responsibility and I am only too happy the Governor has been so cooperative. My father will have to share some of that responsibility. He will be the one taking The 'Prince' to Dutch Guiana to meet those East Indian folks. I am not sure what role I will play in that." I hesitated for a few seconds before asking. "Can you make sure Ben and the others especially Sebastian know how to behave in the 'Prince's' presence? After all they have never met any royalty before."

Matthew was quick to accept that responsibility. I was happy he will be coming a few days after my family.

Diego came to tell me that all is ready for our flight to Triangle. This was the first time I was fulfilling an obligation I undertook so many years ago. I was extremely happy to do it and looked forward to meeting those lovely people again.

When we arrived at Triangle, Sebastian discovered that the river was not safe enough for a landing. There were rocks poking above the surface looking dangerously like icebergs. We circled around looking for an ideal spot. There was nowhere safe enough to land, too many rocks just above the water. Diego told us there is a lake not far away and large enough for us to land.

As we headed for the lake a huge crowd was running trying to keep up with the plane and when it finally landed the cheers went up amid rapturous applause.

Diego's folks were the first to greet us in their boat and they assisted in securing the craft while we made our way to shore.

Manny and Ben hastily prepared a field surgery and I went about fulfilling my obligations. Mission accomplished it was time to return home. No time for a celebration. Diego's folks were disappointed. I, on the other hand, was happy to get back to base and forget about drinking for a while.

We were not allowed to return empty handed many gifts were given for my family. They all promised to come and see us when the dust has settled.

We returned to Sappanam in torrential rain. The entire village were on the river bank looking at the rain watering the fields. Soon it will be time to plant the seeds. I could not help noticing how tall the orange and lime trees had grown. Perhaps they relish the hot sun. I noticed also that Sebastian had put up his sign announcing ownership of the fields. Now is it registered and the rent paid he was a happy man.

At the Rest House Matthew poured us a drink and we sat reviewing all the good news he brought back from the city. His main concern now was to arrange the time for the Rabbi and his delegation to meet us. I suggested when Sebastian goes to the city for the fridge and other essentials he bought, he go with him and arrange the Rabbi's visit. I do not trust Sebastian and his American attitude to handle such a delicate matter. I would have liked to go and deal with this situation myself. As it stands I am too occupied with other important official matters. Matthew understood the situation and as always readily agreed.

We were having a second drink when he suddenly asked. "What are you going to do with those people who attached themselves to you? I could understand Hector helping with the electrics and living independently away from us. Margaret's father, do you really want his services that badly? He will be a liability and I am not so sure he will honour that pledge of never to get drunk. You will have to stop sheltering people and think positively, and not from a charitable point of view. Margaret, on the other hand, is an asset for Christine; she seems a polite and amenable young lady. What about Singh the pilot. Have you heard anything of that venture they spoke of?"

I had to stop him from going further. I explained to him. Hector and D'Costa are useful for the simple purpose that they can both keep the wind charger, Jeeps and stand by electric plant in working order. You or I do not have an infinitesimal idea of anything electrical or engineering. Besides, they can always do something useful to earn their keep. I am glad you brought this up. No definite arrangements have been made and the sooner we put that right the better. Can I leave you to deal with it?"

"Of course you can." He replied. Then he asked the most awkward question "What about Ben?"

"I don't understand what you mean,"

"He is serving no purpose looking after you any longer. Do you really need him around?"

"Discarding Ben is like severing an arm. I am so attached to him being around; it will be disastrous if he were to go his way. He is no financial burden and I will need him in the city to keep an eye on family." I told him.

"I tell you this with great reluctance. You will never be a completely independent person until you get rid of Ben. You said he will be required in the city to look after your family. That is a start. Gradually you will be able to rid yourself of his constant presence. You will have to look to your family for reassurance if you need reassuring. I should be the last person telling you this, considering I was never married." Matthew advised.

"I am sure what you are saying is absolutely right. I do not look to him as a protector any longer. He has become more of an affectionate friend who will never let you down." I told Matthew.

A week later Matthew returned from the city with the household items. Hector and D'Costa took charge of it while I went and greeted the Rabbi and his small delegation. I told him of the dilemma I am facing with the upbringing of a young child in a strange land. I wanted her to continue in the tradition to which she was born. I also made it absolutely clear that I have no intention of going back to Catholicism or to follow the tradition my newly found identity.

"A man must look to something for guidance. Something you can cling to in times of desperation," he suggested.

"I know precisely what you are saying. I may seem unorthodox but I have found a potent means of extricating myself from the misery you suggested. At the same time, I do not wish my family to suffer because of my lack of faith. I will be there when I am wanted." I told him this with total confidence of my conviction.

"What is this rare magic you have discovered that gives you this confidence?" He asked with some interest.

"You know Matthew better than me. I think you will find a more appropriate answer coming from him." I said.

"Ah! I see you have been converted. Say no more. I cannot say I discard such beliefs completely. I am what I am and respect every man for their ideology. Now let's talk some business." He looked at me for a moment and said the strangest thing I heard for a long time. "The world thought that Jews are always talking of money. It is that misconception that brought about the devastation we experienced in Germany. I am not going to hold you on the promise of a generous contribution. I will speak only of the welfare of your child. We have a school that teaches the laws of Judaism and also the curriculum as required by the government."

"We are a private organisation and a small one at that with only about forty families. I do not think the Rabbi need to go further. I am sure you understand the position," a member of his delegation informed me.

"Of course I do that is why I will give the donation I promised. It is not that I wanted special treatment for my daughter but because I just feel right doing it. Will you accept it on those conditions?" I asked.

"Your donation is a separate arrangement altogether. We will do our best for your child whether we get a donation or not. That is our commitment to our people. I think we have covered all that was needed to be discussed." A second member added.

"How about that fishing trip you promised?" Rabbi Solomon smilingly asked.

"Today I will take you dry-fishing. Have you done that before?"

"I can't say I have. If it is interesting then let's go. First you forgot one important thing."

I could not think what the important matter I missed was. I looked puzzled. Then, he suggested that a drink is always important before going fishing. We all laughed hysterically at his comment. I was beginning to like this gentleman. His sense of humour was most pleasant and friendly.

Matthew had disappeared and left us alone to negotiate terms and conditions. When he realised we were finished he quickly joined us. "I sensed someone been telling a funny story." He said as he sat next to the Rabbi. We all pointed to the Rabbi.

Ben and Diego were invited to join us. We did not have a clue of dry fishing. I merely heard Diego mention it as a swift way of getting the himaras. He sent his son for the fishing rods we kept in the store room and showed us how to tie the fly on the hook then he demonstrated the way it is done. It was simpler than conventional fishing. I hope the results will be just as effective.

First, we must have that drink I was reminded about. Ben as usual was quick to oblige. We did not have to walk very far to find the ideal spot where these fish can be found. Diego was the first to get his quarry followed by the Rabbi. It was sometime before Matthew proved his worth. Ben and I were not so lucky.

By late afternoon we devoured the fish and had a few more to drink. It was time to say goodbye to our visitors.

The Rabbi embraced me for a good minute and quietly thanked me. Before leaving he offered a prayer for all of us. "I wondered what Moses would have thought of this place. It's so peaceful it could be your promised land."

Sebastian was given strict instructions to see them safely home as we waved goodbye.

CHAPTER 26

Family Reunion

There were a large gathering of friends and families; actually a convoy of four cars. As is expected in a small colony every little exciting aspect of life becomes a large celebratory event. I did not really entertain this idea. I wanted a private meeting with my family first and then to have introduced them to various friends and relations at convenient stages. I could not say no when said they would be coming to the airport. My mother frowned on these large gatherings especially when it was supposed to be a private occasion.

As soon as the luggage was located and the formalities of introductions were over we sped off with my parents trying to stay as close as possible behind us.

Bell and the other ladies were busy preparing snacks and various flavoured lemonade. In my absence they erected a huge welcoming sign with lots of signatures. I appreciated their efforts.

A semblance of privacy prevailed when we entered the house. Isabella confined herself to the kitchen. As soon as Bell and Margaret were introduced they disappeared.

It was the first opportunity I had to embrace and welcome Christine. She was so tenderly loving embrace that I did not wish for it to end. Bell came and inquired if we needed any help with the luggage. Catherine and Elizabeth were shown their rooms and instantly Elizabeth came running and shouting "I have a shower in my room" Catherine teased by saying "so do I young lady." Turning to me she expressed her delight at the preparation I made for her visit.

It was a long flight. I suggested when they are freshened up and have a bit to eat it would be better to have a good rest to prepare for the evening gathering. Margaret came and joined Bell.

I guess it is normal for curiosity to be a potent urge not to miss anything. I would not deny her the opportunity and took to occasion of properly introducing her to Christine. I told her Margaret would be her constant companion, confidant and a nanny to Elizabeth when Catherine had returned home.

"I heard that, Peter. Planning to send me home already" Catherine joked.

"You are the one mother-in-law that any man would tolerate living in his house." I responded.

We sat on the veranda sipping lemonade. Catherine was ever so pleased with the view. She remarked what a luxury it is to have the sea just a hundred yards away and the breeze was a gift of angels. I thought of inviting the ladies for a much stronger drink Catherine was overwhelmed with my suggestion, both Bell and Margaret went and brought the necessaries. I ask them to send Isabella to meet her mistress. I felt a bit heartless leaving her out. She must know her place from the start; she is the kind of person to get familiar when a little courtesy is extended. As she came in she curtsied as my mother taught her. I told Christine she is the maid and kitchen help with her own flat on the ground floor. She was so subdued I felt she was about to have a fit. She took the opportunity to express her displeasure of sharing the ground floor with the gardener. Catherine dismissed her in a formal manner. I thought we will have to adjust our mannerisms towards her and make her feel relaxed. People in England do treat servants as servants. Here in our little domain we are a bit more relaxed and tried to be more tolerant towards them.

"You have a fine selection of malt here, Peter. Who's selected them for you?" Catherine asked.

"It's that brother of your son-in-law. He taught me to appreciate fine malt. I guess it is one of his great pleasures living out there in the wilderness." I told her.

"Would he be coming tonight?" She asked.

"Or sooner, with the regular crowd, they are with my parents at the hotel right now. Only decency prevented him from rushing here to be reunited with his niece." I told her.

"You must sit down and explain to me all the plans you have for my short holiday."

"Is it a short holiday Catherine?" I asked.

"Oh yes. I cannot leave Jonathan for too long." She replied.

"When is it you are planning to return?" again I asked.

"In two months' time, it should give him enough time to miss me and to realise what an asset I am to him." She said with relish.

Diego, his son and Ben were behind Matthew walking up the stairs. There was a loud cry of welcome from Catherine and it took a good two minutes before they released their embrace.

"Catherine, may I introduce Diego, Bell's husband and this here is Ben. He has been with me for eleven years now. He is going to be staying here while I am at Sappanam. He will be Elizabeth's body guard. I hope they become good friend."

"He is huge." Exclaimed Elizabeth she turned to Matthew and asked "Is he dangerous Uncle Matthew?"

"He is a pussy cat." Matthew told her.

"Good. I love pussy cats." She then went and held his hands and examined his fingers.

Ben was looking rather shy and in one swoop he lifted her off her feet and held her in the air. She was so thrilled she asked that he do it again.

Diego Jr. came and shook her hand quite formally and announced that he has many names.

"What are all your names? Elizabeth asked.

"I am Diego, Matthew, Peter and Ben. Father gave me all his best friends' names." He told her and asked "How many names have you got?"

"I have only one name. But I am named after a princess" She proudly told him.

I asked Margaret to look after them while I entertained my friends. A few minutes later my guests started arriving. They all gave Christine a thorough inspection and asked so many questions she was unable to answer them all at once. We sat on the veranda enjoying the Atlantic breeze and each other's company.

It was Matthew who suggested that he reveal the itinerary he made for Catherine's 'short stay'.

"I will surprise you by announcing we are having a 'Princely' visit in three days. What I suggest is we let Catherine take in as much of the social activities available. Tonight we rest and tomorrow evening you all join me at my club for a second welcoming party. When the 'Prince' arrives we will see what program Gordon has in mind and try to coordinate our movements to make it a pleasant visit.

I think Peter suggested that we visit Berbice when Joseph is ready to take him to Surinam and to treat him to one of his river trips. I think Peter would like to take him to Sappanam to show him how the native South Americans live."

While he was talking my mind was on Christine. Again I found myself twirling the ring she gave me and then I remembered I had a diamond ring I had made using the measurement of her ring.

Father was proposing a toast. He began by saying "Ladies and gentlemen. I am sure you all know how proud Miriam and I are to meet our daughter-in-law for the first time. We did discover that our son was not honest with us when he told us she is rather pretty. We found her not only to be the most beautiful young lady we had the good fortune to meet. Her grace and charm complimented that rare beauty. I welcome you to the house of D'Abrue."

When he finished I took Christine by the arm and expressed my love for her and took the diamond ring and place it on her finger. She looked at it and gasped. "Is this real darling? It must have cost you a fortune."

"It is real and it does cost a fortune but not enough to compensate for the happiness you brought me, my parents and friends."

The ladies took turn to admire the stone a huge fifteen carat diamond. It was not intended for a display of affluence but purely for what it represented, my love for her.

In the morning Christine, her mother and Elizabeth returned from the sea looking disappointed. They told me the water was dirty and not really good for swimming. I told her the facts; the condition of the water is caused by the Amazon and Orinoco rivers. All the silt from these two rivers, dirty the water all along the Atlantic coast and up to three hundred miles out in the sea.

"The Amazon?" Catherine asked in disbelief, "And the Orinoco?

"The Amazon is several hundred miles to the East and the Orinoco is merely a few hundred miles to the West." I explained.

After breakfast I took them to the Tower Hotel for a swim which they enjoyed thoroughly. I made a financial arrangement with the management for them to swim as regularly as they want.

Gordon rang to say he would be visiting to discuss the 'Prince's' visit and hoped that Matthew would be present. I relayed his message to Matthew who was very pleased.

Elizabeth was not happy to be left behind in the care of Margaret. I told her she would not enjoy our party as it was boring and we only did it for her grandma.

"Would grandmas enjoy it?" She quickly asked.

"You would have to ask her in the morning." I said.

Our entourage doubled the entire membership of the club. No one could remember the last time when it was filled to capacity. Matthew had arranged a more modern band to play for us. Which was good as the Guianese band the club hires was a bit out of tune with the times.

Catherine watched in amazement as Inge got hold of Matthew and displayed her tantalising dance and her display of more legs and other parts of her body. I think Matthew got some kind of sensual excitement from it all. When the band stopped he refused to sit and stood there waiting for the next tune to be played. Catherine noticed it too and made it known to my father. My mother pretended she was not observing our merriment. I felt obliged to take her to the floor and was soon joined by Christine and Bell. This softened her a bit and she looked more relaxed. My father came to the rescue and I was free to dance with my darling wife.

The champagne flowed as it never flowed before and when Marina came and ask me for a dance I knew she was in a merry spirit. While we were dancing she whispered in my ear. "I could have been the one wearing that huge diamond ring."

"I hope you are not jealous, Marina?" I asked waiting to hear what she would say.

"There is another thing I discovered yesterday," she continued.

"And what is that?" I asked getting a bit more mystified.

"There is something that is not right. You spent four years in England. Elizabeth is seven. Are you really saying she is your daughter?" Her conversation unsettled me and although it is not impolite to question friends on certain personal matters. I felt offended. I did not want to hurt her feelings. I realise that she regretted she did not take my offer of a date more seriously. I was beginning to think that the English has the right attitude to personal affairs. This is colonial Guiana. I must abide with the terms and conditions society has lain down. I felt I should answer her question when I told her. "One day perhaps you will find the truth and now shall we enjoy ourselves."

She smiled as if content with my answer. I was ever so happy when the tune ended. I can get back to Christine and really enjoy myself.

Matthew and Inge were the stars of the night. He was so happy he invited the members to join in the celebrations. It was an invitation that need not be extended twice.

It was past 2 o'clock in the morning when we arrived home. Tired and in the happiest of mood, Elizabeth came running with Margaret at her heels. She hugged me and asked.

"Was it a really horrible party papa?"

"Why don't you ask grandma? It was a party for her."

"Grandma did you enjoy the party?"

"It was the most horrible party I've been to." She told her making a face of discontentment.

"Fibber, ... Then why you spent such a long time."

"I'll tell you in the morning. Now be a good girl and go to bed."

Tomorrow we have a meeting with Gordon. I forgot to tell Matthew I will have to notify him early in the morning and ask him to deal with it. Right now a good sleep is all I need, my first night with my dear wife in our own home and in my country.

Matthew arrived on the dot of 9 o'clock a few minutes later Gordon arrived. He chatted with Catherine for a long time and inquiring of Jonathan and his well-being. Eventually we sat down and discussed the arrangements. My father was willing to travel to Surinam with the guests and any others willing to accompany him. Gordon told us that he met the Prince a dozen or more times in India and would be pleased to accommodate him. The Governor would keep his promise of having a dinner in his honour on the eve of his departure. It seems we have been through this before and confirmation was necessary. Gordon has extended an invitation for us to dine with him when it is convenient. We can always arrange this within our itinerary.

Finally, he told us he booked the entire Tower Hotel for the duration of the visit and the bill would have to be met by us. Since no one disagreed. It was settled. He stayed for lunch before departing. Elizabeth soon became his friend especially when he showed her a trick of the disappearing coin. She was still trying to work out how it is done long after he left.

Aubrey rang to ask if I could meet him in his office at 3 o'clock, the agreement with the pilot Singh needed my signature and that Sebastian promised to be there. I told him Matthew will have to be present as he is part of the deal. He told me he has to adjust the agreement accordingly and it would not be a problem.

I find his office well above the standards of the lawyers and solicitors occupying Croal Street. The building itself was not impressive. Some of these offices were the chambers of the best legal brains not only in British Guiana but the entire British West Indies.

The young lady at the typewriter was more interested adjusting her skirt than the work she was given. I kept asking myself why do young ladies these days wish to expose themselves beyond the limits of decency and then take a lot of time and energy to cover themselves up. Is it to tell the public that they are conscious of their semi-nudity and will do everything in their power to put it right? I doubt it. I think they are drawing attention by their exposure, hoping to attract a compliment from some admiring young man. I felt uneasy with her wriggling and express it in no uncertain terms. "Miss if you are ashamed of your dress. Why do you wear it? I asked politely. "It is the fashion these days and I do not want to be left out." She replied causally.

Aubrey came out and invited us in his chambers. Singh without asking took the document and started reading it. Matthew took it away and handed it back to Aubrey. "It is the lawyer who will read it to all of us." Matthew told him with a touch of sarcasm. He looked at Matthew in annoyance.

The document was read and each party signed, respectively, on the dotted line.

I told Aubrey to do a separate deed making Matthew the chief executive of this partnership and with conditions that all participants must obey. This will entail Matthew with the authority to scrutinise all incoming and outgoing finances. There were no dissent among the shareholders and Aubrey told me that he had such a document. All that is required is our signatures. This action was brought about by Singh's seemingly dominant attitude earlier. Matthew gave me one of his winks of approval.

As we left the office, I said goodbye to the typist and told her to be herself and not to follow unnecessary trends. She simply smiled and said goodbye.

Matthew wanted us to go to his club. I told him I must return home and spend some time with my family. He departed with the others.

CHAPTER 27

The Prince is Here

Although this was not an official visit, the headlines made it appear so. There were pictures of him standing next to Gordon and Matthew. The motorcade was escorted by four outriders. The Rajkumar and Rajkumari sat impassively at the back while they were motored at speed to his hotel. Gordon and Matthew was immediately behind with me and family at the rear.

This was post war British Guiana and little has changed over the years, except there were cries for a free Guiana. The Governor's hands were tied. Since this was not an official visit there were no alternative but to officially ignore it. However, the presence of four outriders did give the visit a semblance of importance.

It must be remembered that British Guiana, the size of England, had a population of just half a million. It was no wonder that a visit like this would have created immense curiosity. I must give credit to our Governor for dealing so tactfully with the situation and to Gordon acting his part.

There were a police cordon around the hotel and an armed guard stood at the entrance. The 'Royal' couple were escorted into the hotel while we followed and waited in the conference room set aside for this occasion.

The Governor has kindly delegated Gordon to be the couple's companion for the duration of the visit. He was upstairs assisting them to settle down. Matthew decided to order some drinks for us. Christine was ever so patient. She met him once in England. Whether he will remember her is another matter.

I was happy Catherine is not here she might have been bored waiting. She normally has people waiting on her.

The atmosphere changed when they were escorted to the conference room. They were smiling and he immediately recognised me as I paid my respect in the Indian manner. He also recognised Christine, referring her to the lost bride.

As Matthew was presented, The Rajkumar paused and said. "You must be Major Longhorn." Matthew burst out laughing in acknowledgement. He placed a friendly hand on Matthew's shoulder and told him that they must have a private conversation. Matthew nodded in agreement.

It is customary that a lady escorted the Rajkumari and Christine was willing to oblige. Gordon led the way to the dining room where a lavish meal of both Guianese and Indian meals were laid out.

We continued to ask many questions, one important question being asked, Why this visit? I proposed to answer that with what I know.

"The Rajkumar's intense interest lies with the Indians who left their homeland to work on the sugar plantations and with a promise of repatriation at the end of their contract." I started out by saying. "The Rajkumar is interested in their welfare and whether they kept up their religion and culture. This is a delicate situation. That is why it is a private visit. His Excellency, I pointed out do not hold the British government responsible if that part of repatriation was not observed. It was noted in many dispatches to India that offers of repatriation were ignored as many of the immigrants felt that they were happier where they were. His Excellency wanted to confirm that this was true. He felt obliged to satisfy himself. Since the majority of immigrants were from his home state. The relatives of some of the immigrants wanted to know when their relatives would be coming home, he would be the next ruler of his state when his father dies, who I must add is rather fragile and in very poor health. He does not want to start his rule by dealing with dissatisfied citizens. He intended to have written confirmation from those here of their refusal to be repatriated. Perhaps a photographer could be made available to prove this visit did what it set out to do."

"I could not have made that any clearer Peter." He said to me. He then thanked everyone for their support and also to make it absolutely clear that none of what is discussed here will be open to the public. We all understood this.

We were all surprised when the Rajkumari joined in by saying that the Prince's father was old and weak and may die at any time. When that happens his Highness will be the next Maharajah and there will no time for him to embark on a private mission. As she spoke I could not help noticing her glancing intermittently at Matthew and smiling. I know for a fact that I was one of the few people in the room to know of the relationship with her and Matthew.

Gordon then insisted that the couple be left to themselves for a good rest. He will see to their itinerary and make sure it is executed with military precision.

We said our goodbyes and before leaving, their highnesses clasped their hands as if in prayer and said "May the blessings of Rama be with all of you."

I could see Matthew was moved by their blessings and made an abortive attempt to go and shake their hands.

The truth is no one knew exactly how to deal with the visitors. We were not sure how to address them. Rather than looking foolish we all turned to Matthew for guidance. Christine always appeared confident in his presence. Perhaps she can assist with our dilemma. I should have known better and asked. I remembered when in England, we saluted and either stood to attention or spoke only when required. It will look ridiculous doing the same when he is our guest and we are not in uniform. What surprised me most was that in England, when I was invited to tea with him I did not feel I had to behave differently. I felt completely at ease in his presence. Perhaps it is the presence of the Rajkumari that has brought out this uneasy tension.

Matthew was quick to inform us. "He is not really a royal person but the son of a ruler whom Britain refused to acknowledge as royal by the simple fact that the subcontinent already has a truly Royal Emperor. Just treat him with respect and always keep your hands behind you. Trust me he would appreciate courtesy more that royal flattery. I spent quite a long time with a famous Maharajah and I understood what was required. Be yourself but be respectful."

It was a quick lesson but one that put us all at ease. Christine reminded us that we were making a mountain from a mole hill. I felt more at ease with what Matthew said.

Gordon rang to say that he wanted to confirm the travelling arrangements to Surinam and could he come around to discuss that with my father. When he arrived I left Matthew and my father to discuss what plans were afoot.

Gordon told them that he needs to contact the Surinam Government's immigration office of the visit and to get the necessary papers. "I can deal effectively with that." He told them with confidence. "It will take a matter of hours." Sebastian was told he may listen and to make any necessary comments concerning the flights.

He unfolded a map and suggested to them that it would be better to fly with the amphibian aircraft and land in the Paramaribo River. Gordon agreed, and told us he would inform the immigration authorities and to let them know the purpose of his visit.

A few days later, Gordon told us that he had all the necessary papers and he had included my name and Christine's as would be travellers. I was not keen to go but Christine showed such enthusiasm I could not disappoint her. Catherine wanted to know why she was left out. Gordon could not give a reason.

Christine told her she would be more important looking after Elizabeth while we are away. She reluctantly agreed.

The plan was to fly to Berbice, Isabel and Margaret were included. The two visitors will be accommodated at the Governor's mansion in Berbice along with Matthew and Gordon. There they will have the opportunity to interview the East Indians and to receive written confirmation of their desire to remain in British Guiana. This was the easy part. Matthew could handle this. It is important that we travelled further up the Corentyne where a larger numbers of sugar workers lived. I am sure I will be useful in this area. I could also take them to Skeldon sugar plantation where an even greater number lived.

Gordon suggested that since the road is worse than potato fields we take the amphibian to the Corentyne River and ask Andrew to receive us there. It would be quicker. Sebastian thought that we can continue to Paramaribo from there when our interview is over.

On the morning after arriving in Berbice we set out on this complicated journey. Andrew was most helpful and organised a meeting of all the East Indian labourers to meet the visitors.

They danced and sang praises to the visitors and shouting for freedom for India. This appears to embarrass the visitors.

He addressed them in typical Indian fashion and thanked them for their cooperation and asked them to sign the forms stating their intentions. Andrew got some of his own people to take care of that. He later entertained us at his home. I was happy to see Isme who was formally introduced to Christine. The two ladies took the Rajkumari on a tour of the gardens while we freshened up with a drink of fine malt. Sebastian and the visitor were served tea.

Our next stop was the final destination to a country I never visited. The Paramaribo River was smaller than our Berbice River. As we disembarked I saw a sign in Water Molen Straat that said "Alberga Diamonds." This was the gentleman we sold our diamonds to. There was no sign of him.

We were greeted by a few governments' official and escorted in limousines. I guess they wanted to impress us and took us on a tour of the city which I must say was not as impressive as Georgetown but beautiful enough to be admired.

The East Indians were invited to a football ground and there they declared their intentions of remaining Dutch citizens. They spoke in an unfamiliar Indian language. Matthew understood it and explained it to us. They also spoke fluent Dutch, some German and French. Their English was diabolical. It is similar to the Babe English spoken at the villages at home. They call it talkie=talkie.

Gordon took several pictures of all the women who were dressed in their finest saris and gold jewelleries. The men in what looked like tunics and trousers. It was a westernised equivalent to their Indian every day wear. The Rajkumari was pleasantly amused. She placed a hand over her mouth as she smiled.

Written testaments were collected of their new found allegiance. And as they sang praises to them we started our exit.

At the gate was a large crowd, wanting to see what was happening. Among them was our diamond dealer. He noticed Matthew and ran towards him with an outstretched hand. They acknowledged each other and talked for a minute occasionally pointing in my direction before finally beckoning me to come forward. They were too far away for me to respond verbally so I signalled him to say I would be unable to do so. I think he understood and shook Mr Alberga's hand before joining us.

Our next stop was Nickerie. Fortunately, there is a river next to the town. Our presence there caused little stir a handful of farmers were gathered by the harbour. They were less enthusiastic and only paid compliments when the Rajkumari address them. I noticed the crowd was getting larger by the minute. It turned out that most of the late arrivals were at work when we arrived. They looked dirty in their smoke soiled clothes and express apologies for their appearances. Their faces were blackened with the burnt ashes from the sugar cane. It was common practice to burn the sugar cane before cutting. This got rid of all the leaves and also sent the many rattle snakes that thrive on the rats that lived there slithering away to protected areas.

Christine looked scared and asked why they are carrying swords. I told her it is not swords but cutlasses they used for cutting the sugar cane.

Our guests understood the situation and decided not to take any more pictures only the signed declarations were collected.

It was a low-key affair. It suited our visitor's purpose. So I think on the whole the trip was a success.

We boarded the plane for our flight home. When we arrived at the Berbice River, Sebastian told us he could not land the craft in the river. It turned out that dozens of logs tied together as rafts were floating downstream towards the saw mills.

I told him of the Canje River which would be on the right if he turned the plane around. The only problem being, our vehicles were on the stelling. We solved that problem by asking the jetty superintendent to phone the harbour manager and asked that our drivers meet us here.

That evening we attended a dinner organised by Gordon. The mayor was in attendance along with some of his most important councillors.

Gordon like Matthew served in India only at different times. He told us of their regular encounters and the friendship that eventually matured. Unlike Matthew he was not at all interested in the mystical side of Indian life. He also expressed his pleasure of having the opportunity of meeting his friend after so many years. I guess this dinner was in honour of that friendship.

Time was short so father decided not to entertain with his famous barbeque. That was a pity. Christine and the others would have enjoyed it. Catherine would be returning to England in a few weeks' time and I wondered if the opportunity would arise again for her to be treated to such a lovely day out. Most importantly I pointed out to him that I am sure our visitors have never seen a barbeque like his before and what a treat it would be for them. This suggestion flattered my father who immediately changed his mind on condition that I can get Ben here in time.

I asked Sebastian if this was possible. "Nothing is impossible for me when it comes to flying." Then he asked a very pertinent question. "Is it worth flying all the way to Sappanam for one man? Think of the fuel. If you feel it is worth it then I am game to your request."

"If I decided to let you go then I think it would be worth the effort if Diego and his family come along as well." I suggested to him.

"I can see you are determined to let me go so when do you want me to fly there? He asked.

"It's up to you so long as you get back here before tomorrow morning." I told him then I shouted after him. "Dam the cost of the fuel. Happiness comes first."

The barbeque was as always the same as the ones before the same ritual of fishing, hunting, and swimming. The only difference was we had very important guests. The likes of which will not be seen here again. I wish the East Indian couple in their boat who met Gordon previously were somewhere to speak to our guests. It would have thrilled them on ends.

True to his words Sebastian came with his passengers and they all joined in the festive affair. Young Diego was thrilled when Elizabeth asked that they go swimming in the river. Christine was not so sure. Catherine was horrified. Diego promised to look after them. A different feeling was taking hold of me I looked at the two youngsters and thought I would not like any strong feeling developing between them. I knew they were only children; it was a dangerous time for this kind of feeling to formulate. I tried to shrug it away only for it to pop up with alarming conviction. I was beginning to understand how crucial it was to implant the seeds of religion and culture in a young mind and let it take root and grow. I appeased my feelings with the thought that this is a one off encounter and I shall try to avert any unnecessary meeting between to two in future. I cursed myself for having these ideas. I thought the friendship I shared with Diego and Bell did not warrant these cruel thinking.

Formalities prevail throughout the day. We all wanted to climb over that barrier and gave the occasion a chance for total enjoyment. To embrace the 'Prince' in friendship and let him know how much we appreciated his presence. The 'Prince' may have sensed this and came over and decided to take the part of host. Everyone cheered as he poured us all a drink and thanked my father for showing him how to enjoy life in a simpler way. "As heir I have to observe what the advisors of my father suggest. I found it difficult to fit in within the constraints of a natural way of life and heir. I accepted to be his heir not for the power that goes with it but to use that power to bring about change for a more relaxed way of life, as nature intended. This outing has shown me how. For that I am eternally grateful."

"I sensed a change in him, one that I never expected" Matthew whispered to me.

CHAPTER 28

Reliving the Past

Matthew arranged with our visitors to meet at my residence. To be quite honest I was very pleased and I allowed Catherine and Christine to welcome them. Matthew as usual treated my home as his. It was the way he behaved with total confidence that really created the camaraderie, respect, and love for this gentleman. I was always happy to let him have his way. Catherine never knew him until that day she came to Sappanam and a bond of friendship was beginning to show. I was happy with that also.

I joined them in the living room and was amazed when the 'Prince' announced his intention.

"That day at the barbeque has taught me a lesson and what it's like to gather informally and let your hair down. Today I have dispensed with formalities. I see you all as true friends and what could be better than acknowledging it here and now. Turning to Matthew he asked "I hope you would not mind if I address you as Matt."

Matthew smiled and acknowledge with a nod. He then said, "My name is Kumar and my wife is Indera."

Catherine told him her name and unabashed she told him to call her Cathy. The atmosphere changed dramatically. Everyone felt so relaxed. It was like being let out of a cage.

"Now Peter" he said to me "I realise how much effort you and Matt made in making our short stay memorable and happy. I was more impressed with the East Indians in Surinam. I wish those I met here could have provided a better spectacle. Never mind it was all impromptu. The evidence I have will determine whether I have a trouble free state when I return. I have a delicate question to ask Matt. Here in this country as in Surinam the blacks appear to segregate themselves from the rest of the community. Can you explain that?"

"To be quite honest I do not want to let it be seen as if I am degrading one race for the benefit of any other. We the British as in India hold all the responsible posts whether it is in government or other administrative position. For some ridiculous reasons we classified Peter and his kind as Portuguese and not as Europeans. They along with the Chinese are the professionals and merchants. The East Indians are a hard-working people. They plant all the rice in this country. The blacks have a more relaxed attitude to life. They love dancing and celebrate every occasion whether small or important with great enthusiasm. To be fair the blacks were not given the opportunity to succeed. We, the British still treated them as slaves. The inculcation of submissiveness is dying. I can see the future when they will rise and proclaim their rightful place in society and it cannot be soon enough. This picture I expose to you may not be the right one. As an English man sent here over a quarter of a century ago most of my time was spent in the jungle. I had periodical social intercourse with the rest of the population. That did not exclude me from observing their attitudes and way of life when I left India I was with my regiment in Aldershot. My predecessor died from a heart attack and I was asked to replace him. I was told my knowledge of Indians would serve me well. I was shocked when I took up my post to find it was misleading and a million miles from the truth."

"They were not East Indians?" Kumar asked.

"Far from it, as you will see when we take you to Sappanam. These are native South American Indians. We call them Amerindians." Matthew explained.

"Have you married Matt?" Indera asked.

"He never married. He came back to England heartbroken because his Commanding Officer failed to grant his courteous request to marry a princess he was in love with." Catherine told her with confidence.

Both the visitors started laughing with Matthew joining them.

"Did I say something funny?" Catherine asked. There was more hysterical laughter. "Will someone tell me what was so funny about what I said to cause such amusement?" Catherine demanded.

Matthew laughter became uncontrollable and between fits of laughter he asked Indera to explain.

"I was the princess he fell in love with. We wanted to get married. Only now I know why it did not happen. Kumar and I were married not by choice but because of the dictates of our families.

Catherine shook her head in disbelief and profusely expressed regrets to the guests for this social gaffe.

"I am happy it came out this way. I felt my mission would have had emptiness without your intervention, Catherine. Thank you." Kumar said looking a bit happier.

"My, My, Uncle Matthew had a secret no one knew about. I wonder if papa knew." Christine added.

Margaret came in and told us that Elizabeth wanted to meet a "Prince and Princess again. She was not able to converse with them at the barbeque.

"Come and shake hands with our visitors, darling." Christine said. Turning to the visitors she told them it is our daughter.

Isabella came in on a pretext asking if tea is to be served here or in the dining room. Catherine dismissed her. Telling her she will be told when and where it will be served.

I think Isabella should have been granted some privilege of at least meeting the visitors. Somehow I felt I have let her down by not showing the kindness I promised in Berbice. Catherine, on the other hand, was a strict disciplinarian where servants are concerned.

"After all this discussions and secrets revealed I felt like having malt. What about you Kumar would you join us?" Matthew asked.

"Anyone who attended Harrow and declared himself a teetotaller needs his head examined." Was Kumar way of saying yes.

"Matthew and Jonathan went to Eton. Did you know that Kumar?" Catherine joined in

"No I did not. People always believe that Eton was a better school than Harrow. I think it's a myth. Churchill and Nehru attended Harrow and they both turned out to be great politicians." Kumar added.

The ladies left us to our devices and went to have their tea. Elizabeth bravely went and sat next to Kumar holding his hand and admiring his ring with a large stone. He took the ring and placed it on her finger. Of course it was too big. She looked at it and asked if it is for her. When he indicated that it was a gift she hugged and thanked him.

"Are you sure you wanted her to have it." I asked

"It is just a ring with no significance of State authority."

He in turn put his arm over her shoulders and asked. "Do you like your new home?"

"I like it here where it is cool, not outside in the sun, it is too hot. I like listening to the waves from the sea splashing on the beach. At night when I cannot sleep I listened to them splashing and imagine I am swimming. It makes me fall asleep." Holding on to her gift. She told him. "Please excuse me I must have tea with grandma and show her my gift."

Kumar then asked when we would be going to Sappanam. I told him I have a meeting with Rabbi Solomon later in the evening. If Sebastian returns with the amphibian this evening we can go tomorrow morning. He nodded in agreement.

Rabbi Solomon arrived at the same time Sebastian landed and we all went to the veranda to watch him securing the craft.

The Rabbi explained to Christine about Elizabeth's school and what is required of us. Christine asked if it was a school for both boys and girls. He told her there is only the one school and if she wished for Elizabeth to attend a girls' only school it will have to be the Catholic school and she will have to observe their teachings on religion. Christine dismissed the idea and agreed that the Jewish school was the best for our daughter.

Matthew handed him a cheque and I went to the study to prepare mine. When I handed it to him, he looked at it and asked. "Do you want to give that much." I nodded and then added. "If it is too much I can change it."

"No, no, it is not too much. I thank you on behalf of our committee." He said putting the two cheques in his pocket. Matthew offered him a drink which he declined declaring that he has other appointments with some important people.

I explained to Sebastian our plans for the morning. He told me he has a meeting with Singh. He also mentioned that D'Costa was taking to flying as a natural. "I let him fly the plane back from Sappanam." He told me, looking very pleased with himself. He continued.

"A few more lessons are all he needs. It is all coming together. Can you imagine what an asset he will be when this business gets started?" He then explained his meeting with Singh. "We acquired an office that needed some painting and office equipment, Ben is there helping. I will be only an hour to get the phone installed and the office furniture delivered when the painting is done. Once I get all this sorted I will be back before 6 o'clock." He indicated to me his desire of getting a young lady to manage the phone and to register all the people wanting to go on holiday. "We have had so many inquiries about trips to the interior and also to the famous waterfalls. There are also enquiries of trips to Barbados and other West Indian Islands. I tell you Peter this business will be big. I may need another pilot, but that can wait until we get started. Singh has had his friend printing lots of leaflets for advertisements to the local people. We planned to put adverts in the Sunday papers as well and go national." I could see he was all excited. He poured a large drink then had something to eat, before he left he told me that the premises was so large I could set up my surgery in the other two rooms they do not need. "The telephonist could serve us both. What do you think?" Finally, he stopped talking.

I found it interesting the extra rooms for my surgery. It will be ideal for me to have a Surgery in the city. I will have to look at the location and also the feasibility of doing two jobs at the same time. Matthew always knew it was my intention. And I am sure he will not accuse me of neglecting my job at Sappanam. I also knew he loved deputising and exercising his powers when I am away.

When Sebastian left, Matthew and I went to the veranda taking in the Atlantic breeze. The rest of my family soon joined us. Margaret came and dressed in flimsy top and scanty pants. Catherine looked at her and I could see extreme disapproval written all over her face. With a wry smile she told her not to stand upright facing the wind as it might blow her clothing away.

"Why are you dressed like that" I asked.

"It was in the showcase at Bookers stores and it is fashionable. So Isabella and I thought of taking Elizabeth for a stroll at the sea wall." She explained.

"The sea wall" Matthew gasped in astonishment. Do you know a lot of rapes occurred there recently and most of the victims were dressed like that. Are you hoping it happened to you?"

"No Mr Longhorn, I did not plan to go alone. Isabella said she would accompany me. She said in her defence. "I'll go and change it if it suits you."

"Young lady it isn't if it suits me. I am only trying to warn you of the dangers out there." Matthew told her.

Isabella came to fetch her and she was dressed in the similar fashion. Catherine became red in the face. She confronted them in anger. "My granddaughter is to be protected and not subjected to vulgarity. If Christine fails to teach you to dress properly then I will. The clothes you wear to go masquerading down at the sea wall are inviting trouble. This sun and your attire will motivate sexual desires in those virile beasts looking for an opportunity. When they see bare shoulders and very little to cover your legs they lose all senses of decency and want to get intimate with what you are showing. Not only will you lose your pride but dashed all hopes of a decent marriage. I hope you do not consider me prudent."

"No ma'am. I am really sorry if I offended you" She apologised almost in tears.

"Oh dam it." I said "Matthew lets escort the ladies for their stroll. It would be a shame if they were prepared for an outing and their modern attire were to be a hindrance."

"I agree, Let's go." Matthew agreed readily. He then told Catherine. "Young people live in a world different to ours. If we want to be their friends we must try and understand that times are changing."

"It's that blasted war. We never had so much vulgarity in our dress code as these youngsters seems readily to don and exhibit themselves. I tell you Matthew and I am not exaggerating. During the war I saw young soldiers discreetly having sex at the railway station. Can you believe it at the railway station?"

"You must understand Cathy; those men were off to risk their lives. They were not sure of coming home again. If they seize an opportunity no one should blame them." Matthew tried to reason.

Matthew and I took the young ladies for their walk. We deliberately lingered about ten yards behind, observing the situation. It turned out to be a normal walk after all. I even allowed Elizabeth to join them. She was happier in the company of Margaret. I must say she did not take to Isabella.

On our way home, I asked Matthew if he objected to my surgery in the city. He told me in no uncertain terms that all I needed to do is to be seen at my post at regular times and to hand in my reports promptly. I still feel like an assistant Commissioner. The truth is this arrangement is heaven sent. I love being in Sappanam. I also love dentistry there are so many aspects of it. Experimenting was my hobby and I must confess most of it are successful.

Perhaps it is because of that I am looking for further challenges.

CHAPTER 29

'ROYAL' Visitors in Sappanam

We were fast asleep the following morning when Sebastian knocked on the front door. Margaret opened and let him in. I came out to inquire why he came so early. He told me he did not have a good rest and was not sure what time we would want him. I told him to sit on the veranda until we are ready to go.

Matthew would be coming with our guests and Gordon at about 8 o'clock. It was still two hours to go so I went back to bed and invited him to make himself some coffee if he felt like it.

An hour later, I got up and joined the others for breakfast. Sebastian was invited to join us. Half way through, our guests arrived. There was no time to waste. We hurried down the beach and boarded the plane.

Sappanam looked different. I have only been away for a week. Diego and his family were waiting when we came ashore. He was delighted to meet our guests. He helped the guests in the jeep and took them to the Rest House while we walked.

Diego had arranged for the villagers to turn out in their full tribal costume to greet us and did a tribal dance. It was a great honour to be greeted in this way Matthew explained. The chief and some of his elders were introduced. Again Matthew explained why they are called Amerindians. He told our guests that in 1492 when Christopher Columbus discovered the West Indian Islands he thought he had reached India. Hence, the name West Indies and the Natives were given the name they are stuck with. Of course they have their own identity. Our guests were intrigued and asked about Diego again this was explained to him.

"What is precisely your work here, Peter? Kumar asked.

"My job is to see that these people are not exploited and their way of life remains as it were from time immemorial. Loggers and prospectors are discouraged from destroying their habitat. The punishment for any violation is harshly punished. These people need the forests to sustain their lives. I and my rangers make sure that is implemented."

"What sort of punishment do you administer?"

"If it is serious they can be sent to prison, lesser violation can result in confiscation of their equipment and any gold or diamond they illegally mined. That reminds me I must show you a miracle." I said to him.

"A miracle! that is interesting" He asked looking a bit mystified.

"I will let Matthew explain it to you when we get there. First, allow me to show you where the villagers live and the many things they get from the forest to survive."

"I will be able to explain that to him better than you. Peter." Diego told me. "Can I carry on with the demonstrations, if it's alright with you?

The visitors were astounded with the story of how we got rich from gold brought down thousands of miles from the Andes. As usual some gravel were shovelled up and without fail there were some little beauties among them and one was given to each of them as what became our custom.

Catherine told us she wanted to go to the larger Cold Stream for sentimental reasons and we obliged.

In our absence the rain had brought down a lot of gravel not only in the stream but also from the hill which was diminishing in size with every rainfall. Again we were not disappointed. Elizabeth gathered a few and gave it to her grandma.

It was getting late we headed back for The Rest House and after a drink and a meal of pigeons and fish. We flew back to the city.

Our obligations to our guests almost completed. Gordon took them to their hotel. Our final duty will be to see them off at the airport. I can say honestly in as much as I enjoyed their visit I can hardly wait when we finally say goodbye and normality is restored.

I had promised myself that the next time I took Christine to Sappanam we would return to visit the spot where all the magic began. It was very important to me and I knew she would enjoy that reunion. I am delaying that visit for one important aspect and that is to wait when the moon reached it perigee again which is about two days' time.

Christine saw I was in a reflective mood. She sat next to me probing my thoughts. I refused to let her in on what I was thinking. She cuddled me and tried to force it out. I remain stubborn only telling her that if I reveal what was going through my mind it will spoil the surprise I am contemplating for her. This only increased her curiosity. She knew better than to press me any further.

Catherine took Isabel to the city to hunt for tourists gifts and came back with a stuffed alligator, two parrots and a baby squirrel monkey. I told her to let Isabel take them back and she can have the money returned for her effort. She pleaded not to go as the men selling these items will only mock her. I told her to go and if they do, tell them the Commissioner of the Hinterlands will be coming to check their license for selling these forest creatures

"Do they have to get a license to do that?" Catherine asked.

"I am not sure. It will make them think. I will ask the Governor to legislate a law to that effect." I told her.

"I will see to that, Peter." Matthew shouted from the veranda "I will make it become law sooner than you think."

"My, my, My brother-in-law is still a power house even in retirement." Catherine responded "What about my other gifts. Has it met with your approval?" She asked

We did not know who she was addressing so there was no reply.

"I am asking both of you. What about my other gifts. Are they approved to take to England?"

"As long as it isn't a jaguar a caiman or any other wild animals," Matthew responded. I don't think you realise how much effort I exerted when I was in charge to save these creatures from ruthless gift hunters. Let's take a look at the iguanas. You saw them in the market. There are hundreds tied up and put for sale, the majority of them laden with eggs about to be laid. These people have no idea about conservation. In God's name use your discretion; leave a few to allow the species to thrive. Their fat bellies are all they think about. In a few years from now those iguanas will be extinct at this rate.

"You cannot stop the tide. Matthew." Catherine told him. "Has anyone thought of explaining it to these hunters?"

"Common sense should direct them to that end. Peter remembered the time we had a barbeque prior to the one we had last week. There was an East Indian couple with a bucket full of cascadura a prehistorically looking fish and they told us they placed the eggs and leave it there for the male to protect until they are hatched. They are only eaten when required. The egg which is a delicacy is spared for the continued survival of the species. That is what I called natural instincts for preservation." Matthew was in his element telling Catherine his side of the story.

It is true what Catherine said knowledge is the only way forward. I wondered if a program of conservation will help. Maybe I can let Matthew deal with that in his spare time. What better time to ask him now he is in the mood. Perhaps I better leave it for a more appropriate time.

"I will not be going back to Sappanam with you all." Catherine suddenly decided. I want to have some time exploring the city and to meet Gordon and the Governor. Is that possible Matt?

"Everything is possible with Gordon."

"I hope you don't mind Peter. First you must show me your surgery and this tourist business that reckless American is involved with, he and that nutty Indian. By the way I haven't seen Ben for nearly a week. Is he alright?"

"Ben is perfectly happy in this city. He is only keeping away to give me the opportunity to have time with my family. I am sure he is dying to know what is going on. I will have to take him to Sappanam when I go." I told her.

"I thought he will stay here when you are there to keep an eye on the family and the young ladies. Why do you need to take him on this trip especially?" Catherine quizzed.

"Oh! he will like to keep an eye on one young lady if my instincts tells me right. I have asked D'Costa to stay here instead." I replied.

Matthew looked restless. He went and had a shower and later indicated to me if I needed a drink. Christine said she wanted one so did Catherine. Margaret asked if she can have some wine. I told her to help herself. This infuriated Catherine and for a second time she appears to dictate how I behave. I was not angry only observing. I knew she would be gone soon so I tolerated her skirmishes in my private life.

"Did you not approve I let Margaret have some wine Mother-in-law?"

She smiled and said rather lovingly "I am happy when you called me mother-in-law. I am beginning to accept you more dearly as a son." She said kissing me gentle on the cheek

"He was first the son I never I had. Don't you go stealing him from me." Matthew told her in jest. "Now of course he is my nephew-in-law."

"Matt you are not going to let him dodge this issue with the servants. He should explain himself."

"Oh mother! Stop meddling." Christine told her.

"I will explain it to her darling." I said to Christine. Then I turned my attention to Catherine and explained. "Margaret is not a servant as such. I asked her to join us and to be a confidant to my wife and to assist with the caring of Elizabeth. I did not want Christine to feel isolated and alone when I am away and coping with Elizabeth would have had a strain on her in a new environment. We treat her as a member of this family."

"Is that not the nicest thing to do? What a caring husband you are. I am sorry to intervene." Her apologies were rare but this was warranted.

On the veranda, Catherine held Matthew's hand and looked solemnly in his face before speaking. "Matt I never did thanked you for saving us from bankruptcy. Jonathan never told me at the time the reason for giving up your share of the estate. The effects or the Great war was still having a toll on the country and the banks were not in a charitable mood to extend the overdraft facilities we originally had with them. You do not know this, so I better tell you while I still have the courage to do so. One third of the estate in Somerset was sold to pay off the debt. Jonathan worked his butts trying to get the farm and the dairy economically viable. We have a good manager he works on a percentage of the profits and that is what stabilised things. We are now on a good financial footing thanks to you." She kissed both his cheeks before leaving us to go and cry quietly.

Matthew followed her to give some comfort.

Margaret sat next to us and declared her confidence in us and her determination to do her best for the family.

Christine told her that she is still in her late teens and that the idea of having a boyfriend must lay heavily on her mind. She insisted to do all she can to see that she meets with the right young men and have a normal life.

"I do have a boyfriend" She said. "I told him not to see me while I am here. We exchanged letters and I hope that sometime in the future he can visit me here or at the sea wall."

"That's great! Christine told her. "You must arrange for him to come and visit you and give us all a chance to see what he looks like. You can always use the flat below when he visits. I am sure Isabella won't mind."

"That day when Mr Matthew and Mr D'Abrue went with us for a walk by the sea wall he was there looking at me and I signalled him to go away. He is a decent young man. He goes to church every Sunday. Perhaps I can have some time off to go to church with him. The pastor knows of our relationship. I can ask the pastor to visit you to confirm I have your blessings to do so."

"I Am so happy for you if your father knows about this, when we are away to Sappanam he will be staying here. Perhaps this will give you an opportunity to be together. I must warn you. Be very careful. It is up to you to see he behaves himself."

"I am so happy to be with this family I will not do anything to let you down." She finally said. Isabella ran on the veranda and asked why her name was mentioned. "Who invited you here?" Catherine asked brusquely.

"I heard my name mentioned ma'am. I thought someone wanted me." She apologised and departed. Again I could not help feeling sorry for the treatment she getting from Catherine.

Matthew and I decided to stroll down to the premises where Sebastian was. We decided to take Elizabeth with us I wanted to share as much time with her as I possibly can. When life returns to normal I wonder how much time I will have for her and even for Christine. The thought sent tremors of panic through me.

It was as Sebastian said. It was a very large office with three rooms. Ben did not hear entering. He turned around looking very surprised. "I thought you lot forgot about me." He said smiling.

"Who will forget a huge brute like you? Matthew teased. "You better hurry up as we would be returning to Sappanam soon."

"How soon is soon?" He asked.

We inspected the two rooms allocated for my surgery and is more than adequate for the purpose. I took notes and made some rough sketches of how I wanted it to be. On my return from Sappanam I will bring Diego and his family and Hector to help with the plumbing and electrical works.

The idea of having the one receptionist did not appeal to me I prefer to have my own. I will have to put an advert in the local papers when the time is ready.

"Is this where your office will be papa?" Elizabeth asked.

"Not office darling. My surgery" I told her as gently as I can.

Sebastian and Singh came and joined us. Singh asked what I think of the rooms. I told him my thoughts and also of using my own receptionist. This pleased him. He asked if he can come to my outpost when things really started. I had no objections. It must be on the occasion when my family is not there.

He then told me he has the right person as my receptionist and he can arrange an interview whenever I am ready. I told him it is best she be interviewed at the same time as they would be applicants. I know his thinking he is probably doing it as a favour for one of his friends in return for something much bigger for himself. He did not look pleased with my answer.

On our way back home, I thought of visiting Brown Betty an upmarket delicatessen. I have heard a lot about it and everyone recommend its high standard. A lot of Europeans go there for a snack. So I thought of giving Elizabeth a treat of chicken in the rough and milk shake. I was told you will never have milk shake as they do there. I am about to find out.

The recommendation was well deserved. Even Matthew slurped the last drop from his glass, to the amusement of Elizabeth.

CHAPTER 30

A Romance Remembered

D'Costa did not want to remain in the city with the young ladies; Christine quite rightly told him that leaving two young ladies by themselves was not wise. He listened to her and suggested that we can take all of them with us. I was enraged by his suggestion. "Who the hell are you to tell my wife what she must do?" My voice was so loud, it made Isabella think something horrible had happened. She came running into the room her eyes opened wide. I told her everything was fine and she may return to whatever she was doing.

"I am sorry if I upset you Mr D'Abrue." He apologised. "I felt I would be more useful elsewhere. Sebastian told me that he would teach me how to service the aircraft and I was looking forward to that. I do not know if he told you that I can fly the plane and soon I will be in charge of one of them. That is why I was eager to learn. This opportunity you gave me, I am ever in your debt. It's been a long time since I had the opportunity to have a responsible job again. My respect and apologies."

I became subdued with his humility. "Sebastian's business has nothing to do with me. He leased the planes and that is all the connections I have with it. In future I do not want you to contradict my wife. Any problems you have speak to me directly. Is that clear?" I reminded him. I then told him that if I had known of the arrangements he had with Sebastian I would have made other plans. Catherine will be going away soon and my obligation to Kumar is still outstanding. I thought of delegating that to Gordon and Matthew. I realised that if I did not meet him in England this visit would not have taken place. In other words I feel obliged to see him off at the airport. I have a deadline of two days to be in Sappanam to celebrate seven years to the day since

I first embraced my darling Christine on the banks of the Demerara. For some it may seem a frivolous thing to celebrate. For me it remains the most memorable event of my life.

Matthew thought he came up with a brilliant idea. He told me that Catherine can fly out the same time as Kumar. They both have to change planes in Trinidad and I will be free of all obligations. The idea sounded great. I then realised that my mother-in-law would not take kindly to be sent off home earlier than she intended. She will probably interpret it as snub.

Kumar and Indera were given the VIP treatment at the airport. There were several policemen in dressed uniforms at the lounge. Later, when all the formalities of immigration were completed they marched him to the plane. On the steps they both turned around and waved us goodbye.

Sitting on the veranda of my home I thought that D'Costa was right and I should take them all with me. This is going to be like a circus. A situation I am familiar with for most of my life. Matthew was not so sure. He conceded when I explained that the lighting plant was not operating properly and needed some maintenance maybe our engineer will have the chance to see to it at the same time. At this juncture my plans are jumbled and only with the help of careful planning would I be able to extricate myself from the mess I am in.

I comforted myself with the thought that Catherine will help me sort it out. She is a great planner and would relish the idea of untangling me from my dilemma.

That evening we must attend a dinner at the Governor's mansion. It was the celebratory event he planned for the visitors. The next day Christine and I will follow the motorcade to the airport for their departure. That was the big knot in my plans which my mother-in-law was quick to point out. I knew she was a good planner and what a gem she turned out to be.

By midday the next day Ben led the entourage down the beach where we all boarded the amphibian. D'Costa was told to go to the controls and give us a demonstration of his flying capabilities. He proved himself a natural flyer. He brought the craft to a smooth landing keeping clear of the outcrops like an ace. We all cheered. All he needs is his certificate.

At the Rest House I was greeted by two of my most senior rangers. Their faces revealed something serious had happened. I instantly went to inquire. My most senior ranger began to explain. We discovered dozens of greenheart trees had been felled on both banks of the Potaro. It seems that they were being prepared to float down the river to Bartica. I sent Jango up the tallest tree to look for signs of them. I think they must have seen us; we were there for many days and no sign of them.

Then Jango told me that the only way to find them is to send my aeroplane to search the area. "This is the only way to find them and stop the logging."

Out of courtesy I invited Matthew to advise me. I knew he wanted to know what was going on. He agreed with Jango and suggested that as the amphibian is here we can see for ourselves what the situation is really like. He promised we will be back in time to see Catherine off.

Before setting out Sebastian told us he must check the craft and the fuel. We decided to settle down for a well-deserved drink while this was going on.

Sugar Bush came in to ask for Matthew. Catherine eyes popped out and asked in amazement. "Who is that woman?"

She became even more perplexed when Matthew told her she was his partner. "Are you saying you are married to her?" She questioned him.

"Not married in the true sense as you would interpret it but we are bonded. It is their way of being married." Matthew explained.

"Is she not a bit young for the likes of you Matt?" She asked.

"Ten years from now you'll be asking if she is not too old to be my partner." Matthew jokingly replied. Then he told her that genetically these people aged rather quickly after they pass thirty.

When Diego and his family arrived Elizabeth ran to greet the young Diego. He had the young squirrel monkey on his shoulder. It was strange to see Bell had wrapped it up with a nappy. We all knew the reason. Elizabeth and young Diego held each other's hands and disappeared to the veranda upstairs. From there they have a clear view of the river and the newly planted fields. I sent Margaret to look after them. Again the thoughts I had at the barbeque surfaced. I was afraid of a strong bond developing between the two. Diego is half Spanish. Bell is half Chinese They are accepted in certain social circles up to a certain point. I knew deep down in my heart I did not want to entertain these selfish thoughts. I am sure it is the stigma society has created to prevent bastardizing the races that is creating these woeful thoughts. When these ideas are instilled from birth it is almost impossible to ignore. I prized myself as someone tolerant that was the reason I forged a strong friendship with them and Ben who has a touch of Black blood. I did not feel uncomfortable with them even now.

Should I protect my child or allow nature to take its course. If I do, some might see me as a father who neglected his duty to protect her. Others will probably see me as a hypocrite thinking liberally and behaving like a bigot. I needed advice and I am sure the advice I am looking for would not come from Catherine I sensed she shared my concern I could see it from the critical glance she gave as they scampered upstairs. Matthew is the only one I can rely on to give me sound advice to discard such racially motivated feelings. I pray that I can avert any regular meetings between then in order to preserve the friendship and love I have for the family.

I went up to the veranda to see for myself how they are getting on. The innocence of children should be protected from any of society's harsh discipline. Maybe I do not need Matthew to tell me what to do. I will not hurt my daughter's feelings at any price. I left them counting parrots on the silk cotton wood and went and joined the main group.

There was Bell, always smiling and cheerful, busy helping Isabella with the dinner. My heart ached at the sight of her working tirelessly to make us her special meal. Diego was joking and laughing with Christine and Catherine as they sipped some of Matthew's fine wine. When Ben came in to join us I gave him a big hug and called him a big bully. He smiled and asked. "Are you alright you haven't done that to me since you were a teenager." I stabbed him in the chest with my finger and said "Let's find ourselves a drink."

I was beginning to feel much better. Those horrible thoughts seemed a thing of the past. I will do exactly what this trip is about. Enjoy a romantic reunion.

D'Costa decided to take the ladies for a walk by the river. Perhaps he was not ready to cope with the temptation of drinks all around him. I discovered that Catherine was eager to see what a piranha looked like. It was difficult to know whether he succeeded in finding one or not. What was evident the ladies had gone too far and were unwittingly approaching the area where the caimans made their new homes. D'Costa would not have a clue if one of those giants were to be prowling on the bank. So I sent Ben to keep an eye on them. Half an hour later he came back to announce that Diego's family from Triangle had arrived and wanted to meet my family.

This was a surprise. How did they know they would be here? Diego had no answer to that mystery. We invited them to the long house and told them to wait. They brought more gifts and showered praises on the ladies. Later they went and joined the villagers. It then dawned on me that they did not come here specifically to meet the ladies but to join in a celebration of the moon in its perigee. A special event it was the time of the year when all life is reborn and the forest regenerated itself. I was hoping they would keep their celebrations private and away from the banks of the river.

Matthew told me that as Commissioner I must be present for a short while as a mark of respect to their traditions. The ladies insisted on coming. I was there just in time when the chief and his elders exchanged cassiri by drinking from each other's cup. This was passed to me and I pretended to have a sip. I never liked the taste of that drink. This ritual will go on for some time and I asked the chief that if my presence is not required I would like to wish him a successful celebration.

Sebastian finished his examination and told me the fuel was enough.

When Elizabeth and her friend joined us Catherine asked if he tried setting the monkey free.

Bell told her that they tried many times but he only stays away for an hour or two and returns desperate for a hug and a cuddle.

We finished our meal and Catherine began telling us how she will miss this place when she returned home. She also indicated that she would return with Jonathan if only to visit her grandchild. I did not want to get intoxicated and refused several rounds. Ben came and felt my temperature to check if I was running a fever.

They were all puzzled at my abstention. I looked at my watch and it showed a quarter to twelve. I thought if we leave now for the Potaro River it will only take an hour to survey the situation and return in time for my planned reunion.

Sebastian suggested that since we are going to the Potaro we can take the family to see the Kaieteur Falls a stupendous waterfall that was once known as the highest waterfall in the world until the Angel Falls in Venezuela was discovered. I allow the ladies to board the craft Matthew was hesitant. I think the only reason he relented was that he wanted to see this great natural marvel.

Sebastian circled the falls a few times giving the ladies an opportunity to take pictures for their holiday album. Then to the logs they were still lying on the embankments on both sides of the river. It was the Commissioner's policy to seize the logs and sell them to the highest bidder. This was something I let Matthew organise with the help of my senior ranger. I must admit Matthew is more useful to me than I thought he would be. I know he wants to be a part of anything I did and I gladly obliged. At the same time I was wondering if he was not keeping a watchful eye on me.

We arrived at Sappanam with enough time for my plan. When the time was right I asked Ben to follow me and I held Christine's hand and told her to do the same. As we strolled down the embankment Ben realized something was unfolding. He detached himself and went on the higher ground exactly where he walked seven years ago. This time he was parallel with us. When

I reached the spot I held Christine and kissed her as passionately as I remembered and as we lay on the ground I told her it is exactly here that we made love for the first time exactly seven years ago to the very minute. I would imagine it was the years we spent apart and I being oblivious of what was happening to her in England may have intensified my feelings to relive those precious moments.

She opened her eyes and told me she can see the fireworks as it was then. I asked her if she can remember the moon as it was then. She looked at it and told me it is as big as that night and again she asked if I arranged all this just for that memory. She held me tightly and her soft lips caressed mine with the same intensity as that night. She whispered. "I love you just as I did on that night. You are such a romantic I just knew I found the right man to share the rest of my life. It all came to an end when Ben intervened to tell us that a caiman was a hundred yards ahead and coming our way.

Matthew and the others were puzzled by our disappearance. The entire entourage was seen coming towards us. They were warned of the danger ahead. Catherine held Matthew by the hand and said. "My dear Matt, I do not know when we will see each other again. I wish you would come to England and not to hide away in this prison you created for yourself."

"It is not a prison my darling sister-in-law but a sanctuary for peace with one's self and total happiness. If I were to return to England I would be overwhelmed with kindness from the friends I left behind so many years ago. It will turn out to be sad"

"Sad, Matt Why sad?"

"Because they will be disappointed with my new way of life, one they can never understand."

"Well just come anyway and see the estate and how it's thriving.

"I have made up my mind. I will live out the rest of my days here and keep that promise I made to myself and to my Guru of never to return to a world where love of money and other social decadence infiltrate the soul, violating the inner sanctuary of a pure mind and corrupting it.

"I never knew you felt so deep with your convictions. Tell me something truthfully. If you are so immersed in your clean mind; would it not be a good idea to put it to the test to see how it will stand up to the challenges of my world?"

"The challenges you are speaking about is right here in different forms and in the city where your grandchild will be educated. Why go to England for that experience?"

In the morning as we boarded the plane for the city, Matthew came and kissed the ladies goodbye. Catherine stood tall and elegant as ever, waving to the others on the banks of the Demerara River.

THE END

The author

Alford Khan, the eldest of 12 children was born at Adelphi Village in Berbice. He studied at the Berbice High School. After which he worked with his father who was a dentist and tailor. On completion of his tutelage in dentistry. He left for the UK and found employment as a civilian with the Royal Army Dental Corps. In 1968 he established his own dental business in London and is still active in that field. The adage "Jack of all trades" suits Alford Khan to the core, as he acquired varied skills right from plumbing to parenting, cabinet making and designing furniture, and has also written many stories for the The Rotary Club of Geenford's magazine. Alford Khan enjoys his life with his four children (three daughters and one son). He loves adventurous travels and socialising with his friends.

novum 🕮 PUBLISHER FOR NEW AUTHORS

The publisher

> **Whoever stops getting better, will in time stop being good.**

This is the motto of novum publishing, and our focus is on finding new manuscripts, publishing them and offering long-term support to the authors.
Our publishing house was founded in 1997, and since then it has become THE expert for new authors and has won numerous awards.

Our editorial team will peruse each manuscript within a few weeks free of charge and without obligation.

You will find more information about
novum publishing and our books on the internet:

www.novum-publishing.co.uk

Rate this book on our website!

www.novum-publishing.co.uk